L.J. BURKHART

# A Queen in the Ashes

*Realm of Queridian: Book 3*

# Contents

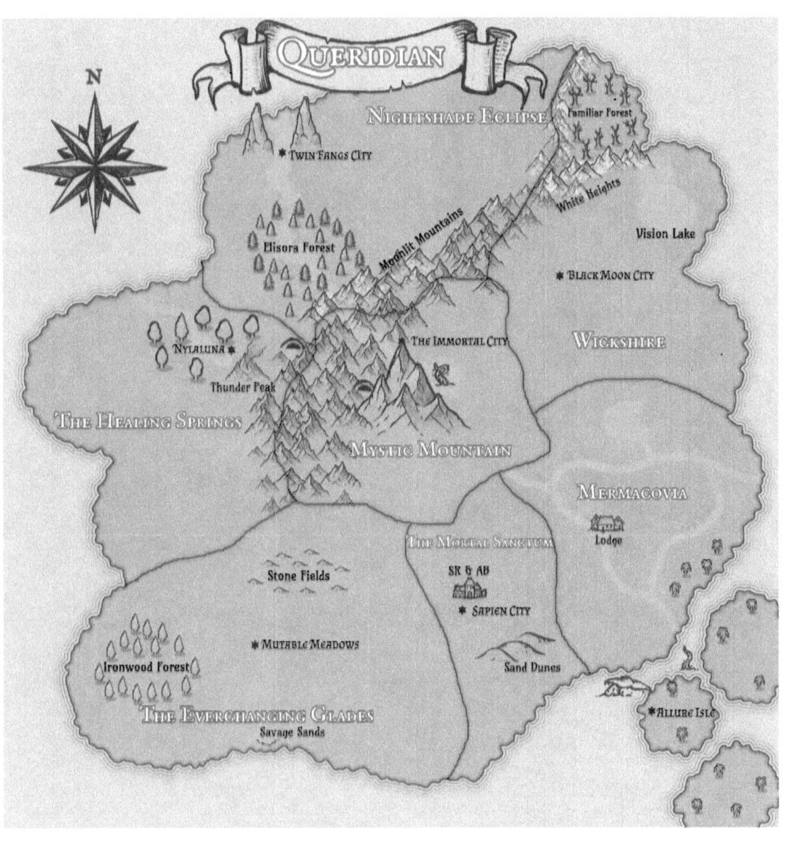

N
QUERIDIAN
NIGHTSHADE ECLIPSE
Familiar Forest
TWIN FANGS CITY
White Heights
Vision Lake
Elisora Forest
Moonlit Mountains
BLACK MOON CITY
NYLALUNA
THE IMMORTAL CITY
WICKSHIRE
Thunder Peak
THE HEALING SPRINGS
MYSTIC MOUNTAIN
MERMACOVIA
Lodge
THE MORTAL SANCTUM
Stone Fields
SK & AB
SAPIEN CITY
MUTABLE MEADOWS
Ironwood Forest
Sand Dunes
THE EVERCHANGING GLADES
Savage Sands
ALLURE ISLE

# 1

## Demonica

I smile to myself as I run out of the throne room. Blood coats my skin from the king, and I revel in the feel and taste of it. I took on the form of a mermaid who was close with the royal family, and from the screams of betrayal behind me, she had been someone important to the young woman. My kin. *Ember.*

I could feel that the girl was my tie to this realm, the reason I was able to sneak past the wards that had kept me out for so long and enter Queridian. We have the same blood in our veins. I'm sure of it.

It had been easy enough. I had been trying to return ever since I'd been banished, wanting to take revenge on the line that had fucked me over so completely. When I was first banished, I had attempted to break through every single day, but in the more recent years, I tried only about every six months or so.

I wasn't expecting much when I headed to the portal we used for funneling in the captives that we fed off of, and I was pleasantly surprised when I was able to travel through without any issue.

I entered the realm in Mermacovia, my allies greeting me with delighted cries and bows. They had been kidnapping people from around the realm for me and my demons for years. The number that we could feed on had dwindled significantly over thousands of years. I originally thought the slaves we were given would be enough, especially once we bred them, but my kind is greedy. There were also some instances of infertility that had cropped up over time.

We need to feed off others in order to continue surviving, having lived longer than our normal life-span. Luckily, just when things were looking pretty grim, the Grand Mistress of Mermacovia came through the portal about a hundred years ago. I was going to kill her until she told me that she was my devoted servant, and she wanted to help me in any way she could.

She had apparently found a hidden record of me and my story buried in the mermaid's territory, and when she discovered it she did what she could to find me, wanting to see me back on the throne. She has since died, but she told her daughter about me.

Coralia took over from her mother, and has even given me more souls than her predecessor, much to my delight. Not many know of me, and even fewer know of what she's supplying me, but she's assured me that if there's ever a war, the mermaids will see me as their true queen and join us.

As soon as I entered the realm of Queridian, I sensed her presence. The one who shares my blood, albeit distantly. It allowed me the passage I needed. I traveled to the center of the kingdom, where the new leader was, and took on the form of a stable boy, feeding off his essence to put him in a comatose state as I staked out the palace in his form.

I couldn't believe my luck when who should approach me but the king himself along with several companions, including my relative. A simple touch to the mermaid she was with allowed me to copy her form. I wasn't always aware of how the mimics copied other forms, but after some "questioning" of the mimic slaves in my realm, I was able to get some answers.

Her mental shields were weak. Well, maybe that isn't the right word considering they were more formidable than most, but they were weak to me. I have the strongest mental shields of anyone, and I broke through them with barely a thought. Then I waited for my moment.

I copied form after form until I was in his throne room. I was delighted when I found him there by himself, and then my relative had to fuck it up and come in when I wasn't expecting her. Luckily, I was in the mermaid's form, so I didn't give myself away. I have to admit that it was delicious to cause her world to crumble so completely when I murdered the king.

I ran out, shifting forms to someone inconsequential as I went. No one was in this part of the building, not that it would have mattered. I would've ripped out anyone's throat that I came across without a second thought. And while that would be fun, it would also cost me precious time.

I head to the nearest window, throw it open, and jump out, shifting into my raven form. I let out a loud croak as I swoop over the territory, letting every being here know that I'm coming for them. I will sit on their precious throne soon enough, and revel in their spilled blood when I do.

# 2

# Pearl

I haul ass to get as far from the palace as I can. Xanto came to our lake to tell me what happened. He immediately knew that I wouldn't have killed the king, that someone had to have been copying my form. He assures me that he will do his best to convince Ember of that fact, but saw what a state she was in after Stavros was murdered. I'm not safe here right now. So I'm running. I have no idea where yet. My first instinct is to go to Mermacovia, but I know that will be the first place she searches for me.

What I really *need* to do is figure out who mimicked my form so that I can clear my name. The problem is that I have no idea who would kill him. Should I head to the Everchanging Glades? See if I can find which mimic copied my form? Whoever killed the king has mimic blood, but they could also be a half blood. *But* if they copied my form, they would have to be very strong. I don't know of many people who would be able to break through my mental shields, and I have them up constantly.

I search my memory to see if I can pinpoint when a stranger touched me and would've been able to gain access to my form. After a few moments it clicks.

The stable boy when we got back from Earth. That is the *only* person

I can think of who's touched me besides my closest party in the last few weeks. And now that I'm focusing on the interaction, I remember him acting strangely. Usually he's completely smitten with me and stumbles and talks too much. He didn't do any of that. I'm sure that whoever killed the king took on his form to get to me. I hope they didn't kill him too.

I finally reach the waters that lead all the way to Mermacovia and launch into them at full speed, shifting as I go. I head deep into the water, trying to make myself invisible from above. It's pretty difficult with my pink tail and white-purple hair.

For now I think my best option is to go to Mermacovia, at least temporarily. I need to get supplies and figure out a game plan. Maybe Coralia has an idea who would've attacked the king.

Mind made up, I swim faster. It's going to be a brutal push, but I'm hoping to make it there within the next few days. It usually takes me a week to make a leisurely journey there. Not this time.

Days later with almost no rest, I arrive at my destination. I stay away from everyone, not wanting to draw attention to myself in case Ember comes looking for me. I head home first. Even though it's an emergency, I don't think Coralia would appreciate me showing up looking like absolute shit. And I doubt she would feed me. Let's be honest, she's a real bitch. The only reason I'm going to see her in the first place is because I have a feeling she knows something.

I burst through the door of my home with Opal. She jumps up in surprise, rushing over to me.

"Pearl! I didn't know you were coming home. What are you doing here?"

"Something really bad happened, Opal. The king was murdered."

Opal's eyes almost bug out of her head. I tell her the little that I know while she fixes me something to eat. I scarf it down since I didn't allow myself to have a decent meal on the road. When I'm finished, she helps me get ready to see Coralia.

"So, who do you think it was?"

"I have no idea. They had to have mimic blood, though, in order to copy my form. And they were *strong*."

"Why are you here, then, instead of the Everchanging Glades?"

"Opal, I have no idea who I'm looking for." I tell her all the thoughts that have been swirling through my head. "And I'm positive Coralia knows something."

"Even if she does, she's not going to tell you. You're close to Ember, and she knows it."

"Well, I have to try."

When I'm ready, I head to Coralia's house. Dread pools in my stomach, and I just know this isn't going to go well. But right now I don't have a choice.

She makes me wait an ungodly amount of time before seeing me, and I curse her in my head a million times over. Doesn't she realize this is urgent?

"Come in, Pearl," Coralia announces finally.

I rush in, even though it's not the best strategy to show her how on edge I am.

"Why are you here?" she asks coolly, as if her voice has the power to freeze me from the inside out.

I quickly fill her in on the situation and watch her reaction closely. She doesn't really look surprised when I tell her the king died, and I think I see a flash of deep satisfaction, but the look is so fleeting I can't be sure.

"Now Ember thinks that *I* killed King Stavros. I thought maybe you might have an idea who's actually behind it."

Her eyes darken. "*Me?* Why on Queridian would *I* know?"

"I just know that you aren't fond of the king and were trying to bring Demonica through to take his place as the rightful queen."

I was originally sent to the palace by her as a spy of sorts for when the timing was right with Demonica. Things have changed drastically since I took my position.

I used to want Demonica on the throne. She's the descendant of Surseiha after all. But then I got to know the king and see for myself how wonderful he was. Then Ember crashed into our lives and I felt even more conflicted. And when I found out she was also from Surseiha's line, my mind changed irrevocably.

Ember is from *both* the royal lines. She should rule. No question about it. But when I tried talking to Coralia, I was immediately shut down. No conversation. No debate. Nothing. I think she realized then where my true loyalties lie, even if I didn't outright tell her.

I debated telling Ember about Coralia's allegiance, but Demonica hadn't found a way to cross into our realm since she was banished. There would be no reason for me to call attention to the fact that I originally was against her father and essentially a traitor and a spy. I know it was cowardly, but I valued my friendship with her too much, not to mention my life at the palace.

Coralia's eyes take on a dangerous glint. "I don't know what you're insinuating, but I will not tolerate it. Get out of my territory. Immediately. If you don't, I will notify the new...*queen* of your whereabouts." Her mouth takes on a disgusted shape, as if she can't even stand to call Ember that.

"Yes, Grand Mistress. I'm sorry to have wasted your time." I turn and leave the room, meanwhile plotting in my head. I can't tell if she actually knows something, or if she wants to get rid of me because I'm close with Ember. Either way, I can't leave yet. I just *know* I'll find answers here. I can feel it. I need evidence in order to clear my name.

I also can't let Coralia know that I haven't left. I need somewhere to camp out without her knowing. My mind immediately goes to a set of underwater caves off one of the islands. I'll have to head back home and see if Opal has anything I can take with me.

I have the urge to look through the mermaid records. I don't know if I'll find anything, but it's worth a shot while I'm here. And the records are kept close-ish to the caves. Plan set, I return to visit Opal.

"How did it go?" she asks cheerfully. I love my twin, but I think she has a false sense of how things work around here. And she holds Coralia in way too high a regard for my liking.

That thought in mind, I figure it's best to watch what I say to her. "Not great. She didn't know anything, and she ordered me to leave the territory."

Her brows furrow in confusion, but she doesn't look upset on my behalf like I would if the situation were reversed. "Why?"

"She didn't say, but I don't think she likes that I'm close with Ember. Or at least was until this whole thing happened."

She nods as if in understanding. "I'm sorry, sister."

I somehow contain my eye roll. "Can I have some supplies for the trip back? I left in such a hurry that I didn't have time to grab anything."

"Of course. Take whatever you need."

I breathe a sigh of relief. I go around the house collecting clothes, some essentials for self-care, and food. I put all of it in a spare underwater bag, feeling a little more settled.

When I'm finished, I hug my sister tightly. "I'm guessing Coralia will soon come to check that I have in fact left," I warn.

She nods. "That's fine. I'll tell her that you're heading back to the palace."

"Thanks, Opal. I don't know when I'll see you again, but stay safe, okay?"

"You too, Pearl."

With that, I'm gone. I head in the direction of the Immortal City, but have no intention of maintaining it. I just need to make sure that if anyone is watching me, they really do think I'm going back to the palace.

As I leave, I run into Proteus. He's just emerging from the ocean, but he glances over at me as he ties his wrap around his waist.

His eyes widen in surprise. "Pearl, what are you doing here?"

I consider feeding him some bullshit answer, but Proteus is really the only person in this territory who I don't feel like is underhanded and always has an ulterior motive. That statement unfortunately includes my sister.

I give him a brief rundown of what happened. I've known him a long time, and while he's close with Ember, he's also close with me. I have faith that he'll believe me and try to help. I, of course, leave out my plan to stay here. I'm not comfortable telling anyone that. Except Xanto, and he's not here.

"Pearl, I'm so sorry." He wraps me in a hug, and I have the sudden urge to break down in his embrace. I also can't help but notice how comfortable I feel in his arms. I've known Proteus my whole life, but we've never had anything sexual or romantic between us. This somehow feels like it's bordering on something more.

This whole experience has been one of the worst in my life, and I haven't had any help or any time to process it. I lost the king, my best friend in the whole world, got kicked out of my home, then traveled all the way here with no sleep, all to be told to basically fuck off and have my twin sister take sides with that evil bitch over me. I'm at my limit, and this kind gesture is going to be my undoing.

I take a deep breath, attempting to rein it in, but it sounds more like a sob. His hand rubs along my back, and I take comfort in his embrace. It feels nice to be supported, even if only for a moment.

"Everything will work out. Ember knows and loves you, she's just upset and can't think clearly right now. Once she's able to get past the initial stage of grief, she'll come around."

"You believe me?"

"Of course. I know you'd never kill the king. You love that man, and his daughter."

"I haven't told Ember that I was sent to the palace by your mother to spy," I confide in him. He knows this about me, and didn't agree with her that it was the right tactic. He's never thought that Demonica was the answer, but his mother doesn't listen to him. She never has.

"She'll come around. Be honest with her. I'll vouch for you if that would help."

I breathe another sigh of relief, glad to have good people on my side. "Thanks, Proteus."

He nods, releasing me. "Now, get out of here before someone finds you." He gives me a look, and I can tell he knows that I'm not returning to the palace. That's okay. I trust him. Just not enough to disclose *where* I'm going.

I head off, diving into the water in search of the caves that no one ever bothers to visit. It doesn't take me terribly long to get there, but I'm relieved when I arrive without anyone seeing me. These are far enough out of the way and not really near anything of interest that most people don't know about them, and the ones that do don't bother coming here.

Mermacovia is a territory where everyone is around each other all the time. It's difficult to find time or space to yourself, and when I discovered this area, I kept it in the back of my mind as a place to escape to. Luckily, I've already spruced up the space a little bit with some decor to make it more homey.

Once I set my things down, I gather up some seaweed from close by to create a soft surface to sleep on. I'm exhausted from the last few days. Once I have my bed made, I lie down and pass out, finally able to relax. I'll do some more research after I've let my mind rest.

# 3

# Ember

"How are you feeling?" Alexei asks me as I put on my dress.

I've intentionally kept my mind off of this all day because there are too many emotions swirling around in my head.

"I don't know," I answer truthfully.

"A lot of things, I'm sure," he prompts.

I sigh. I know he wants me to talk about my feelings, but I am a mess today. "Yes. A lot of things."

Now it's his turn to sigh. "Ember. Seriously, tell me all the things you're feeling."

"Heartbroken, excited, vengeful, motivated, nervous. Probably a few other things, too, that I haven't identified yet."

He comes up behind me, wrapping his arms around me and settling them on my stomach. I meet his gaze in the mirror. "I know you miss him, but this is going to be good. You are going to do wonderful things for this realm. Things Stavros couldn't."

Tears build behind my eyes. I don't want to hear all the things that Stavros couldn't do for this realm. I still haven't told Alexei about Demonica and Domonia, the land of the dead. Every time I'm about to, I remember how Stavros told me I shouldn't until we were married and he was my king.

I'm so conflicted, though, because I feel like he *needs* to know. The other option is marrying him, which I've also toyed with, but then I think about the fact that Stavros won't be able to walk me down the aisle, and I break down into sobs.

Because I have my mate behind me, and it's just the two of us, I voice my other worry. "What if they don't accept me?" I whisper.

"Ember, they're going to love you. Of course there are going to be people that don't like you, but that's true of every leader. You can't be approved of by everyone, but I think the majority of the kingdom will be ecstatic."

I breathe deeply, letting his words soak in. He's right. I know everyone isn't going to love me, but hopefully enough will so that this will be a smooth transition. As smooth as it can be anyway.

I nod, holding my head high. Maybe if I pretend to be confident, others will believe it too. I meet my own eyes in the mirror and see the fire sparking behind them. I let that bolster me. I can feel my familiar inside of me, too, reminding me that I am a fierce bitch, just like her. I wouldn't have a panther if I wasn't.

I take in my appearance one last time, making sure I look "queenly," I try not to dwell on the fact that Pearl isn't here to doll me up. I don't want to fight back tears again. I look good, but I can't help feeling that I would look even better with her assistance.

*No. Stop it*, I chastise myself. I don't need that bitch. She killed my father. She's no friend of mine.

My makeup is done in an equally natural and dramatic fashion, giving me an "I look this amazing all the time" feel. I have bold red lips, eye makeup that has a slight smokey feel but complements my natural coloring well, and a rosy blush that makes me look like I just fed off of someone.

My hair is half down, the bottom half done in loose curls, while the top is pinned back with a large elaborate fishtail braid sweeping back to join the rest. It's going to end up framing the crown that's placed on my head.

And finally, my dress. I don't want to just look royal. I want to look fierce. I want to look like a warrior. It's an armor-style dress. The material is all black, with a few areas of sheer fabric on the torso. It has a bolero with slight wings that extend off my shoulders. The torso is a boned corset and is covered in sequins, embroidery, and jewels. The bolero and the corset are connected by gorgeous rose-gold and diamond pieces. The skirt is made out of silk, tulle, and netting, and is floor length. A few sections of the embroidery and sequins flow down from the corset onto the skirt as well. It's a dress fit for a queen, albeit a warrior queen.

Oh Gods. That thought sends a jolt of panic through me, but I shove it away. I'm not going to let my anxiety get in the way of this.

"I'm ready," I tell Alexei. I release Ebony in the next moment, and she stands at my side, proud and fierce, lending me strength. I considered letting her out of myself for the whole kingdom to see, but I don't want to upset the witches by revealing their secret about familiars. This way, it'll just look like I have a pet panther. No big deal.

He nods, leading me to the throne room. Everyone is already inside, and I try to calm my nerves as Alexei finds himself a seat. The next minute, I hear the song of Queridian being played by the palace quartet, and I know that's my cue.

The double doors open, and even though I knew there would be a lot of people here, I wasn't prepared for the number. I'm overwhelmed by the hundreds, if not a thousand, staring at me. I shake off the uncomfortable feeling, hold my head high and my back straight, and stride forward. I let all of my powers come out to play, releasing my allure, shifting my nails into my mermaid claws, and free just enough fire that it trails behind me. I don't meet the eyes of anyone I pass, not ready to see their expressions.

It takes forever to reach the front of the throne room, and I'm grateful that I made it all that way without tripping. I walk up the three steps, and kneel before Vlad, my vampire ambassador. He's been in the position longer than any of the others, and he's greatly admired among the realm. He's going to give me my crown.

"Do you, Ember Solis, promise to hold the kingdom of Queridian in the highest regard, only doing what is in the best interest of its citizens, swearing fealty to its residents, and devoting yourself to them until your heart stops beating?"

"I do." I'm delighted that my voice stays strong and amplifies throughout the chamber.

With those simple words, he lowers the crown, and I feel the weight settle on my head as well as metaphorically on my shoulders. Relief and panic course through me in equal measure.

"Then rise."

I do and turn toward my subjects. I sink down onto my throne. My skirts pool around me, and I hold my head high, meeting the eyes of every person here, or at least trying to as I smile, showing off my vampire fangs.

My gift picks up on so many emotions in the room, and I read them for a few seconds to get an idea of what I'm dealing with. I sense excitement, fear, reverence, disgust, and so many others. I shut it down before the feelings overtake me. Ebony sits next to me, and I let my hand rest on her head. I can only imagine the picture we're painting right now.

"All hail Queen Ember Solis, first of her name!" Vlad yells.

"All hail Queen Ember!" the crowd parrots.

"Long may she reign."

"Long may she reign!" they yell.

They all sink into a bow, and the part of me that loves power relishes it. I almost let out a purr at seeing them all worshiping me like this. It's then that I realize how dangerous power can be. I really need to be careful and not let this side of me take over. That's not the kind of ruler I want to be.

"Rise," I say, my voice a combination of power and gentleness. That's better.

They do, and with that, the celebration begins. Everyone moves to the ballroom and Alexei holds his hand out for me, inviting me to dance with him. He sweeps me up and around the dance floor in front of everyone, and I'm too wrapped up in him to feel self-conscious.

I'm reminded of our dance lessons so long ago, and I think of how far we've come. I brush the side of his face with my thumb. "I'm so glad you're by my side."

"I wouldn't be anywhere else," he murmurs.

"How does it feel knowing you're going to be king someday?"

"Oh, am I now? Is this a proposal?" he teases.

I roll my eyes at him, and if there weren't so many people watching us, I would swat him. "You wish."

"I do wish," he says, suddenly serious. "I would be honored to be your husband."

"Well, maybe *you* should be the one to propose, then," I say, winking at him.

"Maybe I already have a plan in place."

My heart skips a beat at his words. Does he really? But I don't want the surprise to be ruined, so I just say, "Sure you do."

The song ends and everyone claps. A slight blush comes to my cheeks, but I gesture for everyone to join us. I don't want to be the center of attention anymore, so Alexei and I head to our seats. I had a chair brought up next to my throne so he could sit with me. Apparently it's not customary to do so until you're married, but I don't give a shit. He's my mate and his place is at my side.

Ebony lies at our feet, gazing over the crowd with intensity. A few people give her nervous glances, but most go about their business, dancing, drinking, and generally having a good time. Alexei grabs my hand and squeezes gently. He's been so wonderful throughout this whole process. It hasn't been an easy time for me, but he's been there for me every single second.

I look at him and he meets my gaze. His eyes are full to the brim with emotion. "I love you so much," I tell him.

"I know," he says in typical Han Solo fashion. I make a mental note to make him watch *Star Wars* next time we're on Earth.

"Speech!" someone yells in the crowd. "Speech from our new queen!"

My eyes widen and Alexei smirks but gives me an encouraging nod. I take a deep breath, swallowing down my nerves and clearing my throat.

I stand before them. "Hello, everyone. I know that this change came on us rather quickly and unexpectedly, but here we are. I first want to talk about my father. I only knew him for a short period, but during that time, we were able to get to know each other very well." Tears build behind my eyes, and I struggle to keep my voice even.

"I learned a great deal from him about the kingdom and how to rule. Where I come from, things are done a bit differently, but he was still the best leader I've ever known. I hope to do him, the kingdom, and all of you proud. I know there will still be a learning curve, but I am always open to questions and criticism as long as it's *respectful*.

"In the meantime, I really look forward to not only getting to know you all better, but learning more about Queridian as well. There are some things I think can be improved upon, but I will take any changes slowly to ensure everyone is adjusting. Together, I believe we can make this realm a true utopia, and I can't wait to get started." I raise my glass in the air. "To Queridian!"

"To Queridian," they all echo, thrusting their goblets into the air.

Alexei toasts me, and I give him a relieved smile that that part is over. We drink, but I stay mostly sober as the day continues into night. Most people are getting pretty sloshed, but I keep in mind that I am now their queen. I don't have the luxury of letting loose in front of my subjects. Maybe tonight when Alexei and I get back to our suite.

We're still staying in my same rooms. I didn't feel comfortable moving into my dad's rooms, even though they are technically the monarch's quarters. It doesn't feel right intruding on his space, and I wonder briefly if he felt the same way when his parents passed unexpectedly. They were in an accident that was staged by his old advisor in a plot to take over the crown.

When it's been a sufficient amount of time, I leave. Everyone bows to me as I walk by, and I think it's one of the oddest things that's ever happened to me. Okay, maybe falling through a portal into Queridian takes the cake, but this is definitely up there. I was still adjusting to being a princess. Now I'm their *queen*. It still hasn't sunk in. Obviously.

Alexei and Ebony follow me, and I like the idea of them watching over me. Now that I'm a ruler, I'm bound to have a target on my back. We arrive at our rooms, and Ebony slinks off to lie by the fire. It's interesting how sometimes she prefers to stay hidden inside of me, and how others she enjoys being out in the open.

I pour myself another drink now that we're away from prying eyes. I never realized how stressful this part was, and I have a newfound respect for my dad. Alexei pours himself one too, and we sit in front of the fire.

"Alexei, I think it's time I tell you."

"Tell me what?"

"The big secret Stavros told me before he died."

His eyebrows rise in shock. "I thought I couldn't know that until we got married."

"Originally I agreed with that, but now that my father is gone, my outlook has changed. I just have a feeling that you need to know."

"Fair enough."

I tell him all about Demonica, Domonia, and the conflict that happened thousands of years ago. He listens, enraptured, occasionally asking questions. I answer them to the best of my knowledge, but I don't know nearly enough about the subject.

I wish I could research it, but there are no records. The only people who know anything are the rulers and future rulers. They wiped the realm's knowledge on the subject and essentially erased her from existence.

"I think she's the one I saw in my vision at Vision Lake in Wickshire. The one who said she was me," I tell him.

"Do you think she's somehow finding a way to come through?"

I think about it, but I feel like I'm missing something. Something that's right in front of my face. "I don't know," I answer honestly.

"Thank you for telling me. If we are both aware of it, we can be vigilant and keep an eye on anything out of the ordinary."

Once again, there's that niggling feeling in the back of my mind that I'm missing something important, but the more attention I call to it, the further it slips from me. I roll my eyes at myself and almost growl in frustration.

"Let's go to bed, my queen."

My mate distracts me from my inner turmoil, his words making my core clench deliciously. He holds out his hand in invitation. I lay my palm in his, sparks shooting between us like always, and my mate mark seems to sigh happily in response at the contact.

"I need to pay homage to my monarch."

I smile at him before reaching for my crown.

"No. Leave it on."

My smile broadens and I unzip my dress instead, leaving me in only

my crown, panties, and heels.
   He takes me to bed and *worships* me.

# 4

# Pearl

I wake up surprisingly well rested. For some reason it's easier to sleep in uncomfortable places in my mermaid form. Plus the water is calming and helps me forget about my shit show of a life.

I feel better having slept so well, and I catch myself a quick fish before trying to figure out how I'm going to pull off the next part of my plan. The mermaid records are kept in the ruins of the old underwater palace, and the only reason I know about them is because I came across them while I was exploring. They aren't hidden necessarily, but most don't come out this way and the records aren't broadcasted to the territory.

I don't think anyone will be around, but I need to have a plan in place just in case. I wish I had Ember's shapeshifting powers. That would sure come in handy right about now.

I'll just need to be sneaky, and take it slow. Luckily, there's a lot of debris and seaweed around the ruins. Plenty of spaces to hide.

I finish my "meal," and leaving my things in the cave, I head for the palace. I'm surprised more mermaids don't venture out this way, but there are sometimes predators in this area. While mermaids can fight and are also predators, we try to avoid fights when we can. Our vanity gets in the way, and fights mean cosmetic damage.

I peek my head out of the cave, checking for signs of other mermaids. I'm sure Coralia has let the territory know by now that I'm not welcome here.

The coast is clear, and I slowly make my way to the ruins. It's been a few years, but it's just as I remember. Glorious and withered. Forgotten and abandoned. I make sure to pay special attention to the doorways and things of that nature. I don't want to hit anything and risk more damage. I feel like one swipe of my tail in the right spot would send this place crashing to the ocean floor.

I think I remember where the records are kept, but it still takes me a while to make it there. Some of the hallways and doorways have collapsed, and I feel my anxiety ratchet up with every turn, worrying about either getting trapped here, or coming across an unwanted predator. This area has been abandoned for so long that it only makes sense for nature to reclaim it. Not to mention the walls are so close to each other from partial collapses that I'm beginning to feel claustrophobic.

I finally reach them, and am slightly overwhelmed by the number of books here. I have no idea where to start, and I'm sure it's going to take me days if not weeks or months to find the information I'm looking for.

Of course the books have been protected with a spell that allows them to be underwater, and are therefore in better shape than anything else in this castle. I still am very careful not to damage the precious pages.

I skim through as many books as I can. So far nothing. Some are ledgers and records from when the palace was operational. I skip over those quickly, and learn a little more about the history. Nothing super interesting or relevant to our situation though.

I'm specifically looking for information on Demonica. I know this is how Coralia's mother found out about her, and there might be more here that I can give to Ember. Some clue to help her and to provide evidence of what Coralia is trying to do here. I'm hoping that if I can show her I'm trying to help her and am on her side then she will come to her senses and realize that I didn't kill Stavros.

I search all day, but don't find anything useful. I sigh regretfully, but tell myself that it's going to take time. There's a lot of information here, and of course I'm not going to find anything on the first day of searching.

I head back to the cave, carefully. I don't see any mermaids, but I do spot a shark. However, it doesn't notice me, and I'm able to avoid a run-in. I catch another fish on my way back, and devour it as I swim. When I return, I don't waste any time collapsing on my bed of seaweed, and I'm asleep seconds later.

I spend the next few days looking through countless books. My eyes are strained, and I struggle to stay focused. I wonder for the hundredth time if this is all a waste. Should I be doing something else instead? But I persist. I just have a feeling there's something here that I can show Ember. Something she needs to know.

I head back to the cave, and every night I try to bring something pretty back to add to the decor. I've always loved personalizing my space, and this makes it feel more like a home to me. I'm just finding a place for my newest treasure when a voice in my head makes me whirl around in shock and terror.

*Nice spot*, Proteus says with a smile, admiring my space as he swims into my cave.

My heartbeat calms a fraction. *Proteus, how did you find me?*

*I remembered you used to come here when we were younger. I knew you didn't leave the territory like my mother ordered you to. I had a feeling I would find you here.*

My brow furrows. *You knew I used to come here?*

He smiles at me fondly. *Of course. I've always been infatuated with you.*

Now my eyebrows fly halfway up my forehead. *You have?*

*Was I never clear about it?* he asks, swimming closer to me.

My breath hitches. I've always had a thing for him too. In fact, I was a tiny bit jealous when he and Ember gave it a shot. *No. If you were, I would've been more than happy to accept your attention.*

*Well, I'm telling you now, aren't I?*

*What are you doing here, Proteus?* I ask, trying to decide how to proceed.

He sighs in my head. *I came to check on you and see if you needed anything. I'm also curious what exactly you're doing.*

I stare at him, debating if it's safe to tell him. I have known him my whole life, and I do know that he doesn't agree with Coralia on most things. But she is still his mother.

*I'm not going to tell anyone anything, Pearl. I just want to help you.*

I decide to trust my gut again. I mean at this point, it's essentially guiding my whole life.

*I don't know exactly what I'm doing. I'm looking through the records in the old palace. I just have a feeling there's something important there that I can give Ember.*

He nods thoughtfully. *I can help you. I won't be able to be here all day, but I can help for at least an hour or two.*

The thought is tempting. Even just having company would be nice, but having someone to read through the boring archives to see if there's anything of importance would be incredible. Plus it means that I don't have to be in this creepy-ass castle all by myself.

*Really?*

*Of course. I would like to help you and Ember. And it would be nice to spend some time with you alone.*

A slight blush rises to my cheeks. I'm not usually the blushing type, but I've had a thing for Proteus ever since I was young. I love Xanto, of course, but we've already talked about adding a third to our relationship if it feels right. I can't help the desire that burns through me as he stares at me like that.

He reaches a hand forward and brushes his knuckles across my cheek. Heat blooms through me at just that simple touch.

*Let me help you,* he begs.

I nod and his responding smile is dazzling.

*Until tomorrow, then.* He takes off before I can say anything else to him.

It takes me forever to get to sleep that night, my heart hammering, and my mind running with scenarios of me, Xanto, and Proteus.

The next day, I have an even harder time concentrating. I keep waiting for Proteus to show up, glancing between my book and the entrance to the library, when a light in the doorway catches my eye. A beautiful melody accompanies it, and I'm drawn into its thrall.

I wander toward it, even though a part of my brain is screaming to resist it. I know what this is in the back of my head. A siren. I've never seen one in person, and let me tell you, it's impossible to withstand. Her body is glowing like an underwater star, and her song enraptures me like nothing I've ever experienced.

Her body itself is indistinguishable, blinding in her own light. No one ever knows what a siren actually looks like except for the luminescence that surrounds her and the song she emits, unless they're able to kill them. They all look different underneath their disguise.

I get closer and closer, even though I know I should swim in the opposite direction. I *know* sirens are lethal. This is how they lure their prey. I can't help it though. Her song is hauntingly beautiful, and it's as though I'll die if I don't get to her anyway.

Just when I'm an arm's length away from her and can feel my demise looming, a hand punctures her chest. I gasp as I'm released from her spell. My heart pounds a steady rhythm as I realize how close to death I actually came.

Her light goes out completely as her heart is ripped clean from her chest. As her form falls to the ground, I see Proteus looming behind her, the heart beating its last in his hand, his claws extended with viscera hanging from them. Since her thrall was aimed at me, Proteus wasn't trapped in her web. If he had been with me already, we both would've been dead.

*Oh Proteus, thank the Gods.*

He has a smirk on his face. *I don't think the Gods are the ones to thank.*

*Well, thank you, then,* I remark sarcastically.

We look down at the siren. It's ugly in death. At least this one is, looking truly monstrous. It's similar to a squid or an octopus, but the eyes are bulbous, taking up a good portion of its face, and the mouth gapes wide, razor-sharp teeth lining every inch. It's amazing that something so hideous can emit sounds and sights so beautiful.

*There's some new obstacles since the last time I was here,* Proteus remarks when we've looked our fill at the monster.

*I know. It took me a while to find a suitable path to the library my first time too.*

He swims up to me, and I tense in anticipation. What is he going to do? I want him to touch me again, and he doesn't disappoint. He swims close and brings me into an intimate hug, making my heart hammer against my chest. I'm certain he can feel it.

*It's nice to see you again*, his mind whispers in my ear, making me shiver. *I'm glad I got here in time.*

*Same here.* I roll my eyes at myself. I can't think of anything better to say, and I want to punch myself in the face.

*So, what are we working on?* he asks, pulling away from me. I immediately miss his warmth.

*I left off here yesterday.* I gesture to the bookshelf I'm on.

*Okay. I'll start on the opposite side.*

We get to work, and I feel better now that he's here. I'm able to concentrate since I'm not looking at the door every five seconds.

We read in silence, and even though I'm focusing more now, I'm still very aware of his body and his movements. I wonder how often we'll be here together, and how long it will take us to find something significant.

After about two hours, Proteus sighs, putting away the book he just skimmed through. *I hate to do this, but I have to head back, Pearl. I can't have anyone noticing my absence.*

I nod in understanding. *Thanks for the help.*

He smiles and swims up to me, taking me in his arms again before brushing his lips across my cheek. Kisses underwater aren't the same as they are on land, so it feels different than any kiss I've had in a while, but it still makes my heart rate speed up.

*Proteus?*

*Hmm?*

*I'm with another man. A mimic. His name is Xanto. But we've discussed bringing in another partner...*

*Is that right?* he asks wryly, still holding me. His lips are now moving toward my ear.

*Yes. Do you like men too? Or just women? Because Xanto and I are a package deal.*

*I like men too,* he says as his teeth gently graze my earlobe.

I let out a moan, although it echoes in his mind instead of between us.

*What is his other form?* he asks.

*A stingray.*

*So, he can swim with us?*

I nod.

*Perfect. I'd love to meet him.*

*As much as I want to start something with you now, I don't want to do so without Xanto here. You need to meet him. I would hate for you and I to start a relationship and then it not be a good fit between you and Xanto.*

He sighs, but pulls back. *I understand. We'll have to find something important, then, and head back to him and Ember. I've waited years for you. I can wait a little while longer. Until tomorrow, my lady. And be careful of more predators,* he says, brushing his lips across my knuckles.

We spend the next few days much the same way, close but not too close. He's driving me wild, and picturing him and Xanto together is wreaking havoc on my libido. That and the fact that I haven't shifted into my "human" form for over a week, I'm starting to feel more animal at the moment.

Just when I'm about to give up hope, we miraculously come across something at the same time. Literally the exact same moment. It's so weird and serendipitous that I know it's fate. We're *meant* to find this information.

Proteus finds a book that contains information on Demonica. One that tells her origin story from a mermaid's point of view. Someone named Crissa. It talks about how after Demonica and the other demons were banished, everyone in the realm had their memories erased. Crissa somehow escaped that event and retained her memory, but she wasn't sure for how long, and wanted to document what happened. She talks about how Demonica is the true ruler of the realm and how she intends to do all she can to bring her back. She also mentions the portal that was used to send her to her new realm, Domonia. I know of it, and after this I think that will be my next stop. It also includes a prophecy that seems to be about Demonica, but I'm not positive, and I decide I'll ponder over the crypticness at a later time.

Unfortunately, there's not much else after that other than the rest of her story, which I've already heard. I think this is where Coralia's mother first heard about Demonica hundreds of years ago, passing the knowledge and the obsession down to her daughter. I grab the book from him, intending to take it with me. Ember should have this information.

I found something that I wasn't looking for in the slightest, but I think is maybe not equally as important, but has the potential to be. It's a record of something called Surseiha's Needle. From what I can tell, it was a trident originally of Surseiha's creation. It heightened her powers, and was passed down from ruler to ruler. It can be wielded only by someone with her blood, but was lost centuries ago, even before Demonica was crowned queen.

I know trying to locate the trident seems like trying to find a needle in a haystack, literally, and right now there's no reason for her to need or want it, but I'm drawn to the knowledge, feeling like it's significant in some way.

I put the book I found on top of the one Proteus found. I feel so much better now, knowing that I have something to provide Ember. I don't know if she'll be able to use any of this, but at least I'll be able to tell her about Demonica. I don't *think* she's a legitimate threat. After all, Coralia and her mother have been trying to find a way to bring her into this realm for hundreds of years and didn't accomplish it, but I think it's worth her knowing about.

*So, what do you think? Is this enough to go back to Ember with?* Proteus asks in my mind.

*I think so. I would like to go to the portal though, before heading back home, just in case. I feel like there's something there.*

*I will come with you. Tomorrow?*

I nod. That gives me time to rest a bit and pack what little things I have. If it goes well, I can leave straight from there.

*Then I'll meet you at your cave tomorrow and we can travel there together.*

I smile gratefully at Proteus. I'm glad I didn't have to go through all of this on my own. And if he hadn't been here to help me, I might have found only my information and left. The thought makes me slightly reluctant to leave before reading every book in here, but that would take way too long. We need to figure out who killed the king.

# 5

# Ember

The next few days pass in a blur. There's a lot for me to get used to, and I'm having a hard time adjusting to the specifics of this job. There are a lot of things to approve, supervise, and debate over, surprisingly. I didn't realize how involved my father's job was, although I should've known. He made time for me, but there were always things he had to tend to after our meetings.

Alexei helps me when and where he can, but unfortunately, there's a lot that only I can do. Things will be different when we're married, of course, and the thought makes me want to say vows to him right now. But then my romantic brain kicks in, yelling at me that the reason I'm going to marry my mate is *not* because I need help with clerical work. I hate it when that bitch is right.

I'm in the room I've designated my *office* when I hear a knock. I immediately know it isn't Alexei. He never bothers with knocking.

"Come in."

Xanto's head peeks in, and I almost wince. I've been avoiding him since my father passed. I *know* he isn't the one who killed him, but I can't see him without thinking of Pearl. And I can't think of Pearl without seeing her slit my father's throat.

"Oh, Xanto. Come in."

He does so, and then bows. "Your Majesty."

"Xanto, we're friends. There's no need for that. I feel awkward enough with everybody else doing that."

He chuckles, but nods. "How are you, Ember?"

I sigh. I'm so sick of this question lately. "I'm fine."

"Pardon me for saying so, but I know you aren't."

I try not to bristle at his words. He's my friend, and I know he doesn't mean them maliciously, but they still sting. "Excuse me?"

"Ember, if you were thinking clearly, you would have already figured out what's right in front of your face."

"Xanto, what the hell? You're seriously talking to your queen like she's stupid?"

His brows rise. "You just told me to speak to you like a friend. This is me doing that."

Fuck. He's right. Why did I have to say that? I just didn't want him calling me "Your Majesty." It just reminds me of the fact that my dad is no longer here.

"Fine. What's that supposed to mean?"

"There's something obvious that you aren't thinking about, Ember. It's probably because you aren't from here and have been raised to trust what your eyes tell you, but you're forgetting that here in Queridian you can't always trust your senses."

"Stop being cryptic. What are you talking about?"

"Pearl didn't kill the king."

My heart stops. "What do you mean?"

"Exactly what I said," he says infuriatingly. I resist the urge to throw something at him. Or scream.

"Elaborate, please," I say instead.

"Pearl's form was mimicked."

Fuck. I didn't even *think* of that. How could I not have thought of that? I still am not positive he's right though. "How do you know?"

"Because I know Pearl. So do you. If you were thinking clearly you would realize that she's your best friend in both realms you've lived in. She would never do anything to hurt you. And besides that, she loved your father. She told me many times how much she admired him."

"Why has no one mentioned this to me before? Surely someone would've thought of it."

"A couple reasons. First, mimics don't travel outside of their territory very often, so they're probably just as blind to it as you. The second is because Pearl has incredibly strong mental shields. If they did think it was a possibility, they probably disregarded it."

For the first time since my father's death, I falter. What he's saying makes so much sense. And how many times have I wondered how Pearl could do this to me? How many times have I thought to myself that this was completely out of character for her? Too many to count. Fuck. Hope swells in my chest.

"Not to mention that after his death she was down at the lake. It looked like she had been there for a while. You know how she likes to swim every night for a few hours."

My heart beats harder. "Then why did she flee?"

"Because I told her to. I knew you wouldn't listen to reason after Stavros died. That's understandable. It wasn't safe for her to be here while there was a good chance you wouldn't listen to a word she said."

I frown at that. I like to think that if he had brought this up to me at least a few days after it happened that I would've listened to him. But I was so heartbroken. Honestly, I still am.

"Fair enough. Well, where is she now? I would like to speak with her and hear this from her mouth instead of yours."

"I don't know. She wasn't sure where to go after it happened. She said she would figure it out after she started traveling. I also told her that I would talk to you, so I'm hoping that she'll come back on her own soon."

I let out a heavy breath. "Okay. Thank you for coming to me, Xanto."

"You're welcome, my queen."

"Hey now. You were pretty familiar just now. Don't go backtracking on me."

"You said you didn't want to be called 'Your Majesty.' I thought this was a good compromise."

I roll my eyes but chuckle fondly. "If you *really* want to, I guess I'll allow it."

He smiles at me, and he sweeps me into a warm hug. "I know this has all been really hard on you. I'm so sorry about the king. I promise we're going to find who did it."

Tears clog my eyes, and I feel a frog in my throat, but I push them back and speak through it. "Thank you. I need all the help I can get right now."

"You know, Pearl isn't out there wasting everyone's time. She'll have something for us. I just know it."

What he told me makes sense, but I still haven't fully accepted it yet. I can't get over the fact that I *saw* Pearl throwing a knife at me and then murdering my father in cold blood. But I don't have the heart to tell Xanto that.

"Yeah, let's hope that she finds something that can lead us to who really did it."

"She will."

He's so confident in her that it brings a smile to my lips. The part of me that still loves my best friend so deeply beams at the fact that she found someone like this. Someone who has her back in everything. Someone who has *complete* faith in her.

"Well, thanks for your candor, Xanto. I value your input."

"Spoken like a true monarch," he remarks dryly, making me scoff in return.

"Get out of here."

He gives me a smile before departing. I'm about to go about my business when there's *another* knock at my door. I groan in frustration. Is this what my life is going to be like now? Never having a moment's peace?

"Come in."

To my surprise, Penelope walks in. "Your Majesty," she says, bowing low.

I barely contain my huff. "That isn't necessary, Penelope. The way you addressed me previously is fine."

She wrinkles her brows in confusion, but nods. "Ember, I wanted to speak with you for a moment if that's all right."

"Everyone does today," I say under my breath. "Of course. What can I help you with?"

It's then that I realize I have hardly seen her at all since my father died. She looks awful. She's lost weight, she has bags under her eyes, and her cheeks are gaunt. My face pinches in concern.

"Are you all right?" I ask.

"Yes. I was just curious if you were able to speak with your father before he died?"

I frown, thinking back on that day. Parts of it are a blur, but I do remember him wanting to talk to me about something. I had forgotten about it in the chaos of everything and my quest for revenge.

"No. He called me to him, saying he needed to discuss something with me, but we never got the chance to talk. Do you know what he wanted to talk about?"

She nods as a blush rises to her cheeks. I've never seen her blush. "Yes. I spoke with your father that morning. Right before he went to speak with you, actually."

Tears build in her eyes, and my confusion mounts. What Xanto said was true. I think I would be able to see things much more clearly if I was in my right frame of mind. I feel like past Ember is yelling at me how obvious this is, but I still have no clue what she's about to say.

"Your father and I fell in love. He was about to tell you that the two of us were going to give a relationship between us a shot."

Now that she voiced it, I see all the signs I was so oblivious to before. I was right, too, in thinking that past Ember totally would've picked up on this sooner. It still doesn't stop my surprise.

"You loved my father?"

She nods, tears spilling over onto her cheeks now. "Very much. It didn't happen right away. We started spending time together after I came here. Mostly because we both knew your mother. Neither of us have been able to talk about her with anyone else since she passed, and it was a bonding experience for us.

"Then we realized that we valued each other's company and it became more intimate. We were taking things slow though. We didn't want to make such a big decision and have it not work out. Now I'm regretting that decision," she says sadly.

I stand and wrap her in a hug. She sobs and clings to me. Tears build behind my own eyes, and we hang on to each other for dear life as we fall apart.

We settle after a few minutes, and I pull back to gaze at her. "I would've loved having you as a stepmother," I tell her genuinely.

She smiles sadly. "I would've loved that too, my dear."

"We can still have that relationship. I would very much like to get to know you better."

She puts a warm hand on my cheek. "I look forward to it."

I wrap her in another quick hug, and when she's gone, I'm left reeling. I never pictured my dad with anyone else. He always spoke of how much he loved my mother. I figured he would always be hung up on her and never take another partner. Of course, that was a stupid thing to think. He deserved love more than anyone else I know.

Sadness clings to me at the knowledge that he didn't get that either. Not really. He never had the time with Penelope. I hope that wherever he is now, he's with my mother and they can give their love another chance. They both deserve it so much.

I try to continue doing my clerical work, but after the two conversations I just had, I'm feeling restless. I put it away and head out to the training yard. I've tried keeping up on my combat, but it's been difficult. I need to make it a priority. There's something in me that tells me I'll need to know everything I can, and that time is running out. I don't know where it comes from, but I've learned to trust my witchy instincts.

Luckily, there's no one here, and I'm able to do whatever I want without an audience. Although, I am the queen. If there was someone here, I could just order them to leave. I'm not that stuck-up though.

It's then that I realize I haven't visited Ash in a long time. Poor girl. She probably thought that Alexei and I forgot about her. I teletravel to the stables, scaring the shit out of the stable boy.

He stammers and bows clumsily. "Your Majesty, I'm so sorry. I wasn't aware you'd be visiting today."

"It's fine." I smile at him, hoping to settle his nerves, but it seems to only heighten them. I sigh. "I was hoping you would be so kind as to bring Ash to the training yard for me? I could use her."

"O-of course, my queen. Right away, my queen." He bows a few more times and I fight the urge to roll my eyes. I'm sick of this role already.

I teletravel back to the yard, not wanting to wait and make him more anxious. Instead, I ready my bow and arrow. It feels good to have them back in my hands. I do some light stretching as it's been a while since I did anything physical. I finish up just as the stable boy brings Ash in.

She trots up excitedly, and my guilt intensifies.

"Hi, my pretty girl. I missed you too," I coo as I pet her snout. She snorts happily into my palm, and I smile, making a note to myself to spend more time with her in the future.

"Is there anything else you need, Your Majesty?"

I realize then that I've never learned his name. Jesus. I'm killin' it today. I hope I'm not turning into one of those pompous assholes who doesn't bother learning anyone's names just because she's royal.

"What's your name?"

"My name?"

"Yes." I try not to let my exasperation bleed into my tone.

"Fa-Favian, Your Majesty."

I smile at him. "Favian, would you mind getting me some apples and carrots for Ash here?"

"Of course!" He runs off before I can say another word. I chuckle. Ash huffs at me in frustration.

"I'm sorry, girl. I've had so much going on, and I forgot to visit. I'll be better about it, I promise." I continue petting her and giving her all the love she missed out on, and Favian returns moments later carrying as much as his awkward gangly arms can manage, and I resist the urge to giggle.

"Thank you, Favian. You can set them on the table and head back to the stables."

When he's gone, I pick up an apple and feed it to Ash. She neighs happily, and I smile. I've missed her.

"Ready to have some fun?" I ask her, and she replies with a snort.

"Okay, then." I grab my bow and a quiver of arrows, strapping it to my back. I climb onto her and nudge her into a slow trot.

I nock an arrow and take aim. I remember Alexei's instruction as I breathe deeply and release it on the exhale. To my disappointment, it hits the outer rings. I swear softly, but remind myself that I just need to dust off the cobwebs.

Ash continues walking around the yard in a circle, allowing me to improve shot by shot. After I'm able to hit the two inner rings every time, I turn Ash around and I shoot from the other direction. When I have *that* down, I nudge her into going a little faster.

We practice for a full hour before we take a break. I grab some water and gulp it down and give Ash an apple and a carrot as well as fill a bowl with water. I think about having Favian take her back to the stables and practicing hand to hand or combat, but I missed Ash. I missed riding as well, and the urge fills me to get on her back and ride out into the open for an hour or two.

I mount her again and we head off to the main gates. I wish I could just teletravel both of us to a nice open space without the whole territory watching, but unfortunately my magic doesn't work like that. I briefly consider making us invisible, but with Ash being so big there's a good chance we would bump into someone.

We make our way out of the gates as quickly as possible, and even though the guards don't want me out on my own, they let me pass when I pull the queen card.

"Just tell Alexei that I went out for a ride. He can find me if need be, and I'm fully capable of taking care of myself."

Finally, we are far enough away from the city that Ash is able to stretch her legs. I call Ebony forth as well, and she runs alongside us. She's not normally able to burn off much steam either, and it feels good for all of us to get some fresh air away from the city.

I revel in the feel of the sun on my face and the wind blowing through my hair. I smile as I watch Ebony take off, hunting a rabbit she spots. I don't like to think of her catching it, but I like watching her embrace her true nature. I should do this with them more often. As hard as it is to get away from palace duties, it's necessary to keep my sanity intact.

We eventually come across the lake and waterfall that I swam in when Alexei and I still hadn't made up and he stumbled across me naked. The thought brings a smile to my face, and I dismount, letting

Ash drink from it. Ebony does as well, and I love that the two of them get along. Like they just *know* that they're both important to me.

I strip quickly, wanting to take a swim. I haven't gone since my father died. It reminds me too much of Pearl, but after the conversation with Xanto this morning, some of my hope has been restored.

I dive in, shifting when it's deep enough. My mermaid sighs as she's set free in the cool water. I needed this. So did she. I swim mindlessly for a while, pushing myself at certain times, leisurely wandering at others. When I'm floating on the surface, soaking up the sun, I let my mind drift to Pearl.

Is it really possible that someone copied her form? I mean of *course* it is, but she's a strong mermaid with formidable mental shields. It would have to be someone stronger than her, and I don't know too many people who are. Me, Stavros, maybe Mordecai when he was alive. Probably Coralia. But none of those people besides myself are mimics. Xanto, but I don't know if he's stronger than she is. Not to mention that he's on her side. He made that very clear this morning.

Fuck. I can't believe I didn't even consider mimics. Xanto's right. It's because of the fact that I grew up on Earth. My first instinct is to trust what I'm seeing but it's obvious that with magic at work you don't always get the whole picture.

When I finally make my way out of the lake, I find Alexei sitting on the edge, watching me. His eyes light as he takes in my nudity.

"Well, hello, my queen."

He's the only one I like calling me that. He makes it sound like a dirty promise. My core clenches.

"Hello, mate. What are you doing here?"

"The guards told me that you went for a ride and they were worried about you. I teletraveled around to a few of your favorite places before I found you."

"I'm fine on my own."

"Of course you are, but I couldn't deny the opportunity to get you out of the palace and alone, now, could I?"

I smile at the heat that laces his voice. "And now that you found me, what exactly are you going to do with me?"

He smirks deviously. "Well, I am feeling a little bit hungry if you wouldn't mind feeding me..." He knows I find him drinking from me one of the hottest things in the world.

Wetness gathers between my thighs, and when a breeze blows toward him, his nostrils flare as he scents my arousal. I hear him growl, and then he teletravels right in front of me, pulling me close and claiming my mouth with his.

He guides me down to where he already has a blanket laid out on the ground. When I'm flat under him, he spreads my thighs wide, taking in the juices that are dripping from me.

His eyes turn to liquid fire before he drops down and drags his tongue through my slit. I tip my head back and moan to the sky. There's nothing else in the world except for me and Alexei and the way he's worshiping me. I revel in it, and soon I'm clutching his hair and riding his face, chasing my orgasm. He brings me there in no time at all, and I fight it off as long as possible. I want to bask in this feeling as long as I can.

"Come for me, little doe. I want to feel you coming all over my face."

As much as I try to hold back, his words send me hurtling off the edge, and then I feel his fangs plunge into my mound. I scream, my pleasure surging as high as the sky. I fly there for longer than normal before slowly coming back down.

Before I've fully recovered, Alexei is plunging into me. My body clenches around him, making him growl against my throat. "I'll never get enough of you."

I can't do anything besides meet his thrusts with my hips and let the pleasurable sounds pour out of my mouth. He picks up his pace, and I know he's already close. I feel myself building again from the orgasm I never fully recovered from, and I know that this time I might never come back down.

His thumb glides over the bite mark that's still on my mound, and I sob. I'm so incredibly sensitive, and I never want him to stop. He brings one of my legs up against his chest, changing the angle and hitting a spot inside me that makes me see stars.

His pace becomes frenzied, and I know he's right on the edge. I sink my own fangs into his neck, and his sweet, warm blood fills my mouth along with his power. He groans and bites my shoulder as we come together the way vampire mates do. It sends both of us over the edge, our pleasure spinning between us and building higher and higher. My orgasm continues for minutes, and I can do nothing but ride it out.

Finally it ebbs, and I feel Alexei's hot seed spilling out of me onto the blanket beneath us. "Fuck," he says.

I laugh, clenching around him and making him suck in another sharp breath. "I know what you mean."

He doesn't pull out of me, but shifts us onto our sides so we're facing each other. He smiles softly at me before swiping my hair out of my face. "I love you, mate."

I bring his wrist with our mate mark up to my mouth. "I love you too, mate."

We lounge there for what feels like hours, just watching the clouds pass and the sun move across the sky. It feels like heaven.

"Can we just stay out here forever?" I ask.

"All you have to do is ask, Ember," he answers seriously, and I know that if I really wanted to, he would take me far away so we could live a simple life.

As tempting as that sounds, I know I can't leave. The kingdom needs me, and I will not abandon them.

# 6

## Pearl

The following day, Proteus comes to my cave in the morning, and we head off for the portal, hiding whenever we see anyone. No one can know that we're out here. Especially me.

I've never been to this portal location before, but Proteus has once. It's in a section of caves, the entrance to which is underwater, but the cave itself has an area in a little air bubble, if you will, where the actual portal is located.

*We're getting close*, Proteus says in mind speak.

I swim faster. I don't know why I think there's something here, but it's the same as when I was looking for information in the library.

As we approach, I can hear voices, distorted. Us mermaids don't have the same problem distinguishing noises between above and below water though. Proteus and I cut a glance at each other. I hear them in the cave above us, and it's clear that they're at least not in the water. We will have to be careful because they will potentially be able to hear us in mind speak.

"It took you long enough to meet with me."

That voice sounds familiar. I can't place it, but Proteus goes deathly still, and I'm sure if I could see him better, I would see he was pale.

"I don't answer to *you*. Quite the opposite, actually," another voice cuts in, and that one chills me to my core. I don't recognize it though.

"I'm sorry, Your Majesty. I've just been worried about what will happen next. We don't have a plan in place yet." Coralia. I finally recognize her voice and my blood turns to ice.

"It isn't your plan to come up with, simpleton, but *mine*. I have something in the works, but as of right now, the fact that I'm able to travel through the portal is enough. I've been trying to get through for thousands of years, and I will figure out how to get my army here."

"Yes, Demonica. I mean Your Majesty," she stammers.

I've never heard Coralia sound so docile. Especially after being called a simpleton. My heart beats impossibly faster when I realize who she's talking to.

"Should I tell the other mermaids that you've returned and killed the king to take your rightful place on the throne? I could get the whole of Mermacovia helping you." Oh, fuck. Demonica copied my form and killed Stavros.

"Not yet. I will inform you when I would like you to reveal my presence. Until then, just keep me updated on what's going on in the kingdom. And I'll also need more captives soon. We're running low on people to feed off again."

"Yes, Your Majesty."

Proteus touches me, and I almost jump a foot. He motions for us to leave, and I nod, following him out. It sounds like they're wrapping up and the last thing we need is to get caught snooping. I don't want to think about what the two of them would do to us.

We swim like we have the devil on our tails, and in a sense we do. We don't stop or talk until we return to my cave. We collapse onto the floor, exhausted. When our heart rates have calmed, we finally discuss what we heard.

*Demonica somehow managed to break through the wards. And she killed the king,* I say in mind speak, hardly able to believe that's what we just heard.

*We need to leave now and tell Ember. She needs to know what she's up against.*

*Did you hear what she said about captives?* I ask.

He nods, furrowing his brow in concern and confusion. *I don't know what she meant by that though.*

*I do. There have been people being taken from each territory. No one knows what's happening to them. I think that's what she's talking about. We saw in the records yesterday that demons feed off of other's souls and can stay immortal that way. That must be what they're using them for.*

His face blanches with horror. *My mother is kidnapping people and giving them to the demons to feed off of?*

*It would seem so,* I say sadly, disgusted with Coralia. I knew she was trying to get Demonica on the throne, but I had no idea she was doing this.

*We need to go. Now. Are you coming with me?* I ask.

*Yes. I can't stay here knowing what she's doing.*

I nod in understanding. I would feel the same way. I wish I could warn Opal, but we need to get out of here. I also wouldn't be surprised if Opal condoned what Coralia is doing. She knows about Demonica, and as sad as it is, her moral compass points in a much different direction than mine. On top of that, I'm pretty sure she thinks that Coralia can do no wrong.

*I know we're both exhausted, but we need to get out of here. Ready?* I ask. Just like coming here, we don't have the luxury of taking our time.

*Of course. I'm with you, Pearl.*

I smile and give his hand a squeeze before we take off. We set a grueling pace, and I know that when we get there, I'm going to sleep for a full two days. At least if Xanto was able to convince Ember to listen to me. I have information for her now, and I know exactly who killed her father. I also have Proteus to back me up, which I'm extremely grateful for. She respects him, and I think between the two of us she will trust our word.

My heart pangs when I think of Xanto. I love that man, and I'm excited for him to meet Proteus. I can really see the three of us forming a special bond. As long as they feel a connection too. Fuck, I hope so. I want Proteus. Badly. And with every day we're together, the sexual tension builds higher and higher. It's becoming unbearable.

We rest for short periods when we can, and snack on random fish, but I'm exhausted and starving. Honestly, I've been both since I left the palace in the first place, not getting a true night's sleep or a decent meal in a while.

I can't wait to be back in my nice big bed with a huge glass of wine and a warm freshly cooked meal. I actually miss my legs. I don't think I ever have before, but I'm never in my mermaid form this long. My mermaid will be ready to go into hibernation for a while when I shift back to my land form.

Proteus and I chat a little on the way, but for the most part we're too exhausted and pushing ourselves too hard. I still enjoy his presence, and am happy he's here with me. It's definitely a more pleasant experience than it was swimming here. I'm full of hope now, and I have someone to bring back to Xanto. My heart swells.

Days later, we arrive at my lake. We were able to swim straight here since there are waterways that lead all the way to Mermacovia. We shift back into our land forms, and I'm incredibly relieved when my legs reappear. I missed them so much. I change into the clothes that I grabbed from Opal, and Proteus puts on his signature wrap, covering his glorious body from view. He brought a waterproof bag with him as well, just in case.

I grab his hand and we walk up to the castle. I feel thoroughly self-conscious because I've been underwater for over a week. I don't have any makeup on, and my hair is a wreck, but oh well. Nothing to be done for it now.

As we approach the palace, I worry about how we're going to be received. Are the guards going to arrest me? I don't have long to think about it because we're at the main gates soon enough.

There are shouts when we're spotted, and one of them comes up to us. "Pearl. You are to be taken to the queen immediately," he says. I recognize him but don't recall his name.

"Perfect, because that's just who I need to see."

He grabs my arm lightly, not putting me in handcuffs, but letting me know that it would be unwise for me to attempt an escape. Proteus is still hanging on to my other hand, and he squeezes it in solidarity.

We're ushered into a room that looks like an office. I'm surprised we aren't taken to the throne room, but then I remember Xanto said that's where Stavros was murdered. I wouldn't be surprised if Ember never wanted to set foot in that room again. My heart pangs for her for about the thousandth time since I heard. I wish my best friend never had to go through all this heartbreak. The only good thing that's come of it is that she's been made queen. I just know she's going to do wonderful things for our realm.

We sit down in two chairs that are facing a gorgeous chestnut desk. There are little touches of Ember here, but not many. I'm sure it's taking her a little while to get settled into her new role.

A door opens behind the desk and Ember and Alexei stroll in. Their eyes are hard as they stare at us, and I fight the urge to recoil. I haven't done anything wrong, but I still have to convince her of that.

"Pearl. You have some explaining to do. I won't pardon your crimes until I'm fully certain that you were not the one to kill my father. Speak." Her voice is full of the command, and I know she would have already ripped through my mental shields if I didn't have them open for her. I want her to know that I have nothing to hide. Her brow furrows in confusion and a small glimmer of hope lights in her purple eyes.

"I did not kill the king." I can feel her pouring honesty into me, but it's unnecessary. "I was down at the lake swimming when it happened. You have to know that I would never betray you like that. I think the stable boy we interacted with when we got back from Earth was an imposter. He was acting strangely and he touched my arm."

Ember quietly listens to me, letting me tell my story. Perfect. There's more I need to say.

I tell her everything that happened from the moment I left, including my interaction with Coralia, the records we found and what they included, and what Proteus and I overheard at the portal, including the fact that Demonica plans to bring others with her as soon as she's able. The longer I speak, the more the ice melts from Ember's face. I know she can sense the sincerity in me, but when I get to the interaction we witnessed, her gaze fills with horror. Proteus nods his head along in agreement, silently backing me up.

When I'm finished, she jumps up and runs over to me. Her arms wrap around me tightly and she sobs into my shoulder. Tears build in my own eyes and I let them free as my best friend and I reunite.

"Oh, Pearl. I'm so relieved you are innocent. I was heartbroken thinking that you had betrayed me like that. I'm so sorry that I expected the worst before hearing what happened from you."

"I know. I understand. I probably would've reacted the exact same way." When I pull back, I admire the woman she's become. "You look so lovely. You make a wonderful queen."

She rolls her eyes fondly and snorts. "Hardly."

As much as I want to bask in our reunion, there is one other thing I need to tell her. "Ember, there's something else."

She must sense my dread because she stiffens. "What?"

"I've known about Demonica for a while. Select few were told by Coralia. I swear I didn't know that she was stealing citizens to feed the demons. I only knew that she was trying to find a way to bring her back and put her on the throne."

I take a deep breath as nerves turn my stomach. I hope she doesn't hate me again after this. "I was originally sent here as a spy by Coralia. I was conflicted about it after meeting Stavros and seeing what a great leader he was, and even more so after meeting you. And then you changed and I found out you were also a descendant of Surseiha. My alliances switched then, and when we went back to Mermacovia I tried to tell Coralia that things were different now and she needed to change her allegiance, but she wouldn't listen to me. I haven't been giving her any information for a long time now, but I wanted to be completely transparent with you. I'm so sorry I never told you. I wanted to, but I was so worried that you would want nothing to do with me."

She smiles softly at me. "I understand, Pearl. I get how revered Surseiha's line is to the mermaids. The important part is you tried to do the right thing and convince Coralia otherwise and maintained loyalty to us. I forgive you, and thank you for telling me."

We hug again, and I'm so relieved I almost collapse. She chuckles.

"Head to your room. You must be exhausted."

"Where is Xanto?"

A knowing smile crosses her lips. "Waiting impatiently to come in."

At her words, the door bursts open and Xanto sweeps me into his arms, kissing me fiercely. I almost weep with the joy that rushes through me, and I cling to him. I didn't realize until now how much I missed him.

We break apart, but not far. Xanto still holds me tight and I feel like I can breathe deeply for the first time since I left.

"I missed you," I tell him.

"I missed you too."

I pull back out of his arms, but grasp his hand tightly in mine, not ready to let go yet. I gesture to Proteus, who has a small smile on his face as he watches us. There's no jealousy in his gaze, but his eyes roam over Xanto appreciatively. I hide my smirk.

"Xanto, this is Proteus. He's the son of the grand mistress, and he's been helping me this week. He came back here to assist...and to meet you."

Xanto's eyebrows rise, but he holds out a hand. "Nice to meet you, Proteus."

"Likewise."

I have a hard time not ripping their clothes off seeing them touching each other, even innocently.

"Ember? Can we get a room set up for Proteus?"

"Of course," she says, summoning a servant to escort him to one of the guest rooms.

"Proteus, will you have dinner with me and Xanto?" I ask. I need to talk to Xanto first about what I want and then I would like us all to spend some time together.

He smiles and nods. "As you wish, my lady," he says smoothly before taking off.

Xanto meets my gaze and a knowing look enters his eyes, along with a smirk on his lips.

"Ember, I love you, but I really need to wash up and take a nap."

"Go, go," she orders, shooing us away.

"Glad we have you back, Pearl," Alexei chimes in, speaking for the first time.

I smile before walking over and giving him a hug. He returns it, even though he's never been the most affectionate guy with anyone other than Ember.

"Missed you too, asshole," I tease him with another squeeze.

When I break away from him, Xanto scoops me up and carries me off to our rooms. I squeal in surprise.

"What are you doing?" I ask, laughing.

"You're exhausted from your journey, and I missed you. I'm holding you tight for as long as I can."

I melt at the words. He really is a wonderful man and I'm so lucky. I snuggle into his chest, basking in the warmth emanating from him. He stalks to our room, kicking the door open and making me swoon. He hip-checks it closed and strides to the bathroom, setting me down on the toilet before starting the water.

Soon the bathroom is filled with steam, and I'm so excited for hot water that if I wasn't so exhausted I would be bouncing in my seat. I strip off my clothes and when we're both naked, we step in. The near scalding water beats down on my battered body, and I moan out in pure bliss.

Xanto's hands are on my body, all lathered and smelling of jasmine. He dutifully cleans me, and I let him pamper me, soaking up all the love and affection he has to offer.

When he's finished with my body, I turn to rinse off and he starts in on my hair. I normally like to do this myself since I stick to a specific regiment, but I'm too exhausted to care. Luckily, salt water is extremely healthy for mermaid hair, and since I normally don't get enough of that, this week rejuvenated it.

The scents surround us, and I can't get enough of it. I'm a luxury girl, and it was torture living without my creature comforts.

We stay in until the water starts to cool, and I reluctantly shut off the shower. Xanto picks me up again and towels me off. I laugh, assuring him I'm not so helpless, but he shrugs me off. The next moment, he takes me to bed and we finally give in to the physical need for each other.

He licks me to climax multiple times before finally entering me. I sob in pleasure. Fuck, I missed this. We don't stop for hours, and when we finally lie down to rest, I bring up the subject on my mind.

"What did you think of Proteus?"

A knowing smirk graces his lips. "I don't know him. I only met him for a brief moment."

I huff in frustration. "Did you find him attractive?"

"Why? Do *you* find him attractive?"

I growl at him. "Xanto!"

He chuckles. "Yes I do."

"He helped me out a great deal in Mermacovia. He also confided in me that he's been interested in me for a long time."

"I see. And how do you feel about him?"

"I've always had a thing for him. I think he could make a great addition to our relationship, but I told him we were a package deal, so if the two of you didn't work out then it wouldn't work out with me and him either. I also didn't start anything with him because I wanted you to meet him first."

His eyes soften and warm. "I've always been attracted to men too, and he is a fine specimen."

My core clenches as his words bring the mental image of watching the two of them together, or having both of them worship me. I want to experience all of it with them.

Xanto scents my desire roaring back to life, and we get tangled in each other again.

# 7

# Ember

I'm so relieved that Pearl is back and that I know I can trust her. It was gnawing at me having my best friend turn into my enemy. A small piece of myself mended at hearing her story and sensing her sincerity.

The other part of me was absolutely horrified to discover what *actually* happened. Demonica. Here. Fuck. Honestly, it just brings up more questions. How did she get through the wards? Will she find a way to bring the other demons with her? What does she want? Too many questions and not enough answers.

I'm tempted to bring the fight to *her*, but I don't know if that's a good idea. Especially since I just took over the kingdom. Not to mention I don't know if the mermaids would fight for us or against us. There's a very good chance it could turn into a civil war, especially with Coralia backing Demonica. Then again, Coralia has also been kidnapping fellow mermaids for the demons to feed off of, so hopefully most will be upset that she sacrificed her own people.

I sigh. I can feel a tension headache blooming. There's another aspect my mind immediately clung to that I can't stop circling. If Demonica already made her way through, is there any reason to keep the races segregated? I mean, I'm sure that would guarantee that the other demons could come through into our realm, but I have a feeling that Coralia will figure out a way to make that happen anyway. It's obvious that if we do indeed go to war with Domonia that all the species will have to work together regardless. Maybe it's time that they are told the truth.

Alexei comes into our room as I pace in front of the fire for the millionth time. I'm pretty sure by this time I've gone over the same information with every pass I make over the rug.

"Let's go to bed," my mate says, stopping my path and kissing my neck.

I huff, but let him lay me down. He spends the next hour thoroughly distracting me, and I'm pleased when my mind finally calms. When we're lying next to each other in the afterglow of our lovemaking, I get five minutes of rest before my brain starts back up again.

"Alexei, what do you think we shou—"

"Tomorrow, my love. We can talk and worry about this tomorrow. For now, let's take a shower, have dinner sent up to the room, and I'll exhaust you again before we go to sleep."

His offer sounds all too tempting. "But..."

"Shh." He kisses me before I can say anything else, scooping me up in his arms and heading to the bathroom for the shower he promised me.

The next day, everything feels slightly less overwhelming, and I'm lucky to have a mate who knows exactly what I need. But in the light of day, I realize that something needs to be done. All of my concerns from the night prior seem more clear now, and I decide to call a council meeting with all the ambassadors. I wish I could also include the grand masters and mistresses of all the territories to get their input as well, but I don't have the time it would take for them to travel here. I need to decide what to do *now*.

I send Humphrey to let all of them know that we're having a meeting in an hour along with the kitchen staff. I want them to prepare breakfast for this meeting. Everyone will be much happier with full tummies. I'm also about to send for Penelope when she shows up at my door.

"I knew you needed me here. I don't know why, but I came as soon as I sensed it."

"Thank you for coming."

"What is it you need from me?"

"I'm about to have a meeting with the ambassadors and I would like you at my side."

Her brows rise in surprise. "You want me with you?"

"Of course. You're my royal seer. I value your input."

Tears build in her eyes, but she blinks them back before they can spill over onto her cheeks. She bows. "Thank you, Your Majesty. I won't let you down."

I know her potential was never recognized by anyone of her species and that she carries a lot of self-doubt because of that, but I know what she's capable of. So did my father. "I know you won't," I say, squeezing her hand.

"I'll get ready and meet you there."

Alexei comes in after she leaves, having been getting ready in our room.

"That was thoughtful of you."

"I would be an idiot not to take advantage of having such a witch at my disposal."

"There are no diplomats here, you know? You can tell me the real reason."

"I mean, that is a big part of it."

"What's the other part?"

I sigh. Sometimes I wish he wasn't so observant and didn't know me so well.

"I'm starting to look at her as a mother figure. She knew both of my mothers, and she had started a romantic relationship with my father before he died. I'm upset that neither of them got to actually have the time to enjoy each other like they should've."

He wraps me in a hug. He's never been great with words, but he's always let the contact of his body on mine do the talking for him. It's always exactly what I need.

When it's time, we head down to the conference room. The food is laid out on the table a moment later, and everyone else shows up within the next few minutes. I load up my plate, knowing that they won't eat until I do. Being royal is so fucking weird.

When everyone is fed, I start in. "Good morning, everyone. Thank you all for meeting with me on such short notice. There's been some new developments that I would like to discuss with you all that concern the entire realm. I would like all of your opinions on how best to proceed. As of right now, all of this information is extremely confidential, and therefore cannot be allowed to leave this room. I will make a magical pact with you all to keep it to yourselves until we decide our next course of action."

They all line up in front of me, Pearl and I clasping each other's forearms first. I smile at her. "Do you swear to keep this information to yourself and only those within this room until I say otherwise?"

"I swear." Magic pulses between us where we're touching, and I continue on with each individual here until there is no one left.

"Thank you all for doing that. Please be seated. I know this is different, and I'm sure it is fairly nerve-racking, but you will soon understand why I've called you here."

I take a deep breath before starting with the truth that Pearl was not responsible for the king's death. That her form was mimicked. There are gasps all around, but before they can form even more prejudice against the mimics, I tell them about Demonica, the demons, and the realm of Domonia. I show them the book that Pearl brought me from Mermacovia. There are frantic whispers and shocked exclamations as they digest the information, and just plain fear that floods the room. After I've told them of the history, I explain that Demonica was the individual who murdered the king, and that she's able to travel between the realms, even though I have no idea how. She *shouldn't* be able to. The last piece of information I share is that Coralia is behind the disappearances that have been taking place around the realm, sacrificing her own people for Demonica.

The room erupts into chaos. The information I've shared is too overwhelming for everyone to comprehend. The only ones who remain unaffected are Alexei, Pearl, and Xanto, having already known everything. Proteus is not included in this meeting, considering he's not technically part of my council.

I let them freak out for a moment, knowing they need to get it out of their system, but only a moment. "Enough," I say. I don't even need to raise my voice for them to fall silent.

"I know this is all a lot to digest. That is precisely why I need you all here with me to decide what our next course of action should be. I've had slightly more time to process than you all, and have a few ideas. I would like opinions on them. The first thing I would like to do is to tell the kingdom. It's been long enough, and they have a right to know why they've always been kept separated.

"Second, it's clear that Demonica is able to travel here. I have no idea how she's gotten through the wards, but it raises another concern: can she bring other demons through with her? Thanks to Pearl and Proteus, we know that she's *attempting* to, but we don't know if or when she'll be able to manage it. To mitigate this, I would like to bring the battle to *her* doorstep. She has no idea that we know about her, or that she's been here. We would have the element of surprise. I'm aware that this is drastic, and maybe unwise since I just took over the kingdom, but that is precisely why you are all here. What are your opinions?"

There's a beat of silence before chaos erupts. I raise my hands, catching everyone's attention. "One at a time. I can't understand you when you all speak at once. Who has concerns?"

I sigh when everyone raises their hands. I point to the vampire ambassador. "You first, Vlad."

"Your Majesty, firstly, I would like to say thank you for bringing this to our attention. I understand why none of the past leaders have trusted anyone with this information, but I feel it is best for us all to deal with it. We're here to support you."

There are murmurs of assent and head nods throughout the group. I smile at them, thankful for their support.

He continues, "That being said, I think it wise to tell the people as well. I do suspect there will be some level of panic at first, but they have the right to know why they've been living in the situation they have for so long." He leans back in his chair, and I'm relieved I have at least one person who agrees with me.

The elf ambassador, Anastas, speaks up, "I do agree with the sentiment behind it, Your Majesty, but I do not think it wise. The people could revolt. They could storm the castle. They will be upset that they've never been told about this in the past." The typical elf attitude is present in his words, although his tone is slightly more respectful than I've come to know from the species.

"But they will be thankful that their new leader is telling them. It wasn't her fault that none of the previous leaders did. She's including them in the decision in a way." Pearl speaks up from her side of the table. My heart swells at having her support after everything that's happened.

"That's an idea," I chime in. Everybody goes silent and looks at me. "What if we get the people's viewpoint on what we should do? I mean, of course I will have the final say, but back on Earth we take votes. The people of this realm will be involved in whatever decision we make, they should have a say in our plans."

Everyone looks slightly uncomfortable at the mention of Earth, but Xanto finally breaks the awkward silence that's descended. "I think that's a wonderful idea, Your Majesty. We are very fortunate to have a leader from another realm so we may have input that no one else has thought of before. It will be strange for the people at first, but I think they will appreciate having a voice."

We continue the discussion for hours. I want to be thorough, and hear everyone's opinions. They're all valid, even if some disagree with the points and plans I've brought up, but that's exactly what I need. It's a big decision either way, and I need to make sure I'm making the best choice, and it will help to have my council with me.

"Penelope, what do you think?"

She looks startled that I asked for her input. She hasn't said a word this whole time. "My opinion doesn't matter, Your Majesty."

"It absolutely does. That's why I asked you here."

She swallows uncomfortably. "I think telling the people is wise. I have a good feeling about it."

I understand what she's saying. Her witchy senses are telling her this is the right thing to do. Mine are saying the same thing. The witch ambassador Volina nods from the other side of the table. It's a good sign that all three witches here feel optimistic about this approach.

"Okay. Does anyone have thoughts on the potential war situation?"

Once again, everyone talks at once. I hold up my hand and we discuss things one by one, but this subject seems more split. Some think we should wait to see what Demonica does, and others think we should strike first.

"They killed our king! That in and of itself is an act of war!" Volina yells.

My heart pangs, and Alexei reaches over and squeezes my hand. He's been my rock through this entire meeting. He's let me hear the concerns of everyone here, as well as listened intently, and I'm curious what his opinion will be.

"What of Coralia? You should take action against her, my queen. She is a traitor to the crown and the realm," Vlad pipes in.

"I wholeheartedly agree. How do you propose I go about it?"

"She should be brought before the council and undergo a trial," Anastas suggests.

I nod, having thought the same thing. "Send for her. Maybe then we'll be able to find out more about Demonica and her plans."

After sitting in this room for *hours*, I'm ready for this meeting to be over. "Okay. I think that's all we can discuss for now." Just as I'm about to dismiss everyone, another thought pops up. "Oh wait. I would also like to have a human ambassador. Can someone arrange that, please? That is long overdue. They are a race here just like everyone else, and should have a say."

"I can arrange that, Your Majesty," Volina volunteers.

I smile at her. "Thank you. That's all for today."

Everyone gets up, and soon it's just me, Alexei, Pearl, Xanto, and Penelope left. My inner circle and those I trust most.

"Well, that went well," I say, laughing.

"It actually did, Ember. We're all pleased and surprised that you've included us in what our next steps should be," Pearl says.

I smile, but it's slightly tinged with sadness. Why did no other ruler get other opinions like this? Not even my father?

"Well, I suppose our next step is to tell the kingdom. Can someone please set up a formal address for me in a few days? I want to give a speech to as many people as possible. Alexei and I can teletravel to the other territories as well to give speeches there. For those that aren't able to be there we can transcribe it and send it across the realm. Then we can allow them all to write down their thoughts and concerns and what they think we should do. It's going to be a lot of work, but I value the opinions of my people."

Xanto nods. "I can take care of that."

"Thank you, Xanto."

I know this isn't technically his job, but I want someone I trust to be in charge.

"Do you think Coralia will cooperate?" I ask Pearl.

"Honestly? No. She will come kicking and screaming and won't tell you anything."

I nod. My thoughts exactly. "We need to prepare for the very real possibility that the mermaids won't be fighting for us. I truly don't know what we'll do in that scenario. I can't very well punish an entire territory."

"I know not all the mermaids will back her, but there are a good number of them that care more about power and self-importance than about doing what's right," Pearl says sadly. "Unfortunately, I think Opal is one of them."

I squeeze her hand sympathetically. I don't have siblings, but I can only imagine how hard this is going to be on her.

"We'll deal with it as it comes. In the meantime, it might be a good idea for you and Proteus to go and talk to them, if you'd be willing. Try to garner more support? And Proteus is well-liked by the people. I think out of anyone he would be the best person for the job. And you are the biggest charmer I've ever met."

She blushes. "Oh, stop."

"Do you think that would be something you'd be comfortable doing?"

She nods. "As much as I want to be here with you, I want to help in any way I can. I also was thinking that while we're there, we could also start looking for the trident. That could be a strong asset for you in the upcoming battle. And I don't even know if Demonica is aware of its existence."

Any sort of advantage against her could mean the difference between victory and defeat. "I need all the help I can get," I tell her.

Xanto nods. "Then the three of us will gather some support for you and attempt to find Surseiha's Needle. If it's anywhere I feel like it *has* to be in Mermacovia."

Everyone moves to leave, but I stop Pearl. "We need a girls' night before you leave again. And I want to be caught up on how dinner went with Proteus last night."

She beams, which I take to mean it went well. "Tonight?"

"Yes. Want to take a swim first?"

"What kind of question is that?"

I laugh. "Meet you at the lake at seven."

Alexei and I head back up to our room and I'm comforted that the meeting is over. I strip off my dress and let Ebony free of my flesh. She does what she always does and plops down in front of the fire, giving a dramatic sigh before taking a nap. She looks as exhausted as I feel, and I wonder if being in my body with me causes some of my stress and anxiety to rub off on her. What I wouldn't do for a stress-free day.

My mate comes up behind me and starts rubbing my shoulders. I moan as the tension slowly starts to ease out of my body. "That feels good."

"I can make you feel a lot better than that," he teases, but doesn't stop working his magic hands.

"You can do whatever you want to me," I groan out. I love being intimate with him, but him caring for me like this feels *so* good.

He chuckles and leads me over to the bed. He lays me facedown on it before crawling up and sitting on my ass. His hands roam down my back, kneading away my tightness and stress. After twenty minutes, I'm a melted puddle on the mattress, and about to fall asleep.

There's a knock on the door, and I startle. I wasn't expecting anyone.

"Time for lunch," Alexei says, swatting me gently on the bum.

He returns moments later with food, and my stomach growls loudly. He smiles fondly before setting the tray on the bed in front of me. I ate only a few hours ago, but with the stress of the morning and the little massage I just had, I'm suddenly starving.

We eat together, occasionally feeding each other, and I smile as I think about our trip coming here in the first place. There was a lot of this. While those days were scary and overwhelming, they were much simpler in so many ways.

Alexei meets my eyes, and I'm sure he can read the exact thoughts swirling through my head. "We should take a horse ride soon. Just the two of us. And Ash of course."

Ebony huffs from the floor, glaring at him.

"And you too, Ebony."

She seems pacified as she lays her head back down on her paws.

"That sounds perfect. Maybe you can show me some new moves too."

He smirks. "I can always teach you something."

I swat his chest playfully, and in the next moment we're rolling around on the mattress, wrestling. He, of course, pins me quickly, and then we're making out. We take our time and enjoy each other.

Everything has felt so rushed and stressful lately that it feels nice to just soak in this private moment with him where I'm not thinking about the kingdom or Demonica.

Eventually his hands start to roam, and by the time he sinks into me, I'm soaked. He makes love to me slowly, savoring every second as he stares into my soul. Our marks flare with light and heat, adding to my pleasure, and I swear it's like in that moment we're one person. My soul connects with his at the same time as our magic intertwines, and I gasp at the feeling of him consuming me so thoroughly. It's only cemented further when we feed from each other, our blood circulating between the two of us. The next moment I'm shattering apart into a million pieces as I pull my mate under with me.

# 8

# Pearl

I meet Ember by the lake for our nightly swim. I've missed this. We used to do this almost every night before things got so fucked up. I'm excited to catch her up on everything and hear how her coronation went.

She's already there when I arrive, and we quickly strip and dive into the water. I let the shift sweep through me, and then I'm gliding through the water. We swim for an hour or two, and we're laughing our asses off by the time we make our way out. Ember dries us off with her air magic, and then we're heading back up to her rooms.

She kicked Alexei out for the night, telling him he didn't want to be a part of our girl talk anyway. We order more food up like always, along with copious amounts of wine. It's been too long since we did this, and we are going all out. We have a lot to catch up on. Ember lets Ebony free, and she camps out next to us, sniffing with interest at the food, and soaking up any and all affection.

"So, first things first. Proteus?" She just dives right in. Fuck me.

"You're not wasting any time, are you?"

"Bitch, I've been dying to ask you since you two walked in together looking all cozy."

I laugh. "Well, we met back up in Mermacovia. He helped me with my research and to spy on his mother. He knew of the portal, so it made my mission a lot easier. When we were there, though, he told me that he's always been enamored with me."

"Of course he has. Everyone is."

I roll my eyes at her. "No they are not. But that's beside the point. I never knew, and I felt the same way about him. Either way, I told him that I wanted him to meet Xanto before anything could happen between us. I wanted to make sure that they would be a good fit too."

"And...?"

"We met up with him for dinner last night." I smile before I can stop it.

"Tell me, tell me!"

"They got along really well. And Xanto is attracted to him. We talked about it when we got back to the room."

"You talked about it, or you 'talked' about it?" she asks with a wink.

"You already know the answer to that." I smirk.

She laughs. "So, have you talked to Proteus?"

"We talked a little about it last night, and I think he's willing to give it a shot." Excitement builds in my stomach. I've wanted this for a long time, and I can't believe it took something so horrible to make it happen.

She squeals excitedly and gives me a big hug. "I'm so happy for you, Pearl."

"Okay, enough about me. How did the coronation go?"

"It was fine."

I groan dramatically. "You've got to give me more than that. I need *all* the details. I didn't get to witness your ascent into greatness, remember?"

"Well, I hated not having you there to get me ready. But even still, I don't think I've ever looked better in my life. I also let all my gifts out to play, so they could all see what I was capable of."

I'm a little shocked. "Even Ebony?" She told me about how the witches kept their familiars secret. Most of the realm didn't even know the witches could *have* familiars.

She smiles, and it's slightly savage. The predator in me perks up and takes notice. Not that I didn't know she was a fierce opponent before, but seeing this dark side of her that's come free after her father died is calling to something in me.

"Yes. Although, I let her out before I made my walk down the aisle. I'm pretty sure that everyone just thinks she's a very well-trained pet of mine." Ebony huffs in irritation. "Their shocked expressions were fun to say the least. I wish you could've witnessed it."

"Me too," I say sadly, squeezing her hand. "I haven't had a chance to talk to you alone yet. I'm so sorry. How are you?"

"I'm fine."

I give her an imploring look. I know she's not all right.

"All right, fine. I'm so overwhelmed, I have no clue what I'm doing. My dad who I was just getting close to was murdered in front of me by some crazy demon bitch who impersonated my best friend and made me go all psycho. On top of all of that, I'm considering plunging our realm into war with another realm after just taking over the crown. I could keep going..." Tears well in her eyes, and I pull her into a tight hug before she can get another word out.

She has a bad habit of doing this. She takes too much onto her plate and just keeps going until it gets to be overwhelming, and it inevitably always comes pouring out of her. Speaking of which, I can feel splashes of liquid on my shoulder and I know those tears finally spilled over.

"Well, I'm here now. I'll help in any way I can."

She nods against me, and I squeeze her tighter. I've missed her. "I needed you. And I needed this. Thank you."

After that, the conversation lightens, and we spend the night drinking, chatting, and laughing just like old times. Ebony eats all the food we give her greedily, and gets more rambunctious the more we drink.

When we're thoroughly drunk, she asks me the question I knew she would. "So, when are you guys going to get it on with Proteus? Have you talked specifics? Like how's it going to work?"

I chuckle. "You've never been with more than one partner before?"

"Please. I don't have the lady balls to pull that off. Plus, I'm more of a one man kind of woman. Not to mention that Alexei is almost *too* much for me to handle. But I *am* curious. So spill."

"Well, they both like men as well as women, so all of us will be together. I'm sure at some point I'll have both of them at once, and I'm sure other times I'll watch them with each other and vice versa." I can feel myself flushing just thinking about it. They are going to be so hot together. I can't wait to see it.

"That does sound hot. Although, I'm too jealous to allow Alexei to be with anyone else, even another man."

"I get that. Probably the differences in culture."

She nods, her face red with liquor and probably a little heat from the conversation. "Have you...ever had a threesome with another woman?"

I nod emphatically. "Yes. Many times. Honestly, it's more common than two men and a woman."

"Interesting. Before I got with Alexei I thought it would be fun. I didn't have a ton of sexual experience though, and definitely not serious partners."

"As far as I can tell, the way it works best with people that tend to get jealous but want to try multiple bedroom partners is to have three single strangers get together at the same time. That way no one is jealous or left out."

"That makes sense."

Alexei comes in hours later. "Time for bed, my love."

I swoon at his endearment to her. She does the same as he picks her up and carries her to the bedroom.

"Good night, Pearl!" she exclaims, giggling as she starts sucking on his neck. I chuckle as I make my way to my own quarters.

When I enter, I'm shocked to see Proteus and Xanto there, having drinks of their own and chatting with each other. They're sitting on our couch, and it looks as if they've scooted in closer to each other throughout the night. Now they're within touching distance, and they occasionally reach out to stroke an arm or rest a hand on the other's leg.

They haven't noticed me yet, and I just stand there and admire them, getting hotter the longer I stare.

Proteus finally sees me, and a sexy smirk lights up his face. "Hello, gorgeous. Care to join us?"

I nod, my mouth going dry as I look at their heated expressions. I glide down to sit right in between them, and without any preamble, Xanto starts stroking my leg. Proteus grasps my chin and turns my face to him. It's as if they discussed this before I got here.

Proteus leans in and claims my mouth with a confidence that immediately causes heated liquid to flood between my legs. I moan into his mouth, his kiss so much better than I ever could've imagined it. Xanto's lips skim my shoulder on my other side, his hand tracing a path up to my aching core.

This is all happening so fast, but I have no problem with it as Proteus reaches for the hem of my shirt. I break away from his mouth so he can peel it off my body. His eyes take in my naked torso. He's seen me topless before, but this is different. This is *intentional.*

He claims my lips again before I feel his warm, calloused hands skimming my chest. I whimper as he plucks at my nipples, and I can feel his smirk against me. I pull back, and Xanto kneels before me to drag my bottoms off. Soon I'm bare before them, and their eyes take their fill of me.

Suddenly, I want to see them together more than I want air in my lungs. I stand. "Both of you, clothes off. Now. And kiss each other. I need to see it."

Proteus smirks at me again, and I almost combust from that alone. But then I really do go up in flames when he removes the only clothing he's wearing. His signature wrap around his hips. My mouth waters as I take in his erection, standing proudly at attention. He grasps it with his big hand, squeezing to relieve some pressure.

Xanto undresses as well, and Proteus's eyes turn to liquid fire as he takes him in. In the next moment, their lips meet in a frenzied battle, their cocks rubbing against each other as they get closer. I moan as I watch, and I rub along my clit to soothe the ache building there.

I drop to my knees in front of them, licking up the lengths of both of their shafts at the same time. They groan in unison, their hands resting on my head. They grind against each other and my mouth, and my pussy clenches at the ache and emptiness. *Not yet.* I want to enjoy every moment of this and pay them both the attention they deserve. Both of them have always been so good to me. I want to show them how much they mean to me.

I pull back slightly and turn Proteus so he's facing me. I take him fully into my mouth as I reach my other hand up to grasp Xanto. Proteus hisses between his teeth as I suck on his length, delighting in the way he twitches in my mouth. A bit of salty precum leaks from the tip and I lap it up greedily. He tastes like the ocean, and it makes me feel at home with him.

I break away from him and give my other lover the attention of my mouth, and when I look up, I see them both looking at me with heated eyes.

"Did I say you could stop kissing each other?" I ask sternly. I've always been the dominant one in the bedroom, but Xanto enjoys pushing back against me. I wonder how Proteus will be.

To my delight, they both do what I order them, and dive back into each other with a ferocious passion. I hum my approval against Xanto's skin. I'm just about to switch back to Proteus when he grasps my hair firmly and pulls me up to standing in front of him.

Proteus shoves me onto the bed, and I gasp in surprise.

"It's my turn to taste you." He bends down and takes my clit into his mouth before I can respond.

I cry out as my hips buck off the bed. I wind my fingers through his hair and Xanto meets my gaze at the end of the bed. His eyes are devouring us, and it's so hot that I almost combust on the spot. He doesn't stand there for long though. He scoots under Proteus and in the next moment he's sucking him. Proteus groans against me, and the vibrations bring a whole new level of pleasure to the experience.

He spears his tongue into me, and I fuck myself on his face. He's a typical mermaid and excels at all things sex, oral included. I'm steadily building, but I want more.

"More. Give me more," I command.

Proteus moans, moving his tongue back to my clit as he shoves a finger inside of me. I clench around the digit and I watch as he pistons his hips into Xanto's mouth. The sight has my orgasm crashing in around me, and I splinter into a thousand pieces against his lips, tongue, teeth, and finger.

My orgasm goes on for what feels like forever, and when I finally come down, Proteus licks up my body. He stops to pay special attention to my nipples before continuing up to my mouth. I revel in the taste of myself on his tongue, and I suck on it hard. In the next moment he's pushing his cock into me and I sob into his mouth.

Before I know what's happening, he's flipping us so I'm on top. I plant my knees on either side of him and start to move. He feels different from Xanto. Not as long, but girthier. The way he stretches me takes my breath away.

I feel Xanto's hands stroking my back and I purr and arch into his touch. He bites my earlobe before whispering, "Want me inside you too?"

I nod, greedy for it all. We haven't done this yet. Not that I haven't wanted to, but it just hasn't come up. He pushes me forward so my chest is pressed against Proteus's, and suddenly I feel oil dripping down between my ass cheeks. I hiss in a breath as he pushes a finger inside of me, stretching my tight hole. I move my hips steadily, taking his finger and Proteus's cock with every thrust.

I'm almost hyperventilating when he pushes a second finger into me and scissors his fingers. I know he's prepping me, but I feel so impatient. I want both of my lovers claiming me. *Now.*

"Enough fucking around, Xanto. Give me your cock."

"You don't want me to fuck around with you anymore?" he teases, and normally I would laugh, but I'm too sexually pent-up.

"Get inside me. Now," I demand, and he chuckles.

Before I can growl at him again, he's slathering oil on himself and slowly pushing into me. I groan low in my throat at the fullness. I can't think straight, and I have no desire to. I just want to sink into this ocean of bliss and never come back up to the surface.

"*Fuck.* I can feel you, Xanto. It's like you're stroking my cock through her," Proteus bites out.

They develop a rhythm, and I'm a slave to it. I can do nothing but ride the wave of pleasure between them, and they take me higher and higher with each push and pull of their hips. When one pulls out, the other pushes in. I'm never empty, and I revel in it. Xanto reaches a hand around and strokes my clit in torturous circles and Proteus leans his head to take one of my nipples into his mouth.

It's too much, and at the same time not enough. I want to take everything they have to give me and more. I never want it to stop. I'm making incoherent noises in my throat, not able to put words together, but needing them to know that I'm about to break. That I need more. That it's too much. I'm not sure. All of it. None of it.

"Come for us, my love. Come all over our cocks, and pull us down with you," Xanto whispers in my ear, but loud enough for Proteus to hear. He pinches my clit at the same time that Proteus bites down on my nipple and I splinter. I scream and wail, my whole body convulsing under the force of my climax.

Through the daze, I hear them both groaning, and their hips jerk against mine. I feel so incredibly full as they empty themselves inside of me. I collapse, completely sated between their two hard bodies.

"That was incredible," Proteus says a few moments later when we've caught our breath.

I nod against his chest. He lays a kiss on my forehead, and then I hear him kissing Xanto sweetly over my head. I smile, completely content. We've found it. I know they feel it too. We've found each other.

# 9

# Ember

The next few days pass in a blur. There's so much to do. First, I meet with Proteus. I didn't include him in the meeting with the ambassadors because I already have a mermaid representative, and I really only wanted my council there. That doesn't mean that I don't value his opinion. Especially regarding matters concerning his mother and his territory.

The two of us meet alone for breakfast and spend some time catching up. It's nice to see him again. I forgot how much I enjoy his company, and now that we don't have the undercurrent of sexual tension between us, it's even more natural. We're meant to be friends, no question about it.

"So, the reason I asked you here is to get a better idea of what we should do considering your mother and Mermacovia. She's a traitor to the crown, and I can't let that stand, but do you think she's started swaying the mermaids to side with Demonica?"

He sighs. "It's hard to say. I know she plans to, but when I heard her speaking to Demonica she hadn't yet, which makes me think she's hesitant about something."

"Well, that leads me to my next proposition. Obviously your mother can't continue to be in charge of Mermacovia." He nods in agreement and understanding. "The people love you and respect you. I trust you. I would like to appoint you the new Grand Master of Mermacovia."

For a moment he just stares at me in shock. Although, I don't why it's so surprising. He was next in line anyway, and he knows I can't let Coralia keep her position.

"You really want me to be grand master?"

"Of course. Why wouldn't I? I've seen you with your citizens. They love you. And you care about them much more than your mother."

"I don't know what to say."

"Say you'll accept my offer."

He smiles ruefully. "Is it really that simple?"

"Why not?"

"I don't know. I've always thought about when it was time for me to take over and all I would like to do differently. But now that I'm going to be taking it from her, it feels different. I know she's not a good person, and she's definitely done things I don't agree with in the slightest, but she is still my mother."

I soften. I didn't think about how hard this might be for him. "I understand that."

"There are also a lot of my species that are heartless and back her no matter what. They like her ruthlessness and will resist me taking over. If she were to tell them about Demonica, they would follow her. What would you want to do about them if that were to happen?"

"I think I would like you to have a talk with them first and see if you can get a feel for how devoted they actually are. But I don't know if there's much they can do. Demonica is in a different realm, and I'm assuming none of them can get there. I can also send guards to the portal to make sure they can't manage it."

He nods. "The other thing I have to consider is that I just started a relationship with Pearl and Xanto. I don't want to leave them when we just started something. Do you really want to have your grand master here or your ambassadors in Mermacovia?"

Fuck. I hadn't thought of that. "I don't really like either of those options. I'm sorry that this predicament hasn't crossed my mind. How about we talk to them about it and see what they think? We don't have to make a decision right away. In the meantime, though, I would like to have your mother arrested for treason. Is there someone you think would do well in the position temporarily until we can figure out a solution?"

He nods. "There are a few I think would be good options. Let me give it some more thought and I'll let you know."

"Thank you. I'm so glad you're here. I really value your input. You know that territory better than anyone."

He blushes, clearly not used to this kind of praise. It makes me sad that his mother never told him how well he does with his citizens. It really was amazing to watch him interact with them while I was there.

I head back to my room and sit at my desk. I need to come up with a speech to give the people in regards to Demonica and the coming confrontation. I can feel the pressure of my new position building, and I take a deep breath to calm myself. This wasn't at all what I was expecting to have to deal with, but I just need to take it one step at a time.

I've never considered myself an excellent speaker but I need to make sure that this one is epic. I have to rally the people of this realm behind me, and essentially ask them to back an outsider with combined blood in an upcoming war with an outside threat they never even knew about. Yeah. This will be totally easy.

Alexei joins me not long after. "What are you doing?"

"Staring at a sheet of paper, hoping that my speech to the realm will write itself."

He chuckles. "Having any luck?"

"No. I have no idea what I'm going to say to them."

"Just be honest. The people value honesty in a ruler. Not to mention that you are asking for their opinion. That has literally never been done before. It will be strange for them, but they will be honored that you value their input. I know I would."

His words calm me a bit. "Okay. I can do that."

I start writing what I'm thinking. This first draft is going to be a mess, but I can make it prettier once I have a general idea of what I want to say. At least I'm getting some words down. It's a start.

After working on it for a half hour or so, Alexei comes up behind me, kissing my neck and letting his hands wander along my body.

"I can't concentrate when you're doing that," I moan, closing my eyes and tilting my head to give him better access despite my words.

"You need a break. Let me take your mind off things for a while."

I give in. He's right. I do need a break. And him distracting me right now sounds like the perfect afternoon.

We set the address for three days later. It takes me that whole time to perfect my speech and feel comfortable with it. I also let my ambassadors look it over and suggest any adjustments they think it needs.

The day arrives, and I try in vain to tamp down my nerves. A whole flock of geese is taking off in my stomach. I, of course, have Pearl do my hair and makeup, and my dress is majestic and beautiful, and I have to physically stop myself from wiping my sweaty palms on it and ruining it.

When it's time, we gather before the door to the giant balcony where I'm going to be making my address. The same one that I stood on next to Stavros when he told the kingdom I would be next in line for the throne. It's the perfect space for it. I'm able to speak to so many more people here than anywhere else.

Alexei is on my right side, and Ebony is on my left. I want them next to me through this. They're my strength and support, and I want the kingdom to see that the three of us are a package deal.

I reach up to feel that my crown is in place. I already know that it is, but it's a nervous tick. My breathing starts accelerating, but before I can get too out of control, my mate takes my hand gently in his.

The skin-to-skin contact soothes and grounds me. I take a full deep breath as he meets my eyes and gives me an encouraging smile. I face forward again, looking out over my subjects.

"My good people, I know that I have just become your queen, but I would like to start things off right. Things on Earth, at least in America, where I'm from, are done quite differently than here. The people are given a voice. Their opinion matters. There is a ruler, but we call it a democracy. I want to bring that notion here. Your voices matter to me, and I value your input.

"I have not been here long enough to know how things are done everywhere. I have traveled to all of the territories, and met with the different species, but my knowledge of the realm and its citizens is very basic. You are the best people to make this decision.

"That being said, the information I have to give you is disturbing. It is something that's been hidden from all of the residents in Queridian for thousands of years, and let me just tell you, the decision to give voice to this secret is not one I made lightly."

I take another deep breath. The crowd is utterly silent, waiting with bated breath. My heart pounds faster as my nerves increase. Am I doing the right thing? Would my father be disappointed? He told me not to even notify my mate of the situation until we were married, and now here I am, about to reveal the realm's biggest secret to the entire kingdom.

I internally shake my head at myself. *No.* I made my decision already. This is the right thing. I can feel it in my bones. Especially since I know that Demonica was already able to travel through the wards, and killed my father. That changed so much since the discussion I had with Stavros. If I knew that she wasn't able to get through the wards, I would be honoring his request. As it is, I do not have that luxury.

"The king was murdered by a demon." Gasps of horror and disbelief flit through the enormous crowd, but I raise my hand, silencing them. When they immediately quiet, I'm awed at the respect they already have for me. I then continue to tell them the story of the demons and the demon queen that were banished to the Domain of the Dead. I keep my empath abilities open, wanting to gauge how my subjects are feeling. I'm overwhelmed by the sensations bombarding me, but I wade through them. I feel shock, disbelief, rage, anguish, terror, and self-importance. That last one solidifies my belief that this was the right decision. They're grateful that I came to this with them. And why shouldn't they be a part of this? If this becomes an all-out war, then they will have to fight too.

I then tell them about how Pearl traveled to Mermacovia and overheard Coralia speaking with Demonica, and her plans to sway the mermaids to Demonica's cause. Cries of outrage resound through the open space, and I almost can't believe that they're so behind me on this already. I don't know what I've done to earn their trust and respect, but I clearly have it. Something I do not take lightly or for granted.

"So, my reason for telling you all of this is because we have a crossroads ahead of us, and I need your help navigating it. You all have just as much of a right to be a part of this as I do. Here are our options: we can wait around and see if Demonica is able to bring an army through the wards around Queridian, or we bring the battle to *her*. Either way, war will be upon us soon, but there is a chance that she won't be able to bring anyone else with her from Domonia. The second option is obviously riskier, but we would have the element of surprise, and we would prove to her that Queridian will *not* take this lying down.

"I understand that I've shaken the foundations of our lives. The reason for the segregation that you've been subjected to for all your existence has been kept secret from you, even if it was for your protection. I do believe that we are stronger together. That was why Demonica made that demand to begin with. She *knew* that if we joined forces that we would be unstoppable. But lifetime prejudices are hard to break, I'm aware of that. We need to make this decision quickly, but I want you all to take a few days to think about it. This is an extremely significant choice to make, and one we cannot take lightly.

"There will be parchments sent to everyone's houses. Please fill them out by the end of the week. Tell me which option you think would be best for our realm. I'm also going to leave a space at the bottom for any other ideas or concerns you may have. I appreciate all of your attention and devotion."

I finally stop speaking. I feel exhausted, anxious, worried, and a million other things. But relieved is among them. I will not need to make this decision alone. I also need to recharge quickly, because I need to teletravel all over the realm and make this same speech in every territory. I sigh. It's going to be a long week.

# 10

# Ember

I was right. It's a long week. I start with the mimics. As much as I want to say that there's some sort of strategy behind it, the main reason is because I miss Joseph. I always felt close to him; I spent the longest amount of time there, and since Stavros died, I miss having a fatherly figure in my life.

He knows of my arrival; each territory was informed of my address. So, when I teletravel directly into the capitol and knock on his door, he answers and immediately pulls me into a warm embrace. I break down into sobs as soon as his arms encircle me.

He says nothing, simply pulls me into his chambers, Alexei following behind us and shutting the door. I know I'm a queen, and that I need to be strong, but I can break down with Joseph. And honestly, it feels vital. When my tears finally subside, I pull away, my mate drying the wetness from my face with his thumbs.

"I'm so sorry, Ember," Joseph murmurs.

I take a cleansing breath, getting rid of all the shit that brought up. I do feel like a slight weight has lifted from me though.

"Thank you, Joseph. I missed you."

"I missed you too. It's good to have you back here, even though the circumstances aren't ideal."

I snort. *Not ideal* is the understatement of the century. We chat for a little bit, catching up after our time apart. Nostalgia hits me as I linger in his presence. I know it wasn't long ago that I was here, but so much has changed that it feels like a lifetime. I wish for those days when all I had to worry about was learning how to use my powers. Now I have to deal with not only losing my father and ruling the realm, but dealing with a psychotic demon bitch that wants to steal my crown and suck the lives out of all my subjects. And more than likely kill me while she's at it.

I give my address later that day. The mimics respond similarly to the fae, which gives me hope for the rest of the realm. However, their reactions are a bit more intense because of their animalistic natures. I hear more growls and snarls than in the Immortal City. I smile savagely, grateful that when and if the time comes, I'll have these feral beasts on my side.

Each day, Alexei and I travel to a new territory and I speak to my subjects. It gets easier each time I do it, and I'm more convinced than ever that this is the right decision. For the most part, the reactions I receive are the same.

I was hoping that the witches would have more insight for me, but when I speak to Raven, the grand mistress, she informs me that while they see a lot of war and death, most things surrounding the demons are dark. I wonder if part of their abilities are blocking the witches' sight to some extent.

I know I need to go to Mermacovia to address Coralia's betrayal, but I haven't decided how to go about it yet. I don't want her to continue having power in her territory, and I need to punish her, but on the flip side, I really don't want to give Demonica any inclination that we know about her and her plans. Not until we know more about what the rest of Queridian thinks is best.

I leave the Mortal Sanctum for last, other than Mermacovia, of course, since I still haven't made up my mind. There are other things that need to be done here, and I'll need more than a day to make it happen. First and foremost, I need to select a human ambassador and a grand master/mistress.

My father was a great man, but I'm ashamed to say that he didn't treat them as equals. Even though he was in love with my mother, I think he viewed her as the exception. Then again, he did tend to have his head in the sand when it came to certain things.

I also need to check in on the brothel and make sure all of the women there are happy and healthy.

The most important thing on my agenda with the humans, however, besides the address, is to train them. I have a theory that all humans can access the same magic I use to alter others' emotions, they've just never been properly trained. They've been beaten down by the other species in this realm, and as such, I believe they don't realize their power.

I may be wrong, but it's worth a shot. If war does come, this could be the difference between us winning and losing against Demonica.

My first task isn't easy, and I decide to notify everyone of the available position when I give the address. I want it to be something that people apply for, and then I can meet with multiple candidates for an interview before I decide who I want to take the position.

My second task is much easier, and things at the brothel are running swimmingly. All of the women who have remained are happy. There were some who decided they wanted to leave and pursue something else, but there were a lot of women who heard about the money that was now being offered, and came to join. It's actually more successful now than it ever was before. I make sure they don't need anything else before I leave.

Another oversight to this territory is that there is no capitol. It makes sense that they wouldn't have a fancy building because they don't have a territory leader. I scout the territory's capital, Sapien City, to find a decent location.

The whole of the Mortal Sanctum is incredibly run-down, and it deeply upsets me. I don't know if they've ever had any sort of renovations done. I would imagine not, because it's not a prosperous territory.

I want to build them a beautiful capitol building and do what I can to make it a livable community. I know it's going to take a lot of work, but the good thing about being queen is I can delegate. It will also be a chance to get the citizens work. There's not much to do here besides working in various brothels throughout the territory.

The other sex establishments here don't have conduits working for them, and therefore aren't as successful, but that's what humans are known for, unfortunately. I would like to change that.

I know it's going to take time to make things better for my species, but I'm willing to do everything I can. I think because of our abilities, it might be a good idea for them to be known for their capability to help people sort through their emotions. I wonder if this realm has mental health professionals. I would bet not. As much as I love it here, I feel like they are very behind the times on a lot of things.

The problem with this idea is that I don't know the first thing about therapy. Not enough to teach them how to help people anyway. Maybe there are some who would be willing to go to Earth and get schooling for it? Fuck. There's so much I want to do, but now isn't the time to think about it. Not with war on the horizon.

*One crisis at a time, Ember.*

After I speak to my human subjects about Demonica, I inform them of my special ability. Most are completely shocked, but I can also sense that some are unsurprised. That's encouraging. Maybe there are a few here who have already discovered this ability.

As much as I would love to, there's no way that I can teach them all at the same time. There are too many of them. Instead, I schedule out days that I will be in each of the major cities and those who want to come are welcome.

I do the first day in Sapien City, and I follow the training immediately after my speech. There are more people here than I was expecting, but I'll figure it out. I tell them that I'll be there all day and if they want to leave and return, they're more than welcome to. Most don't take me up on it, which is fine, it's just going to be a bit more difficult.

I amplify my voice and explain to them about mental shields. I don't go into that much, though, wanting to spend the majority of my time here describing how to use this new skill.

I explain it in detail before demonstrating it for them. I spend the rest of the time answering questions.

I teach all day, wanting anyone and everyone to understand how to do this. I have a feeling it's going to make a difference for us. A big one.

By the end of the day, I'm completely drained. I groan inwardly when I think of repeating it for the next three days. I know it's necessary, but I never realized how exhausting training people is. I don't know how Alexei trained me for so long, day in and day out.

The next three days are relatively the same, although it's slightly easier considering that there aren't as many people, and that I've already done it once. I'm able to work in smaller groups a few times, which ends up working better, as I get to watch them practice on each other and give feedback.

From what I can tell, the majority of them don't have the ability, but it's possible they will develop it over time with practice. There are a few that grasp it, though. Overall, I'm pleased with the work that I'm doing here. I find a few people who have taken pretty quickly to my training and put them in charge of helping the others after I've left.

I also have Alexei conduct interviews for the grand master as well as the ambassador. I would like to do it myself, but there just isn't enough time in my day. I trust him completely, and know he will choose only the most competent people.

He ends up selecting a male named Conrad for the position of grand master. I meet with him after he makes his selection, and I can immediately see why my mate chose him. He's competent, patient, well-spoken, and his viewpoints align with what we're trying to accomplish in the Mortal Sanctum.

I know that there is a lot of work to be done in this territory, so I make sure he knows that I will be meeting with him regularly to discuss the progress, as well as things that need to be altered. I'm aware that some of the things we want to do won't work or be well received, but I would at least like to give them a shot.

For the ambassador position he finds a woman who is slightly older. Her name is Claire. Her hair is graying and her face is wrinkled, but she's sharp, and as cutting as a whip. I know that she'll give her opinion freely, and will be honest about things she doesn't agree with. Just the person I need. I don't want a bunch of people kissing my ass.

I arrange for transportation for Claire back to the palace. She's reluctant to leave her family, but is overjoyed when I tell her she can bring them with her. She has no problem leaving this territory behind her. It saddens me that she never loved her home, but when I look around at the land, I'm unsurprised.

I wonder if there would be some way to enrich the land. It's almost like there's an absence of magic in the land here. I make a mental note to ask Alexei later. Maybe if we were to get enough earth fae to work together we could make this a better environment for them.

When Alexei and I have done everything we can for the moment, we head back home. I still need to figure out what to do in terms of Mermacovia, but I think once I have a plan to handle Coralia, I'll have a better idea on how to approach the citizens.

I take a day or two to unwind, needing a break after all the people we've seen and all we've accomplished this past week. Not to mention, I'm still waiting on the votes to come back from everyone.

The ones from Mystic Mountain are likely to come back first, and I will need the help of my council in going through them. I know it's going to be an enormous job, and will take a significant amount of time, but it's important. With any luck, we'll be able to get through one territory before the next one floods in.

I collapse into bed, exhausted beyond belief. Alexei rubs my feet comfortingly, pampering me after my hard week. I melt into his touch, and when his thumb hits a certain spot on my foot, I swear I feel a zing straight to my core. I gasp and he chuckles knowingly.

"Does that feel good, little doe?"

I moan in response, not capable of forming words.

He continues his ministrations until I'm experiencing a strange combination of deep relaxation and pure lust. Either way, I've become a puddle.

"Alexei," I beg.

He smirks at me. "What do you want, little doe?"

"More. Please."

His hands massage up my legs, technically giving me more, but not what I'm wanting. The bastard knows it too. He takes his sweet time getting to my thighs, and with each pass of his thumbs, he grazes my pelvis. It's almost where I want him, but not quite. His teasing is maddening.

I sob in pleasure when he finally swipes his fingers through my drenched folds.

His teasing bites him in the ass when he discovers how worked up I am. "*Fuck*, little doe. You're so ready for me."

"Fuck me. Please."

"Not yet. I want to make you come so many times you forget your own name first."

He plunges two digits inside of me as his mouth latches on to my clit. He has me so strung out that I'm immediately spun into a mind-bending climax. I can feel the vibrations of his groan against my cunt, and it only sends me higher.

He feasts on me relentlessly, making me come so many times that I lose count. He alternates between all of my sensitive spots: my pussy, breasts, and ass. I take all he gives and still want more. I know I won't be fully satisfied until his cock is filling me.

"Alexei, please. Enough. I need you inside me."

"I thought I was," he remarks, twitching his fingers.

I growl, grabbing his hair and yanking him up to me. I seal our mouths together, and I can taste myself on his lips, driving my need even higher. My hand ventures south, sliding over him when I find he's not nearly as unaffected as he wants me to believe.

"If I weren't so desperate for you, I would torture you in the same way you have me," I snarl against his mouth, gripping his length roughly.

His chuckle turns into a hiss as my nails dig in slightly. I look into his eyes and see them flare with just as much heat as mine. Between the two of us, I'm sure we could burn this city to the ground if we wanted to.

He removes his clothes, and I line up his pulsing member with my dripping cunt, and in the next second, he's pushing into me, his patience obliterated. My walls grip him tightly, relief coursing through me at finally being filled like I so desire.

Luckily, his teasing seems to be over, and he gives us what we both want, fucking me with abandon. I cry out in earnest, unable to stop even if I wanted to.

"That's right, my queen. Let the castle hear who owns you."

I'm about to rail into him for the "owning me" comment, but with a wicked smirk on his face, he adjusts the angle of his hips, hitting just the right spot inside of me. I clutch his back, hanging on for dear life. Another climax is building, and this time I feel that it might actually kill me. I've never been this worked up in my entire life.

I'm about to crash over my peak when he pulls out. I garble out an unintelligible complaint, but in the next second, he's flipping me onto all fours, my knees on my edge of the bed, as he presses down my torso to give him better access to me. He makes a long lick up my slit, teasing my clit with little nips, and I whine into the mattress.

He doesn't make me beg anymore though, and his cock is filling me again in the next breath. The angle along with his hands gliding along every inch of my body makes me see stars, my oversensitive nerves zinging.

I attempt to push myself up so I'm no longer tilted downward, but before I can manage it, Alexei's hand cracks down on my ass—hard. I yelp in surprise. He's been so soft and gentle and teasing this whole time that the change in his touch is electrifying.

"Don't even think about it, Ember. I love seeing you like this, ass up, panting for me, and completely at my mercy."

I let out another garbled moan.

"You want to come?"

I nod vehemently.

"Tell me. Say it," he orders.

I don't know where this dominating scene came from, but I'm *loving* it. Especially when I think of how I'll repay him next time.

"I want to come."

"Then come for me. Milk my dick with your cunt."

Before I can follow his command, his thumb plunges into my tight back hole, and his fangs pierce the tender flesh between my shoulder and my neck. That's it. I detonate around him, screaming my release.

His groan vibrates against my skin, and I feel him pulsing hot jets of his seed inside of me.

We collapse on the mattress, completely spent and satisfied. When our breathing finally settles, he pulls out of me and turns me to face him, tucking me gently into the warmth of his embrace. My mind settles for the first time in weeks.

"How did you know that was exactly what I needed?" I ask. I hadn't even known that I needed him to take control like that.

"You've had so much going on. You're literally in charge of the realm now. I figured you needed a break from taking care of everyone else."

Now that he says it, it makes so much sense. I beam at him. I'm so lucky to have a mate who knows what I need before even I do. I kiss him lovingly on the mouth, and with us both cuddled on the bed, we're asleep within minutes.

The votes start flooding in the next day. The council and I hunker down in one of the rooms and go through each one. It's tedious, exhausting, and frustrating, but the number of positive comments I get from my citizens makes it all worth it.

The votes on whether to wait for Demonica to strike or go to war with her first are fairly divided at first, but as we continue through them, the latter option pulls ahead. I smile. This is what I was hoping for. I guess we'll see if the other territories agree.

The thing that is consistent—the comments that flood in about how thankful they are to be included in the decision. And for allowing them to know this secret that's been hidden for thousands of years, even though it affects their lives more than anyone else. They *should* be a part of this. They always should have been.

It takes days to get through Mystic Mountain, which ends up being about 30 percent wanting to wait and 70 percent wanting to strike now and band together with the other territories. Relief pours through me when it's done, but before I can take a break, the next territory floods in.

Luckily, by this point we have a good system going, and it takes less time to get through the votes. The Everchanging Glades are almost unanimously in the latter category, and unless the rest of the realm is thoroughly against going to war, that will likely be the outcome.

After we finish going through the first three territories, Alexei makes me take one day for myself. I object at first, claiming we don't have the time or luxury of taking a break, but then he tells me that I'll be no good to the kingdom if I'm dead on my feet.

It's glorious. I sleep in, have some tea, and read my book on the balcony for a bit before having breakfast by the fire with my mate.

He packs us a picnic for lunch, and we head to our favorite spot by the water. We don't teletravel. Instead, we take Ash and enjoy the nostalgia of when we first met. Ebony races alongside us, enjoying the fresh air as much as we are. I lean against my mate and tilt my face to the sky, the warmth from the sun kissing my skin.

Just when I have the thought that this is the perfect day, we're ambushed before we arrive at our destination.

Thirty masked people surround us after emerging from the trees, arrows flying with zero warning. My magic responds before I do, my air knocking them all away before they make contact.

They look exactly like the group that attacked us in the Everchanging Glades. Although now there's double the number. I growl, and it's echoed by my mate and my familiar.

"Keep one alive to question," I instruct Alexei before teletraveling off Ash. I know it'll be easier for him to keep her safe without me weighing him down. And I can do more damage this way.

My daggers are slashing before I'm even fully formed before them. Ebony is next to me the whole time, traveling with me and sinking her teeth into each opponent in a killing blow before we're gone again.

I keep a solid air shield around all of us, and I give past me a mental high-five when I can sense a hit from behind Alexei and Ash.

My mate is taking out opponent after opponent with expertly placed arrows and strikes of his earth magic.

I can tell the assassins are getting frustrated at being unable to get any hits on us, and I smile viciously at every failed attempt.

"Why won't you fight us like true warriors? You need to hide behind your wall of magic while you attack us?" one yells at me. Their voice is masculine, but beautiful. I have a theory about what species he is, but don't have time to dwell on it at the moment.

"Fight you like true warriors? Is that how you're fighting? Thirty against two? That seems really fair," I spit back, but his remark still nags at me. It makes me want to remove my shield just to show him that I can beat him without it. I could probably end this in seconds with my air and fire magic, but I'm itching for a fight, and I want it to last.

I blow my air magic out and away from me like an explosion, knocking all except my allies on their asses. In the next second, I'm on them, swiping with my daggers and relishing the blood coating my skin.

I feel three coming for me at my back with my premonition, and I throw fire and air their way before they can make contact.

"Am I fighting like a true warrior now, scum?"

His sword swipes for me, and I let it nick me just the slightest so he can see that I no longer have my air shield up. I want this filth to *know* that I bested him, and there was nothing he could do about it. In fact, I want him to be the one that we keep alive.

"Alexei, bind this one up so we can take him with us."

He immediately complies, wrapping the man in vines with his earth magic so completely that only his face is free. I watch, mesmerized by his magic, even after all this time.

I'm so distracted by it that I don't realize an opponent has snuck up on me until their dagger is puncturing my shoulder. I scream out in pain, but turn and burn him to ashes with only a thought.

"Fuck this shit," I say, over it and done playing. I light the remaining enemies on fire until we're the only ones left in the clearing.

"Little doe, are you all right? *Shit*, you're bleeding."

"I'm fine," I tell him quickly. "Can you just pull the knife out so I can heal it?"

He does as I say, but his jaw is tight. I can feel his anger pouring off him in waves. I grit my teeth to hold back my yell of pain as the knife comes free of my flesh, my body gushing blood. I heal it as soon as it's free.

"What the hell was that?"

Alexei's question startles and confuses me. "What was what?"

"Why did you remove your air shield? That was not only completely unnecessary, but also incredibly stupid. You could've gotten yourself *killed.*"

"I didn't need it. I can handle myself without it."

He gestures to the blood coating me. "Clearly you can't." Before I can rip into him, he continues. "And more importantly you don't have to. You have these gifts. *Use* them. Protect yourself."

Shame slithers into my stomach. He's right. It was stupid. "I'm sorry. I just constantly feel the need to prove myself. I want to be strong enough. I want to show everyone that I'm capable and worthy of running this kingdom."

"First off, you are more worthy than any royal we've had in a very long time. Secondly, part of being capable of running this realm is protecting yourself so that you can protect your citizens. Doing risky and unnecessary shit like that isn't doing your duty and you know it."

Tears build behind my eyes. He sees them and wraps me in his arms without another word. I hate being lectured, but everything he said is true. "I'm sorry," I sob into his chest.

"Shh. It's okay, little doe. I understand. But you scared the hell out of me."

He continues to hold me, and the stress finally catches up. Suddenly I'm not just crying about what happened, but *everything.*

I don't know how long we stand there, but when my tears are finally free of my body, I realize that Ebony is standing against my legs, a comforting weight supporting me from behind. I rest my hand on her head, silently thanking her.

I pull away from them both when I feel steady. I'm glad I don't currently have a mirror because I'm sure my face is a blotchy mess of wetness. I wipe my cheeks before we turn and face the only piece of shit left.

"How are we going to get him back?"

"We could drag him behind us," Alexei suggests in a taunting voice aimed at the man. His eyes are terrified, and he shakes his head vehemently, not able to talk through the vine gag.

I chuckle, knowing Alexei wouldn't actually do that no matter how badly he might want to. There would be too great a risk of him dying along the way, and we need him alive.

"Can you lift him up onto Ash with your air magic and then I'll walk him back and you can teletravel there?"

I nod, glad I won't have to be in the assassin's presence much longer. I lift him, doing a few twirls with him out of spite before setting him gently over Ash, stomach across her back, ass in the air. He groans pitifully, and I smile at the small victory.

"Go straight back to the palace," he tells me.

I nod. "Get there as quickly as possible. And if there's another attack, leave this fucker behind. I want answers but not at the expense of your life."

He kisses me softly before nudging me. "I'll be right behind you."

I pull Ebony back into me and we teletravel back to the castle. I alert my council to the events of the last hour as we wait for Alexei to return with the assassin. We've decided to all question him together in case they catch anything I don't. By the time they arrive, I'm itching to see what he knows. I want to see who was dumb enough to fuck with me and my mate.

# 11

## Alexei

My journey back to the castle is uneventful. The traitorous filth lying across Ash is crying and sobbing the whole way, and I know that if I didn't have a gag in his mouth he'd be begging for his life. I punch him in the kidney, pissed that he messed up the perfect day I was having with my mate.

Ember has had such a rough time of it lately. And she's been working so hard. She deserved this break, and this group had to go and fuck it all up.

On the plus side, we will hopefully know exactly who this lot is, and why they keep attacking us. I didn't really think about it much until now, but the fact that we never figured out who attacked us the first time weighed on me pretty heavily. Now at least we'll have answers.

Halfway there, I get so annoyed with my captive that I knock him unconscious. He's lucky I don't kill him, but we need him. We need the information he can give us.

I breathe a sigh of relief when I pass through the gates of the palace. I didn't think another attack would come, but I'm still grateful that I returned safely with my prisoner in tow.

I recruit the help of two guards, instructing them to bring him to the dungeons. He needs to be locked up until we can question him. It also won't hurt to have him fearing for his life.

With him in trustworthy hands, I head off in search of my mate. I find her in the council room with her ambassadors. Her eyes meet mine as soon as I walk through the door, and relief coats her features.

"Alexei," she says, rushing me. She embraces me, and I try to hide my shock. It's not a secret that we're mated and in love, but she typically saves the physical contact for when we're alone. "No trouble getting back?"

I shake my head. "Our captive is nice and comfy in the dungeon. I may have knocked him unconscious."

A smirk briefly touches her lips. "Lovely. He'll wake up in our best accommodations, then."

"Should we bring him in to question, Your Majesty?" one of the council asks.

She shakes her head. "Not yet. I want him to fret a little bit first."

Pride builds in my chest. I think that's the right call, and she came to that conclusion all on her own.

"Yes, my queen."

"Would you like to rest?" I ask her quietly. It's been an eventful afternoon.

She nods. "You're all excused. I'll call on you when it's time."

Everyone departs, and Ember and I head to our rooms. She links our hands as we walk, needing physical contact after our close encounter today.

"I can't wait to get clean. I feel disgusting."

"Who says you'll be getting clean?" I say, smacking her ass.

She lets out a surprised squeak. "Oh, do you plan to dirty me up, mate?"

"I always want you dirty when you're with me."

Her eyes heat, and she grabs my hand to pull me along to the shower.

I make sure that Ember is thoroughly dirtied before I clean her up. When we're finished in the shower, I ensure that she enjoys the rest of her day as planned. I know she's anxious to question our prisoner, but let him drive himself insane with thoughts of what's to come. The piece of shit deserves it. No matter the outcome, I'll kill him for attempting to not only hurt my mate, but kill her. His *queen.* The only thing that awaits him if he cooperates is a swift death.

We dress, and then I grab the picnic basket that I had packed for our afternoon, which somehow remained on Ash unharmed. I grasp her hand and guide her out to the gardens. This is one of her favorite places in the palace, and I know that it reminds her of Stavros. We're in that strange time of year where the weather isn't quite sure what it wants to do. Some days are cold, and some are warmer, the sun shining down liberally. Today it's the latter.

I spread out a blanket in the section that belongs to her mother, and set everything down. When we're comfortable, I take out the food that the kitchens prepared. I requested they packed extra because I know how much my little doe loves to eat.

I pour her a glass of wine while she starts on the cheese and the grapes. I smile reminiscently as I watch her. This was the first thing I fed her, and she still reacts to the food the same way she did that fateful night.

When we're halfway through the spread, she finally slows down enough to speak. "When do you think we should question him?"

"Oh no. There will be no talk of that on our relaxation day," I chastise.

"But—"

I grab the plate she's holding and set it off to the side, and then I push her to the ground, covering her body with mine. Her face flushes with blood, and my fangs—and my dick for that matter—throb at the sight.

"What are you doing?" she asks breathlessly.

"Training you, like you asked me. Get me off of you, little doe." As much as I love having her like I always wanted, a part of me misses how we used to be on the road together. I think she does too. I want to remind her that we're still those people, even though she's a queen now. She's still the woman I fell in love with.

"You think I can't?"

"Eh. I don't think you're as strong as I am," I taunt her, even though it's complete bullshit. She's the strongest person I know. Much stronger than me.

Her eyes flare, and I know I've got her. Instead of her pushing me or throwing me off her with her air magic like I expect, she wraps her legs around my waist. Even though we just made love, I'm still immediately hard at the feel of her wet heat pressed tightly against my shaft. When she moves her hips against me, I groan low in my throat. I wasn't expecting this.

I lean down for a kiss, and that's when she pounces. She rolls us over so she's on top of me, pinning me to the ground. I try to flip us again, but she's prepared, holding me down with her air magic. I grunt against the onslaught. As hard as I try, I can't move an inch. She has me completely at her mercy.

"I'm not as strong as you, huh?"

Before I can respond, her fangs are sinking into my neck. I groan and twitch against her. I know she doesn't need to feed. This is all to prove a point, and I am *here* for it. I never knew what it felt like to be fed from until her. I knew it could feel good, but I never knew it could be like *this*.

She pulls back just when I think I'm going to explode in my pants. She closes the bite, moves off of me, and licks the excess blood from her lips. Without another word, she picks up her plate of food, resuming her meal. I stare at her open-mouthed. Did that just really happen?

She finally looks back at me. "What?"

I shoot up and across the space, claiming her lips with mine in a fierce kiss. She breaks away from me a moment later, chuckling. I love seeing a smile on her beautiful face.

We finish our food, and before she can sneak off to try to do more work, I bring her up to the library. She loves reading, and I don't know the last time she had an opportunity, with the exception of the minimal reading she did this morning. She sighs as she enters, her shoulders relaxing. She wanders the shelves for a while before grabbing what looks like a romance novel, and plopping down in one of the cozy chairs. I smile, grabbing a book for myself and sitting across from her.

Halfway through the afternoon, I step out, and notify a servant that the queen would like some tea and cookies. She hasn't told me, but I know tea helps her settle down even more, and I want to make this day as relaxing as possible for her. When I return, she hasn't moved from her spot, her eyes still glued to the page, and I know she probably didn't even notice my absence.

The servants bring everything in a few minutes later, and her brows rise in surprise. She thanks them as they set the tray down on the table between us. She gives me a knowing look over the rim of her cup. I grab my own mug, clinking it against hers. She smiles before settling back in. She lets Ebony out after the staff leaves to relax with us. She finds a nice patch of sunlight and curls up in it, readying herself for a nap. I know wild cats like her are supposed to be terrifying—which she is—but for the most part, she's basically just a big house cat.

We spend the afternoon lounging and relaxing. I'm proud of her that she stuck to this plan, even though I know she's been struggling being unproductive today. By the time evening rolls around, I can tell she's itching to go down to the dungeon.

"Tomorrow, my love."

"But—"

"Tomorrow."

She sighs but nods. We eat a romantic dinner just the two of us in the dining room, and when we're finished, I lead her to bed. After I thoroughly worship her, I tuck her into my side and she's asleep within minutes. I'm awake a little longer as I look down at my mate. I can't believe how lucky I am to have found her. And even luckier that she forgave me. I will spend every day of the rest of my life making sure she knows just how incredible she is.

Ember wakes early the next morning. I can feel her get out of bed before the sun has even risen in the sky. I'm so tempted to just go back to sleep, but I know she could use my company to keep her even and level.

I reluctantly follow her out of bed. I join her in the shower, and she tenses slightly. "I couldn't sleep anymore."

"I know, little doe. Want to do some combat training before

breakfast? Then we can round up the council and go visit the prisoner."

She relaxes at my words and nods. "That sounds like just what I need."

I can hear her heart pounding, and I know she's anxious about how this is going to go. Physical activity will help keep her nerves down and make her feel more in control. We make quick work of getting ready before heading down to the training ring.

"What do you want to train with today?"

"Swords." Her words are sure, but colored with emotion. Training with swords always reminds her of her father.

I soften even more toward her, but don't say anything. I simply grab my weapon and take my stance. She mimics me, and we begin. This is the form of training she needs the most work on, and I go slow with her at first so she can get in the right headspace. Within the first few minutes she gets in the flow of things, and we really start moving. The work that Stavros did with her in the beginning by separating her arm and foot work was really smart. It really made a huge difference with her training. But she's been so busy lately and had so many different things on her mind that her combat training has fallen to the wayside. She's rusty, and we need to make it a priority.

We practice for about an hour, and by the end, she's sweating and breathing heavily. She has a flush to her beautiful cheeks, and my fangs tingle at the sight. Gods, she's so delectable.

Before I take her back to the room and ravish her, I break my gaze away from her. "Come on, little doe. We have a prisoner to question."

A savage smile lights her face, and we teletravel back to the room to change. She puts on something worthy of the warrior queen she is, her face set in a cold, determined mask. Fuck, she's incredible. She awes me on a regular basis.

"Ready?"

She takes a deep breath and nods. We meet with the council first, making sure everyone is on the same page. Then the guards are bringing him.

I never saw him properly before. His mask was still on when I was bringing him back to the castle, not to mention he was bound head to toe in my vines. There's dirt streaked over his face, and his clothes are worn and dirty, but that doesn't detract from the beauty he exudes. His lavender hair hangs over his forehead, and his turquoise eyes are hard when they enter. *Mermaid.* I'm not surprised in the least. Coralia is out for my mate's blood, especially now that she's queen.

He sits at one end of the table, the rest of us on the other side, which includes me and Ember, the ambassadors, and Proteus. The guards restrain him in his chair, and if looks could kill, we'd all be dead. Especially me and Ember.

Once he's settled, Ember finally addresses him. I'm curious how she'll handle this. If she'll choose to use her powers, or if she'll simply question him and test his honesty.

"So, you're a mermaid."

He scoffs. "Obviously."

Her eyes narrow just a hint. "Did Coralia send you?"

"I'm not going to tell you *anything.* You might as well kill me." His words are an attempt at bravery, but I can hear the fear behind them.

A vicious smile cuts across my mate's face. "Oh, I will. But you'll tell me what I need to know first." The coldness of her voice causes goose bumps to rise on my skin. If I were on the receiving end of her ire, I would be pissing my pants.

He snorts, but a sweat breaks out across his brow, and I can hear his heart beating a nervous pattern in his chest. "You can't make me do anything."

Her eyes twinkle. "You clearly don't know anything about your queen."

"You are *not* my queen. You will *never* be my queen. Long live the true queen! I hope she rips you to shreds."

His words make my blood turn to ice. Demonica.

Instead of letting her composure break, she releases her allure on him. I know she's already broken through his shields and is going to destroy him. I can't wait to see it.

# 12

# Ember

My heart stops when he says the words "true queen." He knows about Demonica. The question now is if Coralia has told only those close to her, or if she's recruited all the mermaids. Only one way to find out.

I break through his mental barriers and release the full force of my gifts onto him. He's a mermaid, so with others he might be able to resist the allure, but not with me. My skin glows with the force of my persuasion, and I push feelings of trust and honesty onto him. In the span of a second his expression morphs from one of distrusting disgust into adoring openness. I smirk to myself. That was easy.

"How do you know about Demonica?"

"Coralia told me."

"What did she tell you?"

"That Surseiha's true heir was trapped and banished to Domonia, her true crown stolen from her, and that to restore her rightful place we needed to kill you."

My blood boils. True queen my ass.

"Who did she tell this to?"

"The entirety of Mermacovia."

I grit my teeth. Fuck. I was hoping she wouldn't have done that yet.

"Are there any that are opposed?"

I have no idea if this piece of shit will be privy to this information, but I'm hoping there will be some mermaids who want to see me rule. I seemed to have quite the fan base when I was there, but the lies that Coralia has spun may have swayed them against me.

"Yes. But I don't know who they are or how many."

He's being so forthcoming. I should've just done this from the beginning. I'm glad that I still have some supporters in Mermacovia. Maybe when Proteus goes back to take over he'll garner even more support.

"Were mermaids behind the attack on me and my mate months ago?"

He swallows, and I sense his attempted resistance, but it's no match for my power. "Yes."

Fury builds inside me. That fucking *bitch.* I can't wait to tear her to pieces. I remember my mate lying on the ground, bleeding out. I was *barely* able to save him, and it's all her fault. The room increases in temperature as my fire power is fueled by my anger.

Before I can explode and kill this asshole, Alexei sets a calming hand on my shoulder.

"It's okay, my love. I'm right here with you," he whispers in my ear. "Don't kill him quite yet. He's a piece of shit, but he may still be able to give us more information."

I take a deep breath, and get my shit under control. I need to maintain calm right now, especially in front of my council. When I've gotten it together, he gives my shoulder another squeeze before backing up again.

"Do you happen to know any sort of plans or timeline?"

He shakes his head vehemently. "We've never been privy to anything like that."

Proteus pipes up from behind me, and I take a brief moment to sympathize with how hard this must be for him. "She will not have told anyone what she's planning. Only a few of us knew of Demonica to begin with, and then she informs only her lackeys of specific tasks she requires from them."

"I can confirm that. She doesn't want any of us to know too much. She also persuades most of them to keep it secret," Pearl chimes in.

I give myself a mental high-five. I was able to override that bitch's persuasion. Suck it, Coralia.

"Fuck," I curse softly before turning back to my captive. "Is there anything else of significance you can tell us?"

"She's going to try to turn the other territories against you. She hasn't visited any yet, and I don't know when she's going to, only that she wants to."

I inwardly seethe. I'm going to rip that fucking bitch to shreds.

"Anything else?"

"No, my queen."

I almost laugh. Only minutes ago he was telling me that I was not his queen and he wouldn't tell me a word. Look at him now.

"Send him back to the dungeons. Maybe something else will come to him."

The guards nod, grabbing our captive and taking him away. When he's gone, I turn to my group.

"We need to go to Mermacovia. I will not let Coralia do any more damage."

They all nod in agreement. I know I'm the queen, and can simply overrule them and do as I wish, but I don't feel comfortable playing that card yet. I care about their opinions, and I'm thankful that I don't have to plead my case.

"What are your plans, my queen?" Vlad asks me.

"We will arrest Coralia for treason, and instate Proteus as her replacement immediately. I will then give them the same speech I gave everyone else. Those that wish to oppose me and want Demonica as their queen can join Coralia." Harsh? Maybe. But I have no idea how else to handle this. I don't want an uprising on my hands, and technically they will be guilty of treason. I will tell them the truth, and they can decide for themselves. I feel bad leaving Proteus to deal with the fallout though.

"Proteus."

"Yes, my queen?"

"Are you comfortable dealing with this after we leave? Should we leave extra security with you?"

He shakes his head. "I believe I will be able to handle the situation, Your Majesty. I know there are those there that are loyal to me. I know who I can trust."

"I'm coming with you," Pearl insists.

"Me too," Xanto says just as vehemently.

We talked about this beforehand and came to this decision. As much as I hate losing two of my ambassadors, it makes me feel better knowing that they'll all be there together. I'll have to talk to Pearl after this. Just the two of us. Even though we already discussed this, it was in the presence of her men.

"I also would like to look for the trident. I think it's in Mermacovia, and I have a feeling that you're going to need it. Somehow I know it's going to be important. I think I can help you more from there," Pearl says.

I take a deep breath, my heart sinking as I nod. I hate the idea of not having her here with me. I take comfort in the fact that I can teletravel to see her.

"How many people do we need to take with us?" I ask. I have no idea how things like this go. I know just Alexei and I won't be enough.

"I would suggest at least a hundred guards, Your Majesty." This is from the witch ambassador.

Sounds reasonable. "Very well." I turn to my mate. "How long will it take to get them all together and ready to travel?"

"Just a few days. And then roughly a week to travel there. We can meet them there when they arrive."

I turn to Pearl, Xanto, and Proteus. "Will that be enough time for you three to get ready as well?"

They all nod. "Proteus, you said there are those among the mermaids we can trust?"

"Yes. I will speak with them directly once we arrive. They will have our backs when you speak to the territory. It will create more of a united front and make them feel less attacked."

That's a wonderful idea. This is why I have my advisors here. They all bring something to the table that I need. Especially since I don't know what the hell I'm doing.

"Perfect. Okay, if no one has anything else to add, I think that's all for today."

Chairs scrape against the floor as everyone stands. Pearl is about to leave but I stop her. "Pearl, hang back a moment."

"I'm going to pick out the guards to accompany us to Mermacovia," Alexei tells me.

I smile at him, giving him a brief kiss before he leaves the room.

When it's just me and my best friend, I drop the queenly mask. "So, you and Proteus, huh?"

She blushes a little. "Yes."

"Pearl, I know we already went over this, but I want to make sure this is what you want. Should I be finding two new ambassadors?"

She audibly swallows. "I think so. Proteus is our third. If his place is in Mermacovia, then so is ours."

Tears build behind my eyes, but I smile at her, squeezing her hand for good measure. "Then I'm happy for you, and I will give you whatever you need."

She leans in and gives me a hug. "I love you, friend. I've never been close to someone like you before."

I clear my throat of the lump that's risen there. "Same here, bitch."

We hang on to each other for another minute before breaking apart.

"So, you think you'll be able to find the trident?"

She nods. "I don't know why. It's been missing for thousands of years, but I feel drawn to it. I *know* I found that information for a reason. I think it's meant for you."

There's something in the statement that resonates within me. I believe she's right, but I don't want to get my hopes up. Anything that could give me an edge in the upcoming war would be immensely beneficial.

"So, you'll come with us to Mermacovia, and then you're going to stay there?"

She nods. "Yes. Xanto and I both feel it. Proteus is meant to be with us. Or I guess in this case, we're meant to be with him."

I smile at her. "How's the sex?" I can't help asking.

Her grin turns wicked. "Unlike anything I've ever experienced. I've had group sex before, but it's never been like this. It's like we're intertwined."

"Isn't that the whole point of sex in the first place?" I tease, knocking her shoulder with mine.

She guffaws. "Absolutely."

"And Xanto and Proteus are together too?"

She nods, fanning herself.

"I can't say that sounds unpleasant to watch," I remark.

"It's definitely not unpleasant, I'll tell you that much."

As much as I want to stay and keep girl-talking with her, we both have shit to do. I'm tempted to tell her that as much as I love watching her work, I have my country's five hundredth anniversary to plan, my wife to murder, and Guilder to frame for it. I know she won't get the reference though. I sigh in regret. Our next trip to Earth I'll have to make sure we watch *The Princess Bride.*

"Why don't you start packing? It'll take you forever to get everything in that room ready to move." I shudder just thinking about the state of her room. She's never been the neatest person.

She scoffs. "Please. I'll have that done in one day."

My anxiety rises just thinking about the last-minute packing that's sure to ensue. "Whatever you say, babes."

We head our separate ways, and I teletravel to my rooms, not really feeling like seeing anyone after the events of the morning. Fuck. I can't believe that on top of everything else, I have to find two new ambassadors. Not that I blame them. If it were me in that situation, I wouldn't hesitate in the slightest to follow Alexei wherever he needed to go.

I wish I could bring Joseph here as my mimic ambassador, but I need him to maintain his position as grand master. I grumble in overwhelming exhaustion. I'm not physically tired. Well, I mean I *am*, but it's more than that. There's been so much change, and I'm in over my head. I have no idea how to do half of this shit.

Ebony pushes at me, wanting to be free of my skin, my anxiety making her restless. I let her out, and she paces in front of me. I feel bad that she takes on my emotions. I know it's because we're so connected on a soul-deep level, but I hate seeing the effect it has on her.

"Why don't you go hunt, girl? Get some fresh air and run it off."

She looks into my eyes, seeming hesitant. I know she wants to, but she doesn't like leaving me alone.

I smile reassuringly, petting her head and making her purr. "It's okay. I'll be fine."

She stares at me for another moment before taking off. I sigh at the feeling of being truly alone. This almost never happens anymore.

She's either with me, or Alexei is. I know I just took a day off yesterday, but I still feel in need of a break.

I call for some tea, and fill the bath while I wait for it to arrive. I add salts and bubble bath, figuring I'll go the whole nine yards. If I'm going to do this, I might as well do it right.

I grab my phone and speaker and get my bath playlist going. Nothing gets me relaxed quite like all the stops I'm pulling out.

My tea arrives a moment later, and I thank my servant—I think her name is Gilda—before returning to the bathroom. I sink down into the water, my muscles releasing for the first time in what feels like weeks.

I don't how long I lounge in the bath, soaking up the relaxation I so desperately need. When I finally make my way out, the water is lukewarm, and my mate or familiar still haven't returned. I have the random urge to watch TV. It's been a long time since I've done something so mindless. What I wouldn't give to watch *Harry Potter* or *Lord of the Rings*. I settle for listening to the soundtracks, and my mind immediately calms even more. Just the music is enough to slow my heart rate.

When I'm tired of sitting around in my rooms, I get dressed in training clothes and teletravel to the training yard. With everything going on, I haven't been training as much as I should. I pick up my bow and a quiver of arrows. I warm up just standing in front of the targets and shooting, but when I've dusted the rust off myself, I up the difficulty a bit. I walk from target to target, firing as I move.

I have an idea then. I haven't practiced archery with my owl form since that first time. It wasn't a huge success because the wind knocked my arrow off my trajectory, but I have air magic. I wonder if I would be able to counteract that problem. Of course I'd have to also focus on keeping myself either in the air, or shifting again before hitting the ground.

I decide to try it without the flying aspect for now. I stand farther from the target than normal, needing the extra time, and this way I can also see if I can pack a more powerful punch with the aid of my magic.

I take aim, and when I release the arrow, I motion with my hand to propel it faster through the air. I can see it's not going to hit the bull's-eye, and I send just a tendril of wind to one side to compensate. I'm delighted when the arrow smacks into the center of the target with a loud *thwack.* I pump my fist in the air in delight.

For the next hour, I intentionally shoot my arrow off-kilter so that I can correct it with my magic. I start small, but by the end of the hour I'm able to make much more significant adjustments, and decide it's time to practice in the air.

I add more arrows to my quiver and take a deep breath before nocking one. When I exhale, I shift into my owl. I fly high into the air and set my sights on my target. When I feel ready, I shift again, shooting immediately. I feel my body plummet, and my stomach lodges itself in my throat, but I focus on all the work I've been doing, letting my body take over. I add more force behind the arrow so it reaches the target faster, and as soon as I've finished casting my magic, I shift back into my owl. I spread my wings, soaring through the air and pausing to see if I was successful.

I hoot in triumph when it hits the target on the second innermost ring. Obviously not my most successful shot, but considering I was falling through the air and using my magic, I'd say it's not bad.

I spend another hour practicing this new technique, and by the end, I'm able to hit the bull's-eye almost every time. I land, shifting back and setting all my things down. I'm exhausted, but it feels good to be training again. I need to be at my best for what's to come.

I hear a slow clapping, and I furrow my brow. My heart picks up an excited pattern when my mate comes into view.

"Impressive."

"You think so?"

He nods. "You must have had an excellent teacher."

"Eh. He was okay. This is mostly all my natural-born talent."

A smirk dances across his lips, but he keeps up the charade. "Is that so? I didn't realize a human would have such an inclination for training."

I know he's trying to rile me up. I haven't been called a human in a hot minute. "Humans are better with physical combat than any other species," I spout.

"Are they now? Care to demonstrate?"

I hold my hand up and beckon him toward me, just like Neo does in *The Matrix.* I can tell he instantly gets the reference.

"No powers?" he asks to my surprise.

I nod. I like this game. In the next moment, he's sprinting toward me. I brace myself and try to anticipate his moves. It's been a while since we've done this, and I know he's going to throw me off. I can feel my witchy sense kicking up, trying to give me a vision of what he's going to do, but we promised no powers. I push it away before making a split-second decision. He taught me this move, but it's fairly complicated, so I've never actually applied it when we've been sparring. I think it will give me the edge I need now.

Right before he reaches me, I fall backward, rolling onto my back and propelling my feet up and over my head. Alexei was moving too fast to be able to slow down when he realizes what I'm doing. My feet push into his torso, shooting him up and over me, knocking him off-balance. He goes tumbling to the ground behind me, and I dart up before he can.

I swipe my foot out to strike him, but he's too fast. He grabs my ankle and yanks me on top of him. I let out an undignified shriek as I fall. He smiles as he rolls us so I'm under him. I can feel how excited he is, and I grind against him, remembering when we were in a very similar position.

"I win," he says smugly, leaning down for a kiss.

Before our lips connect, I flip us again, pulling my dagger and holding it to his throat. "I don't think so."

I let our lips connect then, and I can feel how much I've stunned him. It's funny to me that he's been so distracted by my body since we became mates that I've been able to get the best of him. Honestly, I know that's the only reason I've been able to accomplish it.

When I pull back and meet his gaze, his eyes are blazing. "You're amazing. Do you know that?" he asks.

I give him a sly smirk. "I do, indeed."

I plant another quick kiss on his lips before hopping off him. He groans, but follows me.

"Are the guards going to be ready to leave in a few days?" I ask.

"Yes. I should get back to them though. There's a lot of preparation that needs to be done. I just wanted to take a break and check on you."

"I'm fine. I took some more time to myself today. It was refreshing to just relax and enjoy myself."

He smiles at me. "Good. You've needed it." With that he kisses me and continues to ready the guards.

Within the next few days, we make all the preparations we can. The guards we're taking with us seem excited at the prospect of a potential conflict. After all of the talk of Demonica, I think the kingdom is restless, and this will make them feel like we're making an active move against her. Taking away her only potential allies will be huge.

Alexei announces that everyone is armed and ready to go, and a pit of nervous energy settles in my stomach. I know that we should be doing this, but it's still incredibly nerve-racking, and makes me question everything.

My heart sinks as Pearl gathers all of her things along with Xanto and Proteus. I'm not ready to see her go, and the sight of all of her belongings is just a reminder that she won't be coming back. At least not anytime soon, and definitely not permanently. My best friend will no longer live in the same place as me. No more late-night swims. No more girls' nights with food and booze. No more makeovers. Tears gather in my eyes as she approaches me.

She looks as though she's about to say something smart-ass, but as soon as she sees the moisture gathered in my eyes, she softens. "Bitch. Don't you start. I'm going to see you in a week." Even though her words are harsh, her voice breaks at the end, and I know she's struggling to keep her shit together as much as I am.

"You know it's more than that," I say quietly.

All humor and joking fades from her expression. "I know. I'll come back to visit. And you can be at our home in the blink of an eye. Literally."

"It won't be the same," I whisper. I knew this was coming, and I thought I had prepared for it, but I'm not ready. Pearl was my first female friend. Ever.

Instead of responding, she draws me into her arms. There's nothing to say after all. She knows.

We break down in each other's embrace, and I cling to her with everything in me. She squeezes back just as tightly. After a few minutes, we pull back.

"I'll see you in a week."

I nod. "Alexei and I will meet you at the designated spot."

I hug Xanto and Proteus in turn. "You both take care of her. Do you hear me? If you don't, you will have the wrath of a fucking queen coming down upon you."

Xanto looks like he's about to laugh, and I have the urge to smack him, but Proteus elbows him and looks at me seriously. "We will protect her with our lives. I swear to you."

I nod and wave them off. If they stay any longer I won't be able to let her leave.

They take off, the head of the pack, leading the way. The troop follows, and I'm grateful that they won't be by themselves. I'm also thankful that Proteus is with them. He will have more sway among the mermaids than anyone.

I feel Alexei's warm arms wrap around me from behind, and I sigh as I relax against him.

"We will see them soon," he says, giving me a soft kiss on my neck.

I nod, incapable of saying anything at the moment.

"Come. Let's go do some training."

# 13

## Ember

The next week passes by at a glacial pace. I'm so anxious about the upcoming conflict. Something inside me is telling me that it's not going to go how we think. I try to meditate and trigger a vision, but nothing comes. I practice some divinations, but they're all vague and give me no answers. I growl in frustration. I wish I could just skip ahead in time so I didn't have to wait. That's what kills me the most.

*Finally*, the day comes to leave. We've estimated that the group will reach the coast by today, and to make a united front we'll all be arriving at Allure Isle at the same time. I'm sure people have seen the group traveling through the territory, so Coralia likely knows they're coming, but without us there, it should still be a surprise. I say surprise like it's a good thing and she'll enjoy our company. It's not. And she won't.

When I can't stand waiting another *second*, I tell Alexei. We weren't going to leave for a little while still, but I would rather get there early. He looks at me dubiously, but relents in the end. He can't say no to me. The thought makes me grin as I grip his hand. I'm not sure if I tug him or if he tugs me, but a few seconds later, we're staring at the beautiful waters of Mermacovia.

The sun beats down on us, and I internally thank Proteus for this location idea. There is no one here, just as we were hoping. To be on the safe side, I put an invisibility spell on both of us. We do not want Coralia knowing we're here, and I don't want to risk anyone seeing us. It's a little weird at first, waiting for our group to arrive without being able to see each other.

My mermaid is pushing at my skin, and I feel the urge to take a swim in the sea, but I have no idea if my runes will be visible even though I'm not, and I push the urge to the side, batting my mermaid back. For now. I promise her she will get her chance to swim here, but not yet. That seems to pacify her somewhat.

Instead, I bask in the warm sun beating down on me and the sound of the waves lapping at the shore. It's doing wonders for my nerves. I wonder if I can still get a tan if I'm invisible? The notion is ridiculous and makes me chuckle.

Alexei and I sit next to each other on the beach, and I skim my hands over him. We've been in almost constant physical contact since we arrived, making sure we stay together. The act itself is reassuring. As my hand drifts up his muscled thigh, I come into contact with something that I wasn't expecting. I'm higher on his leg than I thought I was, the action causing me to brush up against his length. I hear him suck in a sharp breath, and it gives me a wicked idea. No one can see us. There's no one here anyway, and we're waiting on a group that could take a day or more to get here. There is one way we could pass the time.

I shift my skirt up my legs in a move that would normally bare myself to him, and straddle him. I feel his hands drift to my waist.

"What are you up to, little doe?"

"I think this could be something fun to try."

"And you want to try now? Here?"

"I need a distraction."

"Ahh. So I'm just a distraction to you, then?"

"An incredibly strong, gorgeous, and charming distraction," I tease him, bringing my mouth to his.

It's a very disorienting sensation. I can feel him. I can hear him. It's bright outside. I *should* be able to see him, but I can't.

He chuckles against my lips. "You say *I'm* the charming one, huh?"

"Oh yes," I stroke his ego as my hand moves down his abdomen, intent on stroking something else. My fingers close around his hardening cock over his clothes, and when he groans it brings a triumphant smile to my face.

The sound causes wetness to pool between my thighs, and I reach up my own skirt to move my panties to the side. I swipe a finger between my cleft, gathering my excitement up for him. I bring my finger to his mouth and paint my arousal over his lips. I can feel his tongue dart out to taste me and in the next moment, he's sucking my finger. We both groan in unison.

"Take me inside you, my queen."

Instead of giving him what he's asking for, I bring our lips together, sucking his tongue into my mouth as I continue to pump his length. He lets me continue for about a minute or so before he breaks away from me.

He doesn't ask again, or order like I thought he would, he pushes his hands under my skirt, desperate to feel me. He shreds my panties as soon as he reaches them, and I moan. That shouldn't be such a turn-on but it is. I'm going to be essentially going into battle without underwear on, after all.

His fingers find my soaked center and he growls. "So ready for me. You just like to tease me, don't you?"

"I don't know what you're talking about," I respond in a breathy voice.

"You know, two can play this game, my love."

"I would win, and you know it."

He chuckles. "Is that a challenge?"

I know I'm going to regret this decision, but I'm enjoying this game too much to stop. "Yes. I bet you cave before I do."

"What do I get when I win?"

"When *I* win, you get to make me a romantic dinner."

"You really would prefer to have something I make you over the royal kitchens?"

I nod. "I miss your cooking."

I can hear the smile in his voice. "Deal. And when I win you'll bake for me," he says.

I smile and nod. He knows I love baking. I thought I would be ready for the full weight of his seductive efforts, but I'm not. It's a little awkward at first because we can't see each other's bodies. Our hands grope and feel for where things are, pulling at clothing we can't see, and mouths meet cheeks and noses instead of lips. But soon, his fingers are plunging into my desperate heat and I'm trembling against him. His thumb finds my needy clit, pushing, swirling and thrumming against it. I let out a keening cry as I feel myself building already. I refocus and double my efforts on him. I need to feel his length inside me, not just his fingers, but I will *not* be the one to lose this battle.

My hand reaches under his waistband, finding silk-encased steel. He makes a husky sound low in his throat when I squeeze, working him with an expert touch. I trace my thumb around the head of him and he hisses at the contact. At this rate we're going to bring each other off before we even get down to the real thing. Then again, that just means multiple orgasms for me. I can live with that. Him, on the other hand, he will not want to spend his orgasm not inside me. I can win this. I just have to push him far enough.

I feel his mouth moving from my jaw down my throat, nibbling and sucking as he goes. My skin is oversensitized, and every touch feels like a spark straight to my core. I whine when his lips close over my nipple. I want him inside me almost more than anything. Not as much as I want to win though.

I reach my hand farther down and give his balls a firm squeeze and he makes a choked sound on my breast. I lick my other palm and take over working his shaft.

"You don't play fair," he pants against me.

I smile knowingly, even though he can't see me. In answer, he pushes another finger inside me, stretching me even wider. Fuck. I'm closing in on my climax. He knows all the right buttons to press to get me there. Literally.

I ride his hand, my body taking over, reaching for the finish line. Just as I'm about to topple over, he pulls his hand free of me.

"No! Alexei, don't stop."

"Do you want me to make you come?"

I snarl at him. "You know I do. I was so close."

"Do you want me inside you when you do? Clenching around me as I stretch you wide with my cock?"

Fuck me. He could send me over the edge with just his words. And I might not be able to see him, but I sure as shit hear the smirk in his voice. He thinks he's won.

"I think that's what *you* want. I can bring myself off just fine." I reach the hands that were touching him and bring them to myself, tweaking my nipple and stroking my clit instead. He can't see me, but I make sure he can feel exactly what I'm doing.

He growls and his hands snap forward and rip mine away from me, pinning them behind my back. "No cheating."

The position has his length pressed up against my core and I find my opening. I may not have my hands, but I don't need them anymore. I shift my hips, rubbing against him. He lets out a needy groan at the feel of my wetness pressed against him. I'm still so close. I moan in earnest, letting him know that within a few rolls of my pelvis, it'll be over.

"Ember…fuck. Ember, stop."

I don't listen. I keep moving. I'm right there.

"Fine. *Fuck.* I cave. Let me in," he growls.

I smile in victory. He lets go of my hands, gripping my hips instead. He lifts me, and in one fluid motion, he's buried gloriously deep inside me. My clit brushes against his pelvis, and with that, I'm thrown over the cliff. My orgasm bursts through me, and Alexei steals my mouth in a kiss to quiet my scream of pleasure. I don't have it in me to keep moving, but he's there, taking control of my body and fucking me with everything he's worth.

It's fast, messy, and needy, but I don't care. This is exactly what I need after the stress of this week. I need to feel this connection to my mate, like we're the only two people in the world, and that nothing else matters.

His hands roam, pinching, caressing, loving, and before I even come fully down from my orgasm, I'm thrust into another one, clenching around his length greedily. I want more. I want it all.

"Alexei, bite me."

He growls his approval as he gives me what I want. His teeth pierce the top of my breast as mine latch on to his shoulder. His pleasure mounts, and when he spills inside me I topple over the edge one final time.

We stay there for minutes, unmoving, our hearts beating as one, breaths intermingling. When I can finally think straight, I realize how dirty I feel. And not in a good way. I knew sex on a beach wouldn't be a good idea. There is sand in places I definitely don't want. I really want to take a swim now.

I look around the beach again. We have not seen one person since we arrived. I think it will be safe.

"I really want to wash off," I tell him.

"Me too. Remind me in the future how unpleasant sand is."

I chuckle and we remove our clothing, setting them in a pile. I reverse the invisibility spell so we don't lose them, and we grab each other's hands before taking a much-needed dip in the ocean. It's incredibly refreshing, and my mermaid delights in the feel of being in Mermacovia waters.

When we're done I dry us off with air magic, and we get dressed in our clothing again. We resume our sitting positions on the beach, and I'm much more relaxed and content than before. That was just what we needed.

The group arrives not long after. I knew it was unlikely for anything to have happened to them on their travels, but seeing them alive and well with my own two eyes is comforting. I rush up to Pearl and wrap her in my arms.

She squeaks in shock and surprise, and I realize that I'm still invisible.

I chuckle. "Sorry. It's just me."

She relaxes against me, returning my embrace. "Ember! I missed you. Let me just tell you, it has been a nightmare traveling with all these *men*," she says in disgust.

I laugh loudly. I hadn't even thought of that. That would be horrid. Especially for someone like Pearl. She likes things pretty and traveling with over a hundred men would not be pretty. Men are disgusting.

"Why can't I see you?"

I reverse the spell on myself and then Alexei. "We wanted to make sure no one saw us while we were waiting for you."

"Well, now that we're all here are we ready to head to the capital?"

I nod even though my nerves are back. "Yes. Let's get this over with."

With everyone except me, Pearl, Proteus, and Xanto unable to shift and swim the distance, we go in search of a ship.

There's a harbor nearby, and we head that way. The closer we get, the more crowded it becomes. I don't know if this is a good idea, but we have no choice. It's really unfortunate that she has to live on a fucking *island.*

There are a few boats in the harbor, but with how many of us there are, we will have to find one large enough. There are two or three that seem to be able to carry only fifty or so, but then I see it. The only one that would be able to get us all there. With my status as queen and his respectful position among the mermaids, Proteus and I decide that we should go to the harbormaster together.

Of course Proteus knows the man, and he spends a few minutes schmoozing and buttering him up before we actually tell him what we need. Proteus is truly the most charming man I've ever met. He could charm the panties off a nun if given the chance, and I have fun watching him work. Within minutes, he has the man smiling and blushing. When he's thoroughly buttered, Proteus tells him that the queen requires safe passage to Allure Isle and that we would make it worth his time, as well as the ship's crew. The man nods enthusiastically before nodding and running off to find the captain.

"Is there anyone you can't get to do what you want?" I ask.

He gives me a cheeky smile. "Just you."

I scoff, bumping him with my shoulder. I'm glad that we can still be friends. He's a wonderful man, and if things hadn't been how they were between me and Alexei, I could've seen myself really enjoying being with him. As it is, I still enjoy his company, and I'm so happy for him and my two other besties. They make the perfect throuple.

The harbormaster returns within ten minutes and tells us that the ship will be ready to escort us in a half hour. I thank him profusely and give him a small fortune for ensuring our passage. He beams at both of us.

Within thirty minutes we are all aboard the *Tipsy Mermaid* and settle into our seats. It's not a long trip to get to the island, for which I'm thankful. The less Coralia knows, the less time she will have to plan or sneak off.

I shake my leg restlessly in my seat. It jiggles up and down and I'm getting side eyes from most of our group. I wish I could stop myself. I shouldn't be showing my anxiety to my subjects, but it's like my leg has a mind of its own.

Alexei leans closer to me and puts his hand on said leg. The warmth immediately helps to soothe my frayed nerves. "Just relax, little doe. Everything will be fine. We will capture Coralia and take back Mermacovia. And after that, we will beat that bitch Demonica back into her shithole never to be seen or heard from again."

I doubt it will be as easy as he's making it out to be, but his assurance comforts me just as much as his touch, and I finally relax for the first time since we made love on the beach. I lean into him, letting his warmth soak into my bones. I can do anything with this man by my side.

Within an hour we're sailing up to the capital. I spot the capitol building, Coralia's headquarters, on the most beautiful section of the beach. I wonder how long ago it was built. Did she have any say in the architecture or the design?

Our group unloads off the boat and I give the crew the money they deserve but probably never see. I tell them to wait for us and that there will be more where that came from. We will need safe passage back, and I'm not sure we'll be able to find another boat that can fit us all. The captain eagerly nods and tells me he was planning on staying in the area for a few days anyway.

When we have our passage secured, I lead the way with Alexei and Pearl and her men at my side. We present a united front, and quite a crowd has gathered.

We arrive and I knock on the door, trepidation churning in my gut. I don't let any of that show on my person, however, internalizing it and shoving it down as deep as it will go for the time being. I can't show an ounce of weakness right now. Everyone seems to wait with bated breath. There's no answer. I knock again, louder this time. Minutes go by, still no answer.

Proteus walks up and opens the door, his magical signature allowing him access, and I'm even more grateful he's here with us. We search the building and find nothing. No one is here. Not even a servant. Fuck. She knew we were coming.

"Where would she go?" I ask Proteus.

He shakes his head. "I'm not sure exactly."

"If she knew we were coming she might've gone to alert Demonica," Alexei pipes in.

My stomach sinks. That sounds just like something she would do.

"We need to go and check out the portal," I decide.

"What about the guards? They can't swim. It will be only the four of us," Pearl says.

I look at Proteus. "Are there any mermaids we could bring with us right now that you trust and would fight with us if it came to that?"

He nods. "We can recruit them along the way."

"I don't like this, Ember. I won't be able to protect you. What if Demonica is there?" Alexei asks, worry evident in his voice.

"I don't like being separated from you either, but this is unavoidable. The group of you can search the island and ask if anyone has seen her. If you find her, capture her and keep her until we return," I order.

Alexei's jaw flexes and I know he wants to argue with me.

I reach up and cup his jaw. "There isn't time for us to think of something else, Alexei," I whisper. "I will be fine. I'll come back to you. You trained me well."

I can see how torn he is. I knew if he was able that he would learn how to breathe underwater just so he could come with me. I can see how torn he is, but I won't risk taking him and breathing for him. If there's a conflict, keeping him alive is the last thing I want to worry about.

"Okay. But be safe. And you come back to me. No matter what."

Tears build in my eyes but I nod.  Before I can say anything, he crushes his mouth to mine in a bruising kiss.  He pours everything into it. All of our love, all of our heartbreak, all of our anxiety. I return it wholeheartedly, making sure he knows I care for him just as deeply, and will do everything in my power to return to his side.

We break away and he gives me one last intense look before he turns and commands the group to move out.

I'm alone with Pearl, Proteus, and Xanto. Pearl lays a supportive hand on my back. "We'll come back. Now we have to go."

# 14

## Ember

We strip as we head for the water's edge. We dive in with no preamble and shift, taking off just as quickly. Proteus leads the way, and within moments we're in the underwater community. The group that Proteus was always talking to is gathered near the large underwater structure I admired when first coming here. He tells them what's going on, and they all nod emphatically. They hate Coralia nearly as much as we do. There are ten of them total, but I wish there were more.

When I tell Pearl this, she tells me there will be. One of the mermaids in the group breaks from the rest and takes off.

*Sherman is going to get more help*, Proteus notifies us.

*Good. For now, this will have to be enough*, I say. I don't want to waste any more time.

He nods, and he and Pearl lead the way to the portal. The farther we swim, the less populated it becomes until eventually there is no one around.

I can feel the nausea start, and I know we have to be close. Although this portal feels different than any other I've encountered. It's dark, and I can sense an evilness pouring from it. There are no fish nearby, or any sea life for that matter, and I wonder if the corruption has tainted the water in the immediate area.

We slow, attempting to make our arrival as quiet as possible. We have no idea if Coralia and her crew are in fact here or not, but if they are, we want to have the element of surprise.

As we approach an underwater cave, I see movement. They're here. I know it. I hold up a hand to the others, stopping them. The area is dark, and there's seaweed around. I motion for them to follow my lead before hiding amid the kelp. We need to do some recon.

We move from patch to patch, and when we're finally close enough, I can see twenty rival mermaids in the water. None of them are facing us, but they have their top halves out of the water and are turned in the opposite direction.

Twenty. That's more than we bargained for. And more than we have among us, even if it's only by a few. But the drive to get to Coralia is strong. And we have more reinforcements coming.

I turn and face my crew. I think we'll be able to risk mind speaking here. It is possible for others to overhear if they're in the vicinity, but since their heads are all above water, we should be fine.

*Let's try picking them off one by one first,* I whisper to them.

They all nod in understanding.

I have an idea then. They will most likely notice if we swim up underneath the group. What if I teletravel directly below them and snag them before they see us. *Or* I could try pushing a feeling onto each individual mermaid to see if I can get them to swim to us on their own. That last option might work. Maybe I can do a combination of the two.

When we are as close as I think we should get, I stop with another hand gesture and lock on to the closest adversary mermaid to me. I feel their sense of duty racing strong throughout them, and excitement about something. I erase all that and push an urgency to explore into her. It's a little strange being in the water. I've never tried to use my empathy this way before, and the colors move through the tide like a rainbow. I can see when the emotion reaches her. I turn back to my group and motion for them to stay put.

Then, without a word, I teletravel closer to her. Not close enough that the others will see me, but close enough that I can snatch her when she inevitably leaves.

She ducks under the water, her tail twitching nervously, and then she takes off. I sneak up behind her and wrap my tentacles securely around her. I take the dagger I had the forethought to bring with me, and I use its handle to knock her unconscious. It happens so quickly that she has no time to struggle or shout a warning to anyone. I swim forward, passing her off to Proteus.

I repeat the same thing with two other mermaids, another female and a male. Their absence is bound to be noticed soon, however, and we still don't know exactly what's going on. But now, the playing field is a bit more even, and I feel more confident in our odds. I gesture our group forward and closer to me. Those along the outer edges have been taken care of, so we should be able to sneak a little closer without being noticed.

We're right at the cave entrance, and I have them stay behind once more as I teletravel to right below the water's surface. I slowly raise my head out of the water. I almost gasp at what I see. Coralia is standing on the ground portion of the cave, a woman standing next to her. The woman has horns, red eyes, and her snow white skin fades to pitch black on her arms. Demonica. In the fucking flesh. The other mermaids have a look of deference and adoration gracing their faces as they listen to her with rapt attention. I also notice with absolute dread that Opal is among the followers. Fuck. Pearl is going to be crushed.

Demonica's voice is smooth as whiskey and as deadly as poison. I can feel the allure coating her words, and I know she must be strong to be affecting mermaids. Although, if these individuals are already loyal to her, it would only heighten their admiration. I try to get a sense of her emotions here with my gift but all I feel is a deep dark void tinged in rage. It's scarier than anything I've felt from anyone yet.

"My faithful followers, you will never know the depth of my gratitude for your loyalty. As Coralia has already explained to you all, my crown was stolen from me. His line still inhabits the throne. Are you willing to be ruled by a descendant of traitorous filth?"

They all shake their heads vehemently, and I can feel the hostility and anger coating the air. Fuck. This is not good.

"Will you help me to restore the natural order and bring me back to my rightful place on your throne?"

The mermaids all shout, and I know my time is up. I duck back under the water and motion them all up. We need to act now while they still don't realize we're here.

They sneak up, and I palm my dagger.  I hate that fucking bitch Coralia, but I need to go after Demonica. If we can end her now there will be no war. I shift into my mortal form and in the next moment, I'm teletraveling behind Demonica. Without another doubt or thought, I thrust my dagger forward, aiming for her heart. Coralia screams and pushes Demonica to the side, just enough that I miss. My dagger still finds purchase in her torso, but the movement jars my weapon, and I miss her heart entirely. Demonica roars, and the sound chills my blood like nothing I've ever felt before, which is significant considering all the monsters I've faced.

She spins and shoots her clawed hand forward, aiming to rip my own heart from my chest. I knock her away, slashing with my dagger hand.  She hisses in pain and outrage when I draw more blood, this time slashing her arm.

The cave turns to chaos around us. Coralia, however, huddles in a corner. Cowardly bitch. Demonica and I match blow for blow. I can tell she's had no formal training like I have. She does however have thousands of years of experience. As we fight, we discover we also have all the same powers, with the exception of our fundamental powers. Demon vs human. Her eyes gleam in the glow of the cave and I feel something happening to me. As if I'm getting slightly weaker, and I don't understand why. I continue slashing at her before it occurs to me that I need to use what weapons she doesn't possess. I pelt fire at her and she laughs maniacally as she douses it with a flick of her wrist. Fuck. She has water magic.

I blast her with a strong shot of air and it throws her into the cave wall. I teletravel in front of her, ready to rip her throat out with my teeth, the razor-sharp incisors already extended. As soon as I bring my mouth to her neck, however, she shoves me off with another blast of water, and I tip off the edge of the ground and back into the water beneath me. I growl in frustration and push her off with me with another blast of air.

We both shift in the next breath as we circle each other in the water. I'm too caught up with her to take note of how the others are faring. The only thing I know is that chaos reigns. I just hope the others are alive.

I take a split second to admire the beauty and similarity of our mermaid forms. Her tentacles are red and black, so close to my purple and black. The runes of Surseiha glow on our skin and light up the water around us.

*So, we finally meet properly, kin,* she sneers at me.

*So we do,* I counter, my tentacle whipping out to slap her across the face.

Blood dribbles from the corner of her mouth and dissipates in the water. Her eyes narrow and she glares dangerously at me.

*I have waited too long and worked too hard for my husband's descendant to fuck this up for me.* She shoots forward, wrapping a tentacle around my neck and squeezing painfully. Her teeth bare in a snarl as her claws reach toward my head. One of my own tentacles wraps around her wrist, wrenching it back painfully. I dig my own claws into the tentacle she has wrapped around my neck. She screeches, finally releasing me, and more blood spreads throughout the water. Black blood. No idea what that means, but it can't be good.

*You killed my father.* I almost tell her "Prepare to die" as well, but figure there's no point.

*Ahh yes. That was a moment I've been waiting for for centuries. It felt so good to have his blood coating my skin. And your despair tasted oh so sweet.*

It dawns on me then. She's feeding off my emotions. That's why I feel weak. I throw up the strongest mental shield I can manage. I block out *all* my feelings, not letting anything but a disinterested numbness settle over me. I don't know how strong her mind is, but just to be on the safe side, she won't be able to feed from me if I'm not feeling anything. I then think of my father's lessons. *Know that your mind is stronger, believe it with everything inside of you.* I know I'm better than this bitch. She might've been through hell, but she wasn't strong enough to come through better on the other side. She came through worse.

*You're smarter than you look, kin. I will give you credit for that.*

I give her a demented smile. I won't be caught off guard by her again. *It's sad that you spent thousands of years waiting to kill a man that literally had nothing to do with your demise. He was so far removed from Theon that the only thing they shared was their name.*

At the name I utter, her body goes rigid and she lets out an unearthly shriek. She lunges at me, but I'm prepared. I teletravel behind her, and in the next second, my fingers are threaded through her hair. I have her head pulled back with my dagger positioned at her throat. Just as I start to drag it across, I look beyond her to see the devastation taking place in front of me. Dead mermaids litter the sea floor and my best friends are locked in intense combat with those left. We're outnumbered. We're not going to make it. This was a mistake. Pearl is still alive and trying to make her way to her twin, but I have no idea what her plan is. It's clear Opal is not on our side as she kills countless of our allies.

My hesitation costs me. Demonica rips my arm away from her throat, and I curse my stupidity. If I had just slit her throat, this would all be over by now. She twists in my hold and brings her face to mine.

*You didn't think it would be that easy, did you?*

I snarl in her face, snapping at her with my fangs since every other part of our bodies are holding each other back. She laughs, and I'm disturbed by how beautiful and lyrical it is.

*Your problem, sweet little kin, is that you get too distracted by your followers.* She brings my attention back to the battle happening behind us. The one that I'm desperate to turn around. *If you did not care for them, and thought only of yourself, you would have been able to kill me and end this whole thing. Your problem is that you have a heart. If you truly want to rule and be the best, you have to place yourself above everyone else. No one else matters, my dear.*

Disgust froths in my gut. The thought of letting those I love die for me while I rise to the top uncaring is unfathomable. I will not do it. And as much as I have in common with this woman, she was wrong when she told me that she was me. We will *never* be the same.

I want to prove that to her. I want to prove that my love for my friends is a strength, not a weakness.

I manage multiple things then. I reach out to my group, pushing strength and courage onto them. I let it fill all of us to the brim. The other thing I do isn't something I even knew I had the ability *to* do. I bellow out a lengthy note, singing long and loud. In it, I pour all of my love and devotion to those around me. I think of Alexei, I think of my father, I think of my mothers. Everyone I've ever cared for. I put all of that emotion and love into that one note. It reaches far and wide, and Demonica's eyes bug out of her head at the sound. She releases me and covers her ears, shaking her head as she backs away.

*No no no no NO!*

I see my opportunity and lunge for her. Before I make contact, however, I'm yanked backward by my hair.

Coralia's voice sounds in my head, her lips poised at my neck. *I thought you said you were going to "deal with me"?*

Demonica takes advantage of the situation, not caring if it's an uneven match. Her claws slash through my abdomen and I cry out in pain. The two women bite me, scratch me, and maul me. They're toying with me. Making an example for everyone who's left. Tears stream out of my eyes and mix with the salt water. I told Alexei I was coming back. I promised. Now we're going to die, and I brought my best friends with me.

Demonica's mouth is at my throat, teeth poised to shred my vocal cords out. I close my eyes and send a silent goodbye to my mate. I wait for the strike to come. For the inevitable pain and darkness to descend, but it never does. Instead, Demonica is ripped off of me, and I open my eyes to see a sword is protruding out of her stomach. I gasp in shock as I see my mate behind her, yanking the thing out. His eyes lock on mine and I sense the worry and panic in them.

We both turn when we hear the other group of mermaids charge in. The ones that Sherman went to rally. I let out an exhale. We aren't going to die today. I turn back, intending on finishing both bitches, even with the sorry state my body is currently in, but they are swimming at full speed toward the cave and the portal beyond, Opal with them. Fuck. I'm about to charge after them, but I meet Alexei's gaze. Shit. He can't breathe. I swim up to him and bring our mouths together. I give him the air he needs, and he sucks it down greedily.

When I know that he is safe, I pull back. We survey the scene around us, and I'm glad to see that with the extra forces we've defeated the rest. There are a few alive and are being restrained. My heart breaks for Pearl that her own twin betrayed her like that.

I get all of their attention and point to the cave. We need to discuss this on land and where there's air for my mate.

I swim us there in record time, and Alexei helps me onto the cave floor. Coralia and Demonica are nowhere to be found, and I know that they escaped through the portal.

"Ember, you're hurt! Gods, they shredded you." Alexei's worried hands hover over my body, clearly wanting to touch me but not wanting to hurt me. Now that adrenaline isn't pumping through my body like crazy, I'm starting to feel the extent of my wounds. My head swims with the blood loss and the pain, but I push past it.

"I know. The bitches were playing with me." I sit and take a deep breath, focusing all my energy on my healing magic. I bring it to the surface and heal every injury I can feel on my skin. When it's all done, I sag in exhaustion.

"How did you get to me?" I ask when he pulls me into his arms on the cave floor.

"I felt your anguish. You somehow telegraphed all your emotions to me. I could sense your panic, desperation, and grief and knew something was terribly wrong. I just teletraveled, knowing my mind would find you. Looks like I got here just in time."

I settle my hand on his jaw, tears building in my eyes. "Thank you. Thank you for coming for me and rescuing me. Again."

"I'll always be there to save you, little doe. Always."

I clutch him to me, unable to believe we almost lost each other. Again. Gods. This has to stop happening.

The rest of our group comes into the cave. "They're gone?" Pearl asks.

I nod. "They took off as soon as Alexei showed up and stabbed Demonica through the gut."

"She has to be dead from that, right? I saw it go straight through her," Xanto remarks, back in his mortal form for the time being after fighting in his stingray form.

I shake my head. "She has elf powers, remember? If she was still breathing she will be able to heal herself. Not to mention that I healed myself after I was already dead. I'm sure she's fine and licking her wounds on the other side of this portal." I eye the thing with trepidation and frustration. The anger still simmering inside of me roars back to life and I stand, suddenly having an abundance of energy. "I'm going after the bitch. Bitches, I guess I should say."

Before I can take off through the portal, Alexei grabs my arm and yanks me back to him. "You will do no such thing," he states firmly.

"Alexei Dreymonde, you will not tell me what to do!" I yell at him, my anger needing an outlet.

"Look, I don't order you around, ever, but I will not budge on this. You would literally be walking straight to your death, and that I will not allow."

"You have so little faith in me?"

His eyebrows rise at my anger, and hurt flashes in his eyes. "You know that I have more faith in you than anyone I've ever known. I know you can do anything you set your mind to, and you'll excel at it. This, however, is a suicide mission. It's not just Demonica and Coralia on the other side of that portal. There is an entire army of soulless demons that have been alive for thousands of years there as well. You would not survive it, my love." His tone gentles at the end.

"He's right, Ember. We cannot take on all of them by ourselves. We need to prepare. And rest and recover, for that matter," Pearl chimes in, she and her men looking a little worse for wear.

I deflate, knowing they're right, but not wanting to let them go when they're this close. I came here for Coralia, and leaving here without her is a hard truth to swallow. Not to mention the fact that I had

Demonica in my grasp and she slipped right out from under me. I could've prevented an entire war, and I wasn't able to.

"You're right. I'm sorry." I turn to my mate. "I'm sorry, Alexei. I didn't mean it."

"Shh. I know you didn't, little doe." Alexei kisses the top of my head as he pulls me to him.

I turn to our crew. I heal them quickly before giving them instructions. "You guys go on ahead. Take the prisoners with you. We will meet you at the capitol soon." I try to rush them out because I feel myself about to break, and I can't do that in front of them. Maybe if it was only Pearl and her men here, but I can't in front of the other mermaids, the few that survived that is. I need to be a strong leader right now. I need to be the queen. Not Ember.

Pearl seems to understand, and leads everyone out of the cave. As soon as they're out of sight, the tears come and the sobs start. Alexei holds me upright when my legs buckle. He scoops me up and sits us back down on the cave floor, gently rocking me back and forth as I break down, not once saying anything, just letting me fall apart with the promise that he'll put me back together.

"I failed," I whimper into his chest.

"You did no such thing. You reclaimed Mermacovia from Coralia. You forced her to retreat. We may not have captured her, but you will get the justice you are owed. I promise you."

His words quiet my sobs just the slightest. His faith in me is greater than anyone's has ever been before. How could I have told him he has no faith in me? The thought brings a fresh wave of guilt and tears. I don't deserve this man.

I don't know how long we stay there, but my tears eventually slow, then stop altogether. With that victory comes another wave of overwhelming exhaustion.

Alexei seems to read my mind, or maybe he just knows me all too well. "You need to rest. Let's head back to the capitol."

I feel him tug me along with him, and we teletravel to just outside the building. We arrive at the same time as Pearl and her men, along with a few other mermaids to help carry the captives. Pearl meets my eyes and gives me a knowing, sympathetic look. I give her a reassuring, if not tired, smile.

"We'll take care of them for now. Why don't you head to your old room and wash up and take a nap?" Pearl offers.

"Yes. I'll have food sent up too," Proteus adds.

"Thank you."

Alexei sets me back on my own two legs, knowing I won't want them to see him carrying me. I trudge to the room, dead on my feet, Alexei's hand a comforting support at my low back.

As soon as we get to the room, Alexei starts up the bath for me. I'm already naked from the swim, so there's nothing for me to take off, and I sink to my ass on the tub floor, none too gracefully, I might add.

Alexei chuckles as he strips off his wet clothes and climbs in behind me. I collapse against him and close my eyes, relaxing in his hold. The events of the day have me so wiped that I can't even function right now. It's been an emotional rollercoaster as well as magically and physically. I'm drained in every possible way right now, and here in the heat of the bath and the comfort of my mate's arms, I can no longer stay awake a second longer.

I wake not long after to Alexei cleaning me. I moan; his attention is just what I need. He's thorough, rubbing a soapy sponge over my body before shampooing my hair.

"You don't have to do all this for me, you know?"

He huffs. "Yes I do, my queen. This isn't for you. It's for me."

I know what he means. Taking care of me is his way of assuring himself that I'm alive and well. His mate bond has to be screaming at him to be a good mate and do everything I could possibly need. I let him because I like it too much. He might say it's not for me, but I'm reaping the benefits more than anyone else.

When I'm all clean, Alexei wraps me in a nice robe and leads me to bed before grabbing the food that was set outside our door. He sits next to me on the bed and we eat everything in record time. I barely even touch my wine because I'm eating so quickly, and when we're finished, I pass out on the bed, completely drained and spent.

# 15

# Ember

The next day, we scrape ourselves out of the bedroom to meet up with Pearl and her men. We need to come up with a game plan and address Mermacovia. They're in the dining room when we emerge, and they look just as haggard as we do.

I meet Pearl's eyes. Sorrow lines her features, and I know that she must be devastated about her twin. I rush to her, wanting to pull her into my arms and comfort her.

She tenses and I can tell she wants me to do this another time, but I can't. My gratitude for her is too much right now, and I need to let her know that even though her sister betrayed us, I'm still here. We aren't sisters by blood, but we chose each other all the same.

I pull her out of her chair and wrap her in a tight hug, and I can feel her deflate in my arms as sobs start racking her body.

"I can't believe she would do this." Her voice is so quiet that I barely hear her.

I hate how small she sounds. Pearl is larger than life. She doesn't deserve this. She shouldn't have to choose between her family and what she thinks is right. But here we are.

"I know," I tell her. "I'm so sorry." The words are cliché, but what else can I say? There's no consolation for the utter betrayal she's feeling right now.

We ignore the fact that there are others watching us and the food is getting cold. We are the only thing that exists. My love for her and the deep need to comfort her.

After a few more minutes, she pulls back and meets my gaze. "I'm sorry she didn't choose us," she tells me.

"Don't you dare. You do not need to apologize for her actions. They are hers and hers alone. Do you understand me?"

She nods, a hardness entering her eyes. I grin at the fight I see boiling in her soul. "That's my girl," I tell her, squeezing her arms tightly.

We sit then and dig into our food. No one mentions the emotions that are so blatant behind each and every one of us. We don't talk about anything yet, we just eat and enjoy each other's company. We need a little bit of normalcy after yesterday.

When the meal is finished, and the plates have been cleared, I look at everyone. "So what are we going to do?"

"You're the queen, you tell us," Xanto remarks like a smart-ass, to which I roll my eyes.

"Well, I think for starters, we need to address Mermacovia," Proteus chimes in helpfully, ignoring Xanto.

"I agree. I think we also need to be prepared that there are going to be more individuals that support Demonica. Just because there were only twenty or so in that cave doesn't mean that those are the only ones," I say, to which they all nod.

"When do you think we should give the address?" Alexei asks.

"The sooner the better. They need to see how powerful you are and to hear how things are going to go from here on out," Proteus says.

I nod in agreement. "Is today too soon? Or should we try for tomorrow?"

"Tomorrow" is the only thing Pearl says.

Relief settles in me more than I care to admit. I want to get this over with, but I don't feel prepared to give a speech today.

"We'll need to give you a makeover too. That will take some time."

Pearl's words would sting coming from anyone else, but I know her well enough by now. Not to mention that she's right. After yesterday, I'm sure I look a hot fuckin' mess.

"What about the prisoners? We should probably question them," Alexei brings up.

I groan in exhaustion and frustration. I know that needs to be done, but I really don't want to. I'm sick of war, and it hasn't even started yet.

"I would tell someone else to do it, but I can get information the fastest," I sigh.

"We'll come with you. You won't have to do it alone," Proteus adds quickly. I give him a grateful smile.

"Will you two also help me with my speech? I want your input since you know the mermaids well. I feel like they're more complex than any of the other species I've addressed yet. Especially with me overthrowing their grand mistress and literally driving her out of the damn realm."

They nod in agreement.

"Well, with that decided, let's go question these assholes."

It turns out, the same scenario plays out with the last mermaid we questioned. The captives know essentially nothing of value, and I curse Coralia and Demonica for playing their cards so close to the chest. It's infuriating. I'm half tempted to kill them because I know they won't be of any further use to me, but I don't feel quite right about it.

I know I need to get used to that kind of thing, this is war and all, but something about the idea of killing members of my realm, even traitorous ones, makes my skin crawl. They're imprisoned and there's nothing they can currently do. I *will*, however, be taking them back to the Immortal City with me. There are too many people in this territory who I can't trust. I'm grateful that I brought an abundance of guards with us so that I don't have to worry about that right now. No one would dare fuck with me with that many trained royal guards here. Unless, of course, the entirety of the territory decided to revolt against me. My stomach bottoms out at the thought. I know it's extremely unlikely, especially considering the mermaids who helped us and fought against their own kind. Their deaths bring a fresh wave of guilt. The battle with Demonica did not come without losses.

It also helps tremendously that I have Proteus on my side. He is well-known and respected throughout the community. He has been more involved than Coralia ever was. He should've been in charge of this territory long ago. The thought brings even more guilt. My father allowed Coralia to maintain her position. As much as I loved him, and I think he was a great dad, he was still a person. He made mistakes. And his ignorance of how things were run in the rest of the realm was definitely an oversight. He became too comfortable in his position, and too reliant on letting others handle the rest of the territories. I will not make that same mistake. I plan to bring the realm together. And I *will* be more involved in how it is run. I want to converse with the leaders regularly and have meetings about what is and isn't working. I desire to *improve* this realm, not just sustain it.

*One day at a time*, I tell myself. I have enough to worry about with Demonica and this war without adding "bettering the realm" to my list right now. Eventually? Yes. Now? No.

After meeting with the prisoners, I gather with Proteus and Pearl. I want their help with my speech. It takes hours to figure out exactly what to say and how to prepare for different reactions, but I think we eventually get something good written. Not good, brilliant. *Why is Ron Weasley in my head?* I chuckle at the welcome distraction of my own mind.

Pearl then helps me pick out the perfect outfit. I had someone retrieve my clothing from the beach, which contained my trunk in one of the pockets. I brought a few different dress options with me because I know that I will need to look killer when I address the mermaids. We set each garment on the bed to air out and examine the options. I want to not only look powerful and beautiful, but also *dangerous*—I think that's important. The mermaid territory not only needs to respect me, but they also need to fear me.

We settle on a black floor-length gown that's mostly sheer with the exception of floral lace that's placed strategically to cover the important bits. Dress picked out, we move onto the makeover portion.

At this point, Pearl and I have done this so many times that we've become a well-oiled machine. I'm no longer uncomfortable with her seeing me in various states of undress. We get rid of every inch of unwanted body hair, scrub me down so I have zero dry skin, and then she washes my hair before applying a hair mask to make it gleam and shine. With the address happening tomorrow, she puts my hair in a silk cap to ensure that it dries without any frizz. The last thing is a mani pedi.

Pearl and I go down and have dinner and drinks with our loved ones when we're finished with my makeover. It's comforting to feel this sense of normalcy with them, and to bask in each other's presence.

We drink wine, eat everything in sight, and joke and make each other laugh. It's perfect. I wish things could be like this all the time. Instead, the threat of war looms over us, tainting everything.

By the end of the day, I'm exhausted and dreading tomorrow. Although we worked out all the possible scenarios, with some obviously worse than others, I still find myself wishing I knew the exact outcome. I try to use my witch sense to get a vague idea, but it's quiet. With so many people attending the address, there are countless outcomes that could come to pass.

Alexei rubs my back when we get to bed, and I sink into his embrace. I let Ebony out as well, and we all cuddle in bed together, one big happy puppy pile. Anxiety threatens to wash away my contentment, but I don't let it. I push it away and focus on the feeling of my mate's arms around me, holding me tight and safe.

I wake early the next morning, my stomach churning with nerves. The address is scheduled for ten, and I simultaneously wish that it was sooner and later. I leave Alexei and Ebony curled up in bed together to start getting ready.

I take my hair out of my cap before getting my battery-operated curling iron and turning it on. I don't use it very often because I don't like wasting the battery, but it will give me curls that no mermaid has seen before. It's going to be something that they envy and respect.

I meticulously curl each strand, I've got time to kill after all, and being busy is helping to settle my nervous energy. Pearl joins me when I'm about halfway through. She admires how I work the iron, just watching. I gave her her own as well when we went to Earth, but she hasn't had the practice or time with it that I have.

While I'm busy, she gets the makeup ready, looking over every shade of eyeshadow she owns. I finish my curls, and she stands and strategically pins some back here and there. The way my hair is styled leaves my neck on display, giving me a tall and regal appearance. Then, she starts on my makeup. She covers every inch of my face with foundation, and then goes in and contours and highlights. She's heavy on the highlighter, wanting to make me look like I have the traditional mermaid blush. She's dramatic with my already bold eyebrows, and then frames my eyes with purple, matching the color of my irises and making my eyes look even more intense. She applies a dark reddish-brown tint to my lips. Lastly, we get my dress and crown on.

I look in the mirror and gawk at her handiwork. I've seen her do this many times, and every time I'm amazed. She manages to make me look like an improved version of myself. Like a million times improved.

With time still leftover before the address, I pace, being mindful to keep the hem of my dress out of my way. The last thing I need today is to trip and fall on my face after all the work we put in to making me look spectacular. Pearl and Alexei both try talking to me to distract me, but nothing works. I just want to get this over with.

Proteus has gone to round up other mermaids who he knows we can trust to support us. While I do trust him, it puts me a little on edge to have mermaids I don't know at my back. I've been attacked by them too many times.

Ten o'clock finally rolls around, and I feel ready to burst out of my skin. My emotions and powers churn beneath the surface, and I take deep breaths to attempt to keep them at bay. Mermaids are predators after all, and they can sense fear just like a lion can.

I try to push some calm onto myself with my powers, and it takes the edge off just enough. I don't know why I'm so nervous, but this feels like the most important address I've given to date. This will determine the future of my relationship with this race.

"It's time, Ember," Pearl says gently.

I step onto the platform in the main square, my closest group, guards, and supporting mermaids behind me. There are thousands of mermaids in front of me, and even more poking their heads up from the sea. I meet as many of their gazes as I can, seeing and feeling a million different emotions playing across their faces. I walk forward, holding my head high, a solemn smile on my lips.

"My fellow mermaids. This is a pivotal time in our history. The future of this realm balances on the edge of a blade. As many or all of you know, Coralia was in league with a former leader of Queridian. Her name is Demonica, and she is a demon that was banished from this realm thousands of years ago. She is a descendant of Surseiha, and I know to many of you, that will encourage you to give her your loyalty. She was also the last queen with mermaid blood. Until me. I stand before you and appeal to you not to forget that I also share Surseiha's blood."

One of the mermaids behind me comes forward with a bowl filled with water from Mermacovia. I dip my hands into it, allowing Surseiha's runes to decorate my skin. I know that a lot of them have seen them and my tentacles while I was swimming. I'm also aware that news travels fast. However, I want there to be no doubt that I am indeed Surseiha's heir, and have just as much of a right to rule in that respect as Demonica.

"I know many of you are no doubt upset that the crown was taken from your race, and believe me, I am as well. But, it stands to reason that it is Demonica's fault. If she had not been as unhinged as she was,

I'm sure the kingdom would've welcomed her back with open arms and rejoiced that their beloved queen was still alive. But they did not. She became mad and dragged the rest of the demons with her. They attacked countless innocent lives in the castle and fed off of them like they were cattle. Is that really who you want back in power? Together, we can defeat her. And with that, we can unite the races. The only reason the species have been segregated for as long as they have is because of her. I have all of the races inside me. I can unify us all, and I *want* to do that. We will be stronger because of it."

I take a deep breath and look over them again, giving them a moment to digest everything I've shared.

"Something many of you don't know is that there was an attack yesterday. We came across Coralia and Demonica planning something nefarious here in your territory. They retaliated and there was an altercation. Mermaids that were against them were killed mercilessly, and the two escaped back through the portal. Now, I know it will not be easy, especially considering that your grand mistress was responsible, but I'm asking you to join me. Together we can defeat her."

I expand my senses, seeing if I can pick up on what people are feeling. Once again, it's a cacophony of emotions, and I struggle to home in on what I'm sensing. Trepidation, distrust, allegiance, gratitude, anger, hope. There is so much, and I can't tell if they're feeling more negative or positive about everything I've said. I decide to move onto happier news.

"On a brighter note, I want to announce something I think you'll all be very happy about. Not only is Coralia stripped of her position, she also abandoned this territory as she fled into Domonia. I have appointed a new Grand Master of Mermacovia. He has long helped those in need, let you air your grievances, and just been a good friend to many of you. As Queen of Queridian, I hereby appoint Proteus Harbor as your grand master." I gesture to him where he stands next to me.

He smiles humbly, stepping forward, and the crowd roars in elation. He has spent years cultivating relationships with the people of this territory, always having their best interests at heart. I can think of no one better suited for this position than him.

"Thank you," he says to both me and the crowd. "I won't make a long speech, but I just want to say that I appreciate the support of this amazing species. I know my mother wasn't the best leader, and I can't wait to make some much-needed improvements. With the support of our queen, and the aid of all of you, I know we can make Mermacovia and Queridian what we've always wanted."

The crowd cheers again, and I smile at their overwhelming acceptance. I knew they would be in support of that decision if nothing else. I'm pleased that we're ending on a positive note. The two of us wave to our subjects, and leave the stage, heading back to the capitol. Alexei and I could obviously just teletravel back, but I want them to see us as a united front. And for them to see that we're comfortable in this territory. Even if I am somewhat fearful of another attack, they can't see that. I want them to feel that I trust them implicitly. How can they put faith in me if I don't return the sentiment?

"Well, that went well, I think," Pearl remarks when we enter. "I told you they would love you," she tells Proteus, rubbing his back soothingly.

"We knew announcing Proteus's promotion would be the easy part. Now we need to wait and see if they are with us or against us." I collapse onto the couch, exhausted from the emotional rollercoaster I've been on today.

"Agreed," Alexei says. "But, we can't wait around to see how they react. We need to go back home and start preparing for war. You know that Demonica will be doing that very thing. We need all the time we can get."

"I don't think you should leave just yet. I think we should start looking for Surseiha's Needle," Pearl cuts in.

"I thought you were going to take care of that, Pearl?" Alexei furrows his brows at her.

"I am, but I was thinking that there may be some secret or something that only Ember can uncover because of her bloodline. There's a chance I won't be able to retrieve it simply because I don't have Surseiha's blood in my veins."

"Is it really that important? I don't think looking for a relic that has been missing for thousands of years is really going to help us. It sounds like a wasted effort to me."

I stand. "Something is abundantly clear, Alexei. Demonica and I are too evenly matched. I don't know if I can kill her. I don't know if I can *survive* her. I need literally every advantage I can get, and if that means we search high and low and in every realm for this trident, you bet your ass I'm going to do it."

Pearl smiles at me, and Alexei nods. When I put it that way, there is nothing more important to him than my safety.

"Okay. We will stay for one more week, but then we have to head back. Do you at least know where to start looking?"

She smiles. "No, but I think I know someone who does."

# 16


## Pearl


Ember and I head to the ocean. The others wanted to come with us, but this is something we need to do alone. Undine is very distrusting of strangers, and she absolutely loathes company. As the oldest mermaid in our territory, she was thrust out of our community long ago. It sounds harsh, but with mermaids being so vapid, we see age and the withering of beauty as a weakness. It's not something any mermaid wants to see. We hate the reminder that we could eventually look anything less than beautiful and perfect.

Undine has long been forgotten. I discovered her only because I loved exploring when I was young. I went way past the borders of the city, and was curious when I came across loose scales floating amid the water. Undine had just gotten into a tiff with an eel, and because of her age, a few of her scales had come loose. I followed them and found her in her cave. At first I was terrified. I had never seen a sight like her before, but I was intrigued too. I wandered into her cave. She didn't seem surprised in the slightest. She didn't seem happy to see me either, but she didn't kick me out. She answered all of my questions, albeit begrudgingly. From then on, I visited her every week. I tried to bring her food when I could, even though she hated taking things from me.

It's been a few years since I've seen her, but I know she's still alive. I'm convinced that crusty old bitch is never going to die. I smile fondly thinking of her cranky ass. Despite everything else going on, I'm excited to see her. I thought about going to her when I had to flee the Immortal City, but I didn't want to put her in danger. Plus I needed to be close to the underwater palace to search the archives.

It takes us about an hour to get to her. My heart beats a little harder at the number of scales I see in the water leading to her home. I know I said she would never die, but I'm suddenly worried that I'm wrong about that.

Ember seems to notice too. *How old is Undine?*

*She's four hundred and two this year.*

Her eyes widen in shock. *How is she still alive?*

*Most mermaids don't live to be over four hundred, but it can still happen once in a while.*

Her eyes stay that way as we continue forward.

My breath snags in my lungs as we enter her home. Most people would ask permission before they just came in, but I've known her for long enough that I know she hates answering the door. She's old, and moving around too much is hard for her.

*Undine?* I call out. She doesn't answer and that pit in my stomach grows just a little. Am I too late? I hate the thought of her dying and no one knowing it. Of me not being here. Even though I hadn't seen her in a while, she had become important to me.

*Undine?* I call out louder. *It's me, Pearl.*

I hear a heavy, tired sigh. *So, you finally came back, huh?* Her croaky voice is less strong than it used to be, but I was right. She's still alive. I sag a bit in relief.

We enter farther and find her sprawled on a couch made of seaweed. I would say she looks the same, but that would be a lie. I didn't realize she could look worse, but she does. To Ember's credit, she doesn't react to her appearance, simply smiles kindly at her. I can see the disbelief behind her eyes, but only because I know her so well. I watch her expression as she takes in all that is Undine.

Undine's tail used to be green, but it's lost its vibrancy, and a good portion of her scales are missing. Even from this distance I can see that in some patches she has what looks like fin fungus. I have the strong urge to keep my tail far away from her. She's lost a lot of body mass as well, including in her tail. Her breasts are shriveled and hang loosely down her chest. Her once-red hair is now completely bleached of any color. Her eyes have turned milky, and I wonder if she's gone blind, but when her shrewd eyes widen upon seeing Ember, I know she's not.

*At last you've come, my queen.* Is that reverence I hear in her voice? *Took you long enough.* Aaaaaand, there she is.

*You know who I am?* Ember asks, surprise and astonishment evident.

*Of course, Your Majesty. I have been waiting all my life for Surseiha's heir to come. Once I give you this information, I can fulfill my promise and go in peace. It's the only reason I've hung on for so long.*

My brows shoot up. I didn't realize there was a reason behind her living so long. *You mean, you didn't hang on to see me one last time?* I ask her, like a smart-ass.

She rolls her milky eyes at me. *You wish,* she remarks, although there's a small smile gracing her lips, and I know she missed me. I also see that all of her teeth are missing. I can't help but grimace.

Ember swims up to her, and plops down on the cave floor. *Pearl, why don't you get her something to drink. Is there anything else you need, Undine?*

I can't wait to hear Undine tell her to kindly fuck off. She hates people getting her things. At least she did whenever I tried.

*I'm a bit cold. A blanket would be nice.*

I stare at her in shock. *What in Triton's name? Why did you never let me do anything for you?*

*It's something called kindness, dear. You never asked me. You just insisted I needed something.*

I'm about to object. I had asked. Hadn't I? Thinking back, I can't think of one time that I did. She's right. I heave a sigh. *I'm sorry, Undine. I'll get you a blanket. What would you like to drink?*

*Liquor. I think I have a bottle of mermish wine somewhere in the kitchen. And get some for you and our queen here as well. It's impolite to let an old woman drink alone.*

I smile. That's more like it. I grab a seaweed blanket from her bedroom and drape it across her lap before going into the kitchen for the wine. Mermish wine is special because it doesn't mix with water. I have no idea how it works, but I'm thanking the genius who came up with it.

I bring glasses for all of us before sitting on the floor next to Ember. When we've all had a drink, Undine tells us the secret she's carried for almost four hundred years.

*Our family dates back thousands of years. To the time of Surseiha's descendants. Surseiha was an extremely powerful mermaid. Partly because of her blood, but also because of her ability to invent magical objects and the blood magic she studied. Not only did she imbue her line with the runes decorating your body, but she also created a magical relic. It's called the Trident Obelisko. It's also known as Surseiha's Needle. The trident was infused with raw power, and it heightened the king or queen's strength. It is partly why her line reigned for so long.*

*There was once a mermaid queen from her line who possessed the trident. She felt like it corrupted her in the way that she had too much power. And because of that, she did not believe that another should possess it until the time came when it would be battled for between two of her line. The most deserving of the trident would be the only one who could obtain it.*

*Our line has long since kept the secret of where information can be found about the Trident Obelisko. That is my task. That is my duty. Now that you are here, my queen, I can tell you the location. Everything else is up to you.*

Ember and I stare at her in shock. I had no idea she would have this for us when I brought Ember here. The only reason I thought she might know something is because of her age. That she not only knows about it, but also has something concrete we can investigate is enormously significant.

*The information you need can be found in the abandoned underwater castle. You will need an object to access it. We have kept it safe for you all these years.*

*What is it?* I ask.

She narrows her eyes in annoyance at me, but answers. *A golden shell.* She points to her bedroom. *There's a secret hole in the cave wall in my bedroom. It is behind a wall of seaweed. Grab it.*

I do as she bids while Ember stays with her. I would never have found it if I hadn't known what to look for. I locate it easily. It's unlike any shell I've ever seen or held. It is indeed gold, and has an iridescent sheen. I wish I was in the sun with it. I bet it would be even more captivating.

*Hurry up, girl! I'm about to die in here,* Undine chides from the other room, making me chuckle and roll my eyes fondly. Despite everything, she's still as feisty as ever.

I bring it into the other room, and Ember gasps when she sees it. She holds her palm out for it, and even though I want to give it to her, I'm reluctant to let go. There's a magic in it that calls to me. Or maybe it's simply because I'm a mermaid and I like pretty things, especially those found underwater.

Undine narrows her eyes at me. I break her gaze and force myself to hand it to my best friend. She grasps it, and as soon as it makes contact with her skin, I know that I wasn't imagining the magic in it. Her eyes shine and reflect the gleaming surface.

*The information you require can be found in the throne room. Underneath the throne itself will be an indent. The shell will fit in there perfectly. Go now, my queen. There is no time to waste.*

Ember meets my gaze. Hope lines her features, and I feel that same emotion swelling inside of me.

*What about you?* Ember asks, clearly worried to leave her alone.

*My dear, I have been alone for many, many years. I like to be on my own. I am the best company after all.*

*I don't want to leave you,* I tell her, guilty she's been alone for all these years. Granted, I wasn't here to visit her since I was in Mystic Mountain, but I still hate it.

*You must. This is much more important than me. And now that I've completed my mission, I can be at peace, whatever may come.*

I've never heard her like this. Cranky? Yes. Annoyed? Check. Surly? Definitely. But this intense woman who has purpose? I've never met her before.

I squeeze her hand. *I've missed you all these years.*

*Oh, you have not. No one in their right mind would want to be around me.*

*Are you saying I'm out of my mind?*

She chuckles before squeezing my hand back. *I do want to tell you that I've always appreciated your company, even if I didn't show it. You brought some light into my days whenever you visited.*

I feel tears well in my eyes. She's saying goodbye. *You're not planning on dying now, are you?*

*Ha! I don't give up that easily. Though I no longer feel the need to stick around like I did before today. I would be perfectly content if the Gods decided to take me tonight. I am awfully tired, after all.*

My heart sinks in my chest, but I hold out hope that she'll stick around for a little while longer at least. We say our goodbyes after she essentially kicks us out of the house. When we're far enough from her home, Ember stops me.

*Are you okay?*

I sigh heavily. *No. Not right now. It's been years since I've seen her, and I didn't realize she would be in that bad of shape. I mean, she wasn't great when I saw her last, but nowhere near like what we saw today. And as surly as she's always been, I've always had a soft spot for her. It's hard coming to the realization that she's not going to be here for much longer.*

I make a mental note to start visiting her regularly again now that I'm back in Mermacovia. I know I'll be busy helping Proteus, but I can carve out some time to see her.

Ember says nothing, simply wraps me in a hug. I sink into her embrace. I'm so grateful to have a friend like her. One who is with me through thick and thin, and supports me no matter what. I've never had that before. It also saddens me, because my twin should've been that for me, and while I thought she had my back for a long time, she was always shallow, and I never felt like I could talk about serious stuff with her. And now, with her betraying us for Demonica and Coralia, my heart is broken.

When I pull myself together, I break out of her embrace. *Thank you. Now, let's go find this trident.*

It takes us an hour to swim to the underwater castle, and during that time, I try to think of all the places Surseiha's Needle could be hidden. I'm itching to get my hands on this information. As soon as I read about it in the archives, I knew I had to find it. I knew from the beginning that I wouldn't be able to wield it, but anything that can give my best friend an edge in this upcoming war is worth all of this effort.

As we approach, tingles erupt along my skin, and I can't discern the feeling creeping over me. Is it remnants of the siren attack I experienced while here? I'm not entirely sure, but I glance around, ready for anything. There are dangerous creatures in this part of the ocean after all. I don't see anything, but I stay on high alert.

*So, where is the throne room?*

I groan. I'm not looking forward to getting to it. *It's in the very middle.*

She seems to understand my less than enthusiastic reaction as she eyes the ruins. *Are we going to be able to reach it?*

*It'll take us a while to get there, but hopefully we can find a path.*

We start forward, picking our way carefully through the debris and hallways. Gods, I really hope what we need is still intact. I don't know what we'll do otherwise.

After what feels like an hour of twisting and turning, squeezing and looping back, we finally enter the throne room. Ember takes it all in with wide eyes, from the ruined chandelier to the crumbling walls.

*It used to be gorgeous,* she states.

I don't know how she's able to tell with it in this condition, but I nod all the same. Somehow, the throne is still where it's supposed to be. I wonder if it was bolted down long ago. Hopefully that doesn't make our job harder.

We swim over to it, and I sigh when I see there's debris everywhere. We will have to clear the area before we can look for the indent for the shell. We get to work, quickly discarding the random stones, coral, seaweed, and everything else you could imagine.

When it's finally clear, I sigh in disappointment when I see the throne has a solid base. We're going to have to move it, and I don't know how difficult that will end up being. Ember and I give each other a look before approaching the throne with trepidation.

We push against it with all of our might to no avail. Fuck. The bottom must be heavily weighted so that it stays put underwater. We push again. Nothing. Again and again. *Fuck.*

Just as we're about to try again, I catch movement out of the corner of my eye. I turn and come face-to-face with a pissed-off eel. It snaps at me with its rows of razor-sharp teeth, and I pull back just in time to avoid it. I swim to the side, drawing it away from Ember.

*Work on the throne. I'll take care of this guy*, I tell her.

She gives me a skeptical look but I wave her off. I've handled pesky eels on my own before. I swim at full speed to the other side of the enormous throne room, checking behind me to make sure it followed. It did. I spin at the last second and shoot back toward the ten-foot-long eel. They don't typically get this big, but it isn't unheard of. They can get up to thirteen feet, but they're usually around four to five. The advantage here is that this won't be able to maneuver around as quickly.

I can see the surprise in its eyes as I flip toward it, claws bared. I swipe at it, nicking its scales. I avoid touching it with my skin considering that they can cover themselves in a toxic sticky substance. No thank you. It rears back before I can do more damage and strikes its head forward like a snake, snapping its teeth at me. I barely avoid it. This asshole is faster than I thought he would be.

I fake one way and dart the other. It falls for my trap and I shoot past it, knocking its long body with my tail as hard as I can. Luckily, my scales offer more protection than my skin, so the substance shouldn't soak into them at all.

It wobbles, stunned before shaking its head and coming at me again. We battle like that for some time, dodging and swiping at each other, and I snarl in frustration. Usually it doesn't take me this long to best these guys, but I think this one is smarter than most. In fact, I can see battle scars on its body and can tell that it's survived more than one scuffle.

I almost feel bad having to kill it, but it did attack me out of nowhere, and we have a mission to get back to. I can't afford to be distracted right now. Done playing nice, I swim up and flip my body upside down before swimming underneath the eel. The move catches it off guard and I'm able to score its abdomen open from neck to tail with my claws, officially ending its life. I try to block out the screech it makes as it dies, but am not completely successful.

I head back to Ember as I scrub at my skin in the water. Bleh. Eels are so gross. When I return, Ember is just moving the throne, and I'm surprised we didn't think of this earlier.

# 17

# Ember

I keep one ear on Pearl as she battles the eel. I know she'll be fine and that she's done this before, but I don't like leaving my friend in danger. It's because of how distracted I am about her that I don't think of the obvious solution right away. When it comes to me, I almost hit my palm against my forehead at the simplicity.

I hold my palms out toward the throne and send air magic out. It's strange since I'm underwater. The effect is much different than what I'm used to, but it does the trick. Somewhat. I have to send multiple blasts of air at it before I can get it to move fully off the area I need to access, but it eventually uncovers what I'm looking for.

Pearl comes back just as the indentation in the floor is revealed. One that looks like an exact cutout of the shell Undine gave me. My heart starts pounding out an unsteady rhythm as I swim forward, sliding the shell into place.

It flares brightly, a shine overtaking the entire chamber before we hear a grinding noise. A section of the floor pulls back and a small stack of papers are revealed. There seems to be some sort of water protection spell on them, like the books that Pearl found in the archives of this very castle.

When I come across something, it triggers a revelation. I gasp in absolute shock.

*What is it?* Pearl asks.

*Apparently, the trident has been deactivated.*

Her face falls in despair and dismay.

*But it can be reactivated. On Earth. And I think I know where on Earth.*

Her eyes grow wide. We start carefully making our way out of the castle, documents in hand. We have to focus on navigating the rough passage so we wait to discuss our findings.

We finally break free into the open ocean and I sigh as my claustrophobia eases. It feels good to be out of that space. I can't believe Pearl went back there as often as she did just to find information for me.

When we're in a safe area with no one around, Pearl stops me.

*So, where's the trident?*

I scan the pages more thoroughly this time. Horror slices through me and I look at Pearl with what I'm sure is panic written across my face.

*Where?* she asks quietly, as if she already knows.

*Domonia.*

Her expression mirrors mine and we simply stare at each other for a long moment, unsure of where to go from here.

Pearl suddenly looks around, scanning the area.

*What's wrong?* I ask, besides the obvious of course.

*I'm not sure. I just have a weird feeling. Maybe it's from that eel attack.* She shakes her head as if to clear it. *Does it at least say where in Domonia?*

*Close to the portal. There's not much water there it says, but there is a lake close by.*

*Wouldn't Demonica have found it by now?*

I shake my head. *It was hidden. Whoever hid it, put it in a very small cave in the lake and piled a mass of stones and rocks in front to seal it off.*

I read from the parchment, seeing if I can find anything else notable. *According to this, they added a golden rock into the blockage so it would be able to be found by the right person.* Me, I realize with a start. *Let's get back to the guys. We can talk about this more with them.*

She nods and we take off, eager to get to our men. We need to figure out some sort of solution, and they'll be able to help us.

Our men are anxiously awaiting our return. Alexei immediately pulls me into his arms when he sees me, and Pearl is squished into a Xanto and Proteus sandwich and looks like she's loving every second of it.

"How did it go? Did she know anything? You two were gone longer than we expected," Alexei says and I feel bad when I see the worry in his eyes.

"We're fine. We had a little run-in with an eel, but Pearl took care of it."

Everyone's eyes shoot to her, and both of her men start checking her over for injuries. She's immediately disgruntled and waves them off.

"Do you think I'm so weak I can't handle a simple eel?" she lectures, even though I know for a fact it was not simple.

The men, however, look thoroughly scolded and give her a quick sorry. I almost burst out laughing and call her out on her bullshitting them, but I would never do that to my best friend.

"What else?" Alexei says impatiently.

"Undine didn't know where the trident was, but she did tell us where to find information about it."

"Apparently, her whole family line has been dedicated to keeping the secret until the right person reemerged," Pearl chimes in.

I hold out the papers to them, but Alexei shakes his head. "Just read it to us."

The first thing I tell them is that the trident has been deactivated. Even if we were able to find it, we would need to go to Earth to reactivate it.

"I actually have a theory about where to do that. The information here says there are three obelisks in the ocean. Well, if we're going with the theory that they left it fairly close to the portal in Mermacovia, then it should be in the mirrored space on Earth which would be in an area we call the Bermuda Triangle." I've been thinking about this since I read that the obelisks were on Earth. My mind was spinning the whole swim back here.

They look slightly confused, but it makes so much sense to me. There would be three, one for each point in the triangle. It could also be responsible for the strange things that occur there. The more I think about it, the more I feel I'm right.

"There are multiple problems we have to consider though," I continue. "The first is that we obviously need the trident in order to activate it, which will be extremely difficult and dangerous considering it's in Domonia. The second is that this states the obelisks are invisible. If my theory about the Bermuda Triangle is correct, then I will know the general whereabouts, but the ocean is huge, and it will take forever to find."

"Will they stay invisible?" Proteus asks.

I shake my head. "According to this, I need to bring the golden shell with me that Undine gave us." I hold up said shell, grateful I had the wherewithal to grab it. "Once I bring it into contact with the obelisk, it will become visible and I'll be able to activate the trident, but only after discovering all three."

"So, really easy, then?" Xanto remarks sarcastically.

We're all silent for a few moments, thinking about possible solutions.

"You know," Pearl breaks the silence first. "I remember hearing about a woman at the black market claiming she can perform a spell on any object that can locate any item you wish to find. It doesn't bring it to you, but it guides you to it."

My brows rise. That's an option, although if Stavros were alive he would tell me it was absolutely not. The thought saddens me, but I push past it. I don't have time to grieve my father right now.

"Okay, let's keep that as an option and perhaps come back to it." The mention of the black market has another idea sparking. "You know, there might be a similar spell in the Epitome Athenaeum. Alexei and I could teletravel there and see if we can find anything. Plus, I should check in on everything there and let the council know what's happened. I also need to find new ambassadors for you two," I groan, remembering just how much I have to do.

Pearl gives me an apologetic look, but Xanto smirks, like he's proud of himself for ditching me to come here. I don't blame him, but it does mean I have more work I need to do.

"Do you trust me?" Proteus asks.

I nod, not even having to think about it. Not after all the support he's given me.

"Good. I can find someone for the mermaid position, if you'd like?"

"Actually, that would be a huge help, if you wouldn't mind."

"Not at all. It's the least I can do after you let me take these two with me."

I smile at them all. They are so good together. I'm glad they've all found what they wanted. "Well, I appreciate the help. I know I've met some of the mermaids here, including those you trust, but I really value your input."

"Anything I can do, my queen." He's always been so polite and genuine. It was the first thing I liked about him.

"Well, we should get back to the Immortal City so we can start our research. We'll be back in a few days. A week at the most," I tell them.

They all come up and wrap me in hugs. Pearl goes last and holds on the longest. We both laugh when we see the guys doing the bro-hug. Then, Alexei and I grab on to each other and teletravel to my castle. He doesn't need to guide me anymore, but it's become a comforting habit of ours.

After everything we just went through, it feels nice to be back home. The smell instantly settles me, and I take a deep breath. It takes only a second for someone to spot us.

"Your Majesty! We were worried about you. You were gone longer than we anticipated," Humphrey says.

"Yes, well we ran into a snag."

"Coralia?"

I nod. "She escaped. With Demonica."

His eyebrows rise in shock, but he recovers quickly. "Well, I'm so grateful you're both all right. What about the rest of the guards?"

"All safe. We lost some mermaids though. We kept the unit there for now. I know there are still mermaids there that support Demonica and Coralia. They'll need guards there that are loyal to me and our cause."

He nods in agreement. "Well, is there anything you require? Food? Tea?"

"Both, please. And some wine. If you could send it to our rooms and notify the council I need to meet with them in about an hour."

"Of course, Your Majesty. Right away." He bows.

"Thank you, Humphrey."

Alexei and I walk to our rooms, and I wish I could just eat and then sleep instead of talking to the council, but it needs to be done. They need to be caught up on everything and our next steps.

Food arrives soon, and we eat before taking a quick shower. I let Ebony free as I'm getting dressed. She hasn't been out in a few days, and I know she wants to stretch her legs and hunt. She nuzzles my leg, purring before taking off.

With it being just the two of us, Alexei pulls me into a tight hug. It was an eventful few days, and we almost lost each other. I melt into his embrace, feeling hot tears sting behind my eyes, but I keep them at bay. There's no time for me to break down again. I have to keep my shit together.

All too soon, I pull away. "Ready?"

He nods and we head for the war room to meet with the council. I debate on what to tell them. They obviously need to know about the showdown with Coralia and Demonica, but I think the less people that know about the trident, the better.

They're all waiting patiently when we arrive. I greet them all, but it's strange not having Pearl and Xanto here.

"Thank you all for meeting with me. And I apologize we're later than expected. We ran into some issues."

They all nod, but I can see the concern on their faces.

"We're fine, as are Pearl, Xanto, and Proteus. But as we were attempting to capture Coralia, we came across her and a group of other mermaids consorting with Demonica herself."

Gasps echo throughout the room as I let that sink in.

"We engaged them in battle. Many were lost on both sides, but in the end Coralia and Demonica escaped through the portal and back to Domonia."

Horror and disbelief are written across their features.

"We did capture who we could and question them. Unfortunately, they didn't tell us any new information, but they are still being held in Mermacovia. We decided to leave the unit of guards there to assist with the unrest in the territory."

"My queen, I'm so grateful you're all right. What do we do now? Do you have a plan?" Vlad asks me.

"Well, there are a few things. In no particular order, I need to acquire new ambassadors since Pearl and Xanto are no longer with us. Proteus is willing to find someone for Mermacovia, but we still need someone for the Everchanging Glades. Since I spent more time there than any other territory, I already have a few people in mind, so I might travel there in the next few days.

"The other thing is that we discovered something that could help aid us in the upcoming war. Now, I can't go into too much detail, but we need to begin searching for it. So, I may be gone a lot. That being said, I need someone to keep an eye on things for me while I'm gone." I look around at them all. I've come to really value them in the short time I've ruled. "And I've decided that instead of one person, I would like all of you to make decisions together if I'm not here. Only if it's an urgent issue, obviously, but I trust you all and know that you have the kingdom's best interest at heart. The queen's council, if you will."

They all look shocked and delighted by the news.

"Now, is there anything that happened while we were gone?"

"The rest of the votes came in. The overwhelming consensus is that they want to go on the offensive and take Demonica down first before she can strike at us."

I nod, grateful that I'm not making a decision that my people are unhappy with. That means, however, that I will have to get my ass moving to find the trident and activate it.

"Very well. Let's get started, then."

And so, the preparation for war truly begins.

Exhausted from our long teletraveling jump, Alexei and I collapse into bed for the rest of the day and through the night. When we wake, I prepare for a day at the library. I'm hopeful that we'll find something, but it takes the pressure off knowing that we can go to the black market if need be. Though, I would like to avoid going if we can. I don't know how we will be received; it won't be like last time where no one recognizes me. Although, with that thought in mind, I could always shift into someone else. But Alexei is still fairly recognizable. Maybe if we were to go to a different one it won't be an issue.

"Do you want to come with me to the library?" I ask Alexei.

"You'd let me?"

"Of course. Why wouldn't I?"

"Well, outsiders usually aren't welcome there."

"First of all, you're my mate. You definitely don't count as an outsider. Second of all, I'm thinking about changing that rule. I feel like our realm would really benefit from the knowledge that the fae have always hoarded."

He looks shocked. "Really?"

I laugh. "I don't know why you're so surprised. You know me well. I hate all the segregation and the fae thinking they're better than everyone else. This would even the playing field and make others feel more equal. Obviously we wouldn't release any dangerous information, but it's their magic. They have a right to use it."

He beams at me, and it solidifies my desire to change some things here. It's not going to be quick or easy, but it will be worth it.

"I would love to come with you, mate."

I smile, grabbing his hand and teletraveling to just outside the library, pulling him with me.

I look up at the mountain and waterfall where the Epitome Athenaeum is housed, the moment bittersweet. This place will always remind me of my father, but after today I'll have some hopefully equally enjoyable memories with my mate here as well.

"This is the library?"

I give him a secret smile before walking toward the waterfall. He follows without question, and I turn to see his expression as he takes in the entrance.

He walks through the water, not quite as taken aback as I was, but that makes sense since he's had his whole life to become accustomed to magic. His eyes widen, however, when they take in the entryway with the book stones across the water, and the door with the book archway. I run my fingers along the spines of those books before opening the door and motioning him forward as I back into the library. I've never seen him look more awestruck.

I let him look his fill, taking in the glory of where we're standing. He spins and doesn't seem to blink for minutes, as if he's trying to absorb every single detail. I'm glad he seems to be just as enamored with this place as I was. Well, am. Because let's be honest, I'm still stunned by the glory that is this library.

When he's gazed enough, well, enough for now, I lead him to the potion and spell room. It still gives me the creeps in the best way possible. We start looking through information for the finding spell, and I can tell he's discovering amazing stuff that doesn't pertain to what we're searching for.

"We can come back when we don't have so much going on," I promise him.

He nods and we keep searching. Hours and hours we search to no avail. The next day, more of the same. I sigh in defeat. I really thought we would find something.

"We're going to have to go to the black market," I tell him. "There's no time left to keep searching when we have a solution, albeit an unpleasant one."

He nods and we teletravel back to the castle. I'm so tired, but there's so much to do.

"Let's get some food," Alexei suggests, and I'm thankful he remem-bers when I forget to do simple stuff like that.

He asks Humphrey to send some food up for us, and then draws me a bath. This man. I don't know how he always knows what I need, but I love him for it. He hops in with me, and I bask in the comfort of my mate's company. It's the little times like this. Especially in the midst of all this war and uncertainty, the instances where we can just relax and enjoy each other are sacred.

He rubs my feet under the water, and I groan, resting my head on the tub's edge. I so badly want to just go to sleep. I feel like I could pass out for a week and still wake up tired.

He gets out a little while after, and I know it's so I can spread out to my heart's content.

Ten minutes later, food arrives and my mouth waters in response. Alexei tells me he can bring it to me in the tub, but I had my relaxation and now I need to get to work. Besides, if I don't get out now, I never will.

We eat quickly. I'm anxious to do what I need to. Alexei can tell that this isn't my normal type of eating quickly. It's not out of enjoyment, and although it is good, I hardly taste it.

"Do you want to head back to Mermacovia now?" he asks.

"Not yet. I need to travel to the Everchanging Glades and line up a new ambassador."

Alexei nods. "Want to go now?"

"Yes. I want to get that out of the way so I don't have to worry about it."

He simply grabs my hand, telling me with his actions that he's with me, no matter what.

We fade before reappearing in the capitol building of Mutable Meadows. This might not be a huge priority compared to the other tasks we have to accomplish, but with all the traveling I'm going to be doing, I want to make sure that I have representatives from each territory. They'll be making some important decisions in my absence, and that means I need to give each species a voice.

There's also a small part of me that really feels the need to see Joseph. With my father gone, he's the closest person who fits that role. Not that anyone can fill my dad's shoes, but Joseph always felt similar to Stavros, and made me feel comfortable. With all the uncertainty of my current situation, I crave that comfort and reassurance. I saw him when I came to address the mimics, but I didn't get to spend much time with him, and the grief was still too fresh in my mind. I feel like this time I'll be able to enjoy his company more.

We walk up to his door, and I can already feel myself settling at the familiarity of it. This is how Alexei and I spent our days here for a long time. The longest out of any other territory we visited.

Joseph opens the door a moment later, and the warmth of his ever constant fire along with the scent of tea drifts out to meet us, loosening my shoulders even more. His eyes widen, but a genuine smile graces his face.

"My queen, what a pleasant surprise." He bows to me.

I tsk at him. "None of that, Joseph." I walk up and wrap my arms around his torso.

He chuckles, but returns my embrace, squeezing me tightly. "It's good to see you, Ember. You too, Alexei."

We break apart, and the men clasp each other's forearms.

"Come in, please. I just had some tea brought up."

Of course he did. Tea is probably his favorite thing in the realm. He never goes without.

I sit in my usual chair as he pours three cups. The scent of spearmint and honey permeates the air, and I breathe it in deeply before taking a sip. I sigh. I missed this.

"What can I do for you, Ember?"

"Well, I need to find another mimic ambassador."

His brows rise. "What happened to Xanto? He hasn't been there long at all."

"He and my mermaid ambassador entered a serious relationship with my newly appointed Grand Master of Mermacovia. So, naturally they moved to Mermacovia with him."

His lips pop open in shock. "Well, good for him."

"Yes. I'm happy for them. But that being said, I'm short two ambassadors. Proteus is going to find a suitable candidate for me, and I'll be heading there in a few days to see who he recommends, but I was thinking about asking Frida if she'd like to take the mimic position. What do you think? You know her better than I do." I'm not dense enough to think that Joseph knows every single mimic in his territory, but last time I was here he mentioned that they knew each other.

"I think that would be a smart move actually. Frida is soft spoken, but she will give her opinion. She's the type of person that likes to listen to what everyone has to say before voicing her own thoughts."

That sounds like exactly what I need.

"Perfect. I thought she would be a good fit too, but I wanted to check with you first. I value your input more than most," I tell him honestly.

He smiles softly at me. "Thank you, Ember. It is a smart leader indeed that takes advice from others when they need it."

I feel a blush rising to my cheeks, but I push past the awkwardness I feel at the compliment. "I know that I'm not from here and that others will understand how to do things better than I will in some instances."

He says nothing but I can feel pride wafting from him and it inflates my broken heart just a bit.

"Is that all you needed from me?" Joseph asks. "I'm reluctant to see you leave so soon."

"We can't stay too long, but we will need to rest before traveling back. I can go speak with Frida and then join you for a meal before we leave."

"I would enjoy that very much. I will let the staff know to have a special meal prepared."

"Why don't you stay here and catch up with Joseph. I have a feeling Frida will be flying and you won't be able to join me," I tell Alexei.

He looks disappointed, but nods all the same. I smile fondly. If that man had his way, he would be at my side every moment of every day.

I leave the men to it and shift, flying through one of the open windows. I see a flash of a proud smile from Joseph. I wasn't always able to shift so naturally. I struggled a lot finding my owl for the first time, and he was instrumental in helping to bring her out. Of course that way was by pushing me off the roof, but it still worked.

I give them a soft hoot before taking off in search of Frida. I met her when I was here for my training, but not until I was able to shift. We met each other in the sky and became fast friends. Her soft gray dove form matches her sweet personality perfectly, and I hoot and call out to her as I fly. She's hard to spot from a distance because she blends in so well, but she usually prefers to fly with others, so I look for flocks.

I finally find her in the third flock I come across. She lets out an excited coo when she sees me and flies toward me. We brush up against each other briefly before she breaks away from the flock and dives down to land, immediately shifting into her mortal form.

I follow her, and as soon as I've shifted, her arms are around me.

"Ember! I've missed you so much. It's wonderful to see you."

"I've missed you too, Frida. How have you been?"

We catch up for a while. I don't want her to feel like I'm not interested in how she is. She calls me on it soon though.

"So, why are you really here, Ember?"

I huff out a laugh. "You're too perceptive for your own good, you know that?"

"Well, there is something, isn't there?"

"Yes. I was hoping you'd want to be my new mimic ambassador." Might as well just come right out with it.

Her eyes fly wide in surprise. "You can't be serious."

"Why wouldn't I be?"

"Because I have no idea what to do. I'm underqualified. There has to be someone who's a better fit for that position than me."

"Now you know how I feel," I chuckle. "Frida, I have no idea what I'm doing either. What I need are people who can give me an honest opinion on what's not only best for the realm but for their species as well. I'm relatively new here, and I know I'm bringing some rather radical ideas forward and there is going to be pushback. I need someone I trust to tell me that, or when something is too soon or extreme. I've already talked to Joseph about it, and he agrees that you'll be a good fit for the position. So, what do you think?"

Her mouth is hanging open, but there's a considering look in her eyes. "Why would you want me?"

"More than anything, I want someone I can trust. I would much rather have you there with me than some random stranger. And I think you will be good at taking everything into consideration before giving your opinion on the matter." The more I think about it, the more I realize this would be a good fit. She doesn't have anyone she's seeing to my knowledge, and while she does have family in the area, she had talked to me previously about wanting to see more of the realm. With the segregation in place, that's never really been an option for her. And even though I plan on changing that very soon, this will give her the opportunity before anyone else.

She stares into my eyes, searching for the truth there. She takes a deep breath before letting out a nervous chuckle. "Okay."

"Okay, you'll do it?" I can't help the excitement in my voice. A large part of me is relieved that I'll have another female friend at the palace. I know no one will replace Pearl, but I really enjoy Frida's company, and I think given time we will become close.

She nods and gives me a smile. I beam back at her before wrapping her in my arms.

"I'm so happy, Frida. I think you'll really enjoy it there. And the two of us can go on regular flights together." It occurs to me then that instead of having my nightly swims with Pearl, I'll have nightly flights with Frida. Or perhaps we will fly in the morning. My heart breaks a little when I think about not being able to swim with Pearl, but knowing I can start a new tradition with Frida makes it more bearable.

"I would love that. When do you need me to start?"

"Honestly? As soon as you can."

She huffs out a disbelieving laugh.

"I know it's short notice and you probably have a few loose ends to tie up here, and that's totally fine. This was just sprung on me as well, so I'm overwhelmed trying to get everything in order, but I don't want you to feel rushed."

She squeezes my arm. "Ember, it's okay. It's just a lot to take in in such a short amount of time. I'll start getting my things together and can probably leave in the next few days and be at the castle in a week."

I reciprocate the gesture, trying to pour all my gratitude into that one touch. "I appreciate you so much, Frida. And I'm really excited that we'll be able to spend more time together."

"Me too. I don't have many friends. Especially women."

Sounds familiar. No wonder we get along.

"Well, I have a spell to teach you so you're able to take everything you need and don't have to worry about lugging heavy trunks with you. This way you can just shrink your trunk and put it in your pocket before shifting and flying."

Her eyes light with excitement, and I make a mental note to teach her more spells. I have a feeling she's like me and will want to learn every single spell she can. I demonstrate it on one of my daggers. It's a little difficult because the dagger becomes so small I can barely see it in my palm, but it does the trick. I have her practice it next, and when

I'm sure she has it down, I tell her I have to get back to have dinner with Joseph. She nods and gives me a hug, telling me she'll see me soon.

Alexei and I have a nice meal with Joseph. We catch up and chat, and the men both make sure to tease me. It's one of their favorite pastimes when they're together. It feels so blessedly *normal.* I miss our days spent here. I feel more at home here than any other territory, with the exception of Mystic Mountain. Before we leave, Joseph brings something up to me that I never thought of before.

"Ember, I had an idea."

"Well, don't keep me in suspense. What is it?"

"With the upcoming war, I think I've come up with the perfect battlefield."

My eyebrows rise in surprise. I wasn't expecting those words to come out of his mouth.

"We don't technically have one fixed portal here because our land changes so much. Occasionally a portal will come into existence when the land gets high enough or low enough to one of the other realms. There have also been instances where the land knows when something is specifically needed, and will therefore change to accommodate those needs."

I nod at him to continue. I think I'm following so far.

"Well, there is an area here that we call the Stone Fields. There is an abundance of natural stones and beautiful gems there that radiate incredible power, and that never change. We could carve runes on the stones, and with the amount that are there, we should have a freestanding portal as long as the land cooperates with us. The land should provide us what we need on the battlefield, and it will give us the advantage of having the high ground."

"That's perfect, actually. Thanks, Joseph."

We continue chatting about unimportant things after that, just basking in the comfortable familiarity. But the night ends all too soon.

"Would you two like to stay the night? Your old room is set up."

I sigh in disappointment. "I wish we could, but we really have to get back."

He nods in understanding. "Very well. Let me know if there's anything you need from me. In the meantime, I will get the mimics ready to fight and prepare the land for our battle."

I smile, thankful to have him at my back. We embrace, and I let myself sink into it for just a moment. Then, Alexei and I grasp hands and travel back home.

# 18

# Ember

We teletravel directly back to our rooms and collapse into bed. Traveling that distance twice in one day has me acutely aware of my exhaustion, and I know Alexei feels the same way. I drift off, though, feeling accomplished and relieved that I was able to at least take care of one of my ambassadors today.

We sleep for a full twelve hours. It's longer than either of us ever normally rest, and I know it's not just from traveling. Our bodies are run down from all the stress and busyness. Not to mention almost dying at the hands of a demon bitch. Oh, and preparing to start a war with said bitch. I hear my mom's voice in my head saying "If you haven't got your health, you haven't got anything" in a fake British accent and laugh.

"When do you want to leave for Mermacovia?" Alexei asks.

As much as I want to reply that we should leave immediately, I know that's not a good idea. We can wait another day or two. "Let's wait for Frida to get here. She should be here soon."

He nods and I can feel his relief. He would be willing to leave now if I wanted to, but taking a few days to rest is what he clearly thinks is the smarter option.

We stay in bed for the morning and eat copious amounts of food, refilling our magic before finally dragging ourselves up and out of the room. Even though I wish I could wear yoga pants and a sweatshirt today, I force myself to dress the part of the queen, albeit a tired queen.

Alexei meets with the guards and the army, making sure they're still on track for the upcoming battle while I meet with the council.

I fill them in on finding a new mimic ambassador and inform them she will be arriving within the next few days, and that after she arrives I'll be traveling to Mermacovia again. I've debated telling them about the trident, but have decided against it for now. The fewer people who know about it, the better. Instead, I inform the council that I'll be gone for a while longer this time, not knowing how long it will take me to find the trident and activate it. There's a good chance I'll have to return between those events.

They catch me up on everything I missed in my absence. It's not much. They continue questioning the mermaid prisoners daily in case they think of anything new to tell them, but so far nothing has come of it. The troops are being readied along with the other territories. I'm about to adjourn for the day when the witch ambassador speaks up.

"Your Majesty, I have an idea." I motion for her to continue. "What if we sent spies to Domonia?"

Silence greets her. None of us have thought or talked about this, and we're all clearly equally shocked.

She blushes but keeps her head high. "Hear me out. What if we sent mimics in their animal forms? They wouldn't need to interact with anyone. They would simply need to see how many are in her forces so we have a better idea of what we're dealing with. If we send birds or small animals they shouldn't be noticed at all."

It's...brilliant. I'm kind of upset that I didn't think of it myself. "I like that idea a lot. The only thing is I'm worried about them being discovered and killed. We have no way of knowing if Demonica has something in place to alert her to people traveling through the portal."

Her eyes soften at that, as if the welfare of the citizens has never been made a priority. "I understand that, Your Majesty. However, we will only recruit those who are willing and understand the risks. We can also make it worth their while for assisting the crown in such a major way. The lives of a few could potentially save thousands of others."

My heart sinks into my stomach. I agree with what she's saying, but I hate the idea of putting any of my people in danger like this. I need to remind myself that this action now could save lives in the coming war.

I finally nod. "Very well. I'll send a letter to Joseph to see if there are any that would be willing to go. If no one has anything else to add, you're all dismissed."

We all head our separate ways, and a strange mixture of dread and certainty coils in my belly. I'm relieved that we're expanding our plan, but the thought of sending my people on such a dangerous mission swirls through me with a nasty mix of guilt and anxiety. Even if it is for the betterment of this war and our realm.

I go straight back to my room, intent on writing my letter to Joseph. I wonder what he will think. I have some tea sent up while I debate on what to say.

*Joseph,*

My quill stalls there. How can I ask him this? It's not fair. Not to anyone. My hatred for Demonica burns brighter in my veins. I've lost so much because of her. I can only hope this doesn't cost me my friendship with Joseph.

I take a drink of the soothing tea and pretend I'm with him in his study. I picture his kind face and warm smile. It gives me the courage I need to write this letter.

*My council has come forth with an idea that has merit. As of right now, we have no idea how many people Demonica has in her army or the state of her troops. It's been brought to my attention that it would be beneficial to send spies there to investigate. Ideally, mimics would make the best candidates because they can travel there in their animal forms or potentially shift into someone in her forces to get more information.*

*Even though it's a wonderful idea, it obviously poses a great risk. I'm reluctant to send anyone seeing as we have no clue if Demonica is able to detect when someone travels through the portal, or if she's able to sense someone not from her realm, but I thought I would bring the idea to you. We would compensate anyone appropriately who is willing to take on this dangerous and important task seeing as it's so risky.*

*I do also value your input immensely, and would love your viewpoint on this plan. Let me know.*

*All my best,*

*Ember*

My breath stutters out of me, and my heart beats quickly as I think of Joseph reading it, but I seal it and stand. I call for one of the vampire messengers, and when he arrives, I hand it to him with strict instructions to give it to Joseph and to wait for his reply. He nods and disappears in the next moment. It used to be that the Immortal City, and all of Mystic Mountain for that matter, was warded against anyone teletraveling in. The ward is still there, but when I became queen, I brought in a few vampires for this very purpose and gave them access to travel in and out, essentially bypassing the ward. At this moment, I thank past Ember for her wonderful foresight. It definitely makes my life easier.

I pace, awaiting my friend's reply. I don't know why I'm so nervous. My letter was well written, not to mention I'm the queen. I can order anything I want, and I didn't even do that. I asked his opinion. Maybe that's why. If he says he doesn't agree or is upset with the idea, I don't know what I'll do. The smart choice is to send the spies. But if I were to go against his advice and send his people into enemy territory, what would it do to our friendship? He means a great deal to me, especially now that my father is gone, and I would never want to jeopardize our relationship.

When I've basically worn a path in the rug in front of my fire, I get a knock on my door. I open it to find the messenger has returned. I take the letter with shaking hands and dismiss him, thanking him for making the trip.

I take a deep breath before opening it, finally sitting down to read.

*Ember,*

*I know you well enough to read between the lines of this letter. Keep in mind that even though we have a close relationship and you value my opinion, you are queen first and foremost. Your duty is to the realm, not to me.*

*That being said, I'm honored that you still ask for my advice, and will freely give it whenever asked.*

*The idea your council proposed is an exceptional one, and I'm only sorry that I did not think of it. I have a group that I think would be perfect for the task, and I will approach them and get those who agree ready to leave within the next week. I shall notify you as soon as we have a date set. I'm sure they will be honored to serve their queen and their realm just as I am.*

*Regards,*

*Joseph*

I let out a breath, and I'm grateful I'm sitting. Even after everything that's happened, I still struggle with confrontations with people I care about, maybe even more so now. I've lost so many people that I want to hang on to everyone I have left with both hands.

I reread his letter again, taking note of the more important details now that I know he's on board with my plan. He said he'll be sending his team in a week or so. The information gives me a thought, or rather an idea.

We still need to travel to Domonia to get the trident. I wonder if it would be easier for all of us to avoid detection if we traveled through the portal at the same time. They would be entering in a different location than we would, and if there is any sort of alarm upon entering, hopefully she'll think it's a fluke if two different locations go off at the same time. That also gives us enough time to make all our arrangements and get back to Mermacovia.

Frida arrives the next day, and I get her settled in her new room. I thought about putting her in Pearl's old room, but it didn't feel right. I'm sure she'll come back to visit, and I want her to be able to stay in her old space.

Frida is incredibly impressed by the palace, and I can't say I blame her. I remember what it was like coming here for the first time. She's confused by the showers, never having seen one before, but she looks fascinated when I turn it on for her. I could, of course, have someone else show her everything, but she's my friend, and I want to make sure she's comfortable before I leave. I'd love to go on a flight with her, but she's been flying straight for two days and is exhausted. I leave her to rest, and tell her I'll meet her for dinner.

I send another messenger to Joseph, telling him that Frida arrived safely, and to stay until they get the information on who is going to Domonia and when. I'll need all of that before we can head back to Allure Isle.

Alexei and I have a relaxing dinner with Frida that night. She's hesitant about the food since it's different from what she's used to, but she eats it all the same. I invite her to come take a swim with me after dinner, but she retires to her rooms to unpack and rest. Alexei joins me instead, and we languidly enjoy the cool water, and the short break.

When we return, so has the messenger. Joseph has found ten people who he trusts for the job who are willing to go. The date is set for six days at midnight. Entering during the night will hopefully allow the team to slip in more subtly. And as a plus, it gives us plenty of time to prepare before we enter at the same time.

Alexei and I plan to leave the following day for Mermacovia after having breakfast with Frida and introducing her to the council. I collapse into bed, exhausted. It will be such a relief when this is all over. I miss this castle, and as necessary as it is, I'm tired of traveling all over the realm. We'll have to travel to two other realms soon as well. I sigh. This is not what I thought being a queen would entail.

"What's wrong, my love?" Alexei asks.

"I'm just tired. I look forward to the days when I simply have to rule and don't need to plan for a war and scheme against a demon queen and go hunting for long-lost artifacts."

"You love that last one."

"Yeah, okay, you have me there. I've always loved finding long-lost artifacts." My mate knows my archaeologist brain well. And I haven't been able to engage it nearly often enough as of late.

"I understand though, little doe. It is a lot. But we will face all of it together. You are not alone. Not only do you always have me and Ebony, but many friends and allies who would die for you. Not because you're their queen, but because they trust and respect you. Because you deserve it. You're giving them the freedom to live the lives they want and you're trusting them by listening to their opinions. It's not something any ruler has done before, and they will follow you into war and die for that. Because they believe in *you*."

His words ignite something inside of me. I've felt like a fish out of water since I became queen. It's not something I *ever* thought I would end up doing for obvious reasons until I told Stavros I would be willing to take over after his reign. But even then, I thought I would have a lot longer to learn from him and not just be thrown into it. From what he's telling me, though, I'm doing well. Pride unfurls in my chest, and I give him an almost timid smile. Even after all this time with him, I'm still not used to getting regular compliments, though he's always been generous with them.

He pulls me into his arms and I fall asleep with happiness bubbling in my chest.

The next day we have breakfast with Frida and then I take her to meet with the other ambassadors. I can tell she's nervous, but she holds herself together well, head held high with a polite smile on her face.

I introduce her to everyone, and am happy to see she seems to be getting along with the witch ambassador. I feel more comfortable leaving her now that there's someone looking out for her.

"How are you feeling?" I ask Frida.

"Good." She gives me a reassuring smile. "I feel a little more settled now that I've met everyone and am set up in my room."

"I'm glad, because I have to leave today," I tell her regretfully.

"I know. It's okay. I'm a grown woman. I'll be fine. When I came here, I knew you were going to be busy and I'd be on my own a lot."

I give her a tight squeeze. "I know I've already told you this, but I'm so glad you're here. Thank you for coming."

"When you get back, we'll start flying together in the mornings."

"I look forward to it."

With that, Alexei and I collect our belongings and teletravel to Mermacovia. Again.

# 19

## Pearl

Being the partner of a grand master is overwhelming. Even more so than being an ambassador.  At least being an ambassador for King Stavros. Ember is better about involving her council, which I think is extremely smart. When Stavros was ruling, there was never much for me to do, other than schmooze random people. Besides, when I first started working at the castle, I didn't take my job seriously. The whole reason I was there in the first place was so that I could spy for Coralia.

Ruling a territory is much more involved. Especially a territory on the verge of a civil war. And while Proteus is technically the official ruler, Xanto and I have been helping him as much as we're able. There's been so much to do. We've been searching for someone to take over my position at the castle for Ember, whipping the territory back into shape after Coralia's negligence and lies, along with setting the house up how we like and getting all moved in and settled. Needless to say, I feel like we've hardly had any downtime. I can't say I mind the busyness though. It keeps my mind off the fact that I'm living back in Mermacovia and my sister is not here. She betrayed me and is now living with Coralia and Demonica in Domonia. My twin in the Domain of the Dead. Emotion and anger clog my throat every time I think of it, and I push it out of my mind for the tenth time today.

I'm impatient for Ember and Alexei to return. When they get back we'll make a trip to the black market before traveling to Domonia to find the trident. I have to say, I'm disappointed we're not going to a different black market since I've already been to this one, but I'm still looking forward to it. I've always had a dark streak in me, and the black market calls to me. I was so upset with Ember when she went without me, but I was also terrified because I know how dangerous it can be.

This time we will go in disguise with Ember being the queen, and Proteus being the grand master. Although now that Ember is able to shift her form, she will have no problem with that. Neither will Xanto. That just leaves me, Alexei, and Proteus to worry about that. I know Ember is going to suggest that she and Xanto go by themselves, but I am *not* missing out on going to the black market again. She promised me, after all.

On the plus side, the three of us have had fun christening the house at every available opportunity. We haven't had nearly as much time as we would like, but we still spend every night wrapped up in each other. Tonight will be no exception.

The boys are busy taking care of territory business, and I spend the time primping. We've been so busy lately that I haven't had nearly enough time to take proper care of my body. I get rid of every bit of unwanted hair I can find, bathe with my favorite scented oil mixed in with the water, polish my nails, and finish by using the special hair curler Ember bought me in the mortal realm. She explained to me that it has a battery and doesn't need electricity. It's taken me some practice to get used to using it, but I think I finally have it mastered.

By the time I'm finished, my skin and hair are gleaming, I smell like heaven, and I'm wearing my sexiest bedroom outfit. I drape myself across our huge bed and wait for my lovers to show up.

I'm amazed with how well I timed things when they walk through the door five minutes later. They're laughing and talking to each other, but they stop as soon as they see me.

"About time you two showed up. I almost left to find myself two other lovers," I tease.

"Is that right?" Proteus asks, prowling forward with a gleam in his eyes. "Xanto, do you think we should leave her to do just that?"

Xanto is staring at me with unadulterated hunger across his face, but he joins in. "Maybe. I bet we can find a woman who will worship at our feet."

Fuckers are teaming up on me. Time to up my game. "Fair enough. Go on, then. I can take care of myself." I trail my hands tauntingly over my breasts, plucking my nipples along the way, before dipping my fingers into my panties and letting out a low moan as my nails drag across my clit.

Both men growl, and I inwardly smile as I close my eyes and continue. Before I can do much more, though, Proteus lunges forward and snatches my wrist, bringing my hand up. I don't realize what he's doing until he wraps his lips around my fingers. He groans at my taste, and my eyes widen in surprise.

"Let me taste," Xanto says from behind him.

Proteus dips his own finger into my wetness before holding it out for him, but instead, Xanto grabs him and brings him in for a fierce kiss, his tongue diving into Proteus's mouth.

Fuck. They're so hot together. I touch myself again. Not to tease them, simply because I can't resist.

"I want to watch you two together," I tell them. The three of us have done quite a lot together, sexually speaking. But I'm usually in the middle of them.

They break apart from each other to look at me with heated gazes. Proteus gives me a wicked smile, while Xanto seems to smolder from the inside.

"What do you think, big man? Want me inside that tight ass of yours?" Proteus asks.

Xanto and I both groan at his words, and he nods his agreement.

"Lick our girl while I open you up and get you ready for me."

I'm panting by this point, and I've hardly been touched. Xanto gives me a mischievous look as he crawls up the bed and pulls my panties down my legs. He leans over and runs his nimble tongue up my slit with his ass up in the air. Proteus doesn't touch him yet, simply stands there, palming his generous length through his clothes while he enjoys the view. Xanto still has his clothes on too, and I'm impatient to see them nude.

"Take off your clothes. And his. You're all too dressed," I whine at Proteus.

He gives me a knowing smile, but obliges me, undressing himself first, his proud length jutting out temptingly, before he roughly yanks Xanto's pants down.

I watch Proteus's face as he takes in Xanto, and the blaze in his eyes is hot enough to set me on fire. I grab the oil bottle from beside me and toss it to him. He catches it and makes quick work of slicking his fingers. With one hand he spreads Xanto open even more to him, and I can feel Xanto's moan vibrate against me when Proteus presses a finger inside.

The ecstasy on Xanto's face makes a gush of excitement flow from me, and he laps it up greedily. I can't see exactly what Proteus is doing to him, but I watch the movement of Proteus's arm as he pumps his finger in and out. It's the hottest thing I've ever seen.

Xanto lets out another strangled sound, and I'm guessing Proteus added another finger. Between Xanto's talented tongue, and the sight in front of me, I'm already close to exploding.

"Xanto, I want to know what he's doing to you. Match him," I order.

He brings his fingers up to join his mouth, and he plunges them into my pussy at the same tempo I can see Proteus's arm moving. I let out a keening cry, so close I can almost taste it. Xanto knows it too, and he gently nips on my clit and I explode around his fingers and mouth.

"I think you're both ready enough. Xanto, get inside of her while I get inside of you. I want to fuck you both at the same time," Proteus says.

If I hadn't just come, I think his words alone would've done it.

Xanto crawls up my body, and I can see a string of precum leaking from his tip. My mouth waters at the sight, but before I can act on my urge to taste him, he pushes into me while bringing his mouth to mine. I moan into his mouth, my essence coating his lips. He doesn't move, just simply kisses me and stays seated inside me. I clench around him, impatient for him to move, but I know he's waiting for Proteus.

I feel more weight settle on the bed, and I break the kiss to stare at my other lover. Xanto buries his face in my neck as I watch Proteus reach down and slowly guide himself inside. Xanto begins panting against my skin, and I stroke his back reassuringly.

"Fuck, you're so hot and tight," Proteus bites out, his voice strained and husky.

Once he's fully seated inside him, he gives him a moment to adjust. I keep clenching around Xanto, distracting him with pleasure to ease the pinch of pain.

"Move. Please move," Xanto begs after a minute.

Proteus winks at me over Xanto's shoulder as he pulls back. I can feel Xanto retreating from my own body at the same time, before they both slowly push back in. It really is like Proteus is fucking both of us as he controls the movements and the pace.

He keeps it slow, and it makes me want to scream in frustration. Every languid slide is delicious and torturous, and every graze of Xanto's pelvis against my clit brings me just a little higher.

"Faster. Please, Proteus," I beg and Xanto nods. I know he's just as desperate as I am.

"Hush," Proteus says gently as he leans over to kiss me. After a moment, Xanto's mouth joins in our sloppy kiss and it feels like we're one person instead of three. I clutch at them both, my heart bursting with the love I feel for both of these men. It's all too much.

Proteus pulls back and continues his unhurried rhythm, but this time when I feel myself building, I know it's going to break me apart. I would be terrified if I didn't know these two wonderful men will be there to patch me back together after.

"Proteus, Xanto," I pant. "Please."

"I'm close," Xanto says.

Proteus keeps his eyes locked with me as he plunges forward again, just a little harder this time and swivels his hips. The movement strokes Xanto's cock over that special spot inside me, and that's it, I detonate.

My body trembles, and I close my eyes as I fall apart completely. I can vaguely sense Xanto shuddering and pulsing inside of me. When I open my eyes, Proteus grunts and stills above us, coming inside Xanto.

We all collapse into a sweaty, sated heap. The men turn and collapse next to me so I don't have their combined weight covering me. We drift off that way, clinging to each other, happy and exhausted.

Ember and Alexei show up the following day, and Ember and I spend a full minute embracing each other. I know it hasn't been *that* long, but after us seeing each other every day, any time away seems like an eternity.

"Did you find a replacement?" she asks after they get settled.

I nod. "We have two candidates. We thought we would let you choose between them."

"Perfect. Let's go meet them and then I'd like to talk about going to the black market."

We thought she would want to meet the candidates as soon as she arrived, so we had them stay here. We wait outside as she meets with each of them individually. One of the candidates is someone I chose, and the other is someone Proteus chose. We both think she will pick ours, but I'm her best friend and know her better than my lover. I'm confident.

She meets with Proteus's pick first. His name is Sebastian. He's nice and all, well, for a mermaid, but my pick is the clear choice.

Her name is Calypso. She's gorgeous. And while she isn't *as* interesting as me, she's close. I've known her for a long time, and she's always been a little off in the mermaid community. She's not as vain and power-hungry as most mermaids. I think that's crucial for my old position. And Calypso has been wanting to see the palace for a long time.

She comes out of the meeting with Sebastian looking polite, but I can see the disappointment on her face. I smile, seeing my victory.

I lead her to Calypso's room. "I think you'll like this one better. I picked her myself," I whisper to her.

"There was nothing wrong with Sebastian," she whispers back.

"I know that. Calypso is just a better fit. I know you." I give her a hip bump and a wink.

She chuckles but gives me a relieved smile. I'm so tempted to follow her in, but she needs to do this on her own.

Even though I know she's going to love her, I'm still anxious as I wait for them to emerge. I try not to show it and sit nonchalantly in the chair outside the room.

"What does the winner get?" Proteus asks me while we wait.

"A sexual favor of the other's choice. Obviously."

"Obviously, huh? We already do that for each other anyway."

I tap my chin with my long nail in thought. He's right. "How about we make it more interesting, then? The loser has to watch while the winner has their own fun with Xanto and can't participate?"

His eyes flame at the challenge in my words. The loser really misses out. They will be all worked up and unable to do anything about it. I give him a saucy smile.

"Deal." His voice doesn't portray any of the excitement I know he's feeling, but I can see the evidence of it tenting his signature wrap.

I almost reach out to give it a teasing glide with my fingernail, but the opening door interrupts us.

Ember emerges with the pink-haired Calypso, both of whom are absolutely beaming. I look at Proteus with victory lining my features.

"Looks like you'll be paying up tonight," I remark.

# 20

# Ember

In the next few days, we get ready to go to the black market. I've tried convincing the group to just let Xanto and me go since we can shift forms, but none of them are having it. I bite back my frustration, but understand. Alexei wants to be there to protect me, Pearl wants to be included since she wasn't able to come with us last time, and Proteus refuses to let Xanto and Pearl go without him.

We do a little more research on what we're looking for. Pearl talks to the mermaid she heard about the spell from. They allegedly are able to put a spell on items, but no one knows what the spell is or where she found it. I'm slightly curious if she was able to invent it on her own. I've never come across that spell in the Epitome Athenaeum. Then again, I haven't read every spell in existence, and I don't even know if inventing spells is possible.

Pearl gets the merchant's name from her contact, and we plan to head to the black market the following evening. In the meantime, we come up with disguises for the other members of our group, and Xanto and I nail down our shifts. This is different from shifting into someone else. We aren't copying anyone's form, but rather, we're making up a whole new person. Essentially taking bits of people we've touched and transforming ourselves into an amalgamation of them. We keep in mind that we're in Mermacovia, so we will blend in more if we give ourselves mermaid features.

I am looking forward to coming up with an entirely new look, and I remind myself that I can do this whenever I want to. I can change the color of my hair with nothing but a thought. I wonder how many women on Earth would kill for this power.

I stand in front of the mirror with Pearl next to me. She's very excited to help with anything related to my appearance, and this is no different.

"What color should I do my hair?" I ask.

"Purple. It will go really well with your skin tone. And it's your shifted color."

I concentrate on my hair, first lengthening it so that it flows down to my waist in soft waves, and then altering the color to a purple so deep and vibrant it reminds me of an eggplant or a glass of wine. I add a little glitter to it, too, so that it shines.

"Gods, it's beautiful. You should wear your hair like this more often," Pearl remarks.

"Okay, what next? I feel like I should change some of my facial features."

She nods. "Eye color. Gold, I think. And then I would get rid of your beauty mark, thin your eyebrows a bit, and upturn your nose."

I do as she says, and watch in fascination as I become unrecognizable. I also make my cheekbones more pronounced and turn my lips a shade or two darker. I look to my best friend when I'm finished.

"Well? What do you think?"

She squeals. "Perfect. No one will recognize you."

Xanto and the guys walk in a moment later. Xanto didn't change his look too much. Mainly just changed his hair to a brilliant blue and the color of his eyes turquoise. He also made himself a bit taller and bulkier.

Alexei stares at me with wide eyes. I stride up to him confidently.

"My, my. Aren't you a glorious specimen." I trail my fingers down his chest, letting a claw out to scrape him lightly. "I bet you're even more glorious below the belt." I toy with the waist of his pants.

He chuckles, his eyes lighting at my game. "Sorry, lovely, but I'm taken."

"Pity," I reply. I meet his eyes and know that we're going to have fun with this later when we don't have an audience. I turn my attention to Proteus. "What are you guys going to do for your disguises? I assume you have a plan?"

"Just your normal stuff. We will all wear cloaks with hoods and I'm sure Pearl would be happy to do our makeup. If we keep our hair covered and change our facial features enough with makeup, no one should know it's us."

I nod. "Have any of you been there besides Pearl?"

They all shake their heads, and Pearl beams. I turn to her. "You remember how to get there?"

She rolls her eyes at me. "Of course."

"Anything we need to know?"

"We have to travel through the water to get there."

Fuck. I won't be able to go in my mermaid form. I'm too recognizable. In fact, we all are. "How the hell is that supposed to work, Pearl? Everyone will know who we are."

She shakes her head. "We won't need to shift. Calm your tits."

I huff out a laugh, holding my hands up in surrender. "All right, then. I trust you," I tell her, even as my stomach clenches with nerves.

The next day, we're all in our disguises, and my hands are sweating. I don't know why I'm so nervous. I've done this before. Although, the last time was a bit more depraved than I was anticipating, so that's probably why. I hear Stavros's voice in my head telling me that I'm not being smart about this, but I ignore it. This is important.

We head outside, and I'm shocked when Pearl leads us to an open wagon with horses instead of the ocean. I'm about to ask her, but she gives me the look that says if I question her she will be thoroughly offended that I don't trust her like I said I did, so I keep my mouth shut.

She takes the driver's seat and the rest of us pile into the back. I settle in next to my mate, letting his presence calm me. He'll never let anything bad happen to us. And no one can recognize us. We'll be fine.

It takes longer than I thought it would before Pearl finally stops the horses. We've traveled fairly far into the center of the island, and I look around expectantly but don't see anything of significance. In fact, there's nothing of interest around. I'm unsurprised though. In my experience, the most interesting things can be found in the most unlikely places, especially here in Queridian.

We all unload out of the wagon, and Alexei places a protection spell on it and the horses, like last time. Pearl leads the way, and we walk a few minutes. There's not much around except forest, but she swears she knows where we're going. This time Proteus asked, not me, and I'm grateful that I kept my mouth shut when she gives him a death glare.

She stops in front of a small pool. It looks as if it's filled with black water, and I cringe away from it. We have to go in there? My mermaid balks.

Pearl shifts one of her fingernails into a claw and slices open her palm, letting her blood drip into the water. Immediately, the water clears. I gasp and peer down. The water is clear as glass, and I can see the deep drop.

I glance up at my best friend to see her with a smug smile on her face, the words *I told you so* in her eyes. She doesn't say anything though.

Before any of us jump in, I take her hand in mine and heal the small cut on her hand. She thanks me in return before turning back to the pool and jumping in.

Proteus and Xanto jump in after her, and I take a deep breath before turning to my mate. "Ready?"

"After you, little doe."

I jump in before I can rethink this choice.

I barrel down, down, down, pulled by some unseen force. I keep my eyes open and take in everything around me, but there's not much to see except earth. Dirt and rock surround me on both sides, and I look down and see something getting closer with every passing second.

Before I'm prepared, I fall, no longer in water but plummeting through the air. I'm about to catch myself with my own air magic and give myself away when magic slows my descent, and I float to the ground.

Pearl and her men are waiting for me, all seemingly dry. What the hell kind of magic is this?

I move out of the way as Alexei splashes out of the water from above me. He looks just as disoriented as I felt.

When we've all landed safely, I look around at our surroundings. It reminds me a bit of the underwater community but without the water and with a more malicious feel to it. I look above us to see a roof of dirt and rock.

"Where are we?" I ask. I *know* that we're at the black market, but my mind can't make sense of what this place is.

"We're technically under the island. We're in a special pocket that's neither on land nor in the sea," Pearl tells me. "Now, don't look too dazed. We're supposed to fit in, remember?"

I shake my head to snap myself out of the spell I feel I'm under. It's like Alice tumbling down the rabbit hole.

Pearl once again leads the way, and we follow behind like little ducklings. I palm my daggers at my sides to reassure myself that if need be, I can defend myself and those around me.

We pass by merchants selling all manner of dark objects, just like in the Immortal City. In fact, it feels very similar, and I even recognize a merchant or two that was at the other location. They must move around to sell their wares to a new group.

When we pass the monsters, I feel that same pang of regret and sadness as I did last time. They have a different selection this time, and I look in awe and terror at the creatures before me. They have sirens in tanks, an abyss hound or two, and nymphs of every kind. They come from Mystic Mountain, and there's one for every element.

The fire nymph keeps transforming between her fiery womanly body and her fire bird form, trying to escape her cage. She shoots flame out, attempting to burn through it, but the cage seems designed specifically with that in mind.

The water nymph stays in her womanly body. She seems to glisten with the water sluicing over her. She doesn't attempt to escape, and I can only imagine that she's already done so and found it pointless.

The earth nymph is a man and seems to be half shifted. His arms are great big tree trunks and he's hitting them against everything he can reach. His rage emanates from him in such powerful bursts, I feel like he should be able to escape simply from the force of it.

I can't see the air nymph, but the cage moves and rattles as if a tornado is locked within.

I swallow deeply past the lump in my throat. I hate this. Alexei squeezes my hand, bringing me back to our mission. Getting our object spelled. Right.

Pearl locates the vendor we need, a woman more beautiful than any

I've seen before, and I'm shocked that someone so gorgeous would be here of all places. She's a mermaid, so it makes some sense, but why is she selling things in the black market? Seems unnecessary for a woman like her.

"We need you to spell an object that can help us locate something we need. Well, a few things, actually," I tell her. I was insistent that Pearl let me interact with her. She doesn't need to draw attention to herself and be recognized.

"Of course. I'm the only person who can spell something for you for that purpose," she replies.

I take out the shell that Undine gave me. "Make sure it's strong. I need to be certain it works."

She gives me a smile filled with greed. "It will cost you."

"I have money."

"It won't just cost you money."

"Well, what, then?" Dread fills my stomach. I remember all the horrible ways Alexei you told me you could pay the last time we were in this situation.

"Your beauty."

I suck in a shocked breath. I didn't even know that was possible. "My beauty?"

Her smile turns sinister. "Yes. I hoard beauty. It's the reason I look the way I do."

I know it sounds vain, but I really don't want to pay this price. I don't want to change my appearance.

Pearl seems to sense my reluctance. "Can you take a little bit from all of us?"

She scans us all. I wonder what will happen with me and Xanto. These aren't our real faces. But then again, she's not taking traits themselves, she specifically said beauty.

"Yes. I would be willing to do that. I will only need to take a small amount from each of you then. You should barely notice it. You will also still owe me money."

I check with my companions for their consent, and they all nod in agreement. I hand the money over, and even though I'm not looking forward to having some of my beauty taken from me, I'm curious about how it's going to work. Will it be like last time when I had to give up a memory?

"You first." She gestures to me.

I step forward hesitantly. She lays her palm against my forehead, murmuring under her breath. I can't hear the words, but in the next inhale I feel a sucking sensation coming from her hand. I gasp as something leaves me and travels into her.

I watch her closely and am amazed and slightly disturbed when her skin shimmers and she becomes even more gorgeous. I vaguely wonder what she looked like before she started taking people's beauty. Was she ugly? Do ugly mermaids even *exist*? I don't remember ever seeing one.

She pulls back, and I'm glad that it's over. That wasn't pleasant. I watch as she repeats the process with the rest of my group. I keep a close eye on whoever she's touching. She's taking such a small amount from each of us that it's hardly noticeable even with my eyes on them. As far as I can tell, they just seem to lose a little bit of their luster and shine. They dull just a hint.

When she's finished, she takes the shell from me and speaks so low none of us can hear her. She motions her hands over the object and I see a faint glow settle into it. She hands it back a moment later and I clutch it to my chest, reluctant to part with it after everything we just went through.

"To activate it, you need only rub your thumb over it three times and speak whatever object you are looking for. You will feel a tug and once you find it, the spell will go dormant until you need it again."

I thank her, and we turn back the way we came.

It will be a relief to get out of here. I don't know what it is about the black market, but it always sets me on edge. As we pass by the monsters again, however, I see the merchant whipping one of the abyss hounds. My blood turns to ice as it shrieks in pain. I'm well aware that these monsters are vicious, but they don't deserve to be tortured.

I stop dead in my tracks. I can't stand here and do nothing. This is wrong. I know it is. The whip sounds again and the pained screech is even more pronounced this time. My blood boils, and I can feel my fury building. One of the nymphs starts crying and yelling.

My hair whips around me with the force of the air building inside me that wants to be released on this sadistic motherfucker. Before I realize what I'm doing, I'm marching over to the vendor. He doesn't even notice me until I'm right behind him. He turns in shock but it soon turns to a malicious-looking glee.

"Hello, lovely. How can I help you?"

I eye his whip.

"You want me to use this on you? I can do that. I'll even give you a discount," he continues talking, not even realizing that he's angering the most dangerous person here. Not to mention that I can feel that my mate is two seconds away from tearing this man apart.

I still don't say anything, and his face starts contorting in frustration. Before he can open his mouth again though, I shift back to my normal appearance and his eyes widen in surprise and recognition. Maybe later I'll regret that I've just blown my cover, but I want to make an example of this mother fucker.

I blast him back with air, essentially trapping him against one of the cages. He lets out his allure.

"*Release me!*" he orders.

I laugh maniacally. "I don't think I will. You're cruel and sadistic, and these creatures do not deserve the treatment you've given them."

"But Your Majesty, they're monsters."

I look back to the creatures, the abyss hound still cowering in the corner of its cage, blood dripping from where the whip made contact through the bars.

"The only monster around here is you. You will release them."

He scoffs. "If I do that they will rip everyone to shreds."

I steal the whip from his grasp, setting it ablaze before everyone. I debated whipping him back with it so he could get a taste of his own medicine, but the last thing I want to do is scare the creatures in the cages behind him. I don't want them thinking that I'm just like he is.

"Open the cages," I order.

He shakes his head vehemently. "No. It will mean death to every person here."

"Oh, so now you care about others? Why do I get the feeling that the only person you care for is yourself?" Before he can respond I release my allure, shredding through his mental barriers while I'm at it. "*Give me the keys. Now.*"

He looks horrified as he starts following my command even though it's the last thing he wants to do. I take them from him and begin unlocking every single cage. When the doors spring open and none of the creatures are able to leave, I realize he has a magical lock on them too.

"*Remove the magical wards.*"

He starts openly weeping and shaking his head violently, but has no choice but to obey. The anticipation is excruciating, and I wait with bated breath as he speaks and motions in the direction of the beasts. If I was more in control of myself I might worry about what will happen once they're free, but as it is, all I can focus on is seeing their suffering end.

As one, they rush out of their prisons, converging on the merchant. I watch in morbid glee as they rip him to shreds. I can hear his agonized screams but those finally taper off with a gurgle.

When it's all finished, there's nothing left of him, and I wonder vaguely what he did to these creatures to invoke such a visceral reaction from the entire group. It's clear he tortured them, but there's no way to know the extent of it. I'm not sure I would even want to know.

My worry hits me then. I just released a gaggle of monsters with no plan for the aftermath. All I knew in the moment was that I absolutely could not just sit there and let them suffer. I might pay for that now that their tormentor is dead.

My stomach sinks in dread as I face them. Then something so shocking happens that I would not have believed it would've ever been an outcome. All of the beasts, *all of them*, slowly sink down to their knees in front of me and bow their heads.

I suck in a sharp breath. They're swearing allegiance to me. For saving them.

"Our queen, we will gladly serve you. Thank you for saving us," the water nymph speaks up. Her voice is like the coolest drink on the hottest day. It flows over me in the most refreshing way, and then her words sink in.

Emotion clogs my throat, but I push past it. This is important.

I turn to the rest of the market. I hadn't realized they were all watching so closely, but they follow suit, falling to their knees as well. "Magical creatures and beasts will no longer be sold at *any* of the black markets. If I find out they have been, the merchants will meet the same fate as this man," I yell loudly as I gesture to where the man was standing before he was utterly demolished. I need to be certain the decree will be adopted throughout the kingdom. News like this travels fast.

I turn back to my new allies. "Please stand, my friends." With that, we make our way out of the black market.

When we all arrive back at the capitol building, my new allies included, Alexei pulls me to the side. "What are you planning on doing with them?" he whispers.

"I don't really know. They would be nice to have on the battlefield."

"Yes, but there are some logistics you need to figure out."

"I know. I've been thinking about it on the ride back." I make my way back to the creatures. "I appreciate all of your allegiance. There is a war coming and I would love to have you all fighting beside me. That being said, I will not force any of you to do that. You have been kept in captivity for long enough and had your choices taken from you. I will not take this one from you as well. The only thing I will demand from you as your queen is that you will *not* attack innocents ever again. I did not release you for you to injure those that do not deserve it. Understand?"

"Yes, my queen," the water nymph answers for all of them again, and I wonder if they can all understand each other.

"So, what will it be? Will you fight for me? Or would you like to live peaceful lives?"

As one, they all move forward and bow to me again. It's the strangest thing to see, especially the abyss hounds. They are not docile creatures, and I remember the sensation of their poison well. Watching them surrender and pledge themselves to me is surreal, and a bit terrifying.

"Very well. The battle will take place in the Everchanging Glades. I'm unsure of the timing, but you had best make your way there. Gather as many supporters as you can on your journey."

"Yes, my queen."

"Do you need anything before you go? Food or water?"

She smiles fondly at me. "No, my queen. We will manage. Thank you."

And with that, they're gone, and I'm left stunned by the turn of the night's events.

"Holy. Shit," Pearl remarks behind me.

I turn. "I know. What the hell just happened?"

"You just convinced a band of monsters to fight for you," Xanto states matter-of-factly, but with awe coating his tone.

"Holy shit is right," Proteus chimes in.

"And, we got the shell spelled. We can go find the trident now," Alexei helpfully adds.

"Even though we're all less beautiful now," Pearl adds dejectedly.

I chuckle despite myself. "It was your idea!"

"Only because I saw how much it upset you!"

That softens me. It also brings me back to our mission. I'm grateful, with the events of the evening, I had completely forgotten why we went to the black market in the first place.

I fish the shell out of my pocket, holding it reverently. This thing already paid off. If we hadn't gone to the black market for the spell in the first place, we never would have gotten a little group of monsters to back us.

"When do we leave?" Pearl asks.

"Day after tomorrow. I want to make sure the mimic spies have enough time to get themselves ready so we can leave at the same time. I also need to send a messenger to Joseph so we can coordinate a time."

They all nod.

"In that case, let's all go get some rest," Alexei says. "I'll go to Joseph. You don't have any other vampires here."

I'm reluctant to let him leave, but I don't have any other choice other than to go myself, and I want to spend my time making sure everything is set for our trip to the other realm.

"Be sure to also tell him about the group of monsters that will be coming his way. Speaking of which, do you think there will be consequences for revealing myself? I probably shouldn't have done it, but it didn't seem important at the moment."

"Honestly, the main reason we disguised ourselves was so we wouldn't be attacked by anyone. The last thing we would need is for you to get assassinated. But instead, you accomplished not only freeing the monsters, but you put fear into the citizens you need to keep in line the most. But if something comes of it, we'll deal with it. Together," Alexei says, calming my nerves instantly.

He kisses me before he disappears from in front of me. I sigh heavily and make my way inside. I wonder if a time will come when we aren't on the go all the freakin' time.

My mate doesn't run into any issues traveling to see Joseph. He confirms the time that the spies will be heading through the portal, and my chest loosens just the slightest bit.

I'm anxious about going to Domonia. The problem is, I'm unsure if it's because I'm just nervous, or if my witch sense is trying to tell me something. I take a deep breath in an attempt to calm myself. When that still doesn't work, I pull out my pouch of scrying bones.

I sit alone in a quiet room. I can't do this if there are others around distracting me.

I pour the bones into my palm, the magic slightly tingling against my hand.

"Will we make it to Domonia successfully?"

Face up. Yes.

"Will we get the trident?"

Yes.

I heave out a breath. I'm about to stop, but another question niggles at me.

"Will we encounter danger?"

This time, the bones are mixed. Half of them are up and half of them are down. Fuck. No straight answer, then. Great.

I try a different divination this time. I put my bones away, and make the room as dark as I can. I sit on the floor cross-legged and focus on my breathing. Maybe I can trigger a vision.

I lose all concept of time. And the only snippet of a vision I receive is a brief flash of Opal. Well, that wasn't much help.

I leave the room and search for my best friend. She might as well know that we're more than likely going to run into her twin.

# 21

## Opal

My time in Domonia has been interesting to say the least. I was originally ecstatic to be in the presence of the true queen, but she's turned out to be a real bitch. And she and Coralia treat me like *their* bitch.

I thought after they asked me to go back home and spy on Ember and my twin, and I returned with the location of the trident, things would improve, but no such luck.

Even though we found Surseiha's Needle, nothing happened when Demonica tried using it. In fact, she was so upset that she threw it at me, hitting me before telling me to get it out of her sight.

I think she meant for me to put it back where I found it, or destroy it, or *something*, but instead, I stashed it in my room.

My feelings toward the two women are slowly but surely changing. This is not at all how I pictured Demonica would be. And the way she talks about my realm and people, I can tell she doesn't care about anyone but herself. That concept isn't foreign to me. The mermaids have always been that way, myself included, but the fact that she's willing to throw away every life she needs to just to gain her power rubs me the wrong way. I know Pearl warned me about them both, but

I didn't listen. I'm starting to regret that choice now. And the look on her face when she saw me with them...that look will stay with me until my last breath.

I also *hate* this realm. Domain of the Dead is right. The landscape is dark and bare with hardly any water. The sun is so dim here that I can barely feel it. Water and sun, the two things mermaids need more than anything. My mermaid soul is shriveling up inside of me.

Not to mention the people here. If you can even call them that. All the demons are incredibly cruel, their blackened souls visible in the changing color of their skin. And the slaves here, the ones the demons feed off of, are essentially catatonic.

The days continue on, and I become more miserable than ever, longing for my land and the company of my twin. I'm so tempted to go back home, but after my betrayal, I know I wouldn't be welcome. I'd be killed or captured on the spot.

I wallow in self-pity every day before something occurs to me. Maybe there's some way I could help my sister. I don't know if she would even *want* my help, but I could try. And after she sees that my allegiance lies with her, maybe she would welcome me back home.

With a plan in mind, I renew my efforts to get back into Demonica's good graces. I sit in on every meeting she allows me to, do everything she asks of me without complaint, and allow her to see how thrilled I am to be here. I learn every bit of information I can that might be even the slightest bit helpful to my sister. I have to make this count, because if I don't, I'm dead. Either by Demonica's hand, or my twin's.

# 22

# Pearl

The day to travel to Domonia has come, and I'm so nervous I feel like I'm going to throw up. I hadn't been feeling too anxious about it until Ember mentioned we will most likely be seeing my twin. I was hoping we'd be able to just sneak in, get the trident, and leave. Apparently, it's not going to be as easy as that.

We've had discussions and arguments about who should come and who should stay. Of course Ember wanted to go by herself, and of course all of us told her that wasn't happening. In the end, we decided that we should all stay together. So all of us it is.

We pack light. We don't intend to stay there for long at all, but just in case we pack enough food and water. You never know when you'll get stranded, and we have no idea if there's going to be essentials available. I mean, there must be, considering so many people live there, but better safe than sorry in this situation.

"Okay. Are we ready?" Ember asks us as we gather around.

We all nod and Alexei says, "Let's go get you that trident, little doe."

She smiles, but it looks a little forced. I know how she's feeling.

We will have to swim to the portal, but it's going to take us longer than it normally would since Ember will have to breathe for Alexei.

That means we'll have to stop every thirty seconds or so so that she can feed him air. Which is annoying. Something occurs to me then before we leave.

"Ember, I just had an idea. What if instead of you breathing for Alexei, you just form a bubble of air around his head?"

She blinks at me, looking taken aback. "Well, that's fucking brilliant. Why didn't I think of that?"

"Probably because you want any excuse to press your mouth to mine," Alexei replies teasingly, nudging her with his elbow.

She rolls her eyes but nudges him back. "Let's try it and make sure it works before we actually leave."

They test it out and I preen when my theory ends up being successful. I'm impressed that I was the first one to think of this. This is a smart group of people. I'm also thrilled that we won't have to take forever to get to the portal.

They give us the thumbs-up, and we all take off. As I knew it would be, our journey is much quicker than we originally anticipated. And much easier. Even with all of that, dread fills me the closer we get.

I know some of the unease is from the effects of approaching the portal. In general, portals make people feel funny and unpleasant, especially this one. I'm fairly certain that the vileness from Domonia has seeped through and permeated the surrounding area. And then of course the other part is the anxiety surrounding my sister.

Part of me wants to see her. I think if I had a chance to talk to her that I could convince her to come back and fight for us. The second part of me is so angry at her for what she did and how she betrayed us that I don't think I'll ever be able to forgive her. The final part of me is terrified of running into her and having to do something that I know I will regret. I don't want to fight my sister. Not in any real sense. Knock some sense into her? Yes. Potentially kill her or seriously harm her? No.

We get to the cave and gather in front of the portal. The area hums with energy, and I feel sick to my stomach, but I push past it. We have more important things to worry about right now.

"Let's go over the plan one more time," Ember says. Even though we've already done this multiple times, I know it's helping with her nerves. "Alexei and I will go through first and quickly and quietly dispatch any waiting guards. Pearl, you'll come through next and get the shell targeting the trident. That should at least put us in the direction of the lake. You boys follow," she says, pointing to Xanto and Proteus. They huff at being called "boys" but don't say anything. "And then we head to the lake, grab the trident, and haul ass back here. Clear?"

Everyone nods.

"We're ready, Ember. Let's do this." It's a lie. I'm not ready. But I don't think I'll ever be. Might as well get it over with. Besides, the plan is simple enough. It should be easy, and I'm more than likely just overthinking it.

She nods, takes a deep breath, and she and her mate travel through the portal. I grab the shell out of my pocket and activate it, rubbing my thumb over it three times and speaking that we want to find Surseiha's Needle. That done, I walk forward, my men behind me.

I tip forward, the world darkens and spins around me, but soon I'm on the other side. I catch myself, and as I do I hear a slight scuffle. Not loud, but enough to let me know that Ember and Alexei are still taking care of the guards. When I get my bearings, I look around to see that Alexei has dispatched the last one. There were five of them in total. Easy for the two of them. They can take out ten with no problem.

I move forward so Xanto and Proteus have room. They enter behind me a second later, and Ember looks back at all of us.

I take a moment to observe my surroundings. My soul feels as though it's rebelling against being here. It's dark, ominous, and altogether just feels *wrong.* I shake off the distress so we can do what needs to be done.

"Where to, Pearl?"

The shell in my hand pulls me in the direction of the trident. I lead the way, letting the others trail behind me. We continue on in silence, not wanting to alert anyone to our presence.

We walk for ten minutes or so before coming upon a body of water. I guess some might call it a lake, but by my standards it's basically a pond. We stop next to it.

"Is this the lake that the trident is supposed to be hidden in?" Ember asks me.

"I would assume so, but the shell is pulling me forward still."

Her brow furrows. "I'm going to go check." She starts stripping off her clothes.

We offer to come with her, but she waves us off and dives in. A moment later, I see a small light beneath the water, and I gasp in amazement. It's coming from Ember.

We wait impatiently for her. I have a difficult time resisting the pull of the shell in my hands, and bounce on the balls of my feet to rid myself of the restlessness. Ember emerges what feels like hours later empty-handed.

"It's not down there. It's already been found. I found the golden rock that was mentioned and the pocket where it was hidden, but it's empty."

"*Fuck,*" Alexei curses behind me.

"Well, it's definitely still in this realm. I can feel it," I say, gesturing to my hands.

"Let's keep following it for now. We might need to reevaluate depending on where it leads us. We want to avoid a confrontation."

We continue on, Ember at my side, and I ask the question I've had since I saw her go under. "How did you have light underwater?"

She smiles smugly at me. "It was fire."

"*Underwater?*"

She nods. "I got the idea from you actually. Had I not made that pocket of air around Alexei's head when we swam here, I would never have thought of it. I just formed a bubble and conjured a flame inside of it."

"Wow," I breathe, amazed.

We continue on, the relentless pull urging me on, and suddenly, I'm stopped, a hand on my arm.

I look over to see Ember with a concerned look on her face.

"What is it?"

"We're at the castle."

I look up in surprise. It's like the shell had me under a spell where I didn't even notice any of my surroundings.

The palace is dark and ominous. And honestly, a bit crude, as if it were slapped together quickly and no one ever bothered to do anything more with it. The absolute *vileness* that clings to the building is evident even from here.

We can see more people now, this area being more inhabited. Thankfully, we still haven't been spotted, but there's no way to know how long that will keep up. We crouch behind some dead-looking trees and foliage. Now we wait.

"Do you think we should try to sneak in?" Proteus asks.

Alexei shakes his head. "No, that will be much too dangerous."

"What if me and you go in, Ember? We can shift and no one will know."

"Or I could turn us all invisible," Ember suggests.

I don't even hear the response, because my sister, my *twin*, is walking out of the castle. I suck in a sharp breath, drawing everyone's attention. The sting of betrayal is sharp, but the hope that surges through me is just as strong. As if she can hear me or sense me, she turns toward us.

Even though we're tucked away, her eyes find mine. So many things pass between us in the span of just a few heartbeats.

Our group tenses as she starts in our direction, looking around. I gesture to them to stay still and calm. I know she won't hurt us. It's a twin thing. She may have betrayed us, but I can feel that she doesn't have any intention of harming me.

The time it takes for her to walk over to us feels like an hour, and I resist the urge to run and meet her in the middle. As if Ember can hear my thoughts, she rests a hand on my arm in silent support.

Opal rounds the copse of trees where we're hunkered down and stops. We stare at each other for a full thirty seconds in silence.

"What are you doing here?" she finally asks.

"Me? What are *you* doing here?" I whisper-yell at her. The fucking *nerve.*

"Look, Pearl, I'm sorry. I know I shouldn't be here. I made a mistake."

I can hear the regret and sincerity in her tone. My sister is never sincere. She doesn't have deep feelings. At least none she's ever shared with me. As much as I love her, she's always been shallow.

"She's telling the truth," Ember whispers in my ear, so low I know no one else can hear. "I can feel her regret."

I deflate a little at the words. "Well, what do you want, Opal? What do you expect to happen now? You betrayed us. We can't allow you to come home."

"I've been gathering intel for you. And I also have something I know you want."

"Oh? And what's that?" My voice is pure ice, and she flinches. I've never spoken to her like this before. She might feel remorse for what she's done, but that doesn't mean I can forgive her.

"The trident."

Ember sucks in a sharp breath.

"That's why you're here, isn't it?" she asks. We don't reply. "Demonica found it in the lake. There's something wrong with it though. She couldn't get it to work for her."

"How did she know where it was?"

She blushes and averts her gaze. I grind my teeth together, wanting to yell and scream and rip her hair out. But I can do none of those things. Not with where we are.

"I came through and spied on you. I overheard you mention where to find it."

"Why are you willing to work against her now?" Ember finally joins in the conversation.

"She's evil. They both are. And this place is awful."

I roll my eyes and scoff. "And you thought she was just so wonderful before you came here?"

"Hey," she whispers sharply. "There was a time when you felt the same way I did. There was a time when you also wanted to see her on the throne."

"That was before!"

"Before what?"

"Before I met the king and Ember. Before I saw Ember in her mermaid form and realized she's Surseiha's descendant too. Before Demonica impersonated me and killed the king. Did you really think that someone that was worth following would do something like that?"

She doesn't respond, but looks down sheepishly. I sigh. This is all so complicated.

"You said you have the trident?" Alexei asks from behind me.

She raises her head and nods.

"And you have intel?" Xanto adds.

She nods again. "I can get it for you and meet you in a better location."

"How do we know you won't betray us again?" I try to keep the hurt out of my voice, but fail.

"Have Ember persuade me if it makes you feel better. But I already told you that I've been gathering information to give you for the past week or two."

"Okay," Ember takes over. "Where should we meet you?"

"By the portal. It'll be safer for all of you to be as close to home as possible."

"Won't Demonica miss the trident?"

She shakes her head. "When it didn't work for her, she threw it at me and told me to get rid of it."

"In that case, *go get the trident and bring it straight back to us. Don't tell anyone we're here or where you're going.*" Ember's voice is full of allure, and Opal doesn't even attempt to resist her.

When she leaves, we all head back to the portal. I pace back and forth in front of it, waiting for my sister to return.

"What are we going to do when she comes back? If she is indeed giving us intel and the trident, should we bring her back with us?" Proteus asks the question we've all been thinking.

Ember looks to me. I don't have an answer. She reads the indecision on my face. Before any of us can answer him, however, my sister shows up, the trident in her hands. It's nothing special, and I'm a little disappointed. I was expecting it to shimmer and shine. To have an ethereal glow to it. Instead, the metal is dull. I know it was just plucked out of a lake where it's resided for thousands of years, but it's magical. It should be immune to that kind of thing, right?

She hands it off to Ember, and I swear it sparks to life just the slightest bit. I doubt I would've noticed if I hadn't been looking so closely.

"Thank you, Opal," Ember tells her sincerely.

She smiles at her. It's sad.

"Do you have information for us?" Alexei asks.

She nods. "Not much because they tend to talk about the important things when I'm not around, but I *do* know that they're planning on attacking from a different portal. Now that the kingdom is starting to come together, the wards are beginning to fail. She can already feel it. So as soon as they do, she's going to strike hard and fast and where you least expect it."

"Do you know the location?"

She nods. "The Everchanging Glades."

Ember sucks in a sharp breath. "Does she have her army in place already?"

"No. The wards aren't failing enough yet, but she is mobilizing her forces at the portal locations. They should be in place in about a week."

"Thank you, Opal. Is there anything else you can give us?"

She shakes her head. "No, but I'll stay here and keep an ear out. I'll let you know what I can when I can."

I tear up at her words. I know she betrayed us and me, but the fact that she's here now and willing to help and stay in this miserable place for us means a lot. She notices my reaction and pulls me to her in a fierce hug.

"I'm so sorry, Pearl. I never should've done it. It's too late now to change it, but I'll do everything I can to make it right."

I pull back. "Be safe" is all I can say to her at the moment. She gives me a sad smile before turning to leave. As we're heading for the portal, I hear a scream.

I turn to see Demonica with her claws deep in my sister's abdomen, Coralia behind her with a slew of guards. No. No. *No.*

"You bitch! How dare you betray me!" Demonica roars, her voice pure demon.

My sister faces me. "Go. *Go!*" She shifts her nails into deadly claws before ripping at Demonica's face, making her let out a blood-curdling shriek. Everyone is filing through the portal, using the precious seconds my sister is giving us to escape, but I can't move. "Go, Pearl! *Now!*"

Ember yanks me back through and I feel the falling sensation just as I see Demonica rip out my twin's throat with her teeth.

My scream echoes through the cave as we land. I fight against the hands that are pulling me into the water and away from my other half, but it's no use. They're too strong. My body shifts without conscious thought, but I'm still being dragged. The fight drains out of me the farther we travel until I'm dead weight, simply letting them pull me along.

I can feel the sting of tears in my eyes, but they're washed away by the ocean, along with the shredded bits of my heart.

# 23

# Ember

I can feel Pearl's anguish hitting me from all sides. She's projecting it outward like she's yelling with her feelings. I wince at the barrage that hits me but block her out as best I can for now. We need to get back now that we have the trident.

As horrible as what happened with Opal was, I'm incredibly grateful to her. If not for her, we wouldn't have gotten the trident, and we wouldn't have known what Demonica's plans are. My thoughts begin swirling with the new information as I try to form a plan. A week isn't much time for us to travel to Earth and find the obelisks to activate the trident. That's another thing. We got lucky that Opal didn't hear about that when she was spying on us. Otherwise I'm sure Demonica would already be defeating us.

Pearl is practically catatonic next to me now, and I drag her along, her men hovering behind her worriedly. I wish I could give her a second to be inactive, but I don't trust Demonica to not come through the portal and attack us and steal the trident back.

"Just a little farther and then you can take a break, okay?" I tell her. She nods mutely beside me.

We hurry back to the house as fast as we can, my heart pounding a relentless rhythm in my chest. We got the trident. Opal died. We know where they're planning on attacking from.

We finally get back, and I nearly collapse in relief. We made it. I put a spell on the trident so no one can tell what it is. I trust only those in my immediate company. Especially here in Mermacovia.

We head straight for the council chamber, and I put a spell on the room so no one can enter or hear us. A cone of silence, if you will.

The brief levity I've found vanishes as soon as I see the devastation on Pearl's face. Her men already have her in their arms, sandwiching her between them as she finally breaks down in sobs.

My barriers are still keeping her out, but I can feel her grief pounding on my walls, trying to force its way in. I cling to my own mate at the realization things could have gone much worse. My own sadness about Opal is weighing on me too. Even though I didn't know her well, we had some fun together, and she was my best friend's twin. I hate seeing her in this kind of pain.

I give her as long as she needs to break down, but when her tears start to slow, I ask her, "Pearl, would you like me to take some of it? Just for some temporary relief?"

She meets my eyes, hers red-rimmed and still brimming with silver. She gives me a hesitant nod. "Just so we can talk through what we need to. I won't be able to focus otherwise."

I nod in understanding. "Come here."

When she's in front of me, I hold my hands out and she puts her own in mine. I immediately suck in a pained breath as her emotions finally break through my shields. Instead, I focus on making her feel calm and focused. I also send out relief and joy to dull the edge of her pain. She instantly relaxes.

"Thank you."

"Of course. It will wear off soon, and I don't think we should do it more than once or twice. You need to experience it all in order to have closure, but for now, it should help."

"Okay, so what now?" she asks.

"I need to go to Earth to activate the trident. I also need to go to the other black markets to release the monsters. I should've done that a long time ago, and it needs to be done no matter what, but if we get the same reaction this time, it would be immensely beneficial. The problem is, I don't know if I have time to do all of that before they get here in a week. We also need to prepare the troops and have them start traveling so they will arrive on time." A headache starts behind my eyes.

"I can go to the black markets for you," Alexei says from my side.

My gaze snaps to his. "I'm shocked you're not insisting on coming with me."

"Believe me, it's not easy for me, and I'm only suggesting it because I know this lot won't let you go alone. I'm the only one who can. No one else can teletravel. And you don't need to stretch yourself thin doing more than you can in the time we have. I'll also have the armies sent out."

Relief and dread hit me at the same moment. It will be so helpful to have him take some of the workload, but I really don't want to be separated from him.

"Are you sure?"

"Like I said, as long as you don't go alone."

"I'll go," Pearl volunteers.

I shake my head. "Pearl, you just lost Opal, you need time to grieve."

Despite the relief I was able to give her, I can see the tears beginning anew, but she pushes them back and shakes her head. "No. Opal died for this. She gave her life so we could defeat Demonica. I will grieve when those bitches are dead and we've destroyed that fucking realm. That is what I need right now."

I'm astounded by the vehemence in her tone, but I understand at the same time. This is giving her purpose and a way to avenge her sister. I won't deny her that.

I nod once. "Very well, then."

"We'll come too," Xanto says for him and Proteus.

I shake my head. "No. Get the armies ready and moving. Pearl and I will be fine on Earth. It won't be anything we can't handle."

They look at each other before turning their gazes to Pearl. She nods and it makes me smile that even though I'm their queen, I know they would go against my orders for her. It's everything she deserves.

"For now, let's all eat and get some rest, and we can all go on our adventures tomorrow."

They all nod and head toward their room. Alexei and I head to our own, and on the way we find servants to bring us food. I'm fighting back tears as we go. Pearl's overwhelming grief, Opal dying, the stress of all that needs to be done, and finally the promise of separation from my mate tomorrow is too much for me at the moment. I feel like I'm carrying the weight of the realm on my shoulders. Fuck that. The weight of multiple realms. Because in my heart I know that if Demonica defeats us, as soon as she's finished feeding off of everyone here, she will make her way to Earth. It might not be anytime soon. Hell, it might not be for thousands of years still, but it will happen eventually.

Panic and anxiety make my chest tight and my stomach clench. My breaths start coming faster, my heart beating quicker. I can feel a panic attack building, ready to explode in my body and wash me away with the tide.

"Little doe. Look at me," Alexei's voice cuts through my spiral just enough. I do as he says only to find warmth and comfort in his gaze. "Everything is going to be fine. I know you feel like things are impossible right now, but you are not alone. We will help you. We're going to do this with you. And with all of us, we *can* do it. I promise.

Just take some deep breaths for me and focus on my hand in yours." He squeezes me firmly to emphasize his point.

My heart rate and breathing start to even out the longer I look at him and feel his skin against mine. After a few minutes, I nod, feeling more composed.

"I don't like that we'll be apart," I tell him.

He squeezes my hand again. "I know. I don't either. But it won't be for long."

When we reach our bedroom, he drags me to the bed and strips me naked. His clothes follow closely after, and when we're both naked, he gently lays me down atop the mattress. My breathing accelerates for an entirely new reason now. A pleasant one. I sigh in contentment and pleasure when his body makes contact with mine, his weight pressing down on me so lovingly.

Yes. This is exactly what I need. What *we* need. He brings his mouth to mine and explores every inch of it with his tongue. It's like he's trying to swallow me whole in the best way possible and I melt into him. Our hands roam over every bit of skin we can reach on each other's bodies, and my nerves are humming with the stimulation. I grow more and more ready with every sweep of his palm.

I spread my legs underneath him, welcoming him. In the next moment he's slowly pushing into me, his hard length stretching me so perfectly that I whimper. His eyes are staring right into my soul, and I couldn't hide anything from him even if I wanted to. He moves inside me, slowly at first, building a steady heat, but I can tell this climax is going to rip me apart in the best way. Alexei will be there to put me back together afterward.

I clutch at his back as his pelvis grinds against mine, rubbing delicious friction on my needy clit, and I can see in his eyes that he knows exactly what he's doing to me.

"Alexei, please," I beg.

"What do you need, little doe?"

"You. Always."

With that, he brings his mouth back to mine and pushes even farther inside, feeling deeper than ever before. I can feel the command he's giving me even though our lips are sealed together. *Come.*

I obey, clenching around him as my entire being splinters into a thousand pieces.

I feel him follow me moments after, pulsing and twitching against my womb, and at that moment, even with the stress of everything going on, I'm *content.*

The next day, our group gathers for breakfast and I put up a privacy spell around us. If the situation with Opal taught us anything it's that you never know who's listening. Pearl looks exhausted and devastated, but determined all the same. I think it will be good for her to have something to focus on during the next week. And after that...

"Okay, so let's go over the plan one more time. Pearl and I will grab the trident and the shell and head through the portal. We will activate each obelisk and be back as soon as we can. Alexei, where are you heading first?"

"Mystic Mountain. I'm the only one besides you that can teletravel there directly. Then I'll go to Nightshade Eclipse and send envoys to the rest of the territories to get their armies moving. Then I'll tackle the black markets one by one. When I'm finished I'll meet you in the Everchanging Glades."

"We will get the Mermacovia army ready and leave tomorrow. Is there anything else you need us to do?" Proteus asks.

I shake my head. "Just be safe."

"Take care of each other," Xanto says seriously, staring at me and Pearl. I expected him to give me a lecture about making sure Pearl is safe, but I'm surprised that he's including me in that statement as well. I know I'm his friend and his queen, but Pearl and Proteus are his life.

We all hug each other, and then I leave Pearl with her men while I say goodbye to Alexei.

"Be safe. Don't take any unnecessary risks," Alexei tells me.

"I should be saying this to *you*. We're just going to Earth. Nothing dangerous there. You're going to be the one freeing monsters from the black market."

"That is not the attitude you need to have. There are still dangerous things on Earth, and you have no idea what's going to happen once you activate those obelisks. Keep your eyes open, your witch senses fully engaged, and your guard up. You understand me?"

He's turning into his possessive macho man again, but I don't have it in me to be upset. He's worried and he hates that we're going to be apart for a week. I feel the same way.

"Only if you promise to do the same."

"I don't have witch senses," he teases me with a twinkle in his eye.

I smack him on the arm. "Alexei, I mean it. I know you're a badass warrior and you can take on a whole army by yourself, but keep in mind that if something happens to you, I might just burn this realm down for spite."

Instead of looking scared, he looks positively thrilled by my savageness. And turned on. "I understand." He's serious all the sudden. "I'll be careful."

He kisses me and I melt into it. I don't think about how this could be the last intimate moment we have before the battle that's about to ensue. I don't think about the fact that we're going to be separated for a week. I don't think about the fact that he's going to be putting himself in dangerous situations and I won't be there to have his back. I just kiss him, pouring all of my love and devotion into it.

He gives as good as he gets, and by the end we're both breathless and have tears in our eyes. One spills onto my cheek, and he catches it with his thumb.

"We'll be reunited before you know it, little doe."

I nod, unable to speak. I give him one last lingering peck on the lips before breaking away. If I don't step back now, I'll never leave him.

I look over to see that Pearl is pulling away from her men too. We meet each other in the middle, but I stare at Alexei until he vanishes from sight, taking my heart with him.

"Ready?" Pearl asks, tearing my eyes away from the spot he was in only moments ago.

"Yes." I have my trunk and the trident shrunken and in a waterproof bag.

We give Proteus and Xanto a wave before walking out. A carriage takes us to the location of the portal, which I'm thankful isn't far away. Once it drops us off, we still have to swim for a while, but it's manageable.

The motion sickness hits me as my necklace flares brightly.

*Here we go*, I tell Pearl.

*See you on the other side.*

With that, we swim into the abyss.

When we reemerge, we're still in the water. I wasn't quite sure what was going to happen. I didn't want to sprout out of the ground like a weed as a tentacle mermaid with a classic mermaid at my side. Naked. No thanks.

*What now?* Pearl asks.

I look around. *Well, let's get the shell out and see if we're close to an obelisk.*

I grab it and activate it. Within moments, it's pulling me forward. I look at Pearl and she gives me a nod.

*Let's get the shell out of here*, I say, laughing at my own pun, even though Pearl is scoffing and rolling her eyes at me.

We take off. I have no idea how long we will be swimming for, but I'm prepared for anything.

We pass by a ton of sea life, some of which isn't present in Queridian. Pearl marvels at them and the differences of the oceans. It must be strange for her to not see any of our kind underwater. The only life present are animals. There's no underwater civilization, no natural lights, nothing magical besides the beauty of the ocean.

After swimming for a few hours, we take a break. We're both hungry and tired. Pearl shows me how to hunt for food, and even though it's not my favorite way to eat, I dig into the raw fish that we catch. I know in my human form I would be thoroughly repulsed by it, but my mermaid delights in the act of hunting our own food and then ripping into it. Savage bitch.

We continue on for another few hours, and I sigh. I was hoping that the entrance to the portal would be close to at least one of the obelisks. I'm anxious to get this over with and get back home to my mate and kingdom, and the fact that we have no idea where the obelisks are or how long this is going to take is not sitting well with me.

When it gets dark, and we still haven't reached the obelisk, we stop.

*Come to the surface and stay there. I'm going to shift and fly around and see if we're close to land.*

Without another word, I shoot up out of the water and shift into my owl. I give a soft hoot and then fly higher. My eyes take everything in. I can see boats but no land. Wait. *There.* I think I can see lights. I take off in that direction, keeping in mind where I came from so I can find Pearl again.

It doesn't take me long to see that the lights are indeed coming from an island. Perfect. That's all I need to know. I turn back around the way I came, swooping low so I can see Pearl better. Once I spot her I dive down and shift again.

"There's an island a few miles that way," I tell her, gesturing. We go back underwater and haul ass in that direction. We're both exhausted and ready to rest. I'm also impatient to see where exactly we are so we'll have a better idea where to find the obelisks as opposed to just following the shell. I'm almost positive that the obelisks make up the three points of the Bermuda Triangle.

Within half an hour, we're approaching the island. We find a section of beach that looks deserted and we shift and walk onto land. It feels a little strange after being in the water for so long.

I quickly dry us with my air magic, and we open the bag and get dressed. I take out my phone and turn it on, grateful I brought it with me.

It takes a moment to boot up, and then I'm able to see that we're in the Bahamas. Perfect. I find a hotel close by and we head in that direction.

The balmy ocean night air is comforting, and I breathe in the humidity. I do always love coming back to Earth for a visit. Thoughts of the last time I was on Earth surface, and soon I'm thinking about Stavros.

I don't have time to think about that too much, though, because we reach the hotel moments later.

"Hello, how can I help you today?"

"We need a room, please. Your nicest one available." We may as well stay in style. I have more money than I'll ever be able to spend here.

He checks us in and we're taken up. Pearl is blown away by the room, and I smile to myself as we get settled. We order room service and while we wait, I bring up a map. The three points of the Bermuda Triangle are Miami, Bermuda obviously, and San Juan in Puerto Rico.

"Right now we're closest to Miami. I think with another day of hard swimming we should be able to get there by tomorrow night."

She nods and I turn on the TV, wanting to enjoy some Earth comforts while we're here. I'm thrilled when I see *Lord of the Rings* is on. Gods, I missed this series so much. The food shows up not long after, and we dig into our food and drinks. I would normally get wine, but being back on Earth, in the Bahamas no less, I get a strawberry daiquiri instead. I told Pearl to get a piña colada, and she's delighting in it. But even with all that, she's not her normal self.

"How are you doing?" I ask.

She looks down at her plate, not meeting my stare. "I'm fine."

"Hey," I say. She finally looks at me. "It's okay not to be okay right now. You've been there for me through all my shit. I've got you, babe."

Her eyes tear up, and I wrap my arms around her, letting her break down in my hold. I gently rock us back and forth, and she clings to me like her life depends on it. I can feel her salty tears soaking through my shirt, but I don't care. My best friend needs me, and I owe it to her to be here. She's carried me through so much, and I want to be right here to repay the favor.

Eventually, her tears slow. When she pulls back, she looks exhausted. I guide her to lie back and gently tuck her in. She's asleep within minutes. I, however, am content to stay up and watch my movie and take a much-needed break from how hectic my life has become. Although, as I watch, I realize the "fantasy" aspect of storytelling has lost some of its allure. I now live in a fantasy world, and the once simple life I lived is long gone.

The next morning, we wake bright and early, getting the biggest breakfast we can. We will need our strength to make the rest of the trip to Florida. When we're done stuffing our faces, we pack up the little that we brought with us and head out. We swim all day in the direction of Miami, and I'm pleased to see that's still where the shell is leading us, proving my theory.

It takes us all day to get there. We once again break around lunchtime, hunting our own meal. I've never swam this long before in my life, and while my mermaid is loving it, I'm exhausted. I also wish I could take a day just to lie on the beach and enjoy the Florida sunshine, but I know we don't have the time for that. I sigh in regret. Oh well. Another time when the world isn't going to shit around us.

When we get closer to land, I pay closer attention to the shell in my hands. The pull is stronger now, as if it's trying to tell me we're almost there. I don't know if they're on land or in the ocean, although since most accidents in the Bermuda Triangle happen in the water, I would guess that they are in the sea. I could easily see boats running into them if they're invisible.

Miami is finally in sight as the sun starts to set. The pull is so strong now that it's the only thing I notice. I don't care that I'm starving or that I've been swimming all day and my tentacles are aching with fatigue. I push forward, Pearl right behind me. It guides us to just east of the shore. I would guess it's about two miles out, and even though we've been swimming above the surface so we can see the land, the shell takes us back under.

We dive, and when we finally reach it, the shell pulses and vibrates in my hands. I touch it to the pillar and the whole thing glows. I feel around and eventually locate an indentation, similar to the one in the old underwater palace. I insert the shell, and the entire obelisk becomes visible. I gasp in amazement.

Just underneath the shell is a Queridian rune. *Power.*

Before I can do anything, like take out the trident, my hands are sucked onto the pillar.

*What the hell is this shit?* I ask, not really having the patience to deal with anything else.

The waves start rolling around us and I can see lightning flash in the sky overhead through the water and my heart rate picks up. Is this because of us?

*I wonder if you have to do something in order to be able to activate the trident.*

*Like what?* I ask, having no clue how to get my hands off this thing. My panic tries to reel me in, but I take deep breaths and don't let it.

*Maybe it's doing some sort of test to see if you're Surseiha's heir?* she guesses, but if that were the case I wouldn't still be stuck to the thing.

*Maybe it has something to do with the rune?*

*Ooh, I bet you're right. It's power, right?*

I nod. I decide to take the most basic approach and just pour my magic into the obelisk. When my hands and the surface of the pillar light up, I know I'm on the right track. I use my allure more than anything considering this is a mermaid test, but I also use a bit of all my other gifts as well. Nothing else happens, and I realize I'm not using enough. The rune is *power* after all. I need to pour everything I have into this thing. I feel like it's ripping me apart, but I keep going.

A hum emanates from the structure, and I briefly worry that I'm destroying it instead. Before I can pull my magic back, however, my hands are released. I sag against the structure, letting out a relieved breath. Thank the Gods that's over.

I take out the trident and reverse the transformation spell. I look at it more closely to see that on one of its prongs is the same symbol, engraved much smaller. I touch the trident to the rune and that prong lights up, making it hum beneath my hands.

I gasp as a current shoots through the trident, and then the obelisk shimmers, turning gold to match the prong on the trident. Then, it starts shifting, rising in the air.

*Holy shit. I didn't think this would happen*, I say as Pearl and I watch it emerge from the water. *We better go before someone comes to check this out.*

She nods and we travel a bit farther north before cutting inland. This area is more populated so it takes us some time to find a good spot to come out of the water and get dressed. I disguise the trident again and put it back in my bag. Can you imagine some random woman walking around Miami with a fucking trident? I don't see that going over well.

We head to another hotel close by and I immediately turn on the local news. I want to know if they're talking about the obelisk yet. I'm not disappointed.

"...reports are coming in of an unexplainable event that happened at

Miami Beach today. We're going live to our reporter Kate at the scene."

"Thank you, Jeremy. As you can see, a great golden pillar has risen out of the water behind me. It happened extremely quickly. Eyewitnesses say they felt the earth shake. Everyone thought it was an earthquake until they started to see this rising out of the water. It apparently only took a few minutes, and no boats or people were near the pillar when it started to rise."

Kate continues talking about the speculation already behind it and how experts are itching to come investigate. I chuckle to myself. They'll never be able to figure it out, and I realize then that in thousands of years, it's going to be like Stonehenge. It's crazy to think that I left my mark on Earth like that. And we still have two more to go. I can only imagine what's going to be said then. Unfortunately, we won't be able to stick around to see.

We once again order dinner, and I turn on something else. I don't want to come back to Earth and watch the news. How boring. Instead, I find a rerun of *Gilmore Girls*. Pearl and I both take a shower. I let her go first, and as soon as we finish dinner, we pass out, exhausted after the events of not only the day, but the week.

# 24

# Alexei

I didn't show my mate how much it killed me to leave and let her and Pearl go off on their own mission. I hate not being with her, but I do know that I'm much more useful to her in this task. I did not like the look on her face after she found out there was only a week until Demonica was planning to attack.

The segregation allowed for the realm to have the protection of the wards, but now that we've told everyone the truth, and Ember has opened the borders and allowed everyone to mix, we no longer have that security. Although it was the right decision to make, it is leaving us scrambling.

I traveled to the Immortal City first. It's a good halfway point, but it also makes sense since other vampires aren't able to teletravel into the territory, with the exception of the messengers at the palace. I notify the army to start making their way to the Stone Fields in the Everchanging Glades. Luckily, I've been preparing for this day for a while now. So have all of the territories. They're ready to go on command.

Needing to let my magic regenerate before teletraveling again, I head to the black market. Might as well get this one over with. Taking the path that I did with Ember last time makes me miss her all the more, but I'm unsure where the other black markets are or how to locate them. I'll have to find someone who knows and can show me. The only other one that I know the location of is in Nightshade Eclipse. I spent enough of my time in that territory that I made sure to learn where all the seedy places were. You never know when you're going to need something that's not available through normal means.

The black market is not nearly as busy during the day, and I'm grateful. I don't want an audience for this.

The monster vendor is in the same place as always, and I scout him and the creatures before I approach. There are five cages in total. One áspro vrykólakas, two fright morphs, one abyss hound, and a vexmouth. My heart rate increases slightly. I know things went well for us last time, but there's no guarantee that it will be the same this time.

The abyss hound rattles its cage, letting out a tortured whine. I wonder how long these creatures have been trapped like this. And they look unhealthy. I doubt they're being fed or watered enough.

"Oh, shut up!" the vendor yells at it, throwing water at it for good measure.

I observe everything and try to come up with a plan. Ember was able to use her allure to get the vendor to unlock the cages last time, but I don't have that advantage. Except...

Fuck. I've used her empath powers before when I've fed from her, but I've never thought to try any of her other powers. I rarely drink blood from another species, so it's not second nature for me to make use of that advantage. How stupid of me. I just fed from her last night. I know now isn't the best time to test this out, but it might be my only option.

I teletravel to right in front of him and he startles. Before he can do anything, I conjure my earth magic and wrap him in vines.

"What the fuck? What are you doing?" he shouts at me, immobilized.

"Here's what's going to happen. By order of the queen, you are going to release these poor creatures."

"Like hell I am! Do you know how hard it was to capture them in the first place? They're worth more than you make in a year."

"Did I sound like I was asking? They aren't property. They are living beings that don't deserve this treatment. They deserve freedom."

I can feel eyes on me from the crowd, but especially the monsters. I wonder how much they actually understand; the ones in Mermacovia understood, so it would make sense these ones would as well.

"I won't do it."

"Did I mention that your *queen* orders you to?"

"Does it look like I give a shit about the queen?" he sneers.

My blood boils. He's talking about my mate. The woman who has done everything in her power to make our world a better place. That anger fuels Ember's blood inside of me, and I can almost feel her with me. He doesn't have any mental shields up, so my next action takes no effort.

"*Release them. Now,*" I order, allure coating my voice as I free him from the vines.

He looks utterly shocked as he stands and does my bidding. I brace for the creatures to attack me or any of the others. They rip into their handler and he's dead within moments. Serves him right. When they turn to me, I brace for their attack, but there's nothing but gratitude in their gazes.

I lead them out of the black market, and when we reach the surface and are in the forest, I address them.

"You are all free to leave. The queen's only condition is that you no longer attack any of the citizens of this realm without cause or self-defense. Do you understand me?"

They blink at me in response, and I can see the intelligence in their eyes.

"There is a war coming. Demons are attempting to take our realm and its citizens for themselves. We would greatly appreciate your help. If you want to leave, that's fine, but know that there are other creatures like yourselves fighting for us. We will be fighting in the Stone Fields of the Everchanging Glades in roughly a week. If you decide to join us and can manage to bring others with you, that would be wonderful."

Another blink. Unlike the nymphs, these don't have the ability to speak. That's okay. I can tell they understand me.

"Enjoy your freedom."

With that, I head back to the castle. After a quick bite, I'm ready to travel to the next territory.

It's been a little while since I've been to Twin Fangs, and upon entering, something loosens in my chest. This was my home for a long time and I've missed it.

The grand master lives in the capitol building. I'm grateful that I know Stephan well and have been here many times.

He seems surprised to see me, but welcomes me in all the same. "What can I do for you, Alexei?"

"A couple things, actually. Firstly, we need to get the armies ready to move out and head for the Stone Fields. Secondly, I need you to send out messengers to the other territories to do the same. They all need to leave as quickly as possible, especially those in Wickshire so they're able to arrive in time. The demons are planning on attacking in a week, and we need to be ready for them."

He immediately gets to work, and I love his no-nonsense attitude. I've always really liked Stephan.

Once I've given my orders, I head to the black market. The experience is essentially the same as the last two times. I'm shocked that these creatures are capable of more than the savage brutality that the realm has always known them for. It makes me regretful for the ones that I've killed in the past, even though the ones I've encountered attacked without provocation. I think back on it, though, and realize that every time I was traveling through their territory. There's a good chance, like any animal, they were defending their space. Something to keep in mind for the future.

After the events of the day, I'm dead on my feet. I wish I could stay in my little hut on the mountain, but there's a guard posted there. That's *his* hut now. The thought saddens me. It would've been fun to stay there and think of the time I spent with Ember when we first met.

Instead, I find a nice tavern, similar to the ones that Ember and I stayed at on our journey. After ordering a meal big enough for two, I bathe, scarf down the food in typical Ember fashion, drink half a bottle of wine, and collapse into bed, completely spent. It's going to be a rough week.

# 25

# Pearl

Ember and I wake early the next morning. We've debated on if we should swim to Bermuda. Ember insists that it's too far, so in the end, we decide to take a flight. She thought we would be able to take a ferry, but there aren't any trips from where we are to where we need to be.

She finds us a flight late tonight. It will take us only three hours to get there once we're in the air, but apparently flights aren't always available, she tells me.

"We're going to get in really early in the morning to Bermuda. I'm thinking we should check into a hotel, take a nap, and then go in search of the obelisk after we've rested. I don't want us doing this on no sleep. It's not a good idea. And we have time." Even though she's reassuring me, I can still see her anxiety.

"Well, what do we do today?"

"I didn't think we would have time to relax, but it seems as though we do. Let's get some swimming suits and lie out on the beach."

"What are swimming suits?"

"Remember how humans don't like to be naked in front of each other? These allow them to go swimming in the ocean without getting their clothes wet."

I harumph. I detest the idea of swimming in anything but my skin, but apparently I would scandalize everyone otherwise. I roll my eyes. Prude humans.

We grab Ember's purse and walk around downtown Miami. There are so many shops that I don't know what to do with myself. I wish I could buy it all. Ember assures me we can buy some clothes considering we will be in tropical climates for the rest of the week. And boy is she right. It is *hot* here. I thought Mermacovia was warm, but being closer to the sun here is so much more intense. We each pick out a bikini along with swimsuit cover-ups, sunglasses, and a big beach hat. We change in the shop dressing room, and then we're heading to the beach.

Ember leads us to some lounge chairs and when we go to sit down, an attendant comes up to us.

"Excuse me? Are you ladies staying at the hotel? These are reserved for hotel guests."

"*Of course we are. You saw us here yesterday, remember?*" Allure is heavy in Ember's voice, and the man looks awed and dumbstruck before nodding.

"Of course. Can I get you anything?"

She looks to me. "Did you like that drink you had last night?"

I nod.

"I'll have a strawberry daiquiri and she'll have a piña colada."

He almost trips over himself in his haste to get us our drinks. We chuckle. It's fun having this advantage with no one else being the wiser. I can see that same excitement in Ember's eyes.

As we're lying on the beach, soaking up the perfect sunshine, grief hits me deeply. I miss my twin. We loved lying out together, and it strikes me that I'll never be able to experience that with her again. Tears silently track down my cheeks, and Ember reaches over and squeezes my hand. I clutch her for dear life. I know she can feel my despair, and for once I'm grateful for it. Not only can she sense it, but she *knows*. She's lost two of the most important people in her life. Recently too. Seeing how she's doing gives me hope that I'll be okay eventually. Even if it doesn't feel like it. I also am grateful that I have this time to feel all the feelings in the midst of all the craziness we're going through right now.

The attendant returns moments later with our beverages, and I take a much-needed drink. The sweet, cool concoction helps me gather myself, and I wipe my eyes under my glasses. I realize how wonderful the shades are. The sun isn't as bright in Queridian, so I'm glad that I have something to dull it a bit.

Ember turns on some music on her phone, and even though it's unfamiliar, I like the beat and I move my foot along with it. When we get too overheated, we take a dip in the ocean to cool off, but even that is strange. The water is so much warmer here. It's like bath water. It's difficult wrangling my mermaid in. As soon as I get into the water, especially salt water, I always shift. It's a different experience swimming with my legs instead of my tail. Much harder too. It gives me a new appreciation for humans.

It's a wonderful day, and I soak it up with my best friend. We order food, drink, lie out, swim, and just generally relax and have fun. But before long, duty calls. We return to the hotel, shower, change, and get ready for our flight to Bermuda.

Ember goes through the same ordeal as last time once we get to the airport since I don't have any form of identification, and Ember doesn't have something called a passport with her. Even though she seems more nervous this time, everything goes smoothly, and soon we're sitting on the plane. We both fall asleep quickly considering it's late and we've been so busy.

We wake only when the plane touches down. We get off the plane and check into another hotel, collapsing into bed the second we walk in. Too much sun, too much alcohol, too much of everything. We wake hours later, slightly hungover, but well-rested. Ember orders us room service and as soon as I eat I feel so much better.

"Okay. Ready to find us another obelisk?" she asks, looking just as refreshed.

"Let's go get it."

We leave everything in the room with the exception of the shell, trident, and room key. We find a section of beach that's less occupied, and we strip off our cover-ups and enter the water in our suits. We make sure there's no one around before also pulling off our bottoms and hiding them under the cover-ups and diving into the water. When we're deep enough, we shift and Ember brings out the shell. She activates it and leads us on.

We swim for hours, and even though we're searching for something important, I still take the time to enjoy the sea life around us. It's even different from the ocean close to Miami. The fish are different, the colors are different, and the predators are different. There have been a few times that we've come across a shark or two, but for the most part they ignore us, seeming to realize that we're just as fierce as they are. Not to mention we aren't nearly as delicious as a seal or something of the like. We're not fatty enough. Ember gets extremely excited when we come across a school of what she calls humpback whales. I've never seen them before, and they're beautiful. She carefully approaches them, and while she says they can be dangerous, these seem incredibly friendly and sweet. We swim with them for a while, and Ember even pets one. It's the happiest I've seen my friend in a while, and I smile at the sight.

There's another time when she spots a group of divers and quickly pulls me behind a grouping of rock formations. It would not be good if humans saw that mermaids actually exist. While we wait for them to pass, she explains to me how they're able to dive and breathe like that underwater. I'm fascinated. Humans on Earth with their technology astound and amaze me. The group takes *forever* to move on, and I'm getting impatient. I can tell Ember is too.

When the group is finally out of sight, we're able to start moving again. Ember tells me that the pull is getting stronger, so we up our pace. With her distracted with the shell, I keep a sharp eye out for more divers. Apparently this is a hot spot for that kind of thing, and we run into two more groups on our swim.

Needless to say, when we eventually find the obelisk, it's a massive relief.

As soon as the shell is inserted, the rune glows bright. *Agility.* Nerves build in my stomach as I wonder what this one will have in store for us.

Suddenly, a strong current pushes me off to the side, and the scene in front of me changes. Ember is trapped in a clear-looking tube, so I can see her, but am unable to help her. She looks around, confused. From where I am, I can see that it's basically an obstacle course. I also realize that the waves are churning again. Lightning strikes above us, and this storm seems more intense than at the previous obelisk.

Ember looks to me, and I point her in the direction she needs to go, but I motion to her that she needs to be careful. I don't know if she understands me, but she nods all the same.

She swims forward, taking the sharp turns with ease. At first I think that this is going to be easy, but then I see what awaits her. As soon as she turns around the next corner, the previous path seals off, and rushing toward her is a metal plate, intent on crushing her flat against the wall now behind her. She stops for a split second to survey, and then she's off, hurtling toward the only opening and escape, a tunnel that branches up. I watch with bated breath as she navigates the twists that try to slow her down. Just when I think that she's not going to make it, she puts on a final burst of speed and surges upward, barely avoiding the metal that whooshes past where she was only moments prior.

I don't celebrate like I want to, however. She's not through it yet, and I know that there will be more obstacles for her.

I'm right, unfortunately, but she seems to be more prepared after the first obstacle. There are two others—one is a shark that she barely manages to squeeze past, using her allure to stop it from following her. The second is a series of swinging blades which she has to dodge. One in particular almost gets the best of her, and I see a lock of hair tumble from her head.

Finally she reaches the end. The current that was preventing me from helping her releases me, and I shoot forward quickly to meet her back at the obelisk.

"Holy shit. That was much more intense than the last one."

"I'd say," I agree. "I thought you weren't going to make it a couple times."

She takes a deep breath and shakes her head as if to dispel the unpleasant experience.

"Well, let's do this, then."

Ember activates the obelisk more quickly this time. The prong lights up again as the obelisk starts to rise out of the water, and the storm finally calms now that the energy from the obelisk has been distributed into the trident.

We haul ass out of there before anyone sees us. It takes us a while to get back to where we started, but not as long as before considering we know where we're heading.

Our clothes are thankfully right where we left them, and we dress quickly. By the time we head back to the room, we're out of breath. It feels like we just escaped a dangerous situation. Ember turns the news on again, and it's essentially the same as Miami. Although now, there's speculation if it will indeed happen again in Puerto Rico considering that those are the three points of the Bermuda Triangle. There's also questions about if there will be any serious consequences to these pillars showing up and what they could mean.

"Two down, one to go," Ember says when she turns off the TV. "I should've known they would figure out that Puerto Rico's next."

"So what now?"

She takes out her phone. "Fly to our final stop. From there I think we can fly to the Bahamas and then swim to the portal."

I nod. Sounds easy enough.

She huffs beside me on the bed.

"What is it?"

"We have to wait for another flight. We can't get out until tomorrow."

"What about flights from there to the Bahamas? Should we book that now?"

"I can look, but I'm worried about not getting the obelisk activated in time."

She begins clicking away on her phone nevertheless.

"Okay. We fly into Puerto Rico tomorrow morning at ten a.m. There's a flight into the Bahamas I could book us at seven. I think that should give us enough time."

"Book it. We can totally find the last obelisk in that amount of time. Even today it only took us a few hours."

She nods and starts clicking away again.

"Okay, we're all set. I guess let's get some more beach time in. It's so weird. This shouldn't feel like a vacation, right?"

"I know. I keep asking myself the same question. Especially after Opal..." My voice trails off with the mention of her name.

"There's nothing wrong with having fun, Pearl. I know you're in your grieving stage right now, but just know that you don't have to be in it all the time. There's no time limit to your grief, and you can still enjoy yourself while you're in it."

A few tears slip down my cheeks, but I nod in understanding. It's so tough without my twin here. Even though we haven't lived in the same territory for the past few years, I still knew that she was alive and well in Mermacovia, living her best mermaid life. I don't have that anymore. She's gone. Before I can stop myself, I'm fully crying again. I growl in frustration. I despise being reduced to this on a regular basis.

"I hate that you somehow look even more beautiful when you cry," Ember tells me, making me laugh through my sobs.

"Oh, shut the fuck up. But yes, I do."

We get to the airport extremely early. Everyone looks half dead and walks around like what Ember says are called "zombies." I have no idea what she's talking about, but she assures me that's what the half dead are called.

Ember gets coffee for herself, and we settle in to wait for our flight.

"I hate all this travel. Flying is my least favorite. Especially after I learned how to teletravel. So much easier."

"Sorry you have to travel the hard way with me around."

"It's okay. The beach time and movies make up for it." She gives me a wink.

We're about to board the plane when Ember sucks in a sharp breath, her eyes going glassy and opaque. Shit. She must be having a vision. A moment later, she comes out of it, but her face is white as a sheet.

"What did you see?"

"Alexei."

"What about him?"

"He's about to be in danger. He's been going around freeing all the creatures from the black markets, and something went wrong. They captured him. Or they're about to."

"Could you tell which territory he's in?" I ask in concern.

"Wickshire. It was frozen. They can probably see him coming so they set up a trap for him. *Fuck.*"

"You need to go home and rescue him."

"I can't! We have to activate the other obelisk. It's the last one."

"I can do it. I've seen what to do, and you already have my next flight booked for me. *And* I have my own allure so I don't even need you to get me through security. I'm an expert by now."

She looks into my eyes, desperation and panic swimming in hers.

"Ember. *Go.* I'll be fine. I'll finish this up and meet you in the Everchanging Glades in a few days."

She huffs in what I can tell is frustration, along with a million different emotions. "Okay, but take my cards and my phone, just in case."

She quickly teaches me how to use it for the flights and tells me to charge the hotel in the Bahamas to the little rectangular card she gives me. I nod, and then our flight is getting called to board. I try not to let her see my nerves, but I'm anxious about having to do all of this on my own. She leaves all of our stuff with me, not that we have a ton, gives me a tight hug, and walks to the bathroom so she can teletravel without people noticing. I take a deep breath. I can do this.

When I'm settled on the plane and we take off, I think about my men. I can't wait to get home to them. It gives me a small measure of comfort to think about how they're traveling at the same moment I am. Not nearly in the same way, obviously, but it still makes me smile. Then I think about Alexei and pray to whatever gods are listening that

Ember is able to find him and rescue him. I'll make sure to give him lots of shit about it when I see him next, but in the meantime, I'm too worried. Our lives have officially crossed over into dangerous territory, and the last thing we need is to lose anyone else.

# 26

## Ember

I'm in a blind panic as I make my way to the airport restroom. I go into one of the stalls, and as soon as I'm away from prying eyes, I teletravel. It's a big jump, but I make it. I travel directly into the ocean where we came out from the portal. My clothes become soaked immediately and I tear them off, not caring. I'm grateful there's nothing around, like a ship or something. It's dangerous what I just did, but all I can think about is my mate.

I shift and swim through the portal, letting out the smallest sigh of relief that I'm at least back in Queridian. I feel horrible for leaving Pearl to handle this on her own, but I couldn't wait for another few days to make it to Alexei.

Unfortunately, doing that big of a jump really drained me, and as much as I want to immediately teletravel to Wickshire, I can't. I growl in frustration. I head to the house Pearl shares with her men. I know they won't be there, but I need somewhere to eat and rest for a few hours. Maybe if I'm lucky I'll be ready in an hour or so, although I highly doubt it.

Servants still occupy the house in their absence, and they prepare a large meal for me. I really don't have an appetite knowing my mate is in danger, but I force myself to eat so my magic regenerates more quickly. I eat everything on my plate even when I feel like I'm going to puke it all back up. As soon as I'm finished, I head to the room I usually share with Alexei and lie down. As worried as I am, I'm also exhausted. I fall asleep within minutes, but it isn't restful. I dream about all the horrible things that could be happening to him while I'm unable to get there.

When I wake a few hours later, I feel more tired than when I arrived. That doesn't matter, though, because I can feel that my magic is full enough to get to where I need to go.

I focus on the frozen wasteland of Wickshire. I'm instantly freezing, and I curse the fact that I wasn't able to wear anything warmer. Not to mention I've been on a beach in the freakin' Caribbean. It's hotter than even the most tropical climate in Queridian, and now I'm thrust into basically Alaska in the dead of winter.

I call my fire magic forth to warm myself before traveling to the mess hall. I know a lot of the witches will be traveling to the Everchanging Glades, but those unable to fight will still be here. Not to mention that I should probably eat again while I find someone to tell me where to find the black market.

Lunch is being served when I enter, and those that are present look startled by my arrival as well as my attire.

"Your Majesty! What are you doing here?" asks a man that I remember from last time. I don't recall his name though.

"Alexei is here and in trouble. I need to find him and rescue him."

His face scrunches up in concern and he nods. "What do you need from us?"

"Food for starters as well as some warmer clothes if you have any that would fit me. And most importantly, I need to know where the black market is and how to access it."

His brows shoot up in surprise. "Of course, Majesty. Why don't you grab some food and eat by the fire. I'll find some clothes and someone who can help with the black market situation."

I sag in relief that I'm going to have help.

I load up my plate, my stomach growling again after another huge jump. I know the only reason I was able to pull it off was because I'm terrified for Alexei. Otherwise, I would've needed longer to recover. But my theory that my mate being in perilous situations allows me to do things I shouldn't be able to is holding up.

The man, whose name I learned is Vincent, returns with clothes and an older ragged-looking woman.

"Majesty, this is Kira. She's been to the black market and can tell you how to get there."

"Thank you so much, Vincent."

He bows and leaves the witch to give me all the information she can while I shovel more food into my mouth. I know I look nothing like a queen right now, but I can't bring myself to care at the moment.

The location isn't far, thankfully. After I've eaten and let my magic refill a bit, I should be able to head straight there. She volunteered to come with me, but I declined. I need to do this on my own.

It kills me to remain where I am for a moment longer. I'm so close to Alexei I can almost taste it, but I need to refuel just a little bit more. I take that time to change into the much warmer clothes, use the facilities, and load up on weapons. I also pack a skein of water and some food. I have no idea how long Alexei has been there or without those things, but just in case, I would like to have them on hand.

When I finally feel ready, I shift my features to match the witches. I don't change into anyone specific. Instead, I change my hair to platinum, my eyes to blue, round my ears, and make myself a little skinnier.

The black market is located in the midst of deep ice caves. As I press my bloody handprint to the ice wall in payment for entrance, I expect it to stain, but instead, the blood *absorbs* into the wall a moment before the entrance opens. The ice gives off a cold blue glow and paints everything in a sickly light. I immediately remember Pearl's words from when Alexei and I went by ourselves to the one in Mystic Mountain. *The one in Wickshire is particularly depraved.* She wasn't wrong. It's worse than the two I've seen by *far*. The vendors seem more vicious, there are many more of them, and they have *everything*. I'm instantly overwhelmed and intimidated. No wonder Alexei got into trouble here. This is not a crowd I want to fuck with. Unfortunately, I have to in order to save my mate. First I just have to find him.

I follow the pull in my heart that seems to be leading me to him. I make my way through the throng of people, careful to keep as far away from them as possible. My heart pounds harder in anticipation and anxiety. Gods, I hope he's okay. If he's not, I swear I will burn this fucking place to the ground. I will quickly and unremorsefully become the scariest bitch here.

I find him a few minutes later. He's in a cage, and his clothes stripped off with the exception of his undergarments. His eye is black and swollen, his lip is split, and he's shivering uncontrollably. My blood absolutely *boils* at seeing him like this. At the fact that they did this to him. My rage builds into an inferno so hot that I'm fairly certain I'm glowing from it. I stalk toward him, not even noticing any other details. When I get closer, his eyes latch on to mine, and despite my altered appearance, I can tell he instantly knows it's me. Relief coats his features, along with shame and fear. I try to project onto him that everything is fine. I'm going to save him, and we're both going to walk out of here okay.

I finally take in the area around him and my breath stutters. There are triple the number of monsters I've seen at either of the other markets. There's also not only one vendor, but five, one of whom has ice blond hair. I bet the witch saw him coming and set up a trap, because normally even five others wouldn't be able to best my mate.

I walk up to the vendors with a sweet smile on my face. They look at me with interest and malicious intent.

"Hello, darling. What can we do for you?"

I take a quick moment to burst into their minds. None of them are skilled enough to even have any sort of barriers up. All except one. I'll need to keep a close eye on him. I let my allure free.

"*Release this man,*" I order, gesturing to my mate.

They look at me in confusion and hesitation, but follow my command all the same. My priority at the moment is getting him out unscathed. Then I can blast these fuckers to kingdom come for daring to harm him.

Alexei slowly gets up and comes toward me, taking my lead. When he's by my side, I squeeze his hand. I suck in a sharp breath at the feel of his fingers. They're *freezing*. My worry comes back in full force even though he's next to me.

"*Now the beasts,*" I command, but my mind is only half on the task at hand.

Only half of them obey, and I realize too late that I've lost my grip on two of them, including the one who resisted me in the first place. Before I can rectify my mistake, he's flinging a dagger straight at me.

His aim is off and I thank the Gods when it sinks into my shoulder instead of my chest. I scream out as it makes contact, losing my influence over the others as well.

They shout their outrage about being manipulated and start fighting back. I breathe deeply to try to regain control, but I'm too overwhelmed. Not to mention exhausted. I have a moment of panic where it's as if I don't remember one bit of my training.

Luckily, my mate is there. Even exhausted and freezing he's still a force to be reckoned with. He unleashes his fury and his earth magic, wrapping all but one in vines. The man who threw the dagger is dead a moment later, his neck snapped by the force of the magic squeezing his throat.

I take back control of the only vendor that's unbound.

"*Release the beasts. Now!*"

I let my allure out full blast. I'm done fucking around. I want to get out of here and take care of my mate, not deal with this shit.

The vendor scrambles to do as I command, wanting to please me. Within moments, all the beasts are free, and I choose that moment to let my appearance return to normal. I call fire to my hands, burning through the vendor's restraints and pinning them to the cages with my air magic.

"You really chose the wrong man to fuck with. Did you not know he was the queen's mate?" Allure no longer coats my voice now that they're immobilized.

"Oh, we knew. He deserved everything he got. Trying to steal from us after doing the same to the other black markets," one sneers as us, venom thick in his words.

"That's right, human bitch," another spits at me.

Alexei snarls at my side.

"Human, huh? First off, would a human be able to do this?" I ask as I form a ring of fire around them, making them sweat with the heat. "Second, humans are much more powerful than you realize." I take that moment to instill as much fear into all of them as I can. They shriek in terror, at least one of them pissing themselves.

I smile in savage delight. It's then that I notice the monsters have encircled them, growling softly. I put my fire out, and the second I do, they pounce, tearing them to shreds.

The others in the market start fleeing and screaming in horror, but I pay them no mind. Soon, the market is empty, save for us and the creatures.

"Thank you," I tell them all, and explain the same thing that I did to the other beasts. They seem to be even more grateful, and it lightens my heart that they're no longer locked up. No creature deserves that. To be used and sold to the highest bidder for doing nothing other than existing, even if they can be a bit scary and dangerous. The same could be said for tigers or bears.

When that's done, and I know we're no longer in any sort of danger, I turn to my mate.

"Are you okay?" I surround us with fire to warm him and wrap my arms around him. Poor guy looks freezing.

He squeezes me to him in what I can feel is relief and comfort. "Yes. Thanks to you. How did you know?" he asks through chattering teeth.

"I had a vision when we were on Earth. I got here as quickly as I could. Sorry it still took me a little while."

"Thank you for saving me, little doe."

He leans down and gives me a heated kiss. I return it before breaking away.

"We need to get you warmed up."

"You were doing a mighty good job of it until you stopped kissing me."

I roll my eyes at him, slapping him lightly on the arm.

"Come on. Let's get back to the village."

"Are you ready to teletravel yet?" he asks.

I frown as I realize I probably need a few minutes. I huff but shake my head. "Not quite yet." I take out the food and water I had packed, handing it over to him. I also wrap my cloak around him, even though he protests. "I brought this in case. I wasn't sure when you were last fed and watered."

He drinks greedily before narrowing his eyes on me. "Watered? Like a horse?"

I chuckle. "Exactly like a horse."

He pinches my backside in retaliation, and I squeal in mock outrage and delight. My mate is safe and I'm back in his company. Even though the circumstances are shitty, I couldn't be more relieved or happy.

When he's finished off the food and water, I finally feel ready to teletravel. We make our way out of the caves before clasping hands and jumping to Black Moon City.

Vincent finds a cabin for us to rest in before we head on our way, and I'm so grateful. Now that everything is as it should be, I realize how exhausted I am. I went through so much magic that I feel as if I could sleep for a week.

Alexei and I take a piping-hot bath, and I spend the whole time healing his injuries and washing him. I know how he felt all those months ago after Coralia injured me. Even though we hadn't gotten back together yet, he *needed* to care for me. I feel the same way now. He seems to understand, and lets me. Maybe *let* isn't the right word, as he's basically purring in my arms.

When we're thoroughly clean and warm, we get out of the bath. Vincent brought some clean clothes for Alexei as well, and soon we're dressed and snuggled under the covers together. I let Ebony out. I could feel her worry for him. She instantly cuddles up against his other side so he's sandwiched between us.

We sleep for *hours*. It's lovely. Even though we don't really have the time to do this, it's necessary. When we wake, however, we finally go over everything that happened while we were apart.

"You first," I tell him.

"I sent out the fae army before traveling to Nightshade Eclipse. I thought it would be more efficient if I dispatched messengers to get the armies moving."

I nod in approval. That was definitely quicker than going to each individual territory himself and having to rest in between each jump.

"Then I went to each of the remaining black markets. Every creature was freed, and I didn't run into any trouble until I came here."

"How did you do it?"

"Well..." he draws out the *L*s at the end of the word. "I used your mermaid abilities."

My eyes widen in shock.

"Remember that we can use other powers when we drink from another species? I had forgotten because I never use that specific set of talents. It was always cheaper for me to drink from other vampires, so I never had the opportunity. Until now. The problem was that when I got to Wickshire, your blood had faded out of my system and I was no longer able to utilize your allure."

"And that's how they caught you?"

"That, and one of them *saw* me coming and prepared a trap for me. As soon as I showed up, they knew who I was and all converged on me using their different powers. Then they put me in that awful cage. I was able to use magic but only in the confines of the cage, so I wasn't able to free myself."

"How long were you there?"

"I think a little over a day."

I shake my head. That could've gone so much worse.

"Enough about me. What happened with you?"

"Well, we found and activated two of the obelisks. It took some time because we weren't able to immediately travel to the next one. We had to wait for flights."

"What about the third one?" he asks.

"Pearl is handling it. She's going to activate the trident and bring it back here when she's finished."

His eyes darken and I can sense his surprise and shame. "You left her alone?"

"I had to. You were in danger. And nothing is going to happen to Pearl on Earth. It is the safest place for someone who has magic. Especially *her* magic. She can coax anyone to do anything for her."

Even as I say the words, I can't help but worry for her still. Activating the trident isn't the easiest thing, although I have all the faith in her. Not to mention the crazy weather that comes along with it. There's no way of knowing what will happen once it's fully activated.

"Good point." His shame is stronger now.

"Alexei, you did so well. You freed all of the black market creatures by yourself. You got the armies to travel to the battle site. I wouldn't have been able to do it without you. We wouldn't have been able to activate the trident, and that could change the tide in this war."

He doesn't meet my eyes. "I didn't free *all* of them by myself. The last one I got myself captured and only escaped because of you."

"Alexei." I'm silent until he looks at me. "You've saved me more times than I can count. You are the fiercest warrior I know. You have nothing to be ashamed of. It just means that the two of us are stronger together than apart. We know this by now, and if circumstances didn't force us to separate there's no way we would've. If Pearl was more experienced with Earth I probably would've let her go with one of her men and stayed with you. As it is, she wasn't quite ready for that yet."

"She is now though?"

I nod. "She's seen how to activate the obelisk and knows how to find them. She's also flown enough to know how to get through security on her own. I also just wanted to confirm my suspicion that the points of the Bermuda Triangle were in fact made up by the obelisks. *And* I was able to book her flights for her, so all she has to do is show up, persuade the agents, and then get on the plane."

He still looks a little worried, and if I'm being honest with myself, I am too. I hated leaving her, but I really didn't have a choice.

"Xanto and Proteus are going to fucking kill me."

He growls. "They can try."

"I thought you liked them."

"I do, but I won't tolerate *anyone* harming or threatening my mate."

"They haven't, but I know they won't be happy with me."

"I think they'll understand," he says.

I raise a single eyebrow in question.

"Okay, maybe not right away, but if circumstances were reversed, they wouldn't hesitate to leave you to save Pearl."

I nod. Good. I'm glad we're talking through this. If I can get them to understand where I'm coming from, they will hopefully see my side.

"So, what now?" Alexei asks.

"We head to the Everchanging Glades. The attack should happen any day now."

"We won't be able to travel all the way there in one jump. It's a long way."

"I made the jump from Allure Isle to here in one."

His brows shoot up to his hairline. "Really?"

I nod. "You were in danger. I didn't have a choice. I wasn't going to rest longer than I had to."

He smiles fondly at me. "If I haven't said it yet, thank you for rescuing me."

I kiss him. "You're welcome, mate," I whisper against his mouth.

He deepens our kiss, pushing me onto my back and settling over me. The time apart has made us both needy, and I crave him so badly.

"We need to leave," I say half-heartedly, hoping he'll ignore my words.

"We will," he says, but continues what he's doing.

I moan into his mouth, grinding against him, unable to help myself. I've missed him, and I want one reunion moment before our world is thrown into chaos again. It might be the last intimate moment we get to have together. *No.* I stop that thought in its tracks. We will not die during this fight. We did not go through all of this *shit* just to have a few months together. We're going to get our happily ever after, we just have to fight for it.

"You're thinking too hard, little doe."

"Make me stop," I beg.

He smirks at the challenge. Instead of returning to my mouth, he trails his lips down my neck, pausing every so often to nip and suck. My hands tangle in his hair as I try to move faster and guide him to where I really want that talented mouth. He tuts at me in disapproval, continuing to take his time. I whine when he reaches my breasts. My clothes are still in the way, but he doesn't seem to care. He suckles at them in turn over the cloth, soaking it and me in the process. It's a different sensation than what I'm used to, and it turns me on more than I was expecting.

When he finally removes my shirt and I feel his mouth on my skin, I'm a writhing mess. He seems to have no issue taking his time with me, even though we have important places to be.

"Alexei, please. I need you, mate."

He growls against my skin, and I know he can never resist me when I call him that. He finally removes the rest of my clothing and moves down to my core, and I almost weep at the relief and pleasure coursing through me. I can feel what a mess I'm making of the sheets under me, but I don't care in the slightest.

He works wonders on my clit, alternating between licking and sucking. I'm building, but not quickly enough. I know he won't enter me until I've come.

"More. Alexei, I need more," I beg.

He groans, the vibrations feeling sublime. When he adds a finger, then two into my soaked cunt, I almost buck off the bed. *Yes.* He plunges them into me mercilessly, seemingly done with teasing me. He wants my orgasm as much as I do.

"Come for me, little doe. Come all over my face and fingers."

I'm a slave to his command and I break apart, blackness taking over my vision. When I finally come back to my body, I feel Alexei poised at my entrance.

"Look at me, mate," he orders.

I meet his gaze, and the love shining in his eyes makes tears pool in mine. What did I do to deserve this man? He pushes into me slowly, stretching me, never once breaking my stare. I feel as if he's staring straight into my soul.

"I missed you," he tells me.

"I did too. I never want to be parted from you again."

He keeps his pace slow. Now that I've already given him an orgasm, he doesn't seem as desperate.

"I want to make this last. I don't want to move beyond this moment. I wish we could just stop time right here."

I nod emphatically, beyond words or coherent thought at this point. Every push and pull between our bodies is heating my blood more and more. It's not going to be a quick release, but I can already feel that it's going to be stronger than the last.

There are no words to describe this act. It's not simply making love. It's our past, our present, our future. It's all the hardships we've endured, it's all the joy we've shared, and everything in between. It's our hope, it's our fear. It's *everything.*

With our eyes still locked, I rip into the skin of my wrist and offer it to him. He holds his out for me as well, and when we drink from each other at the exact same moment, I swear even time itself shatters. Every time that we are intimate I think that it can't get any better, but it always does.

I come around him, and I feel him pulse inside me, his warmth filling me. He drops his forehead to mine, breathing heavily. His weight is so comforting on top of me, and I revel in it. For the first time in days, I feel settled, even with everything that awaits us.

"I love you," he whispers against my mouth.

"I love you so much. I never thought I could feel this way about *anyone.*"

He smiles and gives me a tender kiss.

"Bath?"

I moan. "That sounds heavenly."

He fills the tub, and we sink into it, taking one more moment of relaxation for ourselves.

# 27

# Pearl

I board the flight *on my own.* I didn't let on to Ember, but I'm fucking terrified. I know I told her it was no big deal, and it technically isn't, but I'm nervous all the same. Traveling this way by myself is not something I thought I would ever have to do. Funnily enough, the most important part of this mission doesn't intimidate me in the least. I can swim around and locate that other obelisk and finish activating the trident no problem. It's the whole finding where I'm going in an airport and doing everything correctly that's the scariest.

I've watched Ember enough that I know I'll be fine, but I still hate it. Not to mention that she isn't here to pour calming emotions onto me. I take some deep breaths. It will be fine.

I find my seat with no issues and no assistance, fuck you very much. I'm grateful that she was at least able to come through security with me and help me find the gate. The real test will be when I have to come *back* to the airport and do it all on my own.

Ember left me her phone, so once I find my seat, I turn on some music. I have no idea what I like, but I pick ones at random, skipping them if they aren't to my taste. I don't seem to have that problem too often though. I found an artist that I really enjoy called Yanni. Looking at his picture, I'm struck by his handsome deep-set eyes. The music is calming and it's perfect to settle my nerves on the flight.

I use my allure to get myself a drink—a Bloody Mary. Ember really turned me onto these. When I first tried them, I couldn't make up my mind about them, but they've grown on me.

I'm relieved when the flight lands. I'm anxious to activate the last one and head home. I miss my men, and with the death of my sister and Ember having to leave, I feel lost and lonely.

It helps that I'm busy and have a task to accomplish. Swimming in my mermaid form helps too. I don't feel as many emotions when I'm in her body.

The airport is close to the ocean, so I don't even bother getting a hotel. I also have no idea how long it'll take me to find the last obelisk, but if it's quick, I think I'll hang out on the beach some more and soak up the last of this intense sunshine.

It's once again difficult to find an empty spot to take off my bottoms, but eventually I come across one. This time, I throw it in my waterproof bag and heft it over my head so it's hanging over me cross-body. I swim far enough out that there are no humans close by and then I shift. My mermaid sings her joy at being released. She hasn't liked flying. The air is no place for a sea creature. Unless you're Ember of course.

I activate the shell and let it guide me. The pull already feels insistent, and I have high hopes that means I'm not far from it.

This time is different, considering the last two instances one of us was able to be the lookout while the other navigated with the shell. I don't realize how much more difficult it would be. Especially when I'm hauling ass, minding my own business when I get entangled in a net. *Fuck.* I shriek in surprise and confusion. We don't have many nets in Mermacovia, as most of the fish are caught by mermaids in the actual sea while we swim. I try to untangle myself, but there's no use for it. I'm thoroughly trapped.

It's then that I feel the net pulling me up. Godsdamn it. Good thing I've got my allure to get me through this.

I emerge from the water to the sound of gasps and exclamations.

"What *is* that?" a man asks, awe coating his tone.

"I think it's a...*mermaid.*"

I awkwardly turn in the net so I'm facing them. Luckily, there are only two.

I release my allure full force, not wanting to be in here any longer than I have to be. And the less they see of me, the easier it will be for them to forget me.

"*You will forget this ever happened. Tell no one of this and erase me from your mind.*" The dazed looks on their faces tells me that my persuasion will have no issue taking effect. "*Release me at once.*"

They scramble to get over to me, pushing a button to release one side of the net. I free-fall into the ocean beneath me, grateful when I once again feel the water surrounding and supporting my body.

I rush off, appreciative that I still have the shell in my hands and it wasn't dislodged in that shit show.

I swim for maybe a half an hour, much shorter than the other times. I do everything that I watched Ember do with the last two, but this time, when I insert the shell, I'm immediately pushed back by the strongest current I've ever felt, with perhaps the exception of the last trial. Lightning flashes dangerously close, and there's a cyclone surrounding the pillar in the water. The last two storms were nothing compared to this, and I know it's because it's the last obelisk. I'm knocked far back from the obelisk and I swim toward it. I make the slightest progress when I'm once again blown back. I growl in frustration.

I change tactics. I get out of the current and attempt to circle around the other side. The current immediately switches, keeping me away from the obelisk. Fuck me. This is a trial. The only way I'm going to be able to activate it is to just plow forward as best I can.

I draw on every bit of strength I have, and I'm delighted when I appear to be making progress, albeit slow progress. I snarl when seaweed flows in my path and tangles me up in it. I slash out with my claws, cutting through it like stalks of wheat, but there's so much that it's hindering me even more. I know this is part of whatever magic is at work too, and I curse whoever made these stupid trials. Good thing they're already dead or I would kill them myself.

I eventually make my way through the seaweed, but don't have a chance to be relieved. The current is at its strongest now and it takes everything in me to make the final push. My fin is burning, along with my arms from all the slashing I had to do to get through the obstacles. I'm breathing heavily, maybe heavier than I ever have while swimming before.

When I reach my fingers out and brush the obelisk, everything suddenly stops. I have a terrifying moment where I almost burst into the pillar, but I stop myself in time, sighing in blessed relief. I did it.

When I touch the trident to the rune, this one reading *Stamina*, go figure, the obelisk does the same thing as the last time, but the entire trident lights up and glows. Power electrifies through it, getting stronger and stronger by the second. Once the obelisk is fully raised, the ocean around me starts to charge with the same energy and begins funneling into Surseiha's Needle. I continue holding it, reverently, nervously. I know that even though it's going to be activated now, I still won't be able to wield any of its power. I can *feel* it though. It's the same sensation as the charge in the air before a storm, but it's *magnified.* Just when I think it can't possibly build any more, the power seems to snap, the trident glowing a brilliant blue before the color fades into the object, dimming.

Everything slowly calms and returns back to normal. I let out the breath I was holding, relief and awe pounding through my veins. I did it. The trident is activated. One more tool we can use to defeat the demon bitch queen. A desire for revenge coils tightly inside of me, and the need to release it is so potent I almost choke on it. I close my eyes and take some deep breaths, focusing on the positive—we now have this instrument. We have a weapon to wield against her. I will have my revenge. Ember will ensure it.

When I finally feel composed enough, I open my eyes to see so much activity around me. Boats seem to be coming toward me from every direction. Fuck. I stayed here too long. The humans knew that this was likely going to happen again here. They were ready for it.

Instead of swimming to the surface, I dive down deep, keeping out of sight from any who might be able to see me. The last thing I need is to be captured again and have to persuade them to let me go. As fun as that sounds, I don't have time for it. I need to get back to Queridian and get this back to Ember. Not only do I have to travel back to my realm, but once I get there, I'll also need to travel to the Everchanging Glades. I don't even want to think about how long *that* is going to take me. I just hope I can reach her in time. It's going to be a hard push.

I make my way back to the beach. I was correct and I have some time to relax before I have to go to the airport one last time. I discreetly put my swimming bottoms back on, and disguise the trident and return it to the bag before emerging from the water. I coax my way onto a lounge chair and order a piña colada, and lie out. It's a relief knowing I've accomplished my task and that Ember was able to count on me, and that comfort allows me to relax more than I have in days. Weeks. I finish my drink and close my eyes. Soon I'm napping under the noonday sun.

I wake disoriented, and feeling slightly sick. I look down at my body to see that my skin has turned a pinkish color. When I touch it, it hurts and I suck in a sharp breath. Is this a sunburn? I've heard of them before, but never gotten one. As a mermaid, we're outside in the sun and water so often that our bodies are used to it. However being so much closer to the sun here must have really done a number on me.

I groan and sit up. When I look down at Ember's phone to check the time, I realize I have to leave for the airport. *Now.* I quickly gather my things, triple-checking that I have the trident with me. Can you imagine? Us doing all this work for the ditzy mermaid to leave it behind.

I rush to the airport and my gate, and I let myself relax now that I made it in time. Granted, barely, but it still counts, right?

The flight is uneventful, which is fine by me. I'm impatient to get home. By the time we land, I feel ready to make the final trek to Queridian. I head to the sea, and when I'm far enough out, I shift before taking out the shell one last time. The last thing I need is to be wandering around lost in the middle of the ocean.

It takes hours to get to the portal, and by the time I arrive, I feel so drained. I wonder if it has to do with the fact that magic isn't present like at home. I mean, part of it is how much I've been traveling, my sunburn, not to mention the exhaustion of grief over losing my sister. *Don't think about that now.* Needless to say, when I finally fall into Queridian, I almost feel like I could cry.

I'm not too far from home, and I can eat and rest before deciding how to travel to the Everchanging Glades. I've never wanted to be anything other than a mermaid, but I'm supremely jealous of the vampires right now. I would give almost anything to be able to just teletravel there. Alas, I'm stuck with my fins.

I get home and am instantly warmed by the scents of me and my men. I know they aren't here, but this is comforting enough for the moment. I have one of the few remaining servants prepare a meal for me, and once I'm finished eating, I pass out for a few hours.

When I wake, I pack a new bag, ensuring I have all the important stuff, and then I rally my strength and head to the ocean, deciding to swim rather than take the land route. I think I'll be able to get there faster.

*I'm coming, Ember.*

# 28

# Ember

Alexei and I eat one more time before we leave. We need to be at full strength to make the jump. Nerves dance in my stomach. This is it. When we travel this time, it'll be time to war.

Worry for Pearl also knots my stomach. I hope she's doing okay on Earth. It was hard for me to leave her, but she wasn't in danger. Alexei was. I had no choice. She knew that and was able to push me to go.

When we're ready, Alexei and I clasp hands. I take a deep breath, attempting to center myself.

"Ready, little doe?"

Even though I'm not, I nod. We don't have a choice.

"Hey." I meet his gaze. "Everything will be okay. I can feel it," he reassures me. Even though there's no possible way for him to know that, it settles me anyway.

I let out some of my tension with my next breath. "Okay. I'm ready." I give his hand a squeeze to bring the point home.

We fade as he pulls me with him. The battle is going to take place in the Stone Fields, and seeing as I haven't been there yet, Alexei has to lead us. He's been to almost every place in the realm, and I'm lucky to have him as my guide.

The jump is an insanely large distance, but we make it. I'm comforted to discover that when we arrive, battle isn't raging around us. I would hate to show up late for *my* own war.

A lot of the troops are already in tents surrounding the fields. I sigh in relief. I was worried that many of them wouldn't be here yet.

"We should try to find Joseph. Or Proteus and Xanto."

Alexei nods. "I'll find the guys, you find Joseph."

We take off in opposite directions. I head to the area where the mimics are housed. It seems that even though the borders have opened, and some people are interacting with each other, the majority are still more comfortable among their own species. I remind myself that it's going to take time. Rome wasn't built in a day and all that.

It takes me a solid fifteen minutes to find Joseph, but his face lights up as soon as he spots me. I run over and give him a hug. I'm comforted by his warm, familiar embrace, and I allow myself to sink into it for a moment.

"My queen, I'm so glad you've arrived."

"Oh, stop, you charmer," I tease, giving him a playful shove.

He beams at me. "I'm glad you made it. Do you need anything? You must be exhausted from traveling. We have food and water as well, and I've taken the liberty of having a tent set up for you and your mate."

"I would like to lie down, but first I want to hear about what's happening here."

"Well, most of the armies have arrived. The only ones not here yet are the witches. We were waiting for you to arrive before engraving the rune inscriptions on the stones. Once we start that, the portal will begin to open. We don't want to give ourselves away before we're ready. Also, there have been about a hundred creatures who've shown up to pledge their allegiance to you and our cause."

My eyes widen. "A hundred?"

He smiles. "Yes, Majesty." Now that I'm queen and we're in front of others, he's insistent on calling me by my title. "It seems as though you and your mate have been busy."

"Where are they? Have they caused any trouble?"

He shakes his head. "No. They were insistent on having their own space, so they're on the outer edges of the camp away from the armies. It seems that once they have their own area established and it remains undisturbed, they're amicable."

My relief pounds through me. I was grateful for the monsters to come and fight for us, but I've been worried about them starting trouble.

"According to the information you acquired, Demonica is planning on attacking tomorrow?" he asks.

I nod. "Yes. Although, I don't know if that has changed in the last week. The informant was discovered and killed. I really hope they didn't decide to move to a different location."

"They haven't. The spies we sent out have returned. They're gathering on the other side of this portal."

More relief that I didn't send those spies to die or to be caught and tortured.

"When would you like us to start inscribing the stones?"

I look around. "How long will it take?"

"Not long. I was going to assign each stone to a person and have them all start at the same time. They should all finish within ten minutes or so and the portal will be open."

"And how long to get our armies ready and in position to fight?"

"A few hours."

"Okay. Let's plan on attacking tonight. Once the sun sets. It will be earlier than Demonica is planning on, and we can hopefully take them by surprise. Also, if we have willing candidates, I would like the vampires to feed on any other species. We need every advantage in battle, and if they have more than one power, that will be an incredible leg up."

He nods, bowing. "I'll see it done, Your Majesty. In the meantime, why don't you and Alexei go lie down. I'll have food and water brought to your tent. You need to rest before the battle."

Alexei takes that moment to show up with Proteus and Xanto. They both look exhausted, but otherwise well. With the exception of the worry lining their eyes.

"Is Pearl okay?" Xanto asks.

I nod, guilt turning my stomach, but I push through it. "Yes. She was about to board the flight to activate the final obelisk before I got the vision about Alexei. She should be home by now. I'm sorry I had to leave her. I *had* to save Alexei."

Proteus reaches over to squeeze my hand. "We understand. We would've done the same thing in your position."

Xanto looks less inclined to agree with him, and I know he's unhappy with me for leaving her. I don't blame him. I wouldn't be happy either. But this is war. We've had to make some tough decisions. And I'm sure there will be more before this is all over.

I give him an apologetic look, and he softens just a bit. "I'm glad you're okay."

I smile at him before leaning in for a hug. "Same here. I was worried about you guys. Have any trouble on the road?"

Proteus shakes his head. "None. It just took a while to get here with the whole army. We basically just arrived."

"Want to eat with us before we all get some much-needed rest?" Alexei asks.

The men nod, and Joseph has someone lead us to our tent. It's enormous. The queen's tent, Alexei informs me. Royal tents are always extravagant. Even during war. There's a round table big enough for six people, a massive bed, complete with furs and comfy-looking pillows, and a copper tub. I feel slightly guilty that I have such an extravagant tent while the rest of the army has only the basic necessities, but I shake it off as best I can. I need to get used to the royal treatment eventually, even if it does make me uncomfortable.

We all sit around the table, and Proteus pours us each a glass of wine from the decanter waiting for us. Food is brought minutes later, and even though Alexei and I just ate, we dig in, our magic already burning through our previous meal.

It feels strange not having Pearl here with her bubbly, boisterous personality to give us some levity. As it is, we eat in somber silence, the reality of our situation hanging over our heads like an ax. This could potentially be our last meal together.

When we finish, the men go to their own tent, giving each other an intimate look, and I almost collapse into the bed that's prepared for us, not even having the energy to change.

Alexei climbs in behind me, pulling me tight to him. Even with how tightly strung I feel with the impending battle, his touch instantly calms me, allowing me to relax enough to doze.

We wake hours later to Joseph's voice on the other side of our tent flap.

"Your Majesty, it's time."

Nausea pools in my stomach as I sit up, and I struggle not to lose the contents of my stomach all over the place. Alexei rubs soothing circles on my back, and I sink into his touch like a lifeline.

"Okay, Joseph. We'll be out soon."

"Do you need me to send in someone to assist with your armor?"

"We'll manage. Thank you, Joseph," Alexei says, knowing better than I do. I have no idea how to put it all on, and I will most definitely need his help.

It's then that I see our armor on the other side of the tent. It's on two mannequins, and I gasp at the beautiful metalwork that will protect me. It's black with rose gold detailing. Little swirls and stars decorate it, and while I know it's not meant for beauty, it *is* beautiful.

"Will you help me?" I ask him, but there's no need. He's already taking it off the mannequin and bringing it over to me.

Once it's all on, I twist and turn, marveling at how easy I'm able to move. It doesn't feel heavy either, which I'm happy about. This being my first time fighting in a battle, I really want to make sure I'm not limited.

Alexei is able to get his own armor on without assistance, and I marvel at the smoky gray metal. It's almost silver but it's darker and it's not a consistent color throughout. There's not much design work done to it, but I'm unsurprised about that. Alexei isn't about decoration. As long as it's quality, that's all he cares about.

"You look hot like this," I tell him, stroking my hand over the cool metal on his chest.

His eyebrows fly up in surprise. "Is that right?"

I nod. "We might have to play with it a little after the battle." I wink at him. I'm trying to distract myself from what's coming, and flirting with Alexei always accomplishes that.

"Only if you wear your crown."

My blood heats at the suggestion. "Deal. Now feed from me. I want you to have every advantage possible before we go out there."

His lips latch on to my neck, and instead of the intense pleasure I normally feel from his bites, it's slightly duller. It still feels good, but not as sexual, and I know he's toning it down so I'm not worked up before battle.

He seals the bite and I pull away from him. I could get lost in him for hours, but we don't have that luxury right now.

No. Right now we need to go kick some serious demon ass.

I give him a heartfelt kiss. I won't say goodbye. I can't let myself think of any scenario where the two of us don't make it out of this on the other side.

"For good luck," I tell him, pulling back.

"We don't need luck, little doe. We have each other." He squeezes me tightly before releasing me, and we make our way out of the tent.

Joseph is waiting on the other side. He's dressed in his normal clothing, and at my raised eyebrows, he explains.

"Mimics fight in their animal forms."

I nod. Duh. Why didn't I think of that?

"Is everything ready?"

"All except the runes. I think we should get everyone into position before we do that though. If that's okay with you, of course, Your Majesty."

"Perfect. I agree with that. So the armies are all stationed and ready?"

"Everyone who's here. Still no sign of the witches."

Fuck. I was hoping they would be here by now. Oh well. Nothing to be done for it now.

"Okay." I'm about to tell him that we're ready, but a thought comes to mind. "The humans are here? Let's have them elevated above us if possible. With luck, they'll be able to combat the demons as far as gifts go."

Joseph's eyes widen. Clearly that was something he hadn't thought about. The humans have always been undervalued and underappreciated. The reality is that they could well and truly be what saves us in this war. I've been working with the humans who excelled with their powers, and they've been teaching the others with an affinity for it.

As if the land can hear me, it shifts, creating a shelf above the battlefield on either side. I can hear the commotion of the armies as they're startled by the sudden change.

I use an amplification spell on my voice to make quick work of this. "Humans, make your way above. You'll be using your gifts to push emotions of crippling fear onto any of the demons as well as spread positive ones onto our army whenever you can."

I take in their wide eyes; while they look nervous, they all seem determined to help and happy to be looked upon with some importance for once. I give them a nod, my expression fierce. This is not only about defeating the demons. This is also about sending a message to this realm. The old ways are dead. A new chapter has begun. We won't be looked down upon any longer.

The humans square their shoulders and climb with pride up to the elevated portions.

Alexei sends some archers up there to provide some defense. Most of the humans aren't trained in combat and will need to be protected. I hope they've all been practicing. We're going to need it.

Alexei and I move to the front lines. I will not be one of those rulers that stays back and lets others fight her battles for her. I'm the strongest weapon we have, and I'm damn well going to be used as such. I'm the only one who can defeat Demonica. I know it.

I give Joseph a nod and people stationed at the stones around the field begin working on the inscriptions. As soon as they start, I can feel the power emanating through the field. The feeling of motion sickness grows within me slightly, and I almost groan out loud. That's going to be miserable to fight through. Hopefully I get used to it quickly.

It's a boring and tense ten minutes. The magic grows with each second that passes, and I can feel the anxiety building behind me from the army. I conjure up an enormous cloud of confidence and calm. It gathers in front of me, and I can hear the other humans gasp from above. They can see it too. My beautiful cloud of glittery purple and blue. I expand it as large as I can. And then I see the humans are adding to my cloud. It's soon as wide as the battlefield, and I swing my arms wide, engulfing every person I can. They crow in delight and determination. The monsters, also along the front lines with us, snarl in readiness.

"They will not take us to feed on today!" I yell. "They want to use us as cattle. They want to take what is not theirs like they've done for thousands of years! We will not let them. We're stronger together and they know it. It's why they forced us to segregate. We can defeat them with all of us and we will not be taken today or ever again."

The army roars behind me right as the portal opens. On the other side, I see Demonica and her army, poised and ready for us, a vicious smile on her lips. Without a word, she charges forward into Queridian, her demons and slaves unleashing a mighty battle cry as they follow.

I don't have a moment to wonder how they knew we were coming for them because in the next second, they're upon us.

The monsters burst forward first, releasing their rage and violent natures. I would be utterly shocked by the devastation they're leaving in their wakes if I weren't focused on the others coming toward me.

They come with swords. They come with bows and arrows. They come with all the same weapons we have. The only difference is that they've had *thousands* of years to hone their skills. I can barely keep up with the swipes and thrusts, but I do my best, leaning into all the training I've had from my mate and my father. In that moment, I swear I can feel him next to me, guiding my hand.

It takes me too long to remember I have more weapons than simply my sword and daggers. I don't stop swinging, but I do bring my left hand up and conjure a fire. I sweep out with my air, fanning my own flame and enveloping as many demons as I can. They screech, and the feral side of me sinks into it, reveling in the pain of our enemies.

I'm shocked Demonica hasn't come to me yet. I figured she would've come straight for me, wanting to see me dead so she can conquer my realm and declare herself queen.

Instead, she snuck off to the side, cutting a vicious path through the mermaids. Where she goes, death follows, and I'm devastated to see the destruction she's already wrought. I have to follow her and end this.

I follow the path of bodies that's been left in her wake, although I don't get far before I'm ambushed by three demons. I shriek in frustration, pushing fear onto them. They wail in response. Demonica had a similar reaction when I sang my feelings in our last battle, and I wonder if it's painful for them to experience any emotion at all after being so deadened to them for thousands of years, especially one as miserable as fear. I fill them with it before swiping my blade in an arc, decapitating all three of them. I'm not taking any chances with these fuckers.

Alexei is following closely behind me, even though I'm moving faster than he can easily keep up with. I know he wishes I would slow down. I can see it in his eyes. I can tell that he wants to be right next to me through this entire battle, but I have to do this. This is between me and Demonica, and I'm not going to let her wreak more havoc while I wait for him to catch up.

I continue on, blazing a path through anyone who dares get in my way. I'm on a mission and will not be derailed. I use every tool in my arsenal. I blast them with air and fire, fill them with terror, teletravel from demon to demon, cutting through them like they're stalks of wheat. I can feel the blows that are coming for me before they happen, and I sink into my intuition, letting it guide me. Swipe, dodge, blast, run, teletravel. I am wind. I am air. I am untouchable. I persuade those I can to fight *for* us, not against us. I use every trick I can think of. I don't care if it's dirty or cheap. This is war.

Demonica's destruction cuts up and away from the battle. Fucking coward. I worry she's heading for the humans because she knows that they're her biggest threat on this battlefield.

Fuck this. It's taking too long. I shift into my owl, letting out a shriek to let the bitch know that I'm coming for her. I fly high, searching, searching. Gods. The number of people she killed already. My stomach sinks. Can I really win against her? Against *this*?

There. I spot her. I'm about to dive for her, when she shifts into a huge black raven. She leaps into the sky, croaking and coming straight for me. I have a moment where I almost flee, but I stand my ground. I beat my wings harder, heading for her with my talons extended. I want to rip this bitch to shreds. Unfortunately, she has the same idea and when we meet in the sky, it's violent. We rip into each other with claws and beaks. I aim for her eyes and am satisfied when she lets out a pained sound. Feathers are raining down beneath us, and in the back of my head I wonder how funny this must look.

When I realize that I can't do any true damage to her in this form, I take off. I know she'll follow me. I stay in sight of the fight, but try to remove us from the main battle. I don't want one of her goons sneaking up on me. I also don't want her killing anyone else. This bitch is *mine*.

When I find an open section, I land, shifting as I go. She lands behind me, doing the same. I draw my weapon.

"You know, your pain was so delicious when I killed your father."

I stop short, the scene from that day playing over and over in my head like a movie. I know she's goading me on purpose. And maybe she's even feeding from me now. Was that how she killed all those others so quickly?

Before she can do any further damage, I slam my shields back up. I was so overwhelmed with the battle and I'm so unused to having anyone able to get past my barriers that I didn't realize she had snuck in. The bitch *was* feeding off of me.

"Very good, little human. You only let me take a *little* bit of your essence. Not like those pathetic fucking mermaids. I can't believe they actually used to rule. Complete waste of a species if you ask me. We know the truth though, don't we, darling kin? *We're* the strong ones. Demons and humans. We've been put down since the beginning, always underestimated, always shoved down in the dirt, always used as the whores. They put us down because *we* are the strong ones. And you and I? We're the most powerful of them all."

I know I shouldn't be listening to her dangerous, hateful words, but some of them are true. We are the strong ones and that's why we've always been seen as lesser.

She takes a step closer to me without a weapon in her hands. She doesn't even see me as a threat. Her mistake for underestimating me.

"Can you imagine what would happen if we joined forces? We would be *unstoppable*. We could rule the two realms together, you and I. The humans and the demons on top for the first time in this awful history."

"You'd really want to rule with me?" I ask as I infuse hope into my voice.

Her features soften. "Of course, dear kin. I've been wanting a family for so long. I've never known what it's like. And to have someone just like me. We're *equals*. We could conquer this world and then the next." *Earth.* "Can't you picture it? The queens of the realms. Rulers of all." A dreamy quality takes over her face as she steps closer to me.

I lower my weapon and she takes that as an invitation. Once she's right in front of me, she reaches out her hand slowly. I let her caress my cheek as I imagine the future she's painting.

"Would you continue feeding on the others?" I ask.

"Only those who would defy us."

"I guess you better feed on me, then," I remark sarcastically as I plunge my dagger into her belly.

She shrieks in outrage and pain, every trace of fake kindness and absolute bullshit vanishing from her features. Her nails slice down my face and I feel blood dripping from the stinging gashes.

"You'll pay for that."

Before I can attack again, she vanishes. *Fuck.* That was my chance. I wounded her, but she has elven blood. She'll be able to heal herself, and I have no clue where she went.

I hold my hand to my face, attempting to heal the scratches, but no matter what I do, they won't knit back together. I huff in frustration while worry knots my gut. Did she somehow prevent me from healing?

I curse again before looking out to survey the battle raging. The never-ending tide of demons continues to pour through the portal, and I hope that we have enough numbers to prevail.

I grab the bow off my back and load an arrow before shifting into my owl. I swoop out over the crowd, seeing where I'm needed most. There's so much going on that I feel incredibly overwhelmed. It's also difficult to see who is who. It helps that the demons have the horns, but they also have the braindead slaves fighting for them. It's not easy to tell which side is which in that regard.

I see a massive group of demons going for the mimics, and I make my way there. On the flight, I take a few seconds to shift and shoot an arrow, using my air to hold me up as I reload before shifting again and taking off. I help as much as I can to those I pass, but I can't spend too much time there. I'm needed among the mimics that are overrun.

I spot Joseph in his wolf form battling a particularly large demon male. He's ripping into his leg as I approach overhead, but there's another coming for him from the side. True terror spikes in my veins. I can't lose Joseph. It'll be like losing Stavros all over again.

I shift into my normal form, letting out an almighty roar as I light the motherfucker up. He doesn't even have time to scream before he's burned alive. Joseph makes quick work of ripping the throat out of the demon he was already battling. I use my air magic to land gracefully next to him.

He looks at me with wide eyes, giving me a grateful nod.

"You're welcome, old man," I tell him with a wink.

I can see the retort in his eyes, but I turn from him. We don't have time for this. Too many are dying and I have no idea where Demonica went. But I can't look for her again. Not yet. I need to help my people.

# 29

# Alexei

I have been looking for Ember for what feels like forever. I've lost all track of everything except the movement of my sword, the pull of my and Ember's magic through my body, and the blood I'm spilling. The soil is rich with it, and my vampire senses are going a little crazy with all this blood in the air. I feel high on it, like I'm inhaling the particles.

I know I'm a guard, and I have been for most of my life, but I've never seen battle like this. Yes, I've fought. A good number of people at one time too. But at this scale? Never. The field is overrun with people. The clashing of weapons and the snarling of creatures echoes through the night, and I know that my ears will be ringing for days when this is all over. If I'm even still alive. My arm feels dead from swinging my sword over and over again, blocking blow after blow, but I don't stop to rest. I have to find my mate.

She flew off with Demonica, but they disappeared from where they were speaking minutes or hours or days ago. I saw Ember flying overhead afterward, and I've been traveling in the direction she went, but I don't know exactly where she ended up. If I did, I would simply teletravel to her. I growl in frustration and worry, slicing into another demon.

I don't look at the bodies, dead and broken and surrounding me. Some I know, some I don't, some enemies. I can't. After the first few I wasn't able to reach in time, I made myself shut down mentally. When this is all over, I'll need to process everything, but right now all that matters is surviving and finding Ember.

I use the mate mark on my arm to connect me to her. I let the bond and my love for her fill me up until I'm bursting with it. Then I teletravel. The only time I've ever done anything like this was when she was battling Demonica in the water, but it was different. I simply felt her panic and a pull and traveled. This time I'm pulling on our bond, searching for her with my heart. I can only hope it will work. It has to. I feel myself fading, and as I do, I see her face.

I reappear in the middle of where the battle seems to be raging at an all-time high. But there, right in front of me, is Ember. Relief washes over me, even as I jump back into the fighting. I'm also glad to see that she's fighting beside Joseph. I know he's been keeping an eye on her, and vice versa. She meets my gaze for just a heartbeat and looks just as relieved. I give her a quick smile before we dive back in. She has a nasty gash on her face, but otherwise looks healthy. I wonder briefly why she hasn't healed it, but maybe she's just been too busy. The sight of her blood ignites a rage inside me, and I fight more viciously.

I wrap as many demons up in my vines as I can, but after how long I've been fighting and wielding, my power is starting to flag. Ember jumps right on the opportunity I left for her and burns those I've trapped. They shriek as they die, the horrid sound piercing my ears until they feel like they're going to bleed. The demons turn to ash moments later, but we don't have any time to rejoice. The space is filled immediately by more demented-looking demons. I can feel them battering at my mental shields. They have no finesse whatsoever, so I know they're there, but it feels like my mind is being rung like a bell.

I roar in frustration and exhaustion, although I do feel somewhat revived being back with my mate. Her essence pours through me as we fight side by side, and I revel in how marvelous she is. I can't believe how far she's come. I remember training her for the first time, but seeing her in all her glory now is something spectacular. Of course, I never thought we'd be in this position, but I'm grateful she had the foresight to ask me to train her all those months ago. She never wanted to be helpless again, and now she's the greatest weapon this world has ever seen.

She lets out a piercing note, full of every human emotion she can possibly cram into a tune. It reverberates around the clearing, and every demon within hearing distance whimpers in pain, stopping mid-fight to cover their ears. She gives us a much-needed advantage, and we all take it. We make quick work of slaughtering them while they're essentially incapacitated.

Ember is fully focused on maintaining her gift and is unable to do anything else. I don't know how much magic this is costing her, but I make it worth it, taking out any and all that I can. Moments later, she stops, looking as though she's about to collapse. I rush to her, wrapping her in my arms. Her heroic effort gave us time to regroup.

"Are you okay, little doe?"

"Yes. I just used up a ton of magic with that stunt."

I pull a skein of water out of my pocket and offer it to her. She greedily drinks, letting me support her weight as she attempts to recover. What she really needs is food and to lie down. Unfortunately that's not going to be an option for a long time.

The group around us disbands, going off to help others now that the demons in this area are taken care of.

"What happened with Demonica?" I ask.

"She tried to convince me to join her. Said we could rule *all* of the realms together. After she conquers this realm, she wants to go after Earth too." My stomach bottoms out at the revelation. "I let her think she was getting me drunk on her poisonous words before I stabbed her in the gut. She split open my face with her nails and took off before I could do more. I'm sure she's off nursing her wounds somewhere. I just don't know where."

"We'll find her. In the meantime, I need you to stick by me. Don't disappear like that again. I can't protect you if you're alone."

"Alexei, all that matters is killing her. If I get the opportunity, I'm not going to hesitate to take it."

"I know. But I can help. We can do it together."

"No, Alexei. It has to be me. I can feel it."

I sigh. I knew she was going to say that.

"At least stick by me for now. Until you find her."

She nods, and I know it's the best I'm going to get from her. I take note of her appearance, and am glad to see that while she still looks worn and drained, she at least has some color back in her cheeks and no longer looks like she's about to pass out.

"Are you okay?"

"Yes. I'm ready to move on now."

I nod, taking her hand.

"I don't know how long we can keep this up, Alexei. This battle could go on for days. How are we able to take a break? People are going to need to eat and drink and sleep."

"Just remember that even though they're demons, they'll need to rest and regroup too." At least I hope so. There's no way to know for sure since they've been feeding on others. I don't tell her that though. There's nothing we can do but weather the storm.

I know she can basically hear the thought I didn't voice to her, but she nods anyway, looking somewhat reassured.

"Where to now?" I ask, looking around.

"Let's get closer to the gate. I bet those demons are still pouring in." Her face scrunches, and I squeeze her hand in comfort.

"We've got this, little doe."

She gives me a small smile before I pull her along.

The battle rages for *hours.* I try not to think about how exhausted I am. We all take little breaks and grab water and whatever else we can, when we can, but we're running on fumes. The good news is that the demons seem to be flagging just as much as we are.

There has been no sign of Demonica since Ember stabbed her even though we've been on the lookout for her. I bet she slunk back through the portal to lick her wounds where she knew we wouldn't follow.

Dawn has come and gone. The sun is now high in the sky, and sweat is dripping down my brow. Ember is still fighting beside me. I look around at our troops and see how tired everyone is getting.

"We need to start having people take shifts. We need to rest and refuel. We can't all just keep going at full strength. This battle could last days."

She looks around and nods. "We'll take the first shift. Three-hour shifts. Get some people out and then come back when you're done. I'll come up with some sort of big distraction to buy them time for us to have people break."

With that, she charges back into the fight. I take a second just to admire how strong and brave she is. She is the queen and just as tired as everyone else here. Maybe even more so. Yet, she still insists on other people taking breaks before she does. I find the leaders of each group and have them divide up their soldiers to go off and rest. I don't have the time to ensure that every single person is told to get off the field. I need to return to Ember. I'm soon again at her side, letting her know that everyone who needs to be is informed. She nods.

It looks as though the demons are mainly grouped together in the middle of the battlefield. She takes a deep breath and when she exhales, it's as if she blows fire. She carries the flame on a wind of her own making, surrounding the demons. Other fire wielders join her, making the flame burn brighter, hotter. The demons roar and a few attempt to charge through the fire, but are utterly incinerated.

They push with their horrible feeding magic. I hear others around me whimpering in pain even as I feel my soul start to wither at the edges, and I push back against them, throwing up my mental barriers as strong as I can. Immediately it dims, but it's still an oppressive weight on me. I blast my voice out with magic as loud as possible.

"Mental shields up and strong!" Instantly, the sounds of pain lessen. The fae press their advantage and use the gifts of the elements to bombard the demons. I add mine to it, trapping some in vines, burying others alive in the earth, and some I flood their mouths with dirt. Whatever I can think of to buy us time and give us any edge.

A third of our forces retreat to camp. It's a slow process, but we keep it up for as long as we can, but soon the flames die out and the demons press forward, more enraged than before. The anger has given them a second wind, and they attack with more ferocity.

The mimics with any sort of wings choose that time to swoop down, dive bombing them and ripping them open with talons and beaks. It distracts them enough to divide their attention and we're able to maintain our attack. The whole reason behind it was to give our army a chance at a break, but we may as well press our advantage while we have it.

I give a rallying cry and Ember echoes it. Soon, the whole army picks it up and we charge forward, renewed at the prospect of a chance to soon rest. We have to work twice as hard as we were considering we have fewer people now, but this will allow us to keep going for longer. We won't be able to fight well if we're exhausted. The demons will have to either adapt like we are, or retreat. And soon.

Let's just pray to whatever Gods are listening that we can hold out in the meantime.

# 30

# Pearl

I've never swam so fast in my life. What should take me days to swim takes me only one. I swim along the coast, following the territories from Mermacovia to the Mortal Sanctum, and finally to the Everchanging Glades. I walk onto the beach of the Savage Sands, the black sand feeling coarser than I'm used to. It's then I realize how tired I am. Out of all the things to notice, *that's* what I'm choosing to focus on?

I shake my head and concentrate on the task at hand. I remember Xanto saying his family lived near here. I need a safe place to rest. I was thinking about it on the way, and I have never traveled through this land before. That's dangerous. I can't navigate this territory on my own. People don't wander into the Everchanging Glades for a reason. The land changes so much that most people who don't live here end up getting lost, and I don't really have the luxury of time right now. I need a guide.

I'm hoping Xanto's family can offer me both. Sanctuary and navigation. I know I'm asking a lot, but I don't know what else to do. While his father is fighting with the troops, his mother is not and should be home. At least I hope.

I'm so incredibly thankful for our pillow talk right now, because I know exactly where they live. I approach the house, nervous about my appearance. After all, I've been traveling and don't look like I normally do under the circumstances. I wish I could meet his family looking my best, but once again, it's not a luxury I have.

I stop overthinking it and knock on the door. I hear rustling inside and relief hits me like a tsunami. I really don't have any other options.

The door opens, and a woman answers. She looks older than Xanto and has similar facial features, even though they're confused and full of trepidation at the moment.

I smile warmly at her. "Hello, Odessa. My name is Pearl. I know this sounds strange, but I'm in a relationship with your son, Xanto, and I need your help."

At the sound of her son's name, her face lightens. "Oh yes, Pearl. He's mentioned you in his letters. Won't you come in?"

I almost break down into tears at the offer. Instead, I simply make my way inside, all but collapsing in the kitchen chair she indicates.

"Would you like some tea, dear? You look like you've had a long journey."

I nod. "Yes, please."

She pours me a mug before grabbing some biscuits off the counter and setting those in front of me as well. I know it's extremely rude, but I dig in. I can't help it. I'm starving.

"What can I do for you, dear?" she asks when I finally come up for air.

I tell her exactly what I need. She listens intently, and instead of shutting me down like any sane person would do and telling me to get the hell out of her house, an excited light shines in her eyes. I can also see concern lining her features.

"Go lie down for a while. When you've rested we will travel to the Stone Fields."

"Really?" I can't believe she's so ready to head right into battle.

She gives me a kind smile. One that's also lined with just a hint of mischief. "Yes, really. I think I could use an adventure. It's been a while, and I wasn't happy when my husband left to fight, and I was left here. I'm perfectly capable of fighting too."

Ahh. Now I understand why she's looking at me like that. I return her smile. "Then let's go give 'em hell."

"First, rest," she says in a voice she reserves for her children. It's stern and caring all at the same time.

I chuckle and nod. She leads me to Xanto's childhood bedroom, and I delight in the faint scent of my man surrounding me. It makes me feel just a little closer to him to have this insight into his old home and family.

I dress in one of his shirts and am asleep within minutes.

# 31

# Ember

I trudge off the battlefield hours later. It's finally our turn to take a break, and I'm so relieved I almost fall asleep right on the ground in front of me. I have literally never been more tired in my life. Each step feels like I'm trudging through mud. I would teletravel back to our tent, but both my and Alexei's magics are completely drained.

When we get to our tent, I'm elated to see there's enough food for five people sitting on the table. I collapse into a chair, chugging water that's already been poured for me. When my thirst is sated, I start grabbing food off the platters and shoving it in my mouth, not even bothering with a plate.

Alexei does the same next to me, and when I meet his eyes, he gives me a slightly amused smile.

"I suppose we don't look much like royals right now."

I stick my pinky out as I take another drink. "How about now?"

He chuckles, more amusement dancing in his features. I like that even now, during all of this, I can make him laugh.

"Yes. That made all the difference."

I snort, digging back into my food.

"Would you like me to have hot water sent here for a bath?" he asks.

I eye the tub longingly. I would love a bath, but I also really need sleep.

I finally shake my head. "No. Let's just wipe down with some water and a towel. I don't want to get in bed filthy, but we really need to get as much rest as we can."

He nods and we do just that. When we lie down, however, I'm wide awake. I hear the sounds of battle still raging in the distance and worry knots my stomach.

"Relax, little doe."

"I can't. What if all goes to hell when we sleep? We're barely holding on out there as it is. And Demonica hasn't even been fighting. Not to mention that there could still be more forces on the other side of that portal. There's no way of knowing."

"Sleep, Ember. We won't do anyone any good if we pass out from exhaustion."

I know he's right. Hell, I knew it before he even said it, but I can't make my body unclench enough to give myself the reprieve I need. I'm strung as tight as a bow, and simply lying here is making it worse.

I feel Alexei's lips at my neck, kissing and sucking gently. It's so unexpected after all the violence and killing we've done today that I let out a surprised squeak before melting into him.

"I think I know what you need," he croons in my ear.

I feel myself getting wet as he pushes his hardness into my backside. "Do you now?"

"Mm-hmm." He works down my pants as he continues nibbling on my ear. I arch into his mouth.

His fingers trail over my soaked cleft and I moan at the contact.

"You're going to have to be quiet, mate," he whispers in my ear, his breath tickling me. "Do you understand?"

I shiver but nod, not wanting him to stop.

"You're already so wet for me," he groans so low I almost don't hear him. "Do you want my cock, my queen?"

I nod enthusiastically. He chuckles but lines himself up with my entrance from behind. In one smooth move, I'm impaled on his length. I bite my lip to keep the sounds from escaping.

Our coupling is fast, messy, and rough. We're both so exhausted from battle, but we need this release with each other. We need to feel the connection and the reality that the two of us are still alive and breathing.

His fingers stroke my clit as he plunges into me over and over again. We reach our peaks in no time at all, and I bury my face in my pillow to muffle my shout. Alexei follows me seconds after, and when he stills, my body is so boneless that I am finally able to fall asleep.

I wake from a dead sleep to startled shouts and muffled cries. I bolt upright. Those sound closer than the battlefield. Alexei sits up too, pausing to listen before scrambling out of bed to throw on clothes. He throws mine at me as well, and we dress quickly.

We burst out of the tent to see that the demons have infiltrated the camp. Tents are burning with people screaming inside of them as the demons feed on their pain and anguish.

"Fuck. So much for rest. The bastards snuck up on us," I remark as Alexei and I take off to help the nearest victims.

He growls but doesn't say anything. Instead, he just rips into the nearest demon with his teeth, shredding his throat.

We make our way through the camp, saving anyone we can, but we're overrun. My fear was realized. Demonica had another force ready hiding in the portal. I knew we had yet to meet the full force of her army. She waited until we were all drained and exhausted to release them and take full advantage.

I'm grateful I was at least able to get a meal in and a few hours of sleep. My magic is still refilling, but at least it's not completely empty. I use it sparingly, relying on my steel for now. I need to save up my stores to face Demonica. That battle is coming and I know it's going to take everything I have in order to beat her.

People rush from the tents and face off against the enemy, but these adversaries are fresh. They don't share our exhaustion and look much cleaner than anyone that's been on a battlefield for more than ten minutes. Seems like some of them need to get dirty and bloodied. I grip my already-wet daggers, slicing open anyone I can before moving onto my next opponent.

The sheer mass of their army overwhelms me like a tide sweeping over us. I struggle to breathe. Not only with the amount of effort it's taking to keep moving, keep slicing, keep fighting, but also because the panic starts to creep in. What if we can't beat them? What if I did the wrong thing? Should I have just kept the races segregated like *all* of my previous ancestors? *Fuck fuck fuck.*

Instead of focusing on that, I bring my attention back to the task at hand. That's all I can do right now. Defeat the enemy in front of me. Keep going. Until I can't any longer.

# 32

# Proteus

Xanto and I have stuck next to each other for this entire battle. Every swing of our swords, and every breath. Until now. Somehow we've ended up thirty yards apart. I keep him in my sights as I try to make my way toward him while still fighting my opponent. The problem is that every time I take someone down, three more take their place. It's been like this since the fight started, but now I need it to stop so I can get to my lover.

I'm grateful Pearl isn't here at the moment. I know she would want to fight and then my attention would be even more divided. Knowing us, Xanto and I would probably just tie her down on the bed to ensure that she wasn't able to endanger herself. I don't know how Alexei is doing it. Not only is Ember the love of his life and his mate, she's also his queen.

I get slightly closer to Xanto, but not by much. I feel like I'm swimming upstream against the strongest current I've ever felt in my life. But I keep pushing. I have to. We have to guard each other's backs. I can't do that from over here.

I know he feels the same because we keep locking eyes, our intentions to get closer clear. We're leading the mermaid army, but at this point in the battle, everyone has mixed together for the most part. We have the mimics on one side of us, and vampires on the other. The elves have never really been big fighters, so they've been going around among the troops and doing battle healing when they're able. I was actually pretty shocked to spot the Grand Mistress of the Healing Springs, Serena, in the heart of the action. She can hold her own in battle, so she insisted on being in the midst of everything, declaring that's where she was needed the most.

At the beginning of all of this, our group was using our magical abilities to influence the demons and their mindless slaves into turning on each other, essentially giving us more fighters temporarily. It worked wonderfully until we all started running out of magic. Now, we're able to use only our wits and our strength.

Our turn to take a break should be coming soon, and we need it so bad. If I had any concept of time I would be counting down the minutes in my head. That is, until I hear screaming. Not from the battlefield. From the camp.

I'm about to turn and run that way to help when I'm stopped by the worst possible situation. One second Xanto is battling a demon, sword swinging, sweat beading his brow, and the next second, said demon feints an attack right but thrusts left. I see the trap coming before it happens, but I'm too slow to stop it. I yell out a warning but I'm too late. The sword slices across his belly and I scream in pure terror. Xanto looks down at his torso in disbelief. He brings a hand to his injury, his fingers coming away red. His gaze meets mine, shock evident on his face.

I'm still screaming as I fight with everything in me to make it to him. He falls to his knees in front of the demon. I can see the look of acceptance on his face as the demon holds his sword poised above my lover's head. Xanto meets my gaze again, choosing to have me be the last thing he sees. My heart breaks then and there.

I'm still too far away to do anything. I almost collapse and give up right with him. But then I think of Pearl. Losing both of us would shatter her beyond repair. I have to survive for her.

I mouth to him. One last thing so he knows how I feel about him before it's too late. *I love you.* A tear slips down his cheek as he returns the sentiment.

Then the unthinkable happens. Serena has snuck up behind the demon, and in the next second, his head is separated from his body. Xanto loses consciousness at that moment. He's lost too much blood. He might not be dead yet, but he will be soon with his guts spilling out onto the ground. I'm almost to him now and I utterly destroy anyone who dares get in my way. The blood coating my hands is so slick that I worry my weapon will slip from my grasp.

I *finally* reach him, collapsing on the ground beside him.

"Xanto! Can you hear me? Hang on." I'm sobbing now, able to see how much damage has been done to his stomach.

Serena is now kneeling over him, her hands on his wound. "He'll be fine. I can heal him. He'll just need a blood replenishing potion." She takes out said potion and hands it to me. "Give this to him when he starts coming around."

My hands are shaking so bad that I almost drop it, but I nod all the same. I watch through blurred eyes as his skin begins knitting together under her expert touch and I sigh as the strongest relief I've ever felt hits me. His eyes start to flutter open and I almost vomit on the grass next to us. I can't believe I almost lost him.

"Hey there, handsome," he remarks and I let out a laughing sob.

"Hey yourself. Drink this before you pass out again," I order, holding out the vial.

He drinks it, wincing at the awful taste as Serena finishes up the last of her work on him.

I turn to her, about to thank her for saving him when I watch a sword come down on the top of her head, splitting her skull open. She falls to the ground, the life utterly gone from her eyes.

I roar, standing and running the demon through with my blade, but it's too late. The damage is already done. Serena, the Grand Mistress of the Healing Springs, is dead.

# 33

# Ember

We're overrun. There are too many of them for us to manage. And now we can't even rest. We are so totally *fucked.* I don't have any sort of plan in place for this, and as far as I can tell, Demonica isn't even present. Hasn't been since I stabbed her. I would bet my kingdom that she's going to show up at the last moment, when the battle is essentially already won.

Despite the panic clawing at me, I keep fighting. I keep swinging my sword and using whatever advantage I can. Except my magic. I save that for when Demonica shows up. Because she *will* show up.

I can feel Ebony itching to get out as well, but I don't want to use her just yet. She's my secret weapon and I need to wait for the right moment.

Alexei and I battle back to back. There are too many for us to take on our own, and this way we can see threats from every direction. His solid weight at my back is comforting, and I assure myself that whatever happens the two of us will be together. I will not exist in this world without him. I know he feels the same when he echoes my thoughts moments later.

"I will follow you, little doe. Whenever and wherever. We will never be without each other."

"Until the end and after," I vow.

We unleash ourselves upon the enemy. Death is a song in my blood, and I dance to it. Revel in it. When my sword becomes heavy, I sheath it and remove my daggers. It makes for more intimate kills, but at the moment I prefer it. When even my daggers feel too heavy, I rip into them with my teeth and claws.

Alexei and I give it our all, surrendering every part of ourselves to the fight. For our people. For each other. For our friends. For Queridian. There is no other alternative. I would normally be shocked at the number of enemies we've felled, just on our own. As it is, I can't muster the self-awareness to notice.

Later. What feels like a lifetime, later. The air thickens. The demons become unhinged. The atmosphere seems to darken. And I know. Demonica has arrived again.

She finds me. So quickly she finds me. My stomach tightens in dread while at the same time, my body sags in relief. It's almost over. I can feel it. If she's here then it's almost done with. Whether that means I finally defeat her or I meet my demise. I'm ready.

I notice with no small amount of satisfaction that where I gutted her stomach isn't properly healed. Not how it should have been. I would bet all my money that it's still sore. I tuck that valuable information away for later. I realize then that she's never had proper training. Not like I have. She's had to learn everything on her own. Another important bit of information.

"Hello, darling kin," she purrs, approaching like she's floating on water.

"So nice of you to join us. I was upset that you didn't seem to like my parting gift from the last time we met." I glance pointedly at her abdomen.

She seethes, narrowing her gaze on me. "You act like you're the first one to attempt to kill me. Let me assure you, you aren't. And you won't be the last."

"I will be the last. I'll also be the only one to succeed."

She cocks her head at me. "Are you sure about that? You seem awfully tired to me."

"And you seem awfully rested for someone who should be fully invested in her own war. Have you enjoyed others doing your dirty work for you?"

She gives me a cat got the canary smile. "I definitely am. It's left me fully prepared to defeat you."

I roll my eyes at her. "You talk a lot of shit. Why don't we just get this over with?" I know I should probably try to keep her talking so I have more of a chance to rest and recover, but I want this done and over with.

She looks shocked that someone would dare to talk to her like that, and as I think about it, I realize that no one *has.* Not for thousands of years. She's essentially had all of these slaves and demons under her thrall since she went to Domonia.

I smirk at her. "What's wrong, *kin?* Not used to people telling you what a bitch you are?"

She scowls at me, and brings water to the palm of her hand. The next moment she blasts it at me, aiming for my head. I can only imagine that she's trying to shoot it down my throat and drown me. I counter with a ball of fire and the water hisses into steam. I send a blast of air magic through it and toward her. The steam burns her face and she shrieks in outrage and pain.

The fight still continues around us, but they've given us a wide berth. For now it's as if we're in our own little bubble. I can sense Alexei close by, but he's sticking to his word and letting me handle Demonica.

Demonica doesn't have any weapons on her, and I expect her to attack with magic, so I'm surprised when she surges forward, teeth and claws bared. She slashes, swipe after swipe, backing me up, up, up.

I block as best I can, but she's turned feral. I guess she didn't appreciate me burning her face with steam. I end up missing a block or two. I can feel the slashes on my chest, blood running down my torso.

She backs up a step and meets my gaze, wickedness shining in those depths as she licks my blood clean from her nails. She shudders in delight.

"You know, I've drank a lot of blood, but I've never tasted anyone with all the species before. Maybe after I kill you I'll gorge myself on your blood. I could get *drunk* off of it." Bloodlust swirls in her eyes and I shiver.

While she's distracted, I attempt to get past her mental shields. Without a doubt, they are the *strongest* I've ever come across in my life. It makes Stavros's look like child's play. I take a deep breath, reinforcing mine before focusing on everything my father taught me. All of my training with Alexei. With all of the masters. *This* is what it was for. *This* is why I worked so hard. *This* is the only time it matters.

I am better than her. I am stronger than her. I tell this to myself over and over. I sneak around her mind repeatedly, hoping that she'll slip up and I'll be able to get in. I'll have to stay vigilant. Maybe I can distract her enough that she will let her shields fall briefly. That's all I need. Then I can bend her will to mine.

I blast her with air, pinning her against the rocks behind her, but before I can capitalize on her position, she teletravels. I know she's going to appear behind me. Not only have I done that move countless times, but my witch senses are tingling with it. I spin, wielding my sword. I've already used the daggers against her and know they won't do shit. I have to kill her beyond all doubt. She's brought herself back from death before, just like I have. It has to be decapitation or burning her alive. Maybe even both.

She blocks my blow with her claws, snarling at me. I give her my most infuriating smile. The one that I know drives my mate crazy. She seems to have the same reaction to it, and I inwardly give myself a high-five.

"What's wrong? Upset that you've finally come across a worthy opponent instead of just being able to suck everyone dry and bend them to your will?" I taunt, trying to work her into a frenzy so she's not thinking clearly.

"You call yourself a worthy opponent?"

"I wounded you, didn't I? And from the look of it, you did a shit job healing yourself."

She makes the mistake of glancing down at herself. At the wound she so horribly healed. I spring into action, swiping my blade out. She hisses as she pulls back. I take off a chunk of hair in the process, but unfortunately she was too quick for me to do any damage. She attacks with renewed vigor. She must be upset that she lost some hair.

We battle viciously back and forth but it's becoming increasingly obvious she has the advantage. I'm running on fumes, having exhausted myself over the past few days, hell the last few weeks and months. She quickly begins to overpower me, falling back heavily on her magic. She blasts me with water, teletravels in circles around me, batters her will against my mental barriers. I'm heavily lagging, but I counter as best I can. My magic is still drained, but I'm able to deflect.

My attention is also regularly drawn to the battle around us. I worry for my mate and our armies. We're overrun, and I have no idea how we're faring. I know that if Alexei were seriously in danger I would have a feeling about it, if that were the case, I wouldn't be able to focus on my own battle in the slightest and it would be a fatal mistake.

She seems to be playing with me, seeing that I'm struggling. She knows that she just needs to wait me out until I'm too worn down to properly fight back. I can't let that happen. I need to go on the offensive.

I blast fire in her face before using her trick she's done all night, teletraveling behind her. I sweep my foot out in a move I've practiced hundreds of times with Alexei. He always catches me when I do this, but only because he knows my fighting style. Demonica has yet to learn it, and I've also come to discover that while she's proficient in hand-to-hand combat, she hasn't practiced it as much and relies heavily on her magic.

She goes down, shock lining her features when she quickly flips over. I take full advantage, pouncing on top of her and trapping her underneath me. She attempts to flip me, but I'm well acquainted with this move from my mate as well, and I'm prepared for it. I bring fire to my palms that are holding down her arms and the scream she lets loose is so inhuman that I struggle not to cringe away from her. Even though I feel like my brain is melting, I keep up my flames. But before I can engulf her fully, her fangs rip into my neck. I pull back in just enough time that she's not able to rip it out, but I'm severely injured. Blood pours down from me onto her, coating her face, and she revels in it, licking it off every inch she can reach, moaning in ecstasy.

I scramble off of her, bringing my hands to my neck, healing the damage she's done. Gods, she *shredded* my artery. The only reason I'm not dead is because I pulled back in time and I'm able to heal myself. My vision goes blurry from blood loss, and I'm desperately terrified when she stands in all her bloody glory and walks slowly toward me, looking like the devil's wife.

Ebony, feeling my distress, shifts out of my skin, snarling menac-ingly. Demonica lets out a shocked gasp, backing away from her. I'd been waiting to use her. She's been the trick I've hidden up my sleeve. Releasing her at the right time was crucial. I continue healing myself, using every second of the reprieve Ebony is giving me. Demonica is so busy defending attacks from my panther that she doesn't have time to go on the offensive for the first time since she showed up.

When I'm finally healed, I'm about to stand when a vision hits me full force. Fuck. Alexei is in trouble.

"Ebony, go to Alexei. He needs you more than I do right now."

She looks back at me, hesitance coating every line of her features. She doesn't want to leave me. It goes against her very nature, but I *need* her to save my mate. I'm unable to right now and she's the only one I trust to do so.

"*Go. Now.*"

She reluctantly sprints away from me toward my mate. She bought me the time I needed to gather myself to face off against her again. I just hope the rest of the army can do the same.

# 34

# Alexei

It defies every instinct I have to let Ember face down Demonica alone. But she's right. She needs to do this, and I need to help out the rest of our army. Because there are too many of them for us to fight.

I plunge deep into my magic, wielding it more than ever before. I teletravel to everyone I can find in need of help, tie up others with vines, rumble the earth beneath some to cause them to lose their footing. When my magic starts to dwindle, I rely on my sword. Steel can't run out.

I don't know how many demons I cut down, but the tide is never-ending. I watch too many fellow soldiers fall but make a point not to look too closely at their faces. We can mourn the dead after. If we aren't among them, that is.

Without realizing it, I've somehow moved right into the center of a particularly large group of demons with no ally in sight. I was lured into a trap. Fuck. I attempt to teletravel out, but my magic gutters out. I take a deep breath, raising my sword high. If I go down, I will make damn sure to bring as many with me as I'm able.

I start swinging, falling on every bit of experience I have, every ounce of training that was drilled into me. I keep my mental barriers as solid and tight as I can, even though that's just as exhausting as the physical act of fighting. I can feel the horde battering against my shields.

I shout my rage and effort loudly, making a few of the enemy wince as I cut them down. Just as I think I might get out of this alive, I'm taken down from behind. I attempt to get back up, but there are too many, now all piling on top of me. My breath is shoved out of me, and I have a moment where I wonder if I'll die from suffocation.

I flail, connecting with anything and anyone I can, but it makes little difference. I send out a thought to Ember. My regret and sorrow that I won't be able to spend hundreds of years with her like we were supposed to.

Darkness starts to creep into my vision, and I think I imagine the snarling and ripping sounds that are drawing closer. Suddenly the weight from me disappears. I suck in a much-needed breath, beating the blackness back and giving me renewed strength and hope. I fight harder, able to move more freely now. In moments, I'm free and standing once more, the group that surrounded me nothing more than piles of steaming meat. I look around for the source of my rescue, and come face-to-face with Ebony, blood and gore dripping from her muzzle. Relief and dread hit me at the same time.

"Ebony, thank you. Is Ember all right?"

She blinks those too-intelligent yellow eyes at me and I can see the answer there. She's all right for now, but might not be for long.

The reprieve we have from the battle doesn't last long. The attacks are renewed, and I curse. I look around and realize that our numbers are lessened. How many of us have fallen?

I worry that none will make it out alive when a horn sounds. Our attention shifts to the arriving army. Witches and monsters line the hillside. Too many to count. My relief is immediate and intense.

They plow forward, the huge group of monsters surging to the front and ripping into the enemy. Watching the damage they're wreaking is both terrifying and impressive, and I'm grateful they're fighting on our side. They eviscerate every demon they come across, destroying them with claws, teeth, venom—every weapon in their arsenal. Some are able to call their opponents to them before devouring them, others burrowing into their minds and shredding them apart. The screams echo all around as they plow through the army, taking down everyone in their path and pushing toward the portal where the other battle is raging.

The witches finally dive into the fray, and I'm surprised by the efficiency and skill they possess. I would imagine most of that is from their premonition abilities. And from what Jinx showed me at their training facility, they hone those skills particularly for battle.

Speaking of which, I see Jinx and Mera charging ahead. The former cutting into enemies like they're no more than a nuisance, the latter looking slightly intimidated and out of her depth, but she pushes forward, determined.

"Get back to Ember," I tell Ebony, now that the tide has turned. She needs no further encouragement, taking off the way she came.

I make my way toward the couple we befriended in Wickshire, determined to defend a friendly face. There's still a wide length between us, but I slowly inch my way to them, right in time to see a sword pierce through Mera's chest from behind. She looks down in horror at the tip of the blade protruding from her torso. It disappears in the next moment, and she slumps to the ground, eyes empty and unseeing.

Jinx roars his fury to the sky, and I feel it echo through my soul. That breaking of his heart so completely reminds me of seeing Ember die right before me at my own father's hand.

I'm still unable to reach him despite my best efforts. The man has gone feral. He lunges forward, slicing through the man who killed his lover with ease before taking down every demon around him. He's so enraged and shortsighted that he doesn't see the arrow coming for him until it's too late. Or, perhaps with his gift of premonition, he foresaw his death and chose to embrace it rather than face a life without the woman he loves. The sight breaks my heart further, but even with the aid of the witches, I can't muster the strength for anything beyond fighting. And so I continue.

# 35

# Ember

My duel with Demonica is long, messy, rough, and deadly. We've both already needed to heal ourselves multiple times. It's a relief when I see her beginning to struggle, the playing field is starting to level. I've already tried using my empath powers on her, but she was expecting it after our first battle in the water. Her mental barriers are more impenetrable than the Great Wall of China, but I keep trying to sneak through.

I know, however, that my time is limited. My resources are depleted, my magic reduced to a mere ember, with only my empath and allure abilities remaining—abilities I've barely used since I'm essentially incapable of doing so. I'm running on fumes from fighting for so long, not to mention the exhaustion from traveling and saving my mate from a life-threatening situation. When this is all over I swear I'm going to sleep for a week straight and do nothing except take baths and read.

I can feel Demonica prodding for weakness in my mind, the same way I am with hers. I hiss and burn away her slimy essence and she chuckles.

"What's wrong, dear kin? Don't want me inside that lovely head of yours?"

She's stalling, trying to take a breather while simultaneously distracting me.

"I just don't think you could handle how amazing I am once you see it for yourself. I'm trying to save you the embarrassment of realizing how inadequate you are against me," I taunt her, not able to help myself.

She snarls at me. "You're as much of a smooth-talker as your horrid ancestor, Theon."

"Well, he obviously was a smooth-talker. He convinced you to marry him after all. And then you had to go crazy and attack everyone and turn every demon because someone tried to murder you."

"Not just *someone*, dear kin. Theon. My *husband*. On our wedding night."

That stops me short. Theon killed her?

"It wasn't a random assassin?"

She laughs but there's no humor in it. "No, sweet girl. Theon only married me for my crown. He wanted the fae to rule, and he did whatever was needed to attain that. After we were both crowned and consummated our marriage, he stabbed me in the heart. While I was sleeping, I might add."

Horror slices through me. No wonder she went crazy. Although, even though I didn't go through the exact same thing, there are similarities. She could have made another choice. *Any* other choice, and it would've ended differently.

"That doesn't change the fact that many innocent people have suffered at your hands. Directly because of your actions. Thousands."

"I was innocent when I was killed and taken advantage of!" she screams at me. "Why should they not suffer the same fate?"

I shake my head at her. She's clearly too far gone, which is unsurprising. I knew from the moment I discovered her existence that she needed to die. I just hadn't realized that she had been betrayed so horribly. By my ancestor. Gods. That might take a while to come to terms with. I know it wasn't *me*, but the reality is that my ancestor was a monster. He's the one who set all of this in motion.

"Just because something bad happened to you doesn't mean that you can force that vileness onto others. That's not how it works!" I exclaim as we continue to circle each other.

"Isn't it?" she asks, giving me a smile that chills me to my very core.

Instead of responding, I chuck my dagger straight at her face. She ducks, but not before it scratches her cheek. She glares at me before lunging forward. We're locked in battle once again and I can feel myself starting to get sloppy. She tackles me to the ground and leans up just enough to push water toward my head. I drive my fire back to meet the water. Steam sizzles, forcing Demonica to jump backward. I sit up, taking advantage of the reprieve.

I'm concentrating so hard on my fire magic that I don't realize that my mental barriers have slipped until I feel her sucking my essence from me. I gasp in shock, attempting to push her out, but she firmly grips my mind and I'm too exhausted to fight back.

A victorious smile lights her face as I feel myself weaken even more. The hope drains out of me as despair sinks in. She drinks in my desperation, looking as if she were sipping the finest wine. Ecstasy is etched across her features and she moans in delight.

"I haven't tasted someone as divine as you ever," she remarks in a husky voice.

I'm disgusted, but there's nothing I can do to stop her. I try to fight back with my daggers, with my teeth, with *anything*, but she easily dodges all of my attempts. I whimper. Is this really the end?

Just when I think it's over and am ready to surrender to oblivion, Ebony jumps in out of nowhere, latching her powerful jaws around one of Demonica's legs. The draining instantly ceases and I sob.

"Ember!"

I turn at the sound of Pearl's voice ringing out through the clearing and hope soars in my chest. She's not close enough to hand me the trident, but I can see it glowing in her hand. It's luminous now, no longer the dull relic that was pulled from a lake.

"Throw it!" I call to her.

She does as I say, and I pull it to me with my air magic.

"No!" Demonica screams out.

I catch the trident, and as soon as it connects with my hand, power zings up my arm, filling me with energy and warmth.

Rejuvenated, I reach out for Demonica's mind. The trident aids me in bursting through her shields. I gag on the vileness, darkness, and the overall *wrongness* of her mind.

I picture every emotion I've ever witnessed and experienced, pouring them forward into a cloud in front of me. I bring my voice into the cloud, amplifying it so the whole battle can hear me. The humans join me, our cloud three times as large as when we started. I pour as much of the mist as I can into Demonica, who shrieks and curls in on herself. The humans flood the rest of it onto all the demons. I aid them as much as I'm able, but my main focus is on the bitch in front of me.

She wails, louder and louder, the emotions impossible for her to handle.

"You wanted my emotions so badly, *kin*? Take them." With that, I drive the last of it into her.

She claws at her head and ears, but I don't relent. All around me, demons are shrieking and screeching in unimaginable pain. I push more. More, more, *more.*

With that final burst, Demonica's ears, mouth, nose, and eyes begin to bleed, dripping down her face in crimson tears. The blood gushes out and she eventually falls still on the ground in front of me. I'm about to take a sword to her neck and decapitate her, but Ebony is already there, tearing through her as if she's made of butter. When she pulls back, I hold my hand out and set what remains of her alight. Within moments, she's nothing but ashes blowing in the breeze. I collapse in absolute relief. She's dead. I did it.

I look around the field to see that a similar fate has fallen on the other demons, and the rest of the army is busy decapitating them as well, not willing to take any chances.

The only soldiers left of Demonica's army are the slaves, and our army quickly takes them captive. Maybe with some help from me and the other humans, we can undo the damage the demons inflicted on them, and they'll be able to recover.

At that moment the army hoists up the humans, cheering. My heart swells in my chest. We fucking did it.

# 36

# Pearl

Apparently I arrived just in time to save the day. I should be happy. I should be ecstatic. And I *am*, but, witnessing the devastation on this battlefield, I can't muster up anything beyond sadness.

As soon as I confirm that Ember is safe and has defeated that demonic bitch, I go in search of my men. I won't feel true peace until I know that they're okay. It's disturbing to see so many demons without their heads. It seems our army was thorough in ensuring they are indeed dead, and I don't blame them. After all the grief they caused and the lives they ruined, they deserve nothing less. I'm sure once the fae and Ember regain their magic, they will also be burned, although this will do for now.

I pick my way across the battlefield as quickly as possible, but it still feels like it takes me forever. Or maybe it simply seems that way because I'm anxious about my men. I try not to look too closely at the fallen. I don't have it in me to see how many of them I recognize, especially when I get to where the mermaids seem to have been fighting together. I know this is where my men will be. Even though Xanto is a mimic, our home is now in Mermacovia. He is a partner of the grand master. He will have wanted to be fighting among them, rallying them.

When I see friendly faces, I ask where Proteus and Xanto are, and they point me in the direction they last were seen.

And then I spot them. I cry out in relief. They're alive. I run full speed at them, colliding with both of them at the same moment. They let out shocked noises but wrap me in their arms, Xanto in front of me, Proteus in the back. The three of us cling to each other with everything we have, and I sob as the reality of the last week comes crashing down around me. I've lost so much, but I still have everything I need right here in my arms.

I kiss them both, tasting sweat, blood, and all sorts of horrendous things on their mouths, but I don't care. They're alive. We all are.

When I pull back, I see the blood coating the front of Xanto's shirt and I gasp in shock.

"What the hell happened?"

"I was gutted."

"*What?!*" I exclaim. Of course he doesn't elaborate.

"Serena saved him," Proteus adds helpfully, taking pity on me.

"The elf grand mistress?"

He nods. "Right before she died."

Tears fill my eyes and spill over again. The fact that her last act was saving Xanto is more than I can take right now. I didn't know her well. I met her only a few times, but she gave her life to save his, and even though she's gone, I will be eternally grateful to her. I couldn't face losing either of them, especially so soon after Opal.

I survey the damage. "We will need to put to rest everyone who didn't make it."

They nod, but Proteus says, "There will be time for that later. Now, we need to eat, rest, and celebrate!."

A few mermaids around us hear him, and let out a mighty cheer. If there's one thing mermaids are good at, it's celebrating.

"*The demons are in hell!*" The chant rises up among us, and soon everyone takes it up, the army crowing it mightily.

"I'm a little sad I missed most of the fun," I tell them.

They both give me horrified looks and I chuckle.

"Let's go find the queen."

# 37

## Ember

There's much to do as far as cleanup is concerned, but we don't worry about any of that right now. Everyone is too exhausted and joyous. Instead, we erect more tents for the witches and to replace the ones that were ruined in the ambush.

I send a group of mimics through the portal to check that there are no more enemies in Domonia, and when they return, they report that it's empty. Apparently Demonica didn't believe in sparing those incapable of fighting. She made *everyone* follow her.

The only other people still working are the healers. They make their way across the battlefield, tending to everyone they can find. Others help those with injuries that aren't life-threatening to a medical tent. The healers whose magic has been drained tend to wounds using ointments, salves, and remedies, disinfecting and wrapping until they can be healed properly.

I attempt to help, but no one lets me. Instead, our group is brought food and drinks to my tent, which miraculously remained unharmed, and a water bearer comes in to fill my tub. I'm surprised they have any magic left, but apparently there is just enough left to fill my tub. I'm so grateful I almost cry.

We all sit around the table, ripping into the food that's been prepared for us. It's not the best, but all of us are too hungry to care, including Pearl, who traveled hard and fast to get here.

Xanto was shocked to see his mother. When he tried telling her that she shouldn't be here, she swatted him upside the head and told him to shush. Just thinking about it makes me chuckle. We invited her to join us, but she was on a mission to find her husband. Xanto said he saw him after the battle before he got pulled away by Joseph for something.

After we stuff ourselves full and drink our weight in water and wine, Pearl and her men retreat to their own tent. I face Alexei, finally allowing myself to feel the relief fully. We survived.

He pulls me into his arms, and it hits me all at once. Serena and Mera and Jinx. I'm sure there are more fallen friends who I haven't heard about yet, but those three hit me hard. I can't help but feel that if I hadn't taken over that none of this would've happened. The guilt almost overwhelms me as I sob in my mate's arms. He doesn't say anything, just holds me as I break down.

When my tears finally slow, I pull back.

"Are you ready for a bath?"

I nod, stripping out of my armor and filthy clothes, leaving them in a pile in the middle of the tent floor. Alexei is right behind me, doing the same.

I walk over to the tub and touch the frigid water. With just a thought and a flick of my fingers, I heat the water until it's nearly scalding, some of my magic having been restored from the meal.

I look down at myself and cringe. I'm absolutely filthy. In fact, I don't think I've ever been dirtier in my entire life.

Alexei notices and chuckles. "Don't worry, little doe. I'll help you get clean."

I raise my brows at him. "Will you now?"

He gives me a sexy smile in response, heating my blood despite everything we just went through. We step into the delightful water, and I sigh. The warmth is doing wonders for my battered body. With Alexei behind me, I lean back against him, lacking the energy to do anything else.

He wraps me in his arms, and the feeling of being surrounded by my mate, and the knowledge that we're both safe has me relaxing every muscle in my body. My eyes close, and before I know it, I'm drifting off in the tub.

I wake sometime later to Alexei gently washing my body. I jerk up, but he shushes me, gently pulling me back against him.

"It's okay, little doe. Let me take care of you."

I relax back against him, enjoying the feeling of him washing and caring for me. I try not to look at how disgusting the water is, but with every swipe of the sudsy washcloth over my body, the water becomes more murky and grayish brown. I know we'll need another bath after we sleep, but at least we're getting most of the dirt and blood off of us. I wet my hair, reluctant to use the filthy water, but I'm desperate to wash away the grime.

When I'm as clean as I can be for now, I turn to my mate, needing to return the favor. He tries to wave me off, but I feel the same urge to reassure myself he is safe and care for him as he did for me.

He hands me the washcloth and I lather it up again before bringing it to his skin. He's got nicks and scratches all over him, some deeper than others. I heal every injury I can see as I go along.

When we're finished, we get out of the tub and I dry us off with my air magic before we collapse into bed, completely and utterly spent.

We sleep for so long. I don't know if it's been hours or days, but no one disturbs us, which I'm incredibly thankful for. Our bodies needed to recoup after everything we endured. I'm sure the rest of the army is doing the exact same thing. Everything else can wait until we are all recovered.

More food is delivered, along with fresh water for the bath. This time, Alexei and I are able to thoroughly clean ourselves, and I feel so much better. It's amazing what rest, food, and feeling clean can do for a person.

When we're finally ready, we make our way out of the tent. There's still much to be done. The field has been cleared of survivors. Now comes the tedious and grief-filled task of going through the dead. Distinguishing the friends from the enemies, and notifying the families so they can put them to rest properly.

There are many faces that I recognize, even if I never properly met them. I burst out into tears when I come across Serena, Mera, and Jinx. I make sure Mera and Jinx are together. I know they'd want that. Alexei holds my hand through it, supporting me in his own silent way.

I thank them all, saying I'll miss them and I valued their friendship and sacrifice. They will have burials fit for royalty, I decide.

Once all of our deceased allies are removed, I gather some other fire wielders and we head out to the battlefield. We space out, each taking an area, and then the purging begins. We burn every demon and enemy we can find. It takes hours, and the area reeks of burned flesh, ash coating the air and falling around us like snow, but it must be done. I blow away as much of the ash and stench as I can, helping it scatter to the winds. Other air fae assist me with that, and when it's done, no more demons remain.

As I'm heading back to camp, a nymph finds me. One of the ones I rescued at the Mermacovia black market.

"Your Majesty," she says, bowing. "May I have a word?"

I'm surprised by how eloquent she is. "Of course, my friend. What can I do for you?"

"I've spoken with the other creatures, and after what we've endured, we were wondering if it would be possible for us to relocate."

"Relocate?"

She nods. "We were thinking that since the demons are no longer occupying Domonia, that we could perhaps take it over.  After all, most of the attacks that happen here are because our territories are unknowingly being encroached on. If we were to have our own space, without worries of being captured, I think we would be much happier."

My eyebrows rise in surprise.  I never would have thought of that. And after all they've done for us, I would never dream of making them go somewhere they didn't want to, but it makes a lot of sense.

"Are you sure that's what you all want? After all your help, you all more than have a place here. We can institute sanctuaries for you."

She gives me a sad smile.  "That's very kind of you, Majesty, but we're sure. We need the space to be our own monstrous selves without worrying about injuring others.  We would have that opportunity there."

"You do realize it's not a beautiful place, right?"

She chuckles. "Yes. We can make it fit our needs. Us nymphs can pour our magic into the land."

I nod. "If that is truly what you all want, then I grant you the land. We will always leave this portal open if any of you wish to return. I'll also make sure the portal in Mermacovia is open to you as well. You're more than welcome here. And please, let me know if any of you ever need anything.  I greatly appreciate all you've done for me and this realm. We will never forget it."

She bows. "Thank you, Your Majesty. I will gather the creatures and we will be on our way."

When I return to my tent, Joseph is waiting for me. My shoulders loosen immediately.

"Hey there, stranger," I tell him.

He gives me a warm smile. "Hey yourself."

As soon as we're in touching distance, I walk into his open arms. His warm embrace is so comforting, and for the briefest second, I swear I can also feel Stavros's hand on my back. I had two mothers. It would make sense for me to have two fathers. I smile at the thought.

"How are you doing, old man?" I tease as we break apart.

"Hey, I'm still here, aren't I?"

"You sure are. And I couldn't be more grateful," I say, all traces of teasing gone from my voice.

His eyes soften. "As am I. You fought so bravely, Ember. I know I'm not your father, nor would I ever try to be, but I'm extremely proud of you. I know Stavros would be, too, if he were here."

Tears spill down my cheeks. "Thanks, Joseph."

"Are you heading home?"

"We will soon. We're going to help out more here first."

"You don't have to, you know. You are the queen after all."

"I know. But I'm the one who brought this war to you all. It's my responsibility to make sure that all is well."

"Ember, this war started thousands of years ago. It was a secret that should have been told to us from the beginning. The only thing you did was tell us the truth. Hell, you even let us make our own decision about what to do. Because of you, we are now able to live freely. I think I speak for almost everyone when I say that we are so thankful for you. We are grateful to have a queen who considers us as equals. Who values our opinions. I already know our realm will be a better place with you ruling it."

My tears flow in a steady stream down my cheeks now. It's everything I could've wished to hear. I give him another tight hug, and he returns it, and gives me one last squeeze, then tells me to get some rest.

Alexei and I head home a week later. We've done as much as we can in the Everchanging Glades. I feel slightly guilty that we get to teletravel while mostly everyone else (with the exception of the other vampires) has to make the journey home on foot. Or horseback. Or on the waves. That's how Pearl and her men are getting back. They're staying with Xanto's parents for a few days, and then they will travel home along the coastline.

As such, the Immortal City is far more empty than it normally is. As soon as we arrive, Humphrey is there to greet us, and warmth spreads in my chest at his smiling face. Seeing him always reminds me of my father, and he's always been so kind to me. I wrap him in a hug. He stiffens in shock at first, but recovers quickly, awkwardly patting me on the back.

"Welcome home, Your Majesty. Is there anything you need?"

"Would you send a meal and some tea for us, please?"

"Right away, Your Grace." He bows before taking off.

"It feels good to be home."

"It certainly does," Alexei says as he guides me to our rooms.

I eye the shower longingly as we enter, and Alexei chuckles knowingly.

"Go ahead. I'll get the food when Humphrey brings it."

I squeal in delight. It feels like so long since I've had a shower. I take my time, wanting to savor every second of it. The smell of my shampoo, the heat pounding my back, the ease of washing my hair. It's all amazing, and it makes me never want to get out. The only thing that could make me is the promise of food.

"Dinner's here, little doe," Alexei calls right on cue.

My stomach grumbles loudly, and I sigh in regret, turning off the shower.

I come out, braiding my hair, and see that Alexei has a tray of food and wine on the bed. My heart squeezes as I think about our days on the road when we first met. From the look in his eyes, he's thinking about it too.

"Hungry, my love?"

I chuckle. "Always."

# 38

# Alexei

*One month later...*

I nervously pace the length of our rooms as I wait for Ember to get out of her meeting. I have the whole day planned for us. She's been working so hard getting everything in order after the war with Domonia. She's been brainstorming with her council to help improve relations between all the territories and to find ways to encourage more interaction. It's going to take time, but many people are already excited about exploring the realm and experiencing how other species live.

Ember's also been in contact with all of the earth and water fae she can find. She has big goals for the Mortal Sanctum. We're not sure if it will work, but she's going to try to better the human territory. Right now, it's miserable and severely lacking in the beauty that accompanies the realm of Queridian.  So our plan is to have the earth fae pour their magic into the land and carve out areas for the water bearers to incorporate some humidity into the place so that anything us earth wielders are able to grow doesn't die immediately. It's going to be a big job, but after the treatment they've received over the years, not to mention all they did in the battle against the demons, they deserve nothing less than the best. And the rest of the people in the realm finally see that. Humans are not the weak creatures the realm believed them to be all along.

Obviously, everything can't happen overnight, and it's going to take a lot of time for things to change, but we're on the right path. And Ember is more motivated than ever to make it work. She needs a break. And a special surprise.

I had the kitchen pack us a wonderful dinner full of her favorites, along with a bottle of wine. While she's busy in her meeting, I make sure everything is ready, teletraveling my supplies to our favorite spot.

Ten minutes later, she trudges into the room and I can see how exhausted she is. I'll probably have to coax her into my plan, but that's okay. I have my ways.

"Long meeting?"

She nods. "Yeah, but we're making some progress. I just want to eat in the bath and then collapse into bed for the rest of the week."

My heart sinks at her words, but I push through it.

"I have a different idea."

"Is that right? What did you have in mind?"

"Let's go on a romantic hike and watch the sun set."

Her eyes soften as she looks at me, but I can see the fatigue and reluctance on her face. Normally I would let her relax and do exactly what she wants, but not tonight. She bites her lip as though she doesn't know how to tell me that she doesn't have the energy to go. Maybe this wasn't the best idea, but it's too late to change my mind now.

"Come on, little doe. I know you're tired, but it will be worth it. I promise. I'll even rub your back later," I coax, giving her a wink. "And maybe something else if you play your cards right."

She lets out a chuckle and nods. "Okay, fine. But it better be a long-ass massage. And the 'something else' is going to be all about me."

"As you wish, my queen." I bow low, and she smacks my arm.

"Let me just change first."

When she's ready, we head out, hand in hand. As we continue along, her steps become lighter, her shoulders relaxing.

"You were right. I needed this."

I smile to myself. She has no idea.

"You did. We should start making it a priority to get out of the castle more. You get too cooped up in there."

She sighs. "I know. It's tough when there's so much that needs to be done."

"I know, little doe. But we have plenty of time. There's no deadline."

"Isn't there though? This all should've been done so long ago, and so many have suffered because of it."

"And you're fixing it. The people see that. They know you're doing everything in your power to make this a better world for them, but you need to take care of yourself before you burn out and aren't able to help them at all."

"I know you're right. It's just so hard to make myself a priority."

"Luckily, you have a wonderful mate that cares about your well-being more than anyone else's."

She rolls her eyes, bumping her shoulder against mine, but I can see the warmth in her eyes as she clutches my hand tighter.

"Thank you, mate," she tells me.

I stop her just as we reach the perfect lookout. The sun is just setting, and I couldn't have planned this better if I tried.

I kiss her senseless and when we come up for air, her eyes are hooded and glazed with lust. "Anytime, my love."

We admire the view until the sun dips beyond the horizon, and then I keep pulling her along with me.

"We're not stopping here?"

"You know better than that, little doe. We have a special spot."

She harrumphs, but follows me. I chuckle. I know she's tired. I probably should've done this on a day when she didn't have so much going on, but the woman *always* has something going on.

We finally reach our little oasis. The one that I came upon Ember swimming in all those months ago. When she finally decided not to hate me anymore.

She gasps when she sees what I've done. The area is lit by the fireflies that give off heat as well as some naturally lit rocks. I even threw a few in the water so that glows too. In front of the pool I have a blanket laid out covered with the food and wine the cooks gave me. I also brought her favorite book, music device, and phone so we're able to play music.

Her eyes go a little glassy, and she doesn't say anything for a moment, just stares at the haven in front of her. When tears roll down her cheeks, I know I nailed it.

"Hungry, my love?"

She nods dazedly, and I lead her to the picnic I set up. She turns some music on as I fill her plate up with everything in sight before setting it in front of her. My hands shake just slightly as I pour her a glass of wine. My nerves are trying to get the best of me, but I'm not going to let them.

"Alexei, I can't believe you did this for me. It's perfect."

"*You're* perfect," I say, leaning over to give her a kiss. As I do, I reach into my pocket to pull out the ring that I crafted myself out of my earth magic. Polished wood makes up the band and cradles a large raw rose quartz. One to match the necklace she inherited from her mother. The one that allowed her to find me in the first place. I break the kiss and lean back, bringing the ring with me. "Ember, you toppled into my life, and nothing was ever the same. My world was flipped upside down. Even with everything we've been through, I've never felt happier or more complete. Will you do me the honor of becoming my wife?"

Tears line her eyes, but she doesn't look surprised in the least. She nods furiously. "I would be honored to have you as my husband. My king. My mate. Until the end and after." She holds out her hand, allowing me to slip the ring onto her finger.

When it's in place, I feather my lips over her finger before attacking her mouth in a ravenous claiming kiss. She gives as good as she gets, and I know she's claiming me just as fiercely.

When I finally pull back, I look into her eyes. "Why aren't you surprised?"

"Did you really think that my witchy senses wouldn't be alerting me?"

"You had a vision?" I ask in disbelief. I hadn't even thought of that, and it makes me want to smack myself upside the head.

She nods, a smile and laughter on her lips. "I saw it as soon as we came to the clearing."

"Well, at least you didn't see it before we got here."

"It's beautiful," she whispers against my lips. "Thank you so much."

"I'm glad you like it. Now, let's eat and then you can read while I rub your feet." I wink at her, making her swoon, although I'm sure it's from my words more than my wink. My mate loves food, reading, and being pampered, and I'm offering her all three.

We settle in and I prepare to give her anything she could ever want.

# 39

# Ember



*Five years later...*

I wake up to my husband spooning me from behind, his hand on my belly. I sigh contentedly in his arms. I trace the wedding band on his ring finger with my own as I think about our wedding day.

It was hands down the best day of my life. Everything was perfect. A year after he proposed we got married and had him crowned king. I smile as I think of how the day went...

*Pearl wakes me up first thing in the morning, more intense than usual.*

*"Wake up! It's your wedding day!"*

*I put my pillow over my head as I attempt to get away from her screeching. She doesn't let me though. She rips the pillow from my hands along with the comforter covering my body. I wince at the cold.*

*"Aren't you supposed to spoil the bride on her wedding day? Not make her want to kill you?"*

*"Hey, I'm your maid of honor. As such, I will not let you wallow away in bed when you have so much work that needs to be done to make you beautiful."*

*I roll my eyes, but reluctantly get out of bed. I know she's not going to let me go back to sleep, and I see that she at least brought tea with her.*

*She leads me to the bathroom where she has a steaming-hot bath started for me, oils and salts and perfumes already loaded in the tub, and I sigh in delight. At least she's pampering me.*

*"Get in and drink your tea. I'll do everything else."*

*When she finishes with me, I have to admit, she's outdone herself. It takes hours, but I'm soon looking at myself in the mirror, stunned. I've never looked this amazing, and I doubt I ever will again.*

*Imelda has truly outdone herself with my dress. It looks like spun moonlight. There's multiple layers of fabric ranging in colors from white to silver. She's also somehow managed to infuse sparkles that shine and shimmer as I move. All in all, I look like the moon and the stars in the night sky. Something new. My crown sits proudly on my head, and I appear to glow. I'm also wearing my mother's necklace. It shines brighter than the sun today. Something old. I found a handkerchief of my father's that's worn but beautiful in his office when I could finally bring myself to visit it. It now sits in my pocket that I insisted on having. Something blue. And finally, Pearl lent me a bracelet that her mother had made for her and Opal. They each had one, and now Pearl wears one and I wear the other. It's small and delicate and alternates between pearls and opals. Something borrowed.*

*That, along with not seeing the bride on the wedding day, are the two Earth traditions I bring to our special day. Alexei was not happy when I told him he'd have to sleep elsewhere for the night. They don't understand the sentiments, but I wanted a little bit of my upbringing to be present with me today. A little bit of Earth.*

*I let Pearl plan most of the wedding. She really wanted to, and with the exception of a few details, I didn't care too much about specifics. Besides, Pearl is so great with this kind of thing that I knew it would be incredible.*

*"Ready?" she asks.*

*I nod, even though my heart rate and breathing has accelerated. There's going to be so many people here. People I don't know. My subjects. Fuck fuck fuck.*

*Pearl notices my anxiety. "Let your mental shields down for me."*

*The demand takes me by surprise, but I do as she asks.*

*Her voice is filled with allure as she says, "Take some deep breaths for me."*

*I follow her instructions.*

*"Good. Now look into my eyes and relax. Think about Alexei. Think about your mate and the fact that at the end of the day he will be your husband."*

*I once again do as she says and immediately feel myself calm. My heart rate slows, and my breaths even out.*

*Her allure vanishes. "Feel better?"*

*I nod. "Yes. Thank you. I needed that."*

*"I always know what you need," she teases, giving me a wink. "Now, let's go get you married."*

*I beam at her and we make our way to the room where I first met Stavros. That is where the ceremony will take place. I swear I can feel all of my parents gathered around me at this moment, and I take a second to bask in their presence.*

*Joseph approaches me, looking dapper and unusually put together. I asked him to walk me down the aisle. He's always been like a father to me, and even though my own can't be here today, Joseph is the next best thing.*

*"You look beautiful, Ember."*

*I give him a tight hug in answer. "You're not looking too bad yourself."*

*He chuckles, offering me his arm as my music starts up. I take a deep breath as the doors open. I don't look at anyone in the crowd. The only thing I can see is my mate at the end of the aisle. There are no words to describe how handsome and perfect he looks. His long hair is tied back and out of his face, and he looks dangerous and regal in all black, the night sky to my shining moon and stars. He looks at me in awe, and I preen.*

*The walk down the aisle simultaneously feels like it takes forever and no time at all. When I reach him, I feel like I take my first real breath and he gives me a knowing smile.*

*Most of the ceremony is lost on me as I'm too consumed with my mate, but we say our vows and I cry like a baby. When it's official, we kiss and the crowd cheers.*

*"Until the end and after," he whispers against my lips and I echo it.*

*Then it's time for my husband to be crowned king. We didn't want to have a separate event for this, and since we're married, he's technically king already, but we want to make it official as soon as possible.*

*"All hail Queen Ember and King Alexei Solis! Long may they reign!"*

*The audience roars in delight, and I blush as I look at my new husband, crown and all, and think maybe we should skip the reception...*

The memory brings a soft smile to my face as it does whenever I think of that day. We could've done it much sooner, but there was so much to repair after the war. And honestly, I wasn't in the best head space. The war really took a toll on me, more than I was ever anticipating. I didn't realize that even though it was necessary and the beings that we killed were evil, I would still carry so much guilt. Not only because of the blood on my hands, but because of the fact that if it hadn't been for me, none of it would've happened. Sure, the species would still be segregated, but so many people would still be alive, including my father.

But after some long in-depth conversations with my mate, and seeing how the realm has flourished the last few years, it's made a huge difference. The Mortal Sanctum is now one of the most beautiful territories in the realm after all the work that we've put into it. The land was indeed lacking magic, and needed to be refreshed. I've wondered if something occurred when the demons turned evil in the first place all those thousands of years ago. As if they not only sucked the life out of the people around them, but from the very land itself. I guess we'll never know for certain, but the land is now an oasis. A haven. Not only that, the humans themselves are incredibly respected. They were instrumental in saving us during the battle against the demons, and I think the majority of the population was shocked that the species they considered the weakest was in fact their savior.

We've built them a new capitol building, and they have a grand master just like the rest of the species. And let me just tell you, they are *thriving.* I love watching the realm grow on a regular basis, and while most still live in their original territories, a few have moved and almost everyone has traveled and seen where the rest of the other species live. It warms my heart to see everything we've accomplished in such a short amount of time. I know the citizens were just as ready for these changes as we were.

Alexei starts waking and strokes my stomach. I moan and press up against him, feeling his hardness pinned against my backside.

"Well, good morning," I remark in a husky voice.

He nuzzles my neck, letting out a low satisfied growl. "Do we have time to fool around?"

I chuckle. "No. We need to get up and get ready to see Pearl and her motley crew."

Pearl and her men have been quite busy over the years. They have four kiddos, two of which are twin girls. Pearl broke down into sobs at that news. She named one of them Opal in honor of her own twin.

He groans in disappointment as he thrusts gently against me. "But I thought we could try again while you're still ovulating."

I suck in a sharp breath. We literally *just* started trying for a baby. The past five years have been hectic and stressful, and despite the fact that we're rulers and the pressure was high to continue the royal line, we decided to wait until things calmed down and we felt ready. That finally changed *yesterday*.

The thought of carrying Alexei's child, of bringing someone into the world who was a part of both of us, is exciting and nerve-racking all at the same time, but I realized that I don't want anything more than I want that.

"Well, I guess we have a little bit of time still," I moan out as he nips my earlobe and starts pushing his hands under my clothes.

"I can't wait to see you swollen with our child," he remarks as he strokes my stomach again.

The sentiment makes my heart race and I reach behind to grab him, relenting. I can never resist him. Especially when he wants to get me pregnant.

"Hurry up. We don't have much time," I tell him, impatient to get him inside of me.

"They can wait, little doe. I'm not rushing a second of the forever we have together."

"Forever?" I ask, hope in my voice as I turn to look him in the eyes.

"Forever, little doe. Even when we're gone from this world, I'll find you in the next."

The end.

# Acknowledgments

Wow. It's bittersweet to say goodbye to this series. I've become incredibly close to these characters, and while I'm thrilled they all got their Happily Ever Afters, I will miss them.

To my husband and my family, I love all of you so much and I could never have accomplished this without all of your love and support. It means more to me than you will ever know. A special shout-out to my sister for polishing this piece until it gleamed.

To my word count tracker ho, Iris, you're the best bitch a girl could ask for. Thanks for all of your help with not only this series, but all of my projects.

To my llama ladies, I'm so lucky to have found you all. You are the best group of writers I've ever met, and I love our special relationships and how we always support and help each other out.

To Beth, my editor, thank you for making this series what it is. It would definitely be in much worse shape without you, and I appreciate all your hard work.

To Les, my graphic designer, thank you for delivering the perfect cover art to end this series. It's my favorite of anything you've done for me yet.

Finally, to you, dear reader. I hope you have enjoyed this series as much as I have. Thank you for giving me and my story a chance.

# Also by L.J. Burkhart

<u>The Fire series</u>
    Fire & Ink
    Light Me Up
    The Fire Inside Me

<u>Realm of Queridian</u>
    An Ember in the Dark
    A Blaze in the Shadows
    A Demon in the Dawn
    A Queen in the Ashes

Of Love and Time

Witch, please

# About the Author

L.J. Burkhart is a fantasy and romance author, as she loves all things paranormal and passionate. She has been a lifelong writer, starting with songs and poetry in the third grade, before eventually moving on to novels in her early twenties. When she isn't coming up with dramatic plot twists and steamy sex scenes, you can find her doing yoga, hanging out with her best bitches, baking, or reading, curled up on the couch with her husband and dog with a big glass of red wine.

**You can connect with me on:**

🌐 https://www.ljburkhart.com

**Subscribe to my newsletter:**

✉ http://eepurl.com/hRZzz5